Back in [the Saddle]

Maggie Eckersley is a Polish ro[mance writer who lives] with her husband and two [children. She came to the UK] when she was nineteen years old and fell in love. She isn't sure if it was more with her favourite person who she ended up marrying or the country itself. Maybe a little bit of both. When Maggie isn't daydreaming about the next love story she wants to type out, she's studying Medicine or working as a medical writer. Her weaknesses are great books, food, and single malt whisky. She has a bucket list of Scottish Castles and she will never pass a chance to visit historical landmarks. In 2023, Maggie won I Am In Print Award for the book that became Back in the Saddle. In 2024, she has been shortlisted in I Am In Print Romance competition and longlisted in Penguin Michael Joseph Undiscovered Writers' Prize with another contemporary romance novel.

BACK IN THE SADDLE

MAGGIE ECKERSLEY

avon.

Published by AVON
A division of HarperCollins*Publishers* Ltd
1 London Bridge Street
London SE1 9GF

www.harpercollins.co.uk

HarperCollins*Publishers*
Macken House,
39/40 Mayor Street Upper,
Dublin 1
D01 C9W8
Ireland

A Paperback Original 2025

1

Copyright © Magdalena Formella-Leigh 2025

Magdalena Formella-Leigh asserts the moral right to
be identified as the author of this work.

A catalogue record for this book is available from the British Library.

ISBN: 978-0-00-877037-2

This novel is entirely a work of fiction.
The names, characters and incidents portrayed in it are
the work of the author's imagination. Any resemblance to
actual persons, living or dead, events or localities is
entirely coincidental.

Typeset in Sabon by Palimpsest Book Production Limited, Falkirk, Stirlingshire

Printed and bound in the UK using 100% Renewable
Electricity at CPI Group (UK) Ltd

All rights reserved. No part of this publication may be
reproduced, stored in a retrieval system, or transmitted,
in any form or by any means, electronic, mechanical,
photocopying, recording or otherwise, without the prior
permission of the publishers.

Without limiting the author's and publisher's exclusive rights, any unauthorised use of
this publication to train generative artificial intelligence (AI) technologies is expressly
prohibited. HarperCollins also exercise their rights under Article 4(3) of the Digital Single
Market Directive 2019/790 and expressly reserve this publication from the text and data
mining exception.

This book contains FSC™ certified paper and other controlled sources to ensure
responsible forest management.

For more information visit: www.harpercollins.co.uk/green

To Martyn.
For pulling me into the pages of my favourite love story,
for believing in me when I don't believe in myself,
and for loving me the way I always wanted to be loved.

CHAPTER ONE

Caroline

A pale, smooth circle around her ring finger was the only tangible proof that Caroline had, in fact, been married.

Her gaze lingered on her left hand. If she squinted hard enough in the whisky bar's dim light, she could conjure the eighteen-carat white gold engagement ring with its clear-cut square two-carat diamond sitting on it next to the matching wedding band that completed the set.

A symbol of love and commitment to spending a life together.

Caroline and Finn against the world.

Shame that had only lasted four miserable years.

She laced her hands on top of the bar's chrome surface, peering into the full crystal glass. She hadn't touched her drink yet. Not that long ago, she'd have been petrified that someone might think she was weird, sitting on her own in a bar. But that was *before*.

When she was married to her childhood sweetheart.

When she was still working as an emergency medicine doctor in Glasgow.

Now, across the ocean in Oklahoma, she was another person entirely. Or at least she desperately wanted to be.

So, when she had longed for a taste of home this evening, she'd simply searched for bars in Oklahoma City with reviews mentioning a decent selection of Scottish whisky. From the outside, The Rouge Scot hadn't inspired much confidence. Its edgy interior with rough shapes lacked softness and comfort. It looked nothing like her favourite pubs in Glasgow or Edinburgh, or her native Aberdeen. She had peered inside, her eyebrow twitching as she scanned the outfits of the patrons.

There were men wearing crisp suits, but also those wearing faded jeans and cowboy hats. Some women were wearing tight dresses, others a casual combination of shorts and T-shirts. Those in suits and tight dresses were the type of crowd Caroline had expected to find in a place like this. But the atmosphere didn't seem stiff, at least from the outside. People were chatting, laughing. The entire floor-to-ceiling wall of glass bottles, with many labels she recognised, had made up her mind.

This was the first time she had ever gone to a bar on her own. Not wanting to just sit there and look desperate, she had brought a book. Whisky and a book were always a good idea.

Divorced at thirty-one. Who would have thought . . .

There was no denying that she only had herself to blame. Well, herself and Disney for letting her believe in unrealistic expectations when it came to love. Based on the cartoons she had watched as a child, only one heroine didn't end up with her first love – Pocahontas. Every other princess fell head over heels for pretty much the first man she set her eyes on, and he loved her back deeply. Then, they lived 'happily ever after'.

Caroline knew now why that was the moment all the fairy tales ended. Because 'happily ever after' wasn't so happy after all.

She blew out a breath, wiping her palms on her light denim skirt. She didn't want to look at her bare finger. 'Country's Cool Again' by Lainey Wilson came from the speakers, and Caroline smiled to herself, watching a couple in the corner of the room. The redhead woman giggled and took the man's hat, putting it on her own head.

Her mind wandered back to Finn, the memory of his pinched expression when she had surprised him with tickets for the full three days of Country 2 Country music festival in Glasgow two years ago. She had loved the line up, and couldn't pass up a chance to see Lainey Wilson live.

Isn't country music kind of embarrassing?

He did go with her to the first day but huffed and complained the entire time. Caroline had taken a friend for the remaining two days.

Focusing on the background music and the hum of Friday night conversations, her lungs filled with the air of familiar loneliness. The kind that made you feel invisible in a room full of people.

She picked up her book, re-reading the first paragraph on the marked page for what must've been the third time since she'd taken her seat at the bar.

They'd tried talking. When that failed, they had tried marriage counselling. Months of biweekly sessions inching farther and farther away from each other on the velvet couch in the therapist's office.

Nothing was written down, no papers were signed, but they

might as well have been. Neither of their families knew yet. There hadn't been enough time to fly to Dublin to tell her family before she came to Oklahoma. Dropping a bomb like this was best done in person. So, they had only told their best friends and agreed to sort out all the 'legal stuff' once she got back.

'Is the book good?'

Caroline blinked. As she turned to her right, her forearm knocked her glass. The whisky spilled onto the bar, pooling under her paperback.

It was a good book until you interrupted it, she thought as she picked up a napkin and tried to scrub the wet stain off the cover. It was no use. The light amber liquid had already soaked through the pages. Her eyes pricked with tears again. She had bought this book at the airport on the way here, something to keep Finn out of her mind.

'I don't think that's going to come off.'

She opened her mouth, gaping at the man perched on the bar stool next to her. She hadn't noticed him sit down, concentrating too hard on dispersing her gloomy thoughts and pretend-concentrating on the words on the page. She'd been in Oklahoma City a week, and she'd seen her fair share of handsome men dressed like they'd just stepped out of a country music video. But this one momentarily took her breath away.

His dark, ruffled hair was just long enough to brush the top of his dark green shirt, stretched over what she could see even from here were well-defined muscles, but the most interesting thing about him was his piercing grey eyes. They looked almost silver in the bar's artificial light.

'I'm sorry, do I know you?' she asked.

'Not yet.' The man shrugged with a playful smile. 'I'm sorry about your book. I startled you.'

Caroline's green eyes met his. That warm smile . . . Maybe it was just the fact that his smile reached his eyes, and the effect was interesting overall? Or maybe it was the fact that his smile looked so sincere?

'It's fine, don't worry about it,' she said, feeling a slight pang of emotion. She couldn't remember the last time she'd smiled that way. 'It's just a book.'

'Books are never *just* books,' he said incredulously.

She glanced at him, trying to estimate his age.

He looked like he could be a couple of years or so younger than her. He might be twenty-eight or maybe twenty-six. Or maybe he was thirty. She had never been great at pinning down someone's exact age.

He cocked his head, the cheeky smile still plastered to his face. 'Can I join you? I owe you a drink, too.'

Mid-to-late twenties, she decided. 'You can join me, though I'm not in a talkative mood. And I heard I'm not the best conversation partner.'

His smile widened. 'That is the worst conversation starter I've ever heard.'

'Case in point.'

'Point taken.'

Caroline shrugged. 'Just trying to be honest.'

'Why don't we start again? I can tell from your accent you're Irish, I think.' He paused, observing her reaction. 'I'm right, aren't I?'

Caroline bit back a smile. 'So what if you are?'

He surprised her. She thought her accent was difficult to discern. She had been born and raised in Aberdeen, but both of her parents were Irish. As a result, her accent was a unique mix of soft Irish with some Scottish mixed in.

'But if you told me you were say, Australian, I'd just go

with it.' He clasped his hands on top of the bar. 'Doesn't matter. It wouldn't change the scene we're in.'

'And what scene is that?' She leaned back, not wanting to show how intrigued she was.

He cocked his head to the left and scratched his chin. It was covered with a short stubble, like he hadn't shaved for a couple of days.

'Two strangers meeting in a bar. Sounds like an opening of a romcom.'

Caroline laughed, tucking a strand of her dark blonde hair behind her right ear. She wasn't sure Finn even knew what a romcom was. She pushed thoughts of him away. They were over, and there was nothing wrong with a little flirting.

'Oh, I see. You're not only cheeky; you're presumptuous too.'

'I prefer to call it confident.' He looked into her eyes again and the tension she felt a moment ago was replaced by fluttering. Butterflies? There was just something about him . . . She couldn't put her finger on it.

'If it was an opening scene in a romcom, there'd have to be some chemistry between the characters.'

He let out a low, warm laugh. 'And you don't think there is?'

The air crackled with something equally terrifying and exciting.

Caroline swallowed and changed the topic. 'Can I ask what you're drinking?'

'Glencadam. Fifteen years old.' He brought the glass up to his mouth, taking another sip. 'Yourself? I mean, before it spilled?'

'Knockando. Twelve years old.' She smiled, shaking her head. 'Glencadam's a good choice.'

'You sound surprised.'

She felt her cheeks burning. It was the whisky's fault, she thought. Ignoring the intensity of his gaze, she cleared her throat.

'Well, we're in Oklahoma and you *are* American. Sometimes I wonder if Jack Daniel's is considered the height of what passes as good alcohol over here.'

'We do have bourbon.'

'True, that you do.'

She inhaled, eager to stomp down on her annoyingly beating heart. This was a normal reaction to meeting a handsome stranger who just happened to flirt with her, right? Anyone would get flustered. There was nothing to see here.

He ordered another double for himself and one for Caroline. When their drinks arrived, they clinked glasses and took an appreciative sip simultaneously.

'I always knew Scottish whisky was superior to Irish whiskey, but you've just confirmed it for me,' he said.

Stop staring at him. You're behaving like you've never seen a man before.

'My parents moved to Scotland from Ireland shortly after getting married. So, I was actually born and raised there. But I spent my summers outside Dublin. Guess developing a biased taste for single malt was inevitable, despite my grandfather's best efforts.'

'Not sure I'd call it biased. More like, the right taste.' He bloody winked at her.

Her cheeks heated and she really wished she had a fan stashed in her teal leather handbag. Maybe the air conditioning had stopped working. It had been a stiflingly hot day.

'Careful or my dad will hear you all the way over in Ireland.' She chewed on her bottom lip. 'He moved back when I went to university. And he's decisively patriotic in his drink choices.'

The man propped his elbow on the bar, resting his chin on his open palm. 'So, I'm meeting your dad now? I'm not sure I'm ready for this kind of commitment.'

His laughter was drowned by the high-pitched giggles and excited voices of a group of women walking into the bar.

Caroline narrowed her eyes at a white sash around a tall one's chest. *Bride to be.*

A sudden urge to rip the piece of shiny material, to grab the woman by the shoulders and shake her, to tell her marriage and love were the biggest shams, coiled in Caroline's gut. She tugged on the sleeves of her mauve silk shirt so that her fingers had something else to do. If she wanted to go back to practising medicine next year, she couldn't get arrested for an assault on a perfect stranger.

Maybe the woman was going to be the lucky one and grow old and grey with her partner.

Maybe not everyone's marriage was doomed.

Perhaps it's just me. I'm the problem.

CHAPTER TWO

Caroline

It might've been five minutes or an hour later. Caroline had lost track of time. She exhaled, stashing the thoughts into a black box inside her head. She was in a bar, thousands of miles from home. Tonight wasn't the night to despair about the sad state of her life. There would be time to dance on its ashes later.

'5 Leaf Clover' by Luke Combs was playing now.

Awkward interior aside, The Rouge Scot had both an excellent whisky and music selection.

The handsome stranger didn't leave. He was still sitting on the charcoal vegan leather bar stool, now tapping his fingers against the bar surface. His sleeves were rolled up, revealing a very nice set of forearms.

Caroline swallowed.

Surely, this was some kind of joke. All she had wanted was a peaceful night with whisky and a book to calm her nerves before starting a new job on Monday. Now, her book and peace were both ruined.

Bloody forearms.

His head was turned away from her and towards the bartender. He didn't see the practically ravenous way her eyes soaked in everything about him. From his forearms to his tousled dark hair, even the denim of his jeans and the brown belt he wore. Her mind whirled with vivid images of what she'd see if she untucked and unbuttoned his shirt.

What's wrong with me?

A shiver ran down her spine.

The bartender set a new glass in front of her, taking away the empty one. She gave him a grateful smile, turning to drown once again in the gorgeous grey eyes.

'Damn, where are my manners?' He looked at her with mock severity. 'I never asked for your name.'

'Ah, but you were the one who wanted to dispose with polite etiquette.' She smirked, feeling freer and lighter than she had in a very long time. Something about him, his presence, put her at ease. But then the moment passed, and she coughed, reaching for her glass again. 'I'm Caroline.'

'Hunter.' He raised his glass slightly towards her and took another sip. 'It's very nice to meet you.'

His eyes found Caroline's and she felt another jolt in the pit of her stomach. She looked away first, startled by the strange feeling. She could have sworn she felt him smile beside her.

Tipping the glass back, she closed her eyes and let the Knockando's familiar pale golden liquid coat her tongue. The subtle fresh almond note at the back of her throat spurred an extra dose of courage into her.

She licked her bottom lip. 'So, Hunter. Do you come here often?'

'From time to time. I like the whisky.' He grinned over the rim of his glass. 'What about you?'

'Oh, it's my first time here.'

'Any chance it might not be the last?'

'I'm not sure.' She reached for the tall water glass the bartender had just put in front of her. Her thumb brushed condensation droplets from the cold surface. Lifting it to her mouth, she locked eyes with Hunter. 'There's always a chance.'

'I don't like leaving things to chance.'

'You should have more faith.'

'I don't believe in fate and all the stuff that would make me have more faith. I think life's always what we make of it, the sum of our choices and decisions. Nothing more, nothing less.' Hunter finished off his drink and put the empty glass on the bar. 'Sorry. That's a bit too deep.' He shifted uncomfortably on his stool. His demeanour changed almost instantly from playful and flirty to wistful, somehow older.

'I disagree. I think that although people often have the power to change some things, sometimes the course they're on has been determined from the start. There's nothing they can do to change it. Or, at least, they feel like that.'

'Are you talking about yourself?' he asked quietly.

Caroline froze, halfway through putting the cold glass back on the bar. 'Maybe.'

'Maybe?'

She nodded. 'That's what I said.'

Hunter finally turned back to her and studied her face.

Her heart started beating a little bit faster. Just when she thought she wouldn't be able to stand it a second longer, he smirked.

'I think that such thinking can make people powerless. They can feel like there's no point in fighting for what they truly want, so why should they even try? And if fate is cruel and leaves someone hurt, then they feel like they might've deserved it.'

Something stabbed deep inside her chest. She wanted to ask him about it, wanted to know what caused him pain, wanted to know him.

But you can't, a small voice reminded her, echoing in her mind. *You're only here for one year. Then you're going back home.* Suddenly, Caroline didn't trust herself to be in Hunter's presence. She glanced at the clock above the bar, looking for an excuse to get up and walk.

No, *run*.

That's what she should do. Yet, she found herself unable to move. Her eyes refused to leave his face. When she was debating the fruitless merits of her half-baked escape plan, her gaze wandered to his lips. She had never really thought or looked at lips this way before. Why would she have? She had only ever kissed one man in her life. Her soon-to-be ex-husband.

The music abruptly stopped like someone had decided they'd had enough of upbeat country, and a low rumble of her beloved ballad came on. Chris Stapleton's voice echoed in her mind, slowing down her erratic heartbeat. She downed the rest of her drink, setting the glass back on the bar with a thud.

Suddenly, the fact she had never kissed anyone beside Finn bothered her. It gnawed at her bones, eating its way inside her flesh. What if she died tonight? She couldn't even remember the last time she had been kissed.

She had told herself she'd try new things during her year in Oklahoma.

This would definitely be new and unlike her.

'This is going to sound ridiculous. You need to know that I know it does sound ridiculous,' she mumbled.

Hunter quirked his brow. 'I'm intrigued. We've gone from flirty, to serious to ridiculous now.'

Caroline inhaled sharply. She was so going to regret it.

'Well, this is . . . I mean . . .' She swallowed against a hard lump in her throat. The room was spinning in front of her eyes and Hunter was the only firm and steady thing in her eyesight. 'You can say no, of course.'

'I don't think I could say no to you.'

She snorted, her vision snapping back into focus. 'What if I asked you to take off your clothes and do a chicken dance on the bar?'

His knee brushed hers. Electric sparks snuck through the two layers of denim, rushing up to her chest. 'I'd ask if you want me to make stupid sounds to go with the dance.'

Her breath hitched as she watched his hand drawing close to hers. She didn't pull away. 'What if I asked you to jump off a bridge?'

Hunter chuckled, brushing a calloused finger over her wrist. 'Damn, there are no in-betweens with you, are there? Either a chicken dance or killing myself. I was hoping there were more things in between.'

'What things did you have in mind?'

The tips of his fingers moved down to her palm. 'Well, starting small, I was hoping you'd ask me to kiss you, right here.' He drew a circle over the sensitive spot on her right wrist.

Her eyelids fluttered. A simple touch didn't have a right to feel this good. She pushed her brain to remember the anatomy of the hand and dermatomes, wanting to name a precise nerve she could swear at for putting her in this strange trance, but she came up blank.

'What if I did ask for that?' she said, reason be damned.

'I'd have to oblige you. Otherwise, what kind of gentleman would I be?'

Caroline drew in a shaky breath. Someone pushed against her back as they tried to get through to the bar. The place was getting busier with more locals eager to enjoy the start of the weekend. It was crowded enough that no one was paying them any attention.

She looked up at Hunter. 'Would that chivalry extend to my lips?'

His throat bobbed as he swallowed hard. But the trace of bewilderment drained from his features almost as quickly as it appeared. 'Is that the ridiculous question you wanted to ask me?' His fingers curled into her palm.

Caroline snatched her hand away. 'If it was, would you?'

Hunter jumped off the stool, unexpectedly closing the distance between them. He was even taller and broader than she'd thought when he was sat down. The heat coming off him through the shirt made her dizzy.

He leaned over, his lips brushing the shell of her ear as he whispered, 'Ask me and you can find out.'

'I'm not going to beg you to kiss me.'

'I didn't say anything about begging.' His lips brushed the side of her ear, again.

She shook her arms like she wanted to release all the tension and electricity and things she didn't have a name for. Things she had never felt before.

'Good. Because I don't beg anyone for anything. Ever,' she said, her tone defiant.

His lips peeled from her ear, and he looked into her eyes. 'Never?'

She shook her head.

Hunter let out a low chuckle. 'Well, that sounds like a challenge for another day.'

'All I hear is talk but you still haven't kissed me.'

'I told you to ask.'

'And I told you I don't beg.' She placed her palm against his chest.

Her breath caught. Right there and then, the whole world faded away. She wasn't thinking about her work. And she certainly wasn't thinking about Finn. All she could think about were those gorgeous grey eyes. She held her hand up to his cheek, trailing a finger down to his hairy chin.

He closed his eyes. 'Well then. I think there's only one solution to this.'

Before she could respond, he brought his lips to hers and kissed her. *Really* kissed her. She felt herself falling into the abyss of sweet nothingness. For the duration of that kiss, nothing else mattered. Not the shambles of her life, not her old job, not even her new one.

She grabbed his shirt, pulling him closer. She wanted to remove every remaining millimetre separating their bodies from where they clearly belonged in this moment. Melted together in a dance of a curious lust.

The distinct flavours of single malts they had drunk mixed together in a blended variety worth bottling. He smelled of bergamot, hay and a hint of soil. Like it was a part of him he wanted to wash off but couldn't quite manage to.

She knew that struggle all too well, forever convinced the distinct smell of hospital disinfectants followed her wherever she went.

Kissing a stranger in a crowded bar wasn't something Caroline had ever imagined herself doing. But that crackling attraction had called on something deeply primal in her very core. Something she hadn't had a chance to explore in thirty-one years of her life. Until now.

Maybe the fact that they would never see each other again made it all so much more exciting than it was.

Just as the recklessness made room for the uneasiness, her phone vibrated in the pocket of her skirt.

They jumped apart like someone had caught them doing something they shouldn't be.

Caroline practically fell off the stool. Her legs were made of candyfloss, every bone refusing to support her weight. Blinking to readjust her eyes to the harsh lighting, she threw her handbag over her arm with a flourish. 'I've got to go. But I did enjoy the . . .' Her eyes flicked to his lips, and she had to stop herself from touching hers. They still throbbed, pulsating with a liveliness she had buried deep years ago. '. . . conversation.'

'Likewise,' he said in a low voice.

Their eyes locked and Caroline had to remind herself to breathe. She was quite pleased that he appeared to look almost as ruffled as she did.

'Can I get your number?' Hunter asked. His eyes shone and his cheeks were slightly flushed.

She dropped her gaze. 'I don't think so.'

'You can't blame a man for trying, right? Especially after that kiss.'

She bit back a smile. 'Yes, the kiss was decent.'

He huffed. 'Only decent?'

'Always room for improvement.' She was already walking away from both him and her whisky-drowned copy of *A Lady's Guide to Scandal*. 'Enjoy your night, Hunter.'

Caroline could feel his eyes on her back until she turned the corner. When she was far enough from the bar, she stopped. Smoothing her hair with a trembling hand, she brought her fingers down to her face, pressing into the middle of her lower lip. She closed her eyes, trying to keep her act together. She would never have dared to do this if there was even a chance they would bump into each other again. But what were the odds? As delicious as that kiss was, none of this was on her agenda for the next year. Figuring out who she was without Finn and what she wanted from her life, that's what she needed to focus on.

She was just going to avoid The Rouge Scot for the duration of her stay in Oklahoma.

CHAPTER THREE

Hunter

After a long day at the ranch, all Hunter craved was a hot shower and some peace and quiet. When he used to work alongside the ranch hands, it was a different kind of exhaustion. Physical pain pushing through every single muscle and joint. Hurt like hell, but at least he knew why he was hurting. Now, his days were filled with managing everything. He was no longer spending hours on end on horseback; that had been replaced by making phone calls and shaking hands. But some things hadn't changed, like this part of the day, when it was just him and his favourite horse. If only his entire day could consist of more interactions with the horses instead of pushing through papers and focusing on the cattle . . .

Thinking about what he wanted was pointless. The ranch, his family, needed him to step up to fill his father's boots. So what if he wouldn't have chosen that pair himself?

Maybe he would forsake the quiet evening and head out

to Oklahoma City instead. He couldn't stop thinking about the gorgeous green-eyed woman he had met at The Rouge Scot two weeks ago. *Caroline.*

The memory of her face made him involuntarily grin. Then, the thought of their kiss and her lips on his squeezed his chest tight. Hunter couldn't remember the last time his thoughts were consumed by a woman. It wasn't like him, and he wasn't sure he liked it. Especially as she didn't give him her number – what if he was never going to see her again? Would he be cursed to forever wonder what could've been?

He pushed the thoughts away. He had been back to that damn bar twice now. She hadn't been there.

Forget about her, you damn fool.

'It's OK, Dallas. Almost done. You're doing great, as always.' Hunter stroked the mane of the beautiful black horse and smiled fondly at him.

The horse nickered in response.

Hunter picked up Dallas's front right hoof and gently removed the debris that had got stuck there during their latest training sessions. He repeated the process with the other legs, checking for any signs of cuts or swelling as he did. Everything looked in order. Hunter picked up the curry-comb and brushed in a sweeping motion, working his way across Dallas's body from behind his ear to the top of his tail. Dallas snorted a few times as he got too close to his head and when he went over his spine. As he combed through the mane and tail, he heard slow, heavy footsteps behind him.

'Almost done,' he said without looking to see who it was.

'Good. Mama sent me to tell you that dinner's going to be ready soon.'

Hunter didn't need to turn round to know his sister had her arms crossed. Every member of the Jackson family had found their own way of dealing with the recent uncertainty. They were all sidestepping the impending grief, hoping there would be no reason to turn back and fall into it.

'I didn't say I was staying for dinner,' he said.

Megan snorted. 'She thought you'd say that and said she knows you won't cook anything yourself and that she's starting to worry you're not getting enough hot meals.'

He put the brush away and turned round to face his sister. 'I guess I have no choice then.'

'No, you don't,' Megan said.

Hunter untied Dallas's rope. 'I'll be out in a minute.'

Megan didn't respond. The sound of her boots told Hunter she'd gone outside.

He led Dallas into his stall and closed the gate. When he walked out, he found Megan leaning against the barn's entrance.

'I'm gonna convince Daddy to let me have a glass of red with my steak.' she announced, peeling her back from the red-painted wood.

Hunter laughed. 'Like that's going to happen.'

Megan shrugged. 'I'm eighteen. It isn't like I've never had alcohol before.'

'Maybe don't say that to Dad.' He put his arm around her shoulders and pulled her into a hug. 'It's hard to remember at times how old you are, Meg. Because the older you get, the older I get. I don't know, I just thought that by the time I was twenty-six, I'd have done something with my life. Yet here I am.'

'Don't worry, Buck's practically ancient. You're still a spring chicken compared to him.' She grinned and hugged him back.

Buck was their older brother who lived in Tulsa with his wife, Lorna, and their two children, Morgan and Cody.

'You have time, Hunt. Besides, it's not like you've been stuck here all the time. You've been to college,' Megan added.

'And then I came back . . .'

'Nothing wrong with that. I was over the moon when you moved back home. I'm not sure how Mama and I would've coped if you hadn't been here for us. And for Daddy. It was the right thing to do,' she said in a slow, comforting voice.

His jaw tensed. She was right. It was the only thing to do. As much as he was angry at the universe for the circumstances that had brought him home, he wasn't angry at his father. He could never put even a morsel of blame at his feet.

Megan hit him in the shoulder, snapping him out of his trance. 'What are you thinking about?'

'Dad.'

His simple response wiped her smile away.

Shit. He shouldn't have said that, shouldn't have worried her.

She looked into the distance, where the sun was setting above the treeline.

Hunter followed her gaze. The silhouettes of cattle grazing in the pasture completed the picture imprinted in his memory. Cicadas disturbed the humid July air, the smell of which he doubted he could ever rid himself. Soil, horses, manure and hay. The sturdy fence surrounding the western paddock was only finished last week. A devastating tornado, EF-3 grade, had wiped it off in April. Other structures were higher on the priority list. Hunter assessed the work from where he stood, his eyes moving in a practised fashion to look for any possible escape routes for the horses or weak spots. He found none. Satisfied, he pushed his hands deeper inside his pockets.

Megan was quiet for a minute, deep in her own thoughts. Finally, her lip quivered, and she said in a shaky undertone, 'He's going to die, isn't he?'

Hunter instinctively put his hands on her shoulders. 'Meg, look at me. Please.'

She raised her glistening eyes.

'Dad has a chance. The oncology team has a plan for him, and we just need to be patient. I think it might work,' he added, seeing that she was still on the verge of tears.

No matter how bleak their father's prognosis was, Hunter was going to do what he could to keep her tears at bay. She was still so young, and she loved their father so much. Losing him would break her into a million pieces. Alan Jackson loved all his children, but Megan was the apple of his eye. He'd give her the world if he could. She reciprocated this love in every fibre of her being. Daddy was her hero, her favourite person. He'd got sick when she was just starting high school, and it had distorted her world.

The diagnosis of metastatic melanoma, a type of skin cancer that had now spread to his brain, had pulled the ground from underneath the Jackson family's feet.

Over the past four years, Megan and Hunter had become even closer than before. Shared pain tends to do that to people.

'Do you really believe that?' she asked.

Hunter nodded. 'I do.'

He didn't, not the way he wished he did. But this was his burden to carry. Megan didn't need to know that. If he could put on a brave face for her, protect her somehow, he was going to do just that. Even if it only brought her comfort for a short while.

'There you both are! I was going to walk down to the barn myself if you didn't turn up in the next ten minutes!' Mary hurriedly shooed them inside and closed the door.

Hunter gave his mom a quick hug and a kiss on the cheek. 'Hi, Mom.'

She swatted him away with a white fluffy towel. 'Hi, honey.'

Mary Jackson was a petite woman with short, dark hair. As he hugged her, Hunter noticed her grey roots were more pronounced than the last time he saw her last week. He hadn't remembered ever seeing a single grey hair on his mother's head. Mary took pride in her appearance and visited the hair salon regularly.

Hunter supposed it hadn't been on top of her mind lately. Not that it mattered to him, but the realisation that his mother must be so worried she hadn't done something that he knew brought her joy lodged another stone in his throat.

'I told you I was going to bring him, and I did.' Meg walked up to the stove. 'Mmm, mac'n'cheese. I love when you serve steak with it on the side.' Her wide smile made Hunter chuckle.

'I also made some fries for your daddy. He said they've been on his mind for the past few days. And there's also some salad.'

'Even better, I can eat both!' Megan exclaimed happily, sitting at the table, which was already set for dinner.

Mary shook her head in disapproval, but Hunter saw a small smile on her lips. She put on checkered oven mitts and took out the tray of golden, crispy fries.

'Do you need any help?' Hunter asked, looking around the kitchen.

Mary shook her head. 'No, it's all right, honey. Everything's ready. Sit down and relax. You had a long day.'

He did as she said, taking the seat opposite Megan.

'Al! Dinner's ready!' Mary shouted in the living room's direction.

The distant sound of TV stopped, and a moment later, Alan

walked into the dining area. If someone who knew him before he got ill saw him now, they would never recognise him. He used to be called 'Big Al' by everybody in town due to his height and muscular build. In the past four years, Alan had lost close to forty-five pounds. He rarely had an appetite, and when he did, he often wasn't able to eat much. But stopping chemotherapy had helped a lot with that, and he was enjoying his food again.

Hunter made a mental note to take his father shopping for some new, better-fitting clothes when they were next in Oklahoma City.

'Ooh, steak and fries, that's a Friday night treat.' Alan smiled happily as his wife passed him the first plate laden with food. Then, he turned towards Hunter. 'How's Dallas doing? That horse cost us a fortune. I hope he has as much potential as the old Raffery sang about.'

'He's coming on great. There's definitely potential. I'm thinking he might be ready to go to the Deepwater Springs rodeo.'

'That's what, less than three months from now? You're sure?'

'If we keep making progress, absolutely. It'd be a good occasion to see how he performs in a smaller event. Then maybe next year, we can take him further.'

Alan seemed to be satisfied with this as he responded merely with a curt nod and concentrated on cutting his steak.

Hunter tried to ignore the way Alan's glasses kept sliding down the bridge of his nose. Instead of taking them off, Alan kept pushing them up. He was stubborn that way. Or maybe he was afraid of losing them again. He always seemed to misplace those damn glasses.

The rest of the dinner passed in pleasant small talk, focused mainly on Megan starting college next month and chores that needed to be assigned and done at the ranch. Just as Hunter had suspected, Alan decisively refused to let Megan drink some red wine with the rest of them. She scoffed into her glass of lemonade. Once everyone finished, Hunter piled up the plates and took them to the sink.

Mary followed him into the kitchen. 'Thanks, honey. Just leave them at the side for now. I made a blueberry cobbler for dessert.' She took out the deep casserole dish and started scooping out four portions into shallow bowls.

On autopilot, Hunter opened the freezer and took out a tub of vanilla ice cream. He put it on the counter, and she reached for it and started dishing it out next to the cobbler.

'You know, I'm worried about you.'

Hunter raised his eyebrows. 'Why?'

'It's been five years now. You were so young . . . I mean, you're still very young. But you can't keep yourself closed off to the world forever.'

Not this again, Hunter thought as he let out an exasperated sigh.

'I'm not closed off. I've just been busy. First with finishing college, and then coming back when Dad got sick. It's been a tough time. Dating's been the last thing on my mind, trust me.'

Mary put the ice cream scoop into the sink and faced him. Her eyes were full of sadness, so deep that you could fall into it and drown. She was a beautiful woman, but she seemed to have aged rapidly in the past few years. Her hair wasn't the only feature Alan's illness had touched.

'I know it's been tough. And for what it's worth, I'm sorry,' she paused, shaking her head vigorously as if she hoped the movement could keep her steady. 'I'm so grateful that you're here for him, for *us*. But you also have your own life to live. You know your daddy. He doesn't want you to put your life on hold on his account.'

'Mom, it's fine. You have nothing to be sorry for,' Hunter said in a sharper voice than he intended. It pained him that his mother thought being there for his family was a chore he resented. 'I just haven't met anyone worth my time.'

He winced as the bitter taste of lie flooded his mouth.

Mary looked at him with a sad, knowing smile. 'I'm sure you will.'

The image of Caroline's hypnotising smile flashed before his eyes. He bit his bottom lip. She was definitely someone worth his time.

But she didn't think you were. Otherwise, she would've given you her number.

CHAPTER FOUR

Caroline

Caroline woke up with a start to the sound of a truck reversing outside. Disorientated, she looked at her phone – 7.17 a.m. She yawned, stretching in the double bed. Her alarm was set for half past, so there was no point trying to get back to sleep. She needed to get to work for nine.

It had been two weeks since Caroline had started her job as a research assistant at the Rouken Cancer Center. She had always thrived on challenges and the feeling of satisfaction at the end of the day. So far, the job was great. Intellectually stimulating and engaging. Dr Anna Kennedy, her aunt and the attending oncologist who supervised the exchange programme Caroline got onto, didn't give her any preferential treatment, which was something she had worried about before. She wanted to succeed in the role based on merit, not her family ties.

Two weeks had also passed since she kissed Hunter.

Her cheeks instantly flushed at the memory of his confident smirk and deep voice. She hadn't told anyone about him or the kiss, still too shocked with how brazen she had been. Once or twice, Caroline wondered what would have happened if she had given him her number. Would they have met again? Gone to another bar? Maybe they would've kissed again, too?

Or maybe they would've done more than kissing . . .

A soft knock sounded at the door, pulling her mind from wondering how those calloused fingers would feel pressed against her bare back.

'Come in!' She quickly sat up in bed as the door to the guest bedroom opened.

Gian, her aunt's wife, popped her head in, smiling broadly. 'Do you want some coffee?'

Gian was a tall Korean American woman in her early forties with a warm disposition that made everyone around her feel at ease. Anna and Gian had been together for just over ten years now. They were *that* couple everyone wanted to invite over for dinner parties and game nights. Despite being raised in different cultures and having totally different careers, they were like two peas in a pod.

Caroline smiled. Having been busy with medical school and then the first years of working as a doctor, she hadn't had a chance to spend much time with her aunt's wife before coming to stay with them now. Gian was lovely and Caroline knew they would get along really well. But she was still finding her feet in their interactions. 'Morning, Gian. Coffee would be great, thank you.'

'Sure. Do you want me to bring you a cup or . . .'

'No, that's fine. I'm going to come and sit with you in the kitchen, if that's all right.'

'Perfect, see you there.' Gian closed the door behind her.

Caroline got out of bed and threw on a thin peach cotton robe, tying it around her waist. She was going to jump in the shower before getting ready for work.

She glanced out of the window.

Anna and Gian's second-floor three-bedroom apartment was in a fantastic location with an amazing view of the Oklahoma River. It was on the buzzing doorstep of Bricktown, just east of the downtown business district. The medical school buildings and the Rouken Cancer Center were a stone's throw away as well. Which was apparently the reason they bought it – Anna said she hated being stuck in traffic. From here, she could walk to work, and so could Caroline. At least for another year. Something that wasn't possible in Glasgow, unless you only lived either in the West End or the city centre and didn't need to commute anywhere outside their boundaries. With awful public transport links, having a car was really a must, especially after a gruelling night shift.

When she walked into the kitchen, Gian was already sitting on a pine bar stool at the breakfast bar.

Caroline sat next to her and sniffed the contents of a steaming mug. 'Mmm, I've probably already told you, but I love your coffee. Best coffee ever.' She let out a contented sigh, then raised an eyebrow at Gian. 'Shouldn't you be at the café? You're usually there by five.'

Gian laughed. 'The perks of running a coffee shop. And we're closed today. We're getting new fridges put in. I'm meeting the workmen there at nine.'

'Ah, that explains it. Hope all goes well. You said you're looking to expand your dessert menu, right?' Caroline's stomach grumbled as she thought of Gian's flourless polenta lemon and almond cake.

As if she could read her mind, or maybe she just heard the

sound, Gian walked to the counter and lifted a lid from a plate filled with blueberry muffins.

'Yes, we are.' She put two of them on a small plate and came back to the breakfast table. 'Here you go, I baked these last night. They're Anna's favourite. She's been having a hard time at work lately and I thought coming home to these might cheer her up a bit.'

'You're so good to her.' Caroline grabbed a muffin and took a big bite.

Gian shrugged and lazily peeled the wrap off her muffin, breaking off a small piece. 'We're good to each other.'

Caroline watched Gian's hands. 'How's your arthritis?'

'Fine. I mean, I have good days and worse days. But since I started the new treatment last year, it's been keeping it mostly in check.' She looked down at her hands and flexed the fingers. 'Can't complain.'

'You can if you want to. At least to me.'

Although she hadn't spent much time with Gian before, she knew Gian used to be a piano virtuoso. She attended the San Francisco Conservatory of Music. In her second year, she was diagnosed with rheumatoid arthritis. Gian's words from the first time they met stuck in Caroline's mind.

I could still play but it wasn't at the same level. I didn't want to just be a pianist. I wanted to be a great pianist.

Gian sighed. 'You're just like Anna. Or it is how all doctors are?'

'We get classes on how to be insufferable in med school.'

That made Gian laugh. 'I'd actually believe that.'

They sat in comfortable silence for a moment, savouring the flavours, until Gian popped the last crumb in her mouth and looked at the clock above the microwave. 'Oh, is it that time already? I'll need to get going to the café soon.' She slid off the bar stool and put both mugs in the sink. 'How was your muffin?'

'It was delicious. It was blueberry and . . . orange?' Caroline tried to identify the flavours still tingling the tip of her tongue. She frowned, not convinced she'd guessed correctly.

'Grapefruit, actually. I was experimenting a bit with different citrus fruit in this recipe. Lemon is always the most obvious pairing, but I wanted to see how others taste. Made a batch of blueberry lime last week. Unlikely but delicious.' The way Gian's face lit up every time she talked about baking was positively contagious.

Caroline couldn't help but smile warmly in response. 'Now that you said it, I can tell it was grapefruit. Such a good flavour combination. I loved it! Happy to do any other sampling of your experiments if you need a guinea pig.'

They both laughed heartily.

'Feel free to pop into the café later if you want to, I might have some more then.' Gian was on her way out of the kitchen when she suddenly stopped. She turned round and looked at Caroline, concern in her eyes. 'How are you doing though, really?'

'I'm fine. Still adjusting to the time difference.' Caroline tried to sound casual. Without meaning to, she touched her bare ring finger. It was a force of habit. She had caught herself doing it a lot more lately. 'I think the work's going to be so different from what I'm used to.'

'In a good way or . . . ?'

'I don't know yet. Just different.' Caroline shrugged, looking at Gian. 'I'm trying to decide if I want to continue being a doctor. I mean, as in a practising one,' she added, unclasping her hands as Gian's brow furrowed in confusion.

'Is that why you agreed to take the research position? To see what's out there beyond clinical medicine?'

'Exactly.' She wasn't sure why she was telling Gian that. Maybe muffins were the way to her locked-up anxious soul. Even if it was only a tiny peek into its shadows.

Gian put her keys in her pocket and sat back on the bar stool. She gave Caroline an encouraging smile. 'I can stay another few minutes if you want to tell me more about it. Only if you want to.'

Caroline winced. She didn't know if she was ready to talk about it with anyone. She loved Gian, even though she didn't know her that well yet, but she didn't think she'd understand. It wasn't Gian's fault; it wasn't anyone's fault. Previous attempts at explaining her doubts about her career had left her feeling ungrateful. *But you're a doctor. You studied for all those years. You help people.*

She craved turning time back to the first day of medical school so that she could steal her own enthusiasm and rose-tinted glasses, and sneak them through time into the present. Saving lives and helping people every day were the reasons she applied to study medicine. Eleven years later, she had completed six years of medical school, two years of foundation training and three years of the acute care common stem training pathway. She had been working as a doctor for five years now. Just when she had got onto a higher speciality training and was a mere three years away from becoming an emergency medicine consultant, she stumbled.

One Saturday afternoon before she was meant to go on a night shift, she'd woken up and couldn't get out of bed. There wasn't any single thing she could pinpoint. She supposed she just felt burnt out. If there was even a slight chance she would come back to speciality training, to being a practising doctor, she needed a break.

Caroline didn't know if she had it in her. She needed to know if she missed it when she was in Oklahoma, unable to treat patients under the conditions of her one-year visa and the lack of US medical licence.

Gian's phone rang but she declined the call without checking who it was. She looked at Caroline with a mix of sadness and empathy. 'I'm glad that you were able to take some time off from the training and explore what comes next.'

Caroline rubbed her temple and took a deep breath. 'Truthfully? It saved my sanity.'

'That's good. And you don't have to decide anything right away. Whether you want to quit altogether or just get away from emergency medicine and do something else . . . I hope that these few months working in clinical trials and taking time for yourself will help you make up your mind.' She got up and enveloped Caroline in a long hug.

Caroline felt close to tears. She hadn't been hugged like this in a very long time. Without the weight of broken promises and awkwardness, driven simply by the kindness and feeling.

'Thank you. I really needed that,' Caroline uttered into Gian's black hair before she let her go.

'You know you can always talk to me, right?'

She swallowed her tangled feelings with a sniff. 'I do. Have a great day! I'd better get going too or else I'll be late.'

CHAPTER FIVE

Hunter

Hunter's day started early, but this was the norm on the ranch. The roof of the western barn had suffered some damage during the most recent storm, and it had to be repaired as soon as possible. Anything that was salvageable from its stores would have to be moved elsewhere for the time being. This was normally something the ranch hands did, but Duke and Luke had taken the morning off so they could go to some gig in Tulsa the night before. Plus, he tried to run the ranch the hands-on way he'd seen his father do his entire life.

Halfway through his morning, his brother, Buck, popped in to say hi. He was a truck driver and spent a month at a time on the road, followed by two weeks home in Tulsa. Buck helped to move the last of the stores into another outbuilding, then suggested grabbing some coffee and now, almost an hour later, they were sitting in a small, cosy café in Purcell.

'This is very . . . hipster. Is that the word I'm looking for?'

Buck put his white mug on the table. He leaned back in a high leather armchair and looked around with curiosity. The café was small, with only seven haphazardly arranged tables and mismatched colourful chairs. The walls were a mix of exposed red brick and dark wood panelling, complementing the wooden floor. Soft music played in the background, adding to the overall picture of serenity.

Hunter let out a short laugh and took a long sip of his coffee. 'If you say so. I like coming here. They have great coffee. And it's the only place where the cakes could rival Mom's.'

'Better not tell her that. So, you come here often?' Buck slowly turned his head and looked suggestively at a young woman behind the counter.

Hunter glared at his brother. 'It's just coffee, Buck. Michelle is very friendly. She's the owner's granddaughter. Though I'd probably say she's closer in age to Meg than to me.'

'So? You're only twenty-six. There are tons of guys dating younger women.'

'Like you did?' Hunter asked.

Buck's wife, Lorna, was eight years younger. They met, fell in love, got married and had two beautiful children. They rarely fought and seemed to agree on most things.

Buck grinned in response and drank some coffee. 'Yes, like I did. Although, without my good looks, you might have less luck getting a younger gal to fall for you.'

'You mean your bald head and big forehead? I'm doing just fine with my own, thanks!'

Buck moved closer to him and hit him on the knee.

Hunter instinctively pushed further into his chair.

'Careful, Hunt, you should show some respect to your elders. Anyway, dating is what I wanted to talk to you about.'

Hunter groaned. 'Ugh, not again. Don't tell me – Mom called you?'

'She's just worried about you. You know how she is. She just wants to see you happy again.'

Hunter bit his lip and measured the words. 'Why can't you all get it in your heads? I'm happy as a bunny. I don't need to be in a relationship for that.'

'Don't you, though? You haven't been the same since—'

'Sometimes it's better to mind your own business,' Hunter interrupted.

Buck looked pensive as he nodded several times. 'Mom doesn't know half of it though, does she?'

Hunter didn't meet his brother's stare.

'How you banged every buckle bunny after rodeos when you were in the circuit?'

It was a rhetorical question. Of course she didn't know. What was he meant to do, broadcast it to the world? One-night stands weren't a big deal. He never promised anything to any of these women. And they didn't expect anything of him, apart from a good time and maybe a few drinks. He always made it clear that he wasn't looking for anything that'd last past the morning.

A strange void deep in his gut opened, pouring confusion onto his thinly scarred wounds. Realistically, Hunter knew he couldn't grieve forever. It hit him that he didn't want to. Lately he had started thinking that maybe there was something . . . well, not necessarily missing. He wouldn't say that. He knew better than to try to base his happiness on the presence of another person. No, it wasn't that. But gradually, as the time went on, he started craving the conversation. The morning-after coffee and breakfast. Having someone out there who he wanted to be the first to find out everything good and bad that happened to him.

Luck had it that shortly after that realisation he had met Caroline. And as much as he didn't want to think about her, because he knew there was no point, the other night when 'White Horse' by Chris Stapleton came on the radio in his truck, he could almost taste that kiss again. He thought he would never be able to listen to it again without thinking about her. The buckle bunnies Buck mentioned weren't the same. Maybe because the kissing was always followed by sex.

'As it happens, I decided I might be ready to meet someone new. For real, not just to have someone in my bed on a Friday night,' Hunter finally announced as Buck quirked his eyebrow sceptically.

Just then, Michelle came over and asked if they wanted anything else. Hunter ordered another cup and a lemon bar. Buck just asked for a glass of water. They didn't speak to each other until she brought the order over.

'You actually mean it?' Buck asked. 'You're ready to go on a real date?'

'Well, not sure what you mean by a "real date" . . . but yes. If I meet someone interesting, I'll ask her out,' Hunter said, picking up the steaming mug.

Buck's timid joy disappeared as quickly as it showed in his smile. 'If you meet someone . . .' he echoed, staring at Hunter blankly. 'You're going to set up a profile on dating apps or websites, right?'

Hunter didn't answer, breaking off a piece of a lemon bar instead and chewing it slowly. It was delicious. Just the right level of sweet and sour.

'Hunt, tell me you will. How else are you planning to meet a woman?' Scepticism and concern danced together in Buck's eyes.

Hunter swallowed the last bit of the bar and laced his

fingers together. He didn't look at Buck when he spoke. 'I don't like the idea of using these apps. They sound like a lot of work and not much fun. Whatever happened to chance meetings and connecting with real people?'

'They are *real* people, and you can connect with them in real life after you chat with them online.' Buck grimaced and laughed tensely, disbelief echoing in his words. 'When was the last time you heard of people meeting by chance?'

'You mean, aside from you and Lorna?' he asked, and Buck nodded once.

Caroline.

But something stopped him from telling Buck about her. The sad embarrassment that he was still dwelling on their meeting despite not having any means of contacting her. He had gone back to The Rouge Scot two nights ago, grabbing drinks with his best friend, Mitch. His stomach had flipped whenever a blonde woman walked through the door, just to drop down in disappointment when it wasn't her.

He didn't know if he'd ever see her again.

'I don't know,' he finally said, avoiding looking at his brother.

'Well, I think you might be looking for a very long time.'

'I'm a patient guy.'

Buck raised his empty water glass and clinked it against Hunter's half-full mug. 'Cheers to that, little brother. Can't wait to meet whoever you deem special enough to measure up to your expectations.'

'We're going to be late. I told you we should've left earlier. Now the doc will be annoyed – you know that she has other patients to see, right? She's a busy woman.'

'We won't be late, Dad,' Hunter replied patiently, tightening the grip on the steering wheel. They were on the way to Alan's biweekly visit to the cancer centre. Normally they arrived in plenty of time to find the best parking spot. However, today they had left the ranch late because Alan couldn't find his glasses again. The traffic also seemed to be worse than usual, and as soon as they got into Oklahoma City they ran into pretty much every red light.

Alan was starting to get visibly agitated, drumming his fingers on his thighs. He huffed, fiddling with the brim of the straw hat sitting in his lap. Hunter glanced to the side at the next set of lights and squeezed his father's knee.

'Dad, don't worry. We're almost there. Now, are you really worried about the time or about the visit in general?'

Alan brushed his son's hand away and pointedly turned his head to look out of the Ford F-150's window. When he spoke, his voice was small. 'I know that I don't have much time left. But this clinical trial gives me a sense of purpose, you know? That even if I don't make it, maybe thanks to me and people like me, others in the future will have a better chance.'

Tears welled in Hunter's eyes. His knuckles whitened on the wheel.

It wasn't often that his father spoke about his feelings about his prognosis or dying. Usually, he put on a brave face and brushed off everyone's concerns. Right now, he was probably the most vulnerable Hunter had seen him since they were told his cancer was back.

'Dad, don't say that. It's not over yet. I thought that you'd been feeling better?'

'I've been feeling pretty much the same, which isn't bad. But the doc told me at the last visit that I might feel all right until one day I don't anymore. I'm thankful that this treatment doesn't seem to have many side effects though. And that I can eat real food, unlike last time.' Alan pushed his glasses up his nose.

Hunter bit his lip. This clinical trial was Alan's only option. He'd exhausted all other lines of treatment. He was tired and Hunter couldn't blame him. Most days, it felt like waiting for a miracle, even though no one in the family spoke about it that way. They all tried to stay optimistic, at least as a front.

'It'll be OK, Dad.'

'Yeah . . . I guess it will be, one way or another.' Alan cleared his throat. 'Turn right up here.'

Hunter pursed his lips, holding back from saying he knew. Rouken Cancer Center featured in his nightmares. It was a massive hospital, with a medical school attached to it. All six floors of gleaming white and glass. There was a separate research wing with laboratories and whatnot. Alan had received his care here from the very start of his treatment, which meant that when he enrolled onto a clinical trial, he didn't have to change the doctors or the hospitals. Everything stayed the same. They even recognised the nurses and porters now.

Hunter swallowed as he put the truck in the underground car park.

In. Out. In . . .

He counted his breaths to ten, preparing himself to be there for Alan without the gloom of his own stress hanging over them. Then, he helped his father out of the car and lent him his arm to steady him as they walked up to the entrance.

They made it with enough time to spend a quarter of an hour sitting on the uncomfortable chairs in the waiting area. Instead of inviting them both into her office, Alan's oncologist, Dr Anna Kennedy, came out and said that they had to run some tests today, including an MRI scan of his brain to check if the cancer had spread. Alan also needed to have a full blood workup. Before she had even finished speaking, a nurse appeared seemingly out of nowhere with a wheelchair.

'I'll wait around, Dad. Might grab something to eat in the cafeteria.' Hunter leaned into his father's thin frame and warmly squeezed his arm.

Alan just nodded and the nurse started pushing the wheelchair down the hallway.

Hunter slumped back into a chair and buried his face in his hands. Trying to keep it together in front of his father was hard. The injustice and hurt of it all was always waiting just round the corner of his mind, ready to overtake his mood completely as soon as he was alone.

'Damn it, damn it!' he muttered angrily as he got up. 'Damn it!'

He might as well go to the cafeteria. It'd be a distraction, at least for a little while. As soon as he turned around, he felt a sharp pain in his chest as he collided with something hard. *Someone.* A cell phone and a stack of papers clattered to the floor. The person who walked into him bent down, hurriedly gathering them into their arms. Hunter crouched and mechanically started picking up printed sheets of paper as well as blue folders.

'Oh shit, I'm so sorry. Are you OK?' a female voice asked.

They stood up and looked at each other. Hunter's entire body froze.

He recognised those eyes.

CHAPTER SIX

Caroline

Caroline toppled backwards from the force of the impact. She dropped a stack of folders, loose pieces of paper escaping and scattering to the floor. Forgetting all the manners and professional behaviour, she blurted out, 'Oh shit, I'm so sorry. Are you OK?'

The poor man she had just walked into helped gather the scattered folders before standing straight, towering over her. She got up and looked at him apologetically. He was wearing dark jeans, a brown leather belt with a big metal buckle and heavy brown leather boots. His light blue shirt was tucked in, highlighting his lean, muscular chest and arms. Strands of black hair were visible underneath his camel cowboy hat.

He smirked as he handed her some of the papers. She couldn't quite make out the colour of his eyes due to the shadow cast by his hat and the poor lighting.

There was something familiar about the air around him. About those forearms, the posture . . .

Shitshitshit.

Caroline's mouth went dry. 'Hunter.'

He took the hat off and grinned at her like he couldn't believe his eyes.

Well, at least she wasn't the only one feeling like an idiot. Damn it. What was he doing here?

'Hello, Caroline.' He smiled at her, and an intense feeling of déjà vu hit her. 'I was wondering if you were going to recognise me. Fancy meeting you here.'

'Of course I'd recognise you.' She dropped her eyes to the floor.

How could she forget?

'I'm glad to hear it. Especially since you declared our kiss only "decent".'

Her eyes widened in alarm at the word 'kiss'. She whipped her head round, checking if anyone she knew had overheard them. That'd give something to get people talking, only two weeks into a new job. Caroline hated workplace gossip. She had always made a point of not engaging in any of it herself, nor did she give people a reason to feature in it. And she wasn't about to change that.

She felt herself blush even more as she raised her eyes again and looked up at his face. This was a mistake. Her gaze darted to his lips, her breath hitching at the memory of their tongues crushing together.

'You know the kiss was better than decent,' she murmured.

'Good. I was thinking about it.'

They reached for the same piece of paper, the last one still lying on the floor, and their fingers brushed against one another. Caroline stiffened at the contact. His touch seemed to take away her ability to form a coherent thought or sentence.

You're in so much trouble. So much fucking trouble.

She pulled her hand away, straightening as she stood up. 'I'm so sorry. I hope I didn't hurt you?'

'Don't worry, I'm fine. These things happen.' He grinned. 'Especially if someone's looking at their phone when walking.'

'I was looking up where my next appointment is. I'll be more careful in the future.' She tipped her chin, gesturing to the pile of folders, now safely back in her arms. 'Thank you for helping to pick up these.'

'No problem.' His eyes moved up and down, studying her face intently with those grey eyes she couldn't get out of her head. Their beautiful depth almost made her feel like they were the only two people in the corridor. Everything else seemed to slow down when their eyes locked. Like no one else mattered. Her cheeks were now burning hot, and she felt her stomach do strange acrobatics.

She looked away first, clearing her throat awkwardly. 'Well . . . Erm . . . Yes. Thanks, again. For helping with the folders.' *Don't blush, don't blush.* 'I'd better be going, already late for an appointment.' She readied herself to walk away when his response made her stop abruptly.

'An appointment?' His eyebrows knitted together. 'Hope everything's fine?'

Caroline blinked. *You're in a hospital. He must think you're sick.* 'Oh, yes, I'm fine. I work here.'

Hunter's gaze landed on the stack of the folders back in her arms. 'You're a doctor?'

She inhaled sharply, pushing the wave of anxiety right down to the pit of her stomach. 'Something like that.'

He nodded and she was grateful he didn't push her for more details. She didn't have time to get into it now.

'Can I walk with you?'

She raised an eyebrow in suspicion. 'But you don't even know where I'm going.'

'True. But I have quite a lot of time to kill and don't want to sit around waiting.' He stopped, a shadow of sadness crossing his face.

She realised he was probably waiting for someone who was either having some tests done or was receiving treatment. Considering where they were, whatever the circumstances, they likely weren't the happiest. Hunter didn't look like he wanted to divulge more than he did, and she wouldn't ask.

Her heart ached and she nodded. 'OK then. Walk with me.'

They walked in silence. Caroline kept timidly glancing at him, only to find him already watching her. As they walked into the elevator, she pressed the round button for floor six. She stood with her back to him, pointedly trying to avoid looking at him. Her insides were in disarray whenever their eyes locked, and each time it happened, it untethered her.

'So, what do you do here?' Hunter asked. '"Something like" a doctor is very broad.'

'I'm a research assistant.' She hugged the folders to her chest. 'Probably sounds more exciting than it is.'

'Well, I'm glad I ran into you. Especially since you haven't been back to The Rouge Scot.'

'How do you know that?' she blurted.

'Because I've been there three times since. I was hoping you'd show up.'

Her mouth went dry as she felt his breath on her neck. Turning round, she found herself almost pressed against him.

'I hope you didn't waste too much time thinking about me.'

'Oh, I wouldn't call it time wasted. Maybe I manifested

this meeting. Is that what it's called? When you want something to happen?'

Caroline shut her eyes, blowing off a charged breath.

The elevator stopped as a loud ping signalled the sixth floor. She held its door open. Her mouth formed into a small smile. 'I thought you didn't believe in fate.'

Hunter stepped forward, stopping right in front of her. His brow rose. 'Are you saying it was fate that we met?'

His scent was a lot more hay and soil than bergamot today compared to the night in The Rouge Scot. He fiddled with the brim of his hat. He was nervous, Caroline realised. He had all the smooth talk but she was clearly making him slightly flustered, too.

She chewed on her bottom lip. 'Would that make you a believer?'

He stuck his foot between the door, preventing it from closing. His eyes bored into hers with an intensity that knocked out all the air from her lungs.

The unbearable heat rose in her cheeks, travelling all the way up to the tips of her ears. She wet her lips, which felt absolutely parched.

Hunter must've noticed that as he let out a low chuckle. 'Thirsty?'

She narrowed her eyes at him. 'You're enjoying this way too much.'

'Sure I am. I don't meet women like you every day.'

She raised her eyebrow, ignoring the elevator's grumbling. 'Oh, I see. You're that kind of guy.'

'I don't know what you mean.'

'A guy who thinks women want to hear they're different from the rest. Cheapest trick in the book. No one's falling for that anymore.'

Hunter's eyes widened. 'That's not what I meant.'

Caroline crossed her arms over her chest.

He shook his head, corners of his lips lifted in amusement. 'It was a compliment. Look, were you the first woman I've ever met in a bar? Of course not. The first one I've kissed in a bar? Also no.'

Caroline flinched. *He is nothing to you. You don't even know him. For all you know, he might be a serial killer. Or a con artist.* But even though her imagination provided a myriad of reasons why she shouldn't care, from logical to the most fantastical, something sharp jabbed right between her ribs when he said it. And she hated herself for it.

'Why did you want my number then? If this was nothing to you,' she whispered, a challenge in her eyes inviting him to rise to her bait.

Gently, he took her chin between thumb and forefinger and tilted it up so their eyes were locked in an exchange of sparks. 'You didn't let me finish.' His low rasp raised goosebumps on her forearms. 'Even though I have met and kissed women in bars before, no one has ever asked me to kiss them the way you did.'

Caroline huffed. 'You didn't have to kiss me if you didn't want to.' She tried to turn her head, but his other hand was suddenly cupping her cheek, and she felt herself going boneless.

Hunter bowed his head. 'You're right. But you know I wanted to.'

Their foreheads touched. Caroline could swear she felt the blood pulsing through his veins. Heard the gallop of his heart.

Or was it hers?

'What if I wanted to kiss you again?' he murmured.

The growl of his deep voice vibrated off her lips. She inhaled the sound, not wanting to let it out. It was another moment like in the bar. When all the reasons why this wasn't a good idea evaded her sharp mind. She was a senseless fly caught in the sticky trap of desire.

The elevator hissed its sound again.

His lips hovered over her cheek, his warm breath sending toe-curling shivers down her body.

Focus, Caroline. He's just a good-looking guy. You're a thirty-one-year-old doctor. You've been married. You aren't even legally single yet. Stop acting like a horny teenager.

'Excuse me, are you going up or down?'

They jumped away from each other at the sound of a woman's voice.

Caroline pressed a hand to her chest, willing her heart to stop beating like she was milliseconds away from crossing a finish line of a sprint race.

Shit. The interview with the potential trial candidate. Horrified, she looked at her smart watch. 'I must go, I have a meeting.' She swallowed hard, trying not to focus on how warm she felt.

Barely sparing a glance at a woman impatiently tapping her high-heeled foot on the tiled floor, she stepped out into the corridor and turned left, not daring to look back at Hunter.

'Caroline, wait!' Hunter stuck his head out of the elevator and called after her.

'Seriously?' she heard the woman's irritated voice. 'I don't have all day to wait for you two to figure this out.'

Caroline stopped, heavy breaths flying out of her lips, which were throbbing with the unsatisfied promise of the kiss that didn't happen. Like they remembered how good the last time was and craved more.

He pushed his fingers through his tousled hair, before he put the hat back on. 'Will you give me your number? I don't want to just hope we run into each other again.'

She looked at him. 'And what will you do with that number?'

'Give it to me and you'll find out.' His expression added the context the words lacked. It promised something she didn't know if she was ready for.

'Just give it to him so I can go down and get my car,' the woman said.

Both Caroline and Hunter looked at her.

'What? I don't have time.'

She considered him, thinking quickly. This had 'bad idea' written all over it. Even if she ignored the fact she was still technically married, she was only in Oklahoma for one year. Well, less than that now. Was it really a wise decision to get herself into something that might further add to her general confusion with the state of her life just now? She had fallen off the metaphorical horse years ago and hadn't yet conjured enough strength to push herself back up.

But what if this is exactly what you need to get back into the saddle? What if he walks away, you never see him again and you end up regretting it? He's just asking you for a phone number. That's it.

'Fine. Give me your mobile number. I'll text you if I want to.' She took a pen from her jacket's pocket and scribbled the number he dictated on a piece of paper sticking out from her diary. 'Got it.'

'Don't I get your number too?' he asked in a casual tone, but she could detect a hint of disappointment.

Caroline smiled. 'No, you don't. You'll have it when I text you.'

Hunter shook his head and tipped his hat in a goodbye.

As the metal door closed, she muttered to herself, '*If* I text you . . .'

CHAPTER SEVEN

Caroline

After dinner with Anna and Gian in one of their favourite Thai restaurants, Caroline lay flat on her back on the floor in her room. She put a playlist on her phone and listened in her big green earphones, staring at the ceiling, trying to make a mental to-do list of things she had to get done tomorrow. However, her thoughts kept straying in a direction that made her smile involuntarily. No, 'smile' wasn't the right word to convey what thinking about Hunter did to her. She blushed and grinned to herself like a smitten teenager, swallowing a giggle.

Why did she take his phone number? She knew nothing about him. Nor did he know anything about her. Other than the conversation they'd had at The Rouge Scot, really, which was nothing to go on. She had no idea why he was at the centre today. Maybe he was ill and this whole weird air of confidence and impulsivity that surrounded him was the recklessness of a dying man. Caroline had seen this before. People thinking they had nothing more to lose, wanting to live whatever remained of their lives to the fullest. That'd make sense.

She pressed the heels of her hands to her eyes.

Last year, she was crying in the dark on a bathroom floor mourning the end of a marriage that should've never taken place.

Last month, the tears had all dried up. She and Finn had avoided each other as much as they could while she prepared to leave for Oklahoma. He'd encouraged her to apply for the exchange programme. Told her it was a 'once-in-a-lifetime' opportunity.

She had been here less than three weeks, and she had already kissed a stranger once, almost twice. And now she'd agreed to go on a date? If she really thought about it, she had never been on a real date.

Hunter made it sound so simple. Uncomplicated. When it was anything but these two adjectives.

She shut her eyes. What should she do? It was pointless denying that there was something there. If nothing else, her traitorous body clearly found him attractive. But it wasn't just the physical pull. Both times after she had met him, she'd felt better. Lighter. Like her old self. She missed that Caroline, and she missed that feeling of carefree joy.

Gingerly, she reached for her phone and pressed pause. 'Hey Driver' by Zach Bryan stopped mid lyric. She opened her contacts and scrolled to her best friend, Erin, who had a small green dot next to her name, showing that she was active now. Caroline looked at the time. Erin was an interior designer, but she always worked odd hours. Caroline couldn't count how many times she'd heard her say, *You never know when the muse is going to strike!*

She started typing.

CAROLINE: *Do you remember when I told you about that random guy I met at the bar two weeks ago?*

ERIN: *Of course. It's not every day that you tell me about hot strangers and 'meet-cutes' straight out of a romcom. What about him?*

CAROLINE: *Well . . . You won't believe it but guess who I ran into (literally) today at the centre . . .*

'Read' popped up under her last message almost immediately. She kept looking at the phone, waiting for Erin's reply.

ERIN: *NO WAY! Him?! Really? But . . . How? When? I have so many questions . . .*

CAROLINE: *I probably should've also mentioned that we kissed. At the bar. And kind of almost today, too.*

ERIN: *CAROLINE SIOBHAN O'KELLY. Rithvik's asleep so I can't call you. Send me a voice note. I need details! Will just grab my earphones.*

Caroline laughed and shook her head. She got up from the floor and took her headphones off, trying to listen in for any activity outside her room. All she could hear was the TV in Anna and Gian's bedroom across the corridor, loud enough to drown out her voice. She cleared her throat and sat back down on the floor, resting her back against the bed frame.

In six separate messages, she told Erin everything. She didn't have to wait long for her response.

ERIN: *Holy shit . . . Sorry, I'm just a bit speechless. Can't imagine how strange it was for you! He sounds dreamy.*

CAROLINE: *He kind of is.*

ERIN: *And the kiss was good?*

CAROLINE: *No comment.*

ERIN: *So, that's a yes?*

Caroline started typing her reply, but then caught herself. What was there to say? 'Good' didn't really cover how she felt about that kiss – not then, and not now. It was more than just good.
Biting hard on the inside of her cheek, she deleted the message. She attempted to type out the response twice more but didn't hit 'send'.

ERIN: *I can see that you're typing. It tells me everything I need to know. And you have his number, giiiirl! When are you going to meet up?*

CAROLINE: *That's the thing. I don't think I will.*

ERIN: *Why? You said it yourself, you enjoyed his company. He's handsome, clearly interested in you, and what do you have to lose? It's just one date. If it's a bummer, you don't have to see him again.*

CAROLINE: *Are you forgetting that legally I'm still married?*

ERIN: *Oh, please. That's your excuse?*

She furrowed her brow, confused.

CAROLINE: *My excuse?*

ERIN: *Look. You know I'm always on your side. You know I'm always here to listen, even if I can't solve your problems. And I've never said much about the whole situation between you and Finn. But your marriage is over. It organically dissolved on its own, with or without some handsome cowboy's help. Whatever happens, you'll still be signing the divorce papers once you're back in Glasgow.*

CAROLINE *Yes, but that doesn't mean I can just go off and take up with another guy so soon after.*

ERIN: *And why not? If anyone deserves to let herself a bit loose and have some fun, it's you. You've had a tough time for ages now. You don't even have to see Hunter again for now. Unless you want to, of course. You can just talk a bit. Exchange a few messages.*

CAROLINE: *It still feels wrong somehow.*

ERIN: *Did it feel wrong when his tongue was stuck down your throat?*

CAROLINE: *Erin!*

ERIN: *Car, I love you. But you're too harsh on*

yourself. Sometimes life just puts exactly the right kind of person on your path. Someone who you were supposed to meet.

CAROLINE: *If you're going to talk about soulmates and higher power now, I'm tapping out . . .*

ERIN: *Ugh, you're so infuriating!!! Simple question: do you want to see Hunter again? Yes or no? Don't think about it! Trust your gut.*

CAROLINE: *Yes.*

ERIN: *There you go. Looks like my work here is done. Just in time, too. I feel like I'm going to fall asleep any minute now. Speak soon?*

CAROLINE: *OK.*

CAROLINE: *Hey, Erin?*

ERIN: *Yeah?*

CAROLINE: *You know you're my favourite person, right?*

ERIN: *Ha, I do. But if things keep going how they are, maybe Hunter will trump me on the list.*

She followed her message with a winky face and Caroline shook her head, exiting the app. Despite what Erin thought, it still didn't sit well with her.

Mulling over what she had known she had to do from the start, she finally worked up the courage about half an hour later. Her finger hovered a while on the number. Anxiety rising in her chest, she took a few steadying breaths.

She had to call Finn.

CHAPTER EIGHT

Caroline

Caroline paced the length of the bedroom, working up the courage to press the 'call' button next to Finn's name. She'd had his contact page pulled up for the past twenty minutes. Her mind whirled, playing through the different scenarios of how that conversation could go. What he would say. What she would ask him. Even though the only way she could find out was to actually click her finger and bring the phone up to her ear.

Which she did, though she wasn't sure if there was more intention or accident involved. Maybe it was a muscle twitch. Either way, she couldn't hang up now. She pressed her hip to the windowsill. Flexed her fingers. Rolled her shoulders, like she was preparing to walk into a difficult exam.

Finn picked up on the second ring. 'Car.'

That was all he said.

Caroline tightened her grip on her phone. Hearing Finn's

voice stole her breath away, but not in the way it used to. It wasn't the pulse-accelerating euphoria that she remembered from her teenage years. It wasn't the comfort of being wrapped up in a safe cocoon of knowing she could share the best and worst of her day with her favourite person on the planet of her early twenties. It wasn't even the maddening emotional rage of her late twenties.

Just the resigned acceptance that it was truly over for them.

'Car, are you there?' Finn asked.

She cleared her throat, resting her temple on the cool window. 'Hi.'

'Hi.'

An awkward pause filled her speaker. She could almost see Finn pinching the bridge of his nose, his telltale sign of being uncomfortable. He would probably press his thumbs to his temples next, wishing the unease to wash away from his mind.

If only it was that simple. If only they could have saved each other all that heartache.

She had Googled 'when do you know if it's time for a divorce' several times over the past four years. Each article or response to posts on online forums suggested that thinking about your life after divorce is one of the signs it might be the time. But all the internet experts agreed on one thing: you knew the relationship was doomed when you didn't care enough to fight anymore.

Caroline would never forget their last fight. Pretty much a year ago, to the day.

The beginning of their end.

'How are you? How's the work? Are Anna and Gian well?'

A litany of unimportant yet polite questions.

Caroline smiled sadly to her pale reflection in the window, squinting at the orange and red splashed over the evening sky.

'I'm well. The work's good.' She paused, biting the inside of her cheek. 'Anna and Gian are great. Gian's bakery is doing well, Anna's work is good too.'

'That's great.'

'Yeah.'

Another pause, a longer one this time.

Caroline inhaled like she'd emerged from being underwater for a long time. Her heart hadn't shattered all at once. Sometimes she wished it was something clearcut that had ended things, like Finn having an affair or her falling out of love with him. Maybe if she had walked in on him with someone, she could've hated him. It would've been an open and shut case. Infidelity. A sharp but quick heartbreak. Instead, she'd got the gradual fading of hope and everything she thought she knew – about herself, about Finn. About them as a couple.

One day, she was the happiest person in the room, raising a champagne glass in their honeymoon suite to the start of their lives together. Soon, they were oceans apart.

Hot tears of helplessness pooled in the corner of her eyes. 'I'm sorry I called. This wasn't a good idea. I don't even know why I called.'

Liar.

'No, wait. Don't hang up, please.'

She swallowed, her breath fogging the window.

It was so lively down there, people going about their business, often accompanied by an exciting whoop of conversation and laughter that echoed up to the flat. Anna told her that Bricktown was the city's original warehouse and distribution centre that had been turned into an entertainment district. The excitement and colours of various restaurants and cafés mingled with shopfronts. A large billboard advertising an Indian casino extended a gaudy invitation.

'I never wanted to hurt you, Car.'

'Finn, please. We've been over this. We hurt each other.'

His breath rumbled through her speaker. If she closed her eyes, she could imagine him standing right next to her. 'I know. I'm still so sorry. I should've told you before we got married.'

Thick saliva clogged up her throat. All the 'should haves' and 'could haves' had haunted her dreams for too long. She didn't want to do it anymore. She had drawn a line in their last marriage counselling session, the one at the end of which Finn had asked her for a divorce.

I think it's for the best. We want different things. I can't give you what you want. And I don't want to give up on what I want. It's not fair on either of us.

Not a single tear had trailed down her face. By that point, she was all cried out.

'I don't want to go back to all that. It's over, that chapter's closed,' she said, surprising herself with the firmness to her voice.

Finn sighed. 'I know. S—'

'No more apologies, OK? I feel like we've apologised enough for a lifetime, and then some.'

'Roger that.' He laughed and the sound brought a small smile to her face. 'Why are you really calling?'

Caroline turned away from the window, leaning against the violet wall. She dragged her teeth over her bottom lip, buying herself time to think, though she had mulled over this for long enough. In the end, she decided that the kindest – and easiest – thing would be to rip off the bandage.

'I met someone.'

Something crashed at the other end of the line.

Finn swore. 'Hold on a second, need to clean up the glass. Be right back.'

Caroline let out a half-relieved, half-exasperated breath. But she didn't hang up.

'I'm here.' Finn paused. 'That— I mean, I thought it might happen but didn't expect it'd happen this fast.'

'It's not like that.'

'You've just told me you met someone.' His voice shook. 'Not sure there's another angle to interpret it from.'

'I only meant that I met someone. A guy. He asked for my number.'

'And you gave it to him.' The pain in Finn's voice sent an army of needles right into her heart.

'He gave me his number. I told him I'd message him.'

Silence stretched across the Atlantic, hooking the consciousness of two souls that used to fancy themselves mates.

'Will you go out with him?'

Caroline slid down, sitting cross-legged on the mahogany floorboards. She pushed her head against the wall. 'I don't know.'

An image of Hunter's face leaped into her mind. The sparkle in his eyes. His confident smirk. The inexplicable pull she felt towards him – she wasn't an idiot. She knew it was just pure attraction. But she had never felt something like this before. It was different. Exciting, even. She'd be lying if she said she wasn't intrigued. Perhaps she'd even come to regret it.

'Yes. I do want to go out with him,' she added, not even an echo of hesitation wrapped around the words. 'I wanted to let you know. Not to be cruel, I hope you know that. It just didn't feel right. I know we agreed on a divorce. I know we're sorting out all the paperwork and once I'm back from Oklahoma, that'll be it. But—'

'You didn't want to feel like you were cheating,' Finn

finished. There was no judgement or snarl in that statement. Just brutal honesty.

Caroline stared at the plush teal rug in the middle of the bedroom. Her eyes were dry, heart struggling against her chest like it was fed up with the paces she had put it through.

When are you going to be done? When is it enough?

'I just wanted you to hear it from me. It might end up being one date. Or might not even get to a date. But still.'

'Yes, still.'

She squeezed her eyes shut. They had lost each other, signed and delivered the end of a love that had started when they were still kids.

'Car, I'm glad you're moving on. I . . . I just need a moment to process that. I hope you have fun, really.' He blew a shuddering breath into the microphone on his end. 'And I'd have never thought you cruel. Thank you for telling me. I appreciate it more than you'll ever know.'

The unspoken words hung between them, caught in the frosted cobwebs of broken feelings.

I love you. I'm not in love with you, but a piece of my heart will always belong to you. I should've told you. You should've told me.

The heavy knowledge that if love was enough, they wouldn't be having this conversation. She would be marking the days off from the calendar, counting the days until Finn flew to visit her. They would have planned a trip while he was here, somewhere nice. She wouldn't have kissed Hunter. She wouldn't have even met him, and if she had, she'd have acknowledged he was a charming cowboy. That would've been it.

But love wasn't enough.

'Be well, OK? You know you can always call or text me, right?' Finn asked.

She pressed a trembling hand to her mouth, holding back a sob at his kind serenity. 'Yes. Same goes to you.'

'Bye, Car.'

'Bye for now.'

The sound of the call disconnecting beeped through the speaker. Caroline dropped the phone like it burned her hand. She pulled her knees to her chest, wrapping her arms around them tightly. Tears flew freely, just when she thought nothing could shake her again.

How foolish of her.

Everything that had happened in the last four years – her work, marriage, longing for things she didn't even know she had been missing – it had been too much. It had pushed her off balance, knocked her down.

But no more. It was time to get back in the saddle of her own life.

CHAPTER NINE

Hunter

Techno music blared from all directions. The DJ was wearing a fluorescent orange costume with pink flashing antlers as a headband. If this was what a fashionable club looked like, Hunter would be glad never to set a foot in one again. But Mitch had wanted to check it out, and after Hunter suggested The Rouge Scot last time, he couldn't have said no.

'What did you say?!' Mitch leaned in, almost bumping his forehead into Hunter's face.

'I said it's *too loud*! Can we not leave and just find a bar?' Hunter shouted into the ear of his best friend.

A waitress walked by their table and Mitch motioned to her to lower the tray. He took two shot glasses of vodka and put the bills back on the tray. The waitress flashed them both a smile, but her eyes lingered on Hunter. He was almost sure that she winked at him.

Mitch must've noticed it as well because as she walked off,

he put his arm around Hunter's shoulder and squeezed him. 'You're such a lucky bastard, you know that? How do you do it?'

'Do what?' Hunter asked, though he knew perfectly well what Mitch meant. He didn't want to sound cocky.

Mitch rolled his eyes impatiently. 'Have this effect on women. And you don't even try.'

Hunter only shrugged in response to that. What could he say? None of it had done him any good in recent years.

Mitch just laughed and shook his head. He pushed both shot glasses towards Hunter and his eyes gleamed. 'Bottoms up, bro!'

'I thought one was for you,' Hunter raised his voice as the DJ started mixing another track. The thunderous bass practically made the furniture vibrate.

'Nah, I've had enough. Have work in the morning. Driving up to the van der Moltens' ranch to check up on their new foals.'

Hunter smiled, mostly to himself. Mitch was four years older than him. They had met while Hunter was in his final year of college at Texas A&M University. At the time, Mitch was studying veterinary medicine and came over to give a talk about the DVM programme and the life of a student vet. Hunter had approached him afterwards to ask a few questions and they'd ended up grabbing beers. They'd been friends ever since. Mitch had moved to Oklahoma City after he graduated and set up his practice on the outskirts of the city.

There was a time when Hunter had felt rather jealous of Mitch and the life he had. Not that long ago, he'd wanted to be in his shoes.

Hunter eyed the clear liquid in the shot glasses and hesitated. He wasn't a big fan of vodka. It was one of those things that you thought you liked when you were young, but as you grew older, and in this case wiser, you realised it was not for you. He wasn't driving back to Purcell either. Crashing on Mitch's sofa in Oklahoma City every time they went out for drinks had become a pattern they had both fallen into. Hunter still asked if he could stay, even though by now the question was likely redundant.

What the hell. Two shots of vodka were just two shots of vodka. He downed them both in quick succession.

As the empty glasses clanked on the table, Mitch started cheering.

'That's my man! Do you still want to go to a bar? We could chat.'

He caught a flint of worry in Mitch's expression. Ever since Alan's health had started deteriorating, Mitch had been the only person Hunter confided in. He didn't want to add to his family's burden with his own feelings. It wouldn't do any good.

At home, he kept up the pretence of optimism and hope. He tried to be positive, to lift the spirits of his mother and Megan. Hell, even Buck.

But the truth was that Hunter was scared. And exhausted.

He knew that there was a very high chance that his father was going to die. He knew that he was an adult and that this was the natural order of the world. Parents grew older and eventually they passed away. Despite having time to come to terms with Alan's diagnosis, he still hadn't. Because he refused to imagine never seeing his father again. Never hearing his laugh, never seeing his disapproval at something completely unimportant. Then, there was his mother. He knew Mary would shatter to pieces. His parents had had the blessing of finding and holding on to the kind of everlasting love that could withstand all. One that only seemed to grow stronger with time.

And Meg was only eighteen. Her world would completely fall apart. Then there were Cody and Morgan – they'd lose their beloved grandfather, who had taught them both how to ride their bikes and always had a bedtime story to tell when they stayed overnight at the ranch.

Hunter tried to keep it together for all of them. He felt a responsibility to ensure everyone was all right. Even though he wasn't the oldest, even though he probably wasn't even the right person for this job. But Buck had his own family. He had enough burden on his shoulders.

How could he put all of these dark clouds hanging over his head into coherent words? This was neither the time nor the place. Besides, Mitch knew. He might appear outgoing and fun to people, but Hunter knew that underneath the party-loving exterior, Mitch had a sensitive and loyal heart. He had been there when Hunter was stuck in a mudslide of grief and needed a hand to prevent him from sinking to the bottom.

You could tell him about Caroline.

A smile formed on his lips at a mere thought of her and their meeting earlier at the cancer centre. The almost-kiss in the elevator. The way his body reacted to her in some kind of sweet oblivion. Maybe it was because he hadn't been with anyone for months now. Despite what Buck believed, he had left the rodeos and buckle bunny days behind. Thinking about it now, it must've been what, five months? Six?

He furrowed his brow. Definitely longer than he had thought.

He didn't have a habit of sharing details of his 'dates' with Mitch. As sincere as he was in speaking about his father and everything else, this was a more private part of his life. Something he didn't like discussing.

Not in the last five years.

Hunter shook his head, pushing the thoughts away before they had a chance to take root and ruin the rest of his evening. There was no point in mentioning Caroline, not yet. Not to Mitch, not to anyone else. He knew that his family – and Mitch – would make a big deal out of nothing.

Maybe there would be no reason to mention her at all. Though, damn him, he hoped she would text him.

He was already wary of the influence she had over him, based on just two brief meetings. He thought about her beautiful green eyes, her lips, her soft dark blonde hair. Even the two scars on her face, one on her cheek and another on her temple. He wanted to know where they came from. He wanted to know what made her laugh, what made her sad.

He wanted to know her.

Pulling his mind back to the hazy club and Mitch's suggestion on changing venue, Hunter waved his hand dismissively. 'Let's just stay here. Next round of drinks on me. You can get yourself a club soda or coke if you don't want to drink.'

'Sounds good. I might get a single beer. I don't have to be at the ranch until ten.'

Hunter smiled genially and stood, walking off towards the bar. He weaved through the sweaty bodies on the dance floor, coughing once or twice as overwhelming floral scents assaulted his nostrils. Someone had gone a bit overboard with the perfume.

He reached the bar, flagging the bartender and ordering two beers. As he watched the glasses being filled, he felt a small hand on his bicep.

'I could use another drink, too,' a sweet female voice said.

Hunter turned and looked at the woman who had squeezed his arm.

She was attractive, with luscious black waves and light eyes. The shimmering gold dress hugged her figure, the plunging V neckline leaving little to the imagination. Her red-painted lips turned in a seductive smile. 'You could buy me one.'

Hunter smiled back but shook his head. 'The only person I'm buying drinks for tonight is my friend.'

The woman tilted her head, still eyeing Hunter. 'A friend or a *friend*?'

Hunter paid for the drinks and grabbed both glasses. 'Friend. One I'm getting back to. Excuse me.'

She pouted but moved, letting him pass. 'Enjoy your night.'

Hunter tipped his head in response before navigating the mess of a dance floor back to the booth.

Mitch was typing on his phone when Hunter reached the table. He sat back down, sliding one of the beers towards Mitch.

'Thanks man.' He nodded, his eyes glued to his phone's screen.

Hunter grinned. There was only one person who could elicit the stupidly happy and goofy expression on Mitch's face.

'What's Eve up to tonight?'

Mitch looked up with a smile. 'She's in Galveston. There are three more shows before the tour wraps up.'

'I bet you can't wait.'

'Yeah. It's been four months. I know I saw her in Stillwater last week, but it isn't the same, you know?' Mitch put his phone back in his back pocket. 'The band is there and all these other people. She's busy and I feel guilty pulling her focus away from work.'

'How long will she be home for?'

Mitch shrugged, reaching for his beer. 'No idea. Think they want to record a new album.'

Eve was a tour manager for an up-and-coming country music star, Lionel Webster. Grandson of country music legend, Ritchie Webster. Mitch had met her two years ago when she'd brought in an injured deer to his practice. They got together soon after that. It had been nice, seeing Mitch happy and in love, even though at times it drummed up a hint of jealousy in Hunter.

You could have had all that, too. You did have it.

The muscle in his jaw tensed. Absentmindedly, he took a long swig of beer, letting the fizzy liquid wash down his throat.

'And it's all going well with you two?' Hunter asked.

Mitch beamed at him. 'Yeah, man. So, well. I'm honestly the luckiest man. Eve's just amazing.'

'Glad to hear.'

'You know, she has some spare tickets to see Lionel in Tulsa in the fall. It's a one-off event, some kind of sentimental tribute to his grandfather or something. Sounds like it's going to be quite a show. I could get you a pair, if you wanted?'

Hunter grunted, though he didn't think Mitch could hear him over the deafening music. 'Sure, why not? Might take Meg.'

Mitch's green eyes reflected the pink strobe lights. 'Or you could bring someone else?'

Hunter's mouth went dry. 'Maybe I could.'

They looked at each other but neither said anything else. Mitch appeared pleased with himself. A month ago, Hunter wouldn't have said that. There was no one he would even consider bringing to a show. But now . . .

Don't get ahead of yourself. She might not even text you. And you're already thinking of asking her to go to a show in the fall. What is wrong with you?

That was an excellent question.

Instead of dwelling on the answer, he reached for his beer again, settling comfortably in the booth and watching the crowd bobbing to a fast song that sounded a lot like some chalk being dragged across a blackboard.

CHAPTER TEN

Caroline

Getting lost on her way to the office had become a norm in Caroline's morning. The inside of the Rouken Cancer Center reminded her of an elaborate maze she had got lost in on a trip to Austria once. Which was also the first time she had experienced a panic attack.

At least the Centre had semi-helpful signage.

She passed a water fountain by the elevator on the fourth floor and stopped, looking around for the arrows pointing towards the clinical trials offices. The cancer centre connected to the main hospital building via a glass-covered walkway. Outside, underneath the structure, there was a small courtyard with large concrete blocks serving as flower containers. They overflowed with varying shades of pink and violet flowers, surrounded by greenery. Caroline didn't know much about flowers aside from knowing she loved lilies and disliked roses in her vases. Flowers and gardening were her father's forte.

She had recognised Ronan's favourite flower the other week when she'd walked out to grab an iced coffee from a food truck in the courtyard – Supertunia 'Vista Bubblegum'. The characteristic cascades of bright bubblegum-pink flowers reminded her of stretching on a blanket in the garden of their Aberdeen home, shielding her eyes from the rare sun with a book. Not that the Scottish summers had anything on Oklahoma's heat in August.

The memories were the only thing she had left. After her mother died, Ronan had sold the house and moved to Dublin. Both her sisters followed in his steps, making Caroline the only member of the O'Kelly family left in Scotland.

She slowed her pace as she reached midway across the walkway. Looking down through the see-through floor, she smiled at the flowers. They weren't easily distinguishable from this height but knowing they were there, a connection to her father despite him being thousands of miles away, warmed her heart.

She fished out her phone from her pocket, firing a message to her older sister, Clara.

> CAROLINE: *Do you have time for a catch up? I got to work early and would love to see you. And Vic, of course.*

The reply came only moments later as she dropped her handbag on the desk in the office.

> CLARA: *Sure. Give me five minutes, I'll FaceTime you.*

Caroline smiled at her phone, looking around the empty office. It had just gone 7.30 a.m. Neither of the other research assistants would come in for at least another half an hour, though it'd probably be more like an hour. After last night's conversation with Finn, she had struggled to dissociate. When she had finally fallen asleep, her dreams trembled with anxiety. She had woken up after 5 a.m. and couldn't get back to sleep.

There were always things she could busy herself with at the office. Research papers to read to brush up on colorectal cancer and melanoma, the main tumours the team at the Rouken Cancer Center conducted clinical trials on. She would speak with Clara and browse through the pub alerts she had set up.

She pulled on a smile and clicked on the incoming call button. 'Hi!'

Clara's face popped on the screen. Short chestnut hair framed her face, with an exact replica of Caroline's green eyes gleaming in the camera from underneath stylish bangs.

'Hi yourself! All the photos you send make me wish I could hop on a plane and join you.'

Caroline laughed. 'I've only sent you a few snaps of Oklahoma City. Haven't had a chance to venture out yet.'

'But you will, right?'

'Sure. Anna said I can borrow her car whenever, she doesn't really use it much. Thinking of checking out some of the state parks in the area over the weekends. Maybe venturing out somewhere for an overnight stay later.'

'That's great, Caroline.' Clara beamed.

Caroline shrugged, twisting from side to side in her swivel chair. 'Yeah, I'm glad I came here. Think this year's going to be good for me.'

Clara nodded overenthusiastically. She didn't know about Caroline and Finn's split yet, but she was up to speed with how Caroline had been feeling with regards to her career.

'And the work must be interesting! Remind me, what do

you actually do there? Victoria, honey, I'm on a phone to Auntie Caroline. What do you have on your face?!'

A head of blonde curls popped up in the camera view. Victoria, Clara's six-year-old daughter, looked very pleased with herself and giggled loudly in response to her mother's strained voice.

'It's chocolate,' she crowed. 'Yoummy, yoummy chocolate!' Her face lit up with glee.

Caroline smiled and had to stop herself from laughing alongside her niece.

Clara, on the other hand, didn't look remotely impressed. 'I'm going to go get a towel to wipe this off.'

She disappeared from the video, leaving Victoria alone in front of the laptop.

'What chocolate did you have, Vic?' Caroline asked, feeling the familiar tug of homesickness.

Not being able to see her family more often was the hardest part of living in another country. Even though Scotland and Ireland were a short flight, with all her commitments it hadn't been easy making regular trips to Dublin to see them. And that was how she'd felt in Glasgow – Oklahoma was even further away. She always tried to make up the distance with frequent video calls whenever she had time, but that was now even trickier due to the time difference.

'It was milk an' raisin! So tasty. I ate it all,' Victoria said, starting to giggle again.

'I'm jealous. I love milk chocolate with raisins.'

'I can share with you when you visit us. When will you come? I want to see you.' Victoria's happy expression was replaced with a sad frown. She turned to check that her mother wasn't back yet and moved closer to the screen. 'I love you most of all my aunties.'

Caroline chuckled, warmth spreading in her chest. 'Don't

let Auntie Caitlin hear that. I love you too, poppet. But I can't visit just now. I'm staying with Auntie Anna, remember? Mum told you about it.'

'Yes. And Daddy showed me on the map. It's all the way across lots of water!'

Caroline nodded. 'It is.'

Victoria thought about it for a moment, and then she smiled again. 'That's OK then. But come soon?'

'What do I hear you're telling Auntie Caroline she's your favourite? You said the same to Caitlin the other day.' Clara walked back into camera's view. She was holding a wet face cloth and started washing the remains of chocolate off Victoria's face.

'You did? I'm so, so sad now.' Caroline put her hand on her heart, pretending to be deeply hurt.

Victoria patiently let her mother clean her nose and shrugged. 'Well, I want all my aunties to feel special!' As if it was an obvious answer.

Both sisters shook their heads good-naturedly.

Clara kissed her daughter's cheek, now chocolate free.

Victoria pushed her away, appalled. 'Mum! Not in public!'

'Oh, my apologies. Go ask Daddy if you can help him with anything.'

'OK. Bye, Auntie Caroline, love you.'

Caroline waved to the camera. 'Bye, Vic, love you too.'

Victoria waved with a flourish and ran out of the room.

Clara settled comfortably in her office chair, looking into the camera. 'Sorry about that. She has so much energy, some days I wonder how we're going to keep up with a second one.'

'Are you pregnant?!' Caroline opened her mouth, delighted. She knew Clara and Sean had been trying for a second baby, but it had been a few years now. They had initially wanted to have both children in quick succession – *'so we only go through the nappy phase once and it's done!'*, as Clara used to say. They got pregnant when Victoria was two. Sadly, they lost the pregnancy at only eleven weeks.

'I wanted to tell you before you went to Oklahoma, but it was still early and . . . Well, we wanted to wait until we were further along. Dad, Nora and Caitlin don't know yet. We're going to tell them on Saturday. They're coming over to celebrate Sean's promotion.' Clara's cheeks were red, pure happiness written all over her face.

Caroline felt her eyes watering, smiling from ear to ear. 'I'm so, so happy for you. And Sean. Vic's going to be an excellent older sister.'

'Thank you. She doesn't know, we'll tell her after we tell the family. You know how she is – she'd just blab it out to everyone she meets, including the postman or Amazon delivery driver.'

They both laughed because this was exactly what Victoria would do.

'How far along are you?'

'Only eight weeks. I honestly can't wait to find out if it's another girl or a boy this time. Sean hopes it's a girl, he says that boys are nothing but trouble. But then I'm sure Dad would disagree.'

'Oh, I'm sure he would. He's always said that four women in the house would drive him to an early grave. I wish Mum was here to see what an amazing mother you became.'

Clara sniffed and pressed a hand to her face, covering her eyes. When she spoke again, her voice was thick with emotion. 'She'd ask Vic to call her "auntie" because she'd think she's too young to be a grandmother. But she'd secretly love it.

She'd encourage her to take ballet lessons and introduce her to the opera. And she'd make sure she read all of Jane Austen's novels, in *"the correct order"*. Of course, she'd make sure everything was age appropriate. She wouldn't buy a new copy of *Mansfield Park* until Vic was at least ten years old.'

'Don't worry, Clara. I'm going to make sure Vic knows who Edmund Bertram is. And Mr Darcy, as *Pride and Prejudice* is the best Austen novel.'

Clara must've been feeling pensive as she didn't jump to her usual protests that *Persuasion* was so much better. She dabbed a few lonely tears away with a tissue and tried her best to smile. 'Anyway, putting my daughter's literary education aside, where were we before Vic came in? Ah. You were meant to tell me about your work.'

'Well, no day is really the same,' Caroline started, pausing to check if the footsteps she heard behind her didn't head into the office. 'I'm involved in preparing screening questions for potential participants in these trials and interviewing them. So, it's checking if people who want to take part in the trial are eligible for it. Each trial has very specific criteria,' Caroline said. 'I must check that they fit all of them. I also do some lab work on pre-clinical studies, and last week, Anna asked if I'm interested in teaching pre-med students.'

'But that's great! It sounds right up your street. You always said you wanted to spend some of the time teaching, right?'

Caroline smiled. 'I did. Really excited for that.'

'Who else do you work with?'

'Jake and Amira. The rest of the team are oncologists. They both have a PhD and want to work in research. They—' she turned back to check that she was still alone in the office, 'aren't thrilled that I'm here. I think they think I got the job just because I'm Anna's niece.'

'Pfft, screw them.' Clara's raised voice startled Caroline. She was always very protective of both her and their youngest sister, Caitlin.

'I mean, I get it. Their colleague flew over to the UK to spend a year working on clinical trials in London, and they got me. I think they both applied for that exchange, too. They must think I somehow cheated, or Anna just fast-tracked my application,' Caroline said.

Clara's brow twitched. 'But you *didn't* cheat. There were like, what, a hundred applications?'

'A hundred and thirty-four,' Caroline said without thinking. The research assistant position came with a one-year employment visa, and it was paid at a good rate.

A once-in-a-lifetime opportunity. Just as Finn had said.

Clara folded her arms over her chest, leaning back in a high leather chair. 'Well, exactly. And they chose you.'

'And how's Dad doing? Still seeing his physiotherapist, I hope?'

Clara let out a roaring laughter. 'Oh, that is a true carry-on. You know how he is. Keeps grumbling about it but I do think he's getting better.'

'So, he keeps saying he won't be going?'

'After every session. Then Nora tells him off, and he still goes,' Clara said.

Nora was their father's second wife. She was a lovely woman, and the marriage had been good for Ronan. Together, they were a personification of a 'grumpy and grumpier' romance trope.

'Glad you're all doing well. And Clara, I'm so excited about your news,' Caroline said.

'Will you be able to come see me when the baby's born, do you think?'

Caroline blinked. It had only now hit her she would still be in Oklahoma when her second niece or nephew would be born. 'I'll certainly try.' She glanced at the clock. 'I think I'd better go. I'll call you soon?'

'Sure, bye!'

They hung up and Caroline pulled up a spreadsheet to key in the most recent blood test results. When she entered the same number for the fourth time in a row, she realised she was messing it all up. With a sigh, she backtracked, clearing the fields.

Clara and Sean were pregnant.

Caroline smiled, resting her head against the back of the chair. They were amazing parents, and it was what they had wanted for so long. She was truly bursting with joy for them.

Sometimes, she wondered what it'd be like to be a mother. Children liked her. She was patient, caring and liked to play with them. Throughout her twenties, she had tried to grow into the idea of one day being a mother. Finn had always said he wanted children. So, for a long time, Caroline had just assumed that was the next step on the cards for them. Graduation, setting up their careers, moving in together, marriage and children. All neat and tidy. It was a question she should've asked herself and answered honestly before they got married. Probably even before they had got engaged. Somehow, subconsciously, she had decided she didn't want that life. She didn't want children of her own. Not now, not ever.

The thing she should've told him.

One of the two big reasons their marriage was now dissolved in a puddle of regret and leftover fondness.

Initially, Finn had thought she would change her mind. His unhelpful mother had said the same thing. Her colleagues at hospital had said it. And some of their mutual friends.

Women always change their mind.

Caroline had changed the topic, awkwardly biting her tongue. She'd chewed her lips, bit her fingernails afterwards and asked herself if there was something wrong with her.

He's going to leave you. Every man wants to be a father, eventually. If you don't give him a child, you'll watch him find someone who will.

Once or twice, she had almost convinced herself that maybe, just maybe, she could do it. That maybe it was the right thing to do.

Maybe it would've saved them.

But she couldn't do it. She didn't want to. Not to herself, not to Finn, and most of all, not to a potential child.

Then, she had found out the secret Finn had been keeping from her. And she was able to breathe again, knowing she wasn't the only one uprooting the anchors of their marriage.

The Excel spreadsheet rudely winked at her, challenging her to get back to work. Caroline stared at it, resigned.

She pulled her phone and opened the contacts. Scrolling through, her finger paused on the screen, where she had reached 'H'. Second from the top, underneath Henry Adler, her colleague from Glasgow, was the name she wanted.

She checked the time. 8.30 a.m. wasn't too early to send a message to a guy she had kissed once, almost twice, right?

Chewing on the inside of her left cheek, she opened a new message and started typing.

Hi, Hunter. You wanted my number? Well, here it is.

Hurriedly pressing 'send', she hid the phone in the drawer of her desk, equally terrified of both possible outcomes: his reply and the lack of it.

CHAPTER ELEVEN

Hunter

Hunter's forearms ached from leaning over the wooden fence. He straightened his back, cracking his neck. His white T-shirt stuck to his skin. He took off his hat, wiping beads of sweat from his forehead with a polka dot handkerchief. Glancing at his watch, he put his hands to his mouth in a circular shape and shouted, 'Cody, time's up!'

A lanky boy with straw-blonde hair sat atop a dun mare. His face turned in an unhappy scowl. 'I don't want to go yet!'

Hunter pursed his lips, trying to keep a smile from forming on them. His twelve-year-old nephew was a natural rider. Since he was the one who had helped him into the saddle the very first time, his pride was twofold. It was always a joy to see Cody riding.

If it was up to him, the boy could spend all day right here. But then Hunter would get in trouble with Lorna. His sister-in-law was a very kind woman, most of the time. Especially if someone didn't know her. Having been at the receiving end of her stern glare more than once, Hunter wasn't in a rush to get on her bad side again.

'I said time's up,' he repeated calmly.

Cody pouted but tugged on the reins, approaching the exit to the paddock.

Hunter walked up to him, taking the reins from his small hands and helping him get down. As his boots hit the ground, a low cloud of dust raised from the dry sand. Looking up at the cloudless sky, Hunter winced. It hadn't rained in over a week.

'Mom always spoils my fun,' Cody whined, stalking beside Hunter and the mare towards the barn.

'She doesn't want you to get heatstroke. It's really hot today.'

Cody huffed, crossing his arms over his chest. 'It's summer. Of course it's hot.'

Hunter bit back a smile. Cody's personality had started changing from 'sweet child' to 'young teen with an attitude'. Cody and his younger sister, Morgan, had been spending a lot of time over summer at the ranch. By extension, Cody had been trailing after Hunter, day in, day out. Buck kept saying he didn't know where he got 'that cheek'. Hunter conveniently stayed quiet whenever the topic was brought up.

'Well, you can take it up with your mom if you want.'

'Can you not talk to her, Uncle Hunter?'

Hunter laughed and shook his head. 'No chance. You're on your own with that.'

They entered the barn and Ray, one of the younger ranch hands, jogged up to them. 'Hi, boss.'

Hunter passed him the reins. 'Ray, can you take Twinkle to her stall? She'll need a good hose down too; it's scorching out there.'

'Sure thing, boss.' Ray nodded and led Twinkle away.

Hunter turned to Cody. 'I agree with your mom. You need to rest up, the worst of the sun is about to hit.'

Cody's lip quivered and he looked at Hunter pleadingly. 'But we're going back home tomorrow. Please, Uncle Hunter.'

Hunter's shoulders slumped in defeat. He sighed. 'All right. If you go up to the house for some rest now, I'll come get you later on when it cools down. You can have another half an hour on Twinkle.'

Cody's brown eyes shone with excitement. 'An hour.'

Hunter put his hands on his hips, summoning the steeliest air he could. 'Forty-five minutes.'

Cody didn't blink. 'An hour. Please,' he added, his voice softening.

Hunter chuckled. He was starting to understand what Buck meant by 'that cheek'.

Only now he remembered his phone had vibrated earlier that morning, when he was busy. He fished it out, blinking at the notification.

1 new message from an Unknown number.

'Fine. An hour. Now, off you go. I'm sure Grandma has some food and iced tea waiting for you,' he said, eyes flicking up just in time to register his nephew's smug expression.

The boy didn't need to be told twice. He rushed off, disappearing from Hunter's view up the path to the main house.

Sometimes, a stray thought of whether he'd ever want to have children popped into his head. He adored Cody and Morgan, but the only way he could picture himself was as a fun uncle, never a father. The older he got, the more at peace he was with that way of things. Happy, even. He supposed it was something he should keep in mind to bring up, now that he decided he was open to a possibility of a relationship again. Because there was no point in stoking romance if two people wanted fundamentally different things in life.

Hunter briefly wondered whether Caroline wanted kids. *You're getting ahead of yourself. Again.*

Hunter looked around the barn. Ray must've taken Twinkle out the back as there was no sign of him inside. The only sound came from the horses in their respective stalls.

Sitting down on a three-legged stool pushed against the beam, he opened the message.

Hi, Hunter. You wanted my number? Well, here it is.

He grinned, re-reading the message like he wanted to memorise it. He swallowed through a miniature butterfly of joy hoping to escape from his gut.

Who is this?

The reply came almost instantly, which he didn't expect.

The woman who did NOT force you to kiss her.

His smile widened, as his thumbs moved at a record speed to type: *Ah. Caroline, hi. I have a proposition for you: a date. And not just any date, but one of your choosing.*

He watched the screen like a hawk as the three dots appeared.

How genteel of you.

A low chuckle rumbled deep in his chest. *I told you I was a gentleman.*

His heartbeat picked up as he stared at his phone. The seconds it took for another message to pop up felt like hours.

I think you're a cocky cowboy. Do you know Robbers Cave State Park?

Hunter cocked his head as he wrote: *I grew up here. Of course I do. Great views, decent hiking trails. Though I must say, I didn't take you for a nature lover.*

He breathed in and out, waiting for her reply. Why were his palms sweatier than they had been outside by the paddock? The inside of the barn was cooler than the unforgiving noon sun.
The phone vibrated in his hand.

Oh, Hunter. You don't know anything about me.

He chewed on his bottom lip. *I know more than you think.*

Yeah? Like what?

Hunter leaned back against the beam, exhaling sharply. Staring in the distance, he watched Dallas peering over his stall. He smiled at the horse, even though he knew it must've looked silly.

When he gathered his thoughts, he started typing: *You like reading fiction because working in a scientific field sharpens your logic too much during the day. You like to escape into another world. You're Irish, as we've established, but you grew up in Scotland. You have a good relationship with your father. You have good taste when it comes to whisky . . . And men, since you're going to go out with me.*

He sent the message, pushing his hand through his damp hair. His mouth was dry.

So, you have me all figured out, huh? P.S. I was right about the cocky cowboy label.

Hunter smirked at the phone as he got up from the stool. He typed as he walked towards the tack room, where they had a mini fridge stocked with water bottles.

On the contrary, these are just things I've noticed. I hope to uncover a lot more of them on our date, in Robbers Cave State Park, if that's where you want to go. How is Sunday for you? P.S. Happy to be the cocky cowboy if that label comes with another kiss.

The bottles rattled in the door as he opened the fridge. He grabbed one of them, unscrewed the cap and took a large gulp of water. The immediate cooling sensation ran through him, sending a shiver down his spine.

He set the bottle on top of the fridge, reading Caroline's reply.

Careful, Hunter. Or else I'll assume you're all talk and not much more. Sunday's fine. What time?

Eight o'clock.

In the morning?!

He chuckled to himself. *Yes, Caroline. If you want to go walking, we need to set off earlier before it gets too hot.*

That isn't a date. It's a torture.

It'll be fun, I promise.

I'm going to hold you to that. See you Sunday morning. Send me the pin for the parking spot?

Hunter smiled at the screen as he told her he would. Pushing his hands in the pockets of his jeans, he hummed a tune, unsure where he had picked it up from, as he leisurely strolled back into the barn.

CHAPTER TWELVE

Caroline

Caroline pushed her aviator sunglasses up the bridge of her nose, watching the rolling flat landscape outside the car window.

'So, what exactly are we doing?' she asked.

Anna laughed from the driver seat. 'You said that you wanted to take your mind off things at the centre, what better way to do it than by getting out of the city?'

'And we're going to an actual ranch?'

'Yeah. I know you used to really enjoy horse riding. I thought you might like to get back in the saddle again.'

Caroline's head snapped up. She stared at Anna with a mix of panic and excitement. 'It's been a long time since I rode. I'm not sure I remember how.'

'Don't worry, my patient's son is amazing with horses. Used to be a rodeo star. Now, he's taken over running the ranch but sometimes he still gives lessons.'

'OK. But is your patient fine with us just turning up?'

'I wouldn't have come up with this unless I'd checked with him first. Plus, the place is massive. We probably won't even see him.'

Caroline let out a sigh. It seemed like the matter was settled. She shouldn't be grumpy. Anna just wanted to cheer her up. Even though she was only in Oklahoma for one year, she already missed her life in Scotland. There were times she longed for the easy camaraderie with her colleagues at the hospital. Or going for a walk in one of the country parks near Glasgow. Sometimes, she even missed the weather, even those famous four-seasons-in-an-afternoon days.

She shifted in the car's leather seat, stifling a yawn. In a very irresponsible turn of events, she had stayed up until 2 a.m. last night messaging Hunter. She didn't mean to send him another message after they agreed to meet tomorrow at Robbers Cave State Park. But Chris Stapleton had popped up on her playlist and her mind had immediately rushed to The Rouge Scot and their kiss. And she had stupidly messaged him, just before midnight.

Now, she knew that he thought *The Godfather* was overhyped. He liked reading psychological thrillers. And he was afraid of reptiles.

They're just so weird and slimy.

A song came on the radio and Caroline found herself bopping along.

One thing that was amazing about being in Oklahoma, aside from being able to spend time with her aunt and Gian, was the abundance of country music. The number of amazing artists on the radio always flooded her heart with warmth. Without thinking, she reached to volume control and turned it up.

'He's good.' Anna smiled, moving her head to the rhythm of the music.

'Agree, amazing voice,' Caroline paused, listening to the chorus. She unlocked her phone and typed the first line of lyrics into the search engine. 'Bailey Zimmerman, this one's called "Religiously".' The song finished shortly after, but Caroline had already managed to download his album on the app to listen to later.

'Oh, I love this!' Anna turned up the volume even higher and started dancing in her seat, both hands on the wheel. 'Come on, Caroline. Sing with me, I know you know it.'

Caroline laughed, joining Anna's 'Wagon Wheel' singalong. As the song finished, she looked out of the window, wanting to stay in this moment. There were definitely some things that Oklahoma did right.

Anna turned the radio down and turned to her. 'Welcome to Purcell, also known as the heart of Oklahoma.'

It took them a little longer to reach their destination, which lay just outside the city's limits. They turned right off the main road onto a wide dirt track. As the buildings came into a clearer view, Caroline noticed a wooden sign outside the gate that read *Jackson's Ranch*.

Anna parked the car outside one of the outbuildings and Caroline got out, looking around in awe. 'How big is this place?'

'Just over two thousand acres.'

She almost jumped as she heard a male voice behind her.

The stranger laughed and extended his hand. 'I'm sorry, I didn't mean to scare you. I'm Duke. And you must be Big Al's oncologist?'

Caroline shook his hand but looked to Anna. 'Nice to meet you, Duke. That'd be my aunt, over there. Dr Anna Kennedy. I'm Caroline O'Kelly.'

'Ah. How d'you do, ma'am?' He tipped the brim of his leather cowboy hat in greeting. 'Al told me you were coming and hoping to do some horseback riding?'

'That'd just be Caroline. I've never been on a horse. Probably best not to start at my age.' Anna laughed nervously. 'She used to take horse riding lessons when she was younger. She's visiting from Scotland, and I wanted to show her a true Oklahoma ranch.'

Caroline's cheeks flushed. This was an exaggeration. True, she had taken riding lessons when she was younger. She'd started in primary school and continued all the way into high school. But once her mother got sick, she stopped. Every moment with her mum was precious and she didn't want to waste it on something as indulgent as horse riding. She had never found a way to get back into it.

Duke crossed his arms over his chest and looked at Caroline. He seemed to measure her up from top to bottom. Finally, he nodded approvingly. 'All righty. You seem to be dressed for the ride already.'

Caroline smiled in response. She didn't know she'd be getting up on a horse today but figured one couldn't go wrong with jeans, a shirt over a tank top and a pair of brown leather cowboy boots she had bought the first weekend here. 'Follow me, then, ma'am,' he said to her and then looked at Anna. 'Big Al said he would like to see you in the house. I think Mrs Jackson baked a cake as well.'

'Well, who can say no to a cake? I'll see you later. Hope you have fun!' She waved to Caroline and went off in the direction of the house.

Duke waited for her to disappear and motioned to the left. 'Ladies first.'

The two of them walked towards a set of three tall, red-painted wooden bars on a wide path. Caroline spotted a muddy quad bike parked in front of one of the barns. She glanced back at the vast open space, covered in yellowed grass and contained only by the fences. The soft snickering of horses carried on the air, along with the scent of freshly mowed grass.

Smile tugging on the corners of her lips, she turned and gazed up at the barns in front of her. 'You keep horses in all three of these?'

Duke gave a short nod. 'Yes, ma'am. We have separate ones for the cattle and two more at the back of the ranch for horses, although they aren't the stock we use for training and breeding.'

'What do you use them for?'

'Few years ago, the ranch started to buy ex-rodeo horses. They come here for what you can call retirement, I guess. They get to roam in the pastures and get the food and all. They have a good life. And we keep them here until, you know, they pass.'

'That's a wonderful thing to do,' Caroline said.

Duke shrugged as if he hadn't really considered it before. 'I guess it is, isn't it? New boss has a soft spot for horses, always has. When he came back to help with the ranch, he wanted to do something good, as he put it.'

Caroline assumed he meant Alan's son, the one that Anna had mentioned. 'He sounds like a nice guy.'

They reached the wide entrance to the barn and walked inside. The smell of horses and hay filled Caroline's nostrils. She closed her eyes, remembering the feeling of pure joy and peace when she was younger. A long neigh came from a horse in a nearby stall.

Duke continued the conversation as they walked towards the back of the building. 'Yep, he really is.' They reached a stall where another man was brushing the mane of a beautiful black horse. He was standing with his back to them. Duke stopped, raising a hand in a greeting. 'Hey, boss! This is the woman Big Al wanted you to take out riding.'

As the man turned round, Caroline's heart stopped.

You've got to be kidding me, she thought as her breath hitched.

Hunter seemed just as surprised as she was. He dropped the brush and didn't bend to pick it up. His eyes fixed on her. 'Caroline?'

She collected herself, raising her brow. 'Hi, Hunter.'

Duke looked between them. 'You two know each other?'

Hunter ran a hand through his thick, dark hair. He still didn't take his eyes off her face.

Scraps of their text messages yesterday sloshed in her mind. The memory of the nervous energy zapping through her body when she'd started typing and retyping the first message last night, just to delete the letters with one vicious swipe of anxiety. This was uncharted territory for her, being flustered by a guy. It was as unsettling as it was exciting.

She gave him an unsure smile, not certain how to speak to him when Duke was standing right there.

Hunter seemed to have read her mind. 'Thanks for bringing her, Duke. Can you see if Rory needs any help in the eastern pasture?'

'Sure thing. It was nice to meet you, ma'am.' Duke tipped his hat towards her and bowed slightly. As he walked away, Caroline let out a breath.

Hunter stepped forward, the grin that had already imprinted

itself in her consciousness back on his lips. 'Well, this is a nice surprise.'

'I'm sorry, I didn't know this was your ranch.'

'Technically it's my father's,' he said, his voice strained. 'No need to apologise though. It's not like I wasn't thinking about you anyway.'

Caroline's cheeks heated and she looked down, quite convinced that if she didn't break their eye contact, there was a real risk she could burst into flames on the spot. The out-of-control feeling consuming her body, from the inside of her chest to the very ends of her hair, was a fire hazard.

'Anna, I mean, my aunt, told me you took over running the ranch after your father got sick.'

'Dr Anna Kennedy is your aunt?'

She nodded.

'Small world.'

Indeed, Caroline thought, trying to ignore the odd rush of breathlessness. Her lungs twisted into a tight knot. She was certain she could hear her heartbeat.

Hunter looked up. Even when he didn't say anything, his eyes did.

And the temperature inside the barn had risen.

Caroline took a small step forward, her legs deciding they were teaming up with the butterflies in her gut instead of her brain. The knot in her lungs grew smaller with every step.

'So.'

He bit his bottom lip, his eyes crinkling with amusement. 'So.'

She took a deep breath, feeling the weight of his eyes on her profile. 'Anna was my mother's younger sister,' she blurted.

Hunter's smile fell. 'Was?'

'My mum passed away when I was nineteen.'

'I'm very sorry for your loss.'

She took a deep breath, feeling the weight of his eyes on her profile. 'Thank you.'

It wasn't a topic she brought up in a casual conversation. Why did she even say it? From the first time they had set eyes on each other, easy conversation and flirting had been the common denominator to their interactions. That should be the track she kept to. Because whatever happened next, however many messages they would exchange and however many times they went out, it wouldn't change the inevitable outcome.

This time next year, the exchange programme would be finished and she would be back in Glasgow.

And anything that passed between them would be just a memory. There was no future here, the main criteria Caroline used when thinking about relationships. Or dating. So, this could never be either for her.

She inhaled sharply, realising this was probably something she should tell him – that and other things buzzing around her like a swarm of annoying flies.

'Look, Hunter, before anything else happens between us—'

'I won't lie, I like that you're already thinking of things happening between us.'

Caroline stared at him. '*If* anything was to happen between us.'

He didn't seem rattled by her stony expression. 'Right. Go on, then.'

Standing so close to him was messing with her thoughts, tangling them into loops and hoops, making it harder to string a straight sentence together.

She took in a deep breath, taking a step back. 'I'm only in Oklahoma for one year. On the first of July next year, I'll be on a plane heading back to Scotland.'

Hunter's brows knitted together. 'I don't understand. I thought you worked at the cancer centre.'

'I'm on a clinical research exchange programme, working on clinical trials as a research assistant. It's something that several UK and US cancer research centres take part in annually. A doctor from somewhere in Georgia, I think, is in Glasgow while I'm here.' She shrugged. 'It's very popular and a great thing to add to your résumé.'

'So, you're a doctor. Not a scientist.'

She winced. 'Yeah.'

Either Hunter didn't sense she didn't want to elaborate further, or he decided to ignore it. 'But you aren't working as a doctor just now? While you're in Oklahoma, I mean.'

Caroline shook her head. 'To practise clinically in the US, I'd need to pass USMLE – it's a medical licensing exam. The licence to practise from the UK doesn't automatically give me the right to treat patients here. Same rules apply the other way round, and in other countries.'

Hunter nodded slowly. 'That makes sense.'

She laughed. 'It does but it's a lot of hassle if I did want to take it. Luckily, I have zero interest in working in the US after this year. I wouldn't want to work in a country without universal healthcare. It would go against my values both as a doctor and just a regular person.'

She spotted a flicker of an unease in his steely grey eyes.

'Of course.' He turned his back to her, gazing into the distance.

Caroline wished she could see his face. What was he thinking? Would he say there was no point in their date tomorrow, now that he knew there was zero chance for any kind of future for them? Even though her logical brain agreed with it, her traitorous body had a mind of its own.

And it wasn't rattled by the set end date to whatever this could be.

Stop being fanciful. One kiss, some flirty messages and a walk in a state park are hardly 'a future' material.

She cleared her throat. 'I understand if you don't want to meet tomorrow.'

He turned to her sharply. 'Why would you think that?'

'Because I'm only here for another ten months.'

The smile he flashed her would get toothpaste commercial companies interested if they were looking for a new model. 'A lot can happen in ten months.'

Caroline quirked her brow. 'If you say so.'

Hunter laughed. 'I do. Besides, that kiss made it impossible to not think about you.'

Caroline's breath caught in her throat. The mention of the kiss snapped her out of the strange haze in which both time and place were unfocused. She remembered why Anna had brought her here, and, more importantly, that she'd want to get back home soon.

She decided to change the topic. 'Duke told me about the ex-rodeo horses you buy. That's really sweet.'

'We have tons of space so it's the least I can do.' He shrugged like it wasn't a big deal. Like filling stalls that could house working horses with ones needing peaceful pastures was something every ranch did.

Caroline smiled. 'Can I meet them?'

'Sure. Follow me.'

CHAPTER THIRTEEN

Hunter

Hunter led Caroline outside. 'We keep them in the barn at the back of the property. It's quieter out there.'

She stopped in the middle of the wide path, putting up her hand to shield her eyes from the sun. 'I thought that Mr Fraser's farm was large. This is like four of them put together.'

'I'm sorry?'

Caroline shook her head. 'I grew up in Aberdeen, but we used to visit this farm outside Ballater. They had sheep and chickens. We'd buy free range eggs from there.' She reached to her jeans pocket and took out a pair of sunglasses. 'It was the biggest farm I've ever been to. Until today.'

Hunter watched as she tucked a strand of her hair behind her right ear. She put the glasses on and looked around.

'Well, this is a ranch.' He couldn't help himself. He knew that if he teased her, she was going to give him the look he already associated just with her. Playful but slightly stern. He was unable to keep a grin from his face whenever he caught her glancing at him that way.

'Americans and your love for standing out,' she said slowly, piercing him with the look.

He grinned, right on cue. 'I didn't come up with the name. Sounds like your Mr Fraser had a ranch too. Farms are where the crops are grown.'

Caroline pushed her hands in her pockets. She walked right past him, heading up the path. 'Are you coming?'

'You aren't going to argue with me?'

She chuckled, not turning back. 'I'm a doctor who knows nothing about ranching or farming.'

Hunter jogged up, catching up with her. 'So, you only like to disagree with me when kissing is involved.'

She pressed her lips together. 'We've been through this. It wasn't about kissing itself.'

Hunter took his bottom lip between his teeth. 'What if I asked you for a kiss? Would that be allowed?'

She snorted. 'Horses, Hunter. That's what I'm interested in in this present moment in time.'

'You want to kiss a horse? Well, I wouldn't have picked you for that kind of woman.'

Even through the dark lenses he could see her narrowed eyes drilling a hole in his face.

'I told you, there are a lot of things you don't know about me.'

Hunter's cheeks hurt from grinning. He couldn't remember the last time he had smiled this much. Caroline seemed to have brought out the side of him he thought he had put inside a locked bulletproof container. Somehow, it felt like she had found a key and pulled it out. She had no idea what it meant to him.

Learning that she was only staying in Oklahoma until next summer had taken him aback. Not that he thought there was anything beyond flirting and a good time on the cards for them. There was no space in his life for love. He had to keep the ranch going, he had his family to think of. He had his father's cancer always lurking in the shadows. There was no time left for distractions. Dates themselves could be fun, but dating as in like a relationship wasn't something he was ready for. And he didn't deserve to be happy again. Not after what happened the last time. The guilt he felt hadn't disappeared and he didn't think it ever would.

He sighed, freeing the unwanted thoughts into the August air.

Reaching the entrance to the barn, he looked to Caroline. 'Ladies first.' He sidestepped to let her through.

'Maybe I was wrong and you are a gentleman after all.'

As she walked inside, her hip brushed his thigh. Hunter swallowed hard as at the place her body touched his – just a small area, through two layers of denim – his muscles tightened, decisively ungentlemanly thoughts filling his head.

'The Retirement Yeehaw? Please tell me you didn't come up with this name.'

Hunter's gaze travelled to the metal lettering at the opposite side of the barn. 'Sadly, I can't take the credit. My niece, Morgan, did.'

Caroline walked to the wall. 'Who took these?' She pointed to the row of framed pictures in sepia underneath the name.

Hunter leaned against a beam, watching her from a distance. 'My grandfather, most of them. He's the one who bought the ranch.'

She slid the sunglasses off her nose, examining the frames closely. 'Is he in these?'

'Third photo from the left,' Hunter replied automatically. He stalked to stand next to her. 'It was the first time my father placed in an event. Calf roping.'

Young Alan Jackson was smiling into the camera, an older man wearing a proud expression standing beside him. The photo was missing a corner, it always had. Someone must've ripped it before Hunter found the old albums in the basement when they were building this barn. Four full albums of photos and rodeo trophies. He had asked his father what he wanted to do with them. Alan had waved his hand, saying he had forgotten all about these. He'd told Hunter they could go in the bin. They weren't important.

One evening two summers ago, Hunter had gone through them with Buck and Megan. In the flickering light of citronella candles and to the melody of cicadas, they'd chosen their top twenty. Alan sat on the porch, rocking in the chair and watching them with an expression Hunter couldn't decipher back then.

A week later he told the family his cancer was back.

Hunter drove to Purcell with the box of photos, got them framed, and put them up on the newly painted wooden wall in The Retirement Yeehaw. When he'd brought Alan to see the place after it was finished, they were both lost for words: Alan from thick tears, Hunter from the visceral knowledge one day soon these photos would be the only thing left of his father.

'You look like him.' Caroline's voice brought him back to the present. 'You have the same cheekbones and nose.'

Her elbow brushed his.

He tugged on the collar of his shirt. 'I'm flattered you studied my face closely enough to notice.'

He felt her posture tighten. 'What can I say, you have a pleasant face.'

'Decent kiss, pleasant face . . . I sense a pattern here. Don't think there's any chance of my ego getting too big with you.'

Caroline chuckled, turning to face the row of stalls. 'I've been told before I have a grounding influence.'

His eyes flicked to her profile, drawn to the thin silver lines on her cheek and temple.

She pressed her fingers to her cheek. 'You're looking at my scars.'

'Sorry. Didn't mean to make you uncomfortable.'

'It's fine. I used to be very self-conscious, tried to hide them under layers and layers of make-up. But I grew out of it. Or, rather, the dripping foundation doesn't mix with working in hospital, especially surgical masks.' She took her hand away, so he could look at them.

'How did you get them?'

'Car accident.'

Hunter's blood froze in his veins. He inhaled sharply but his lungs didn't want to expand to release the breath.

Caroline must've thought he was giving her space to talk, because she continued. 'It was stupid, really. I was nineteen. I crashed into a stone wall in bad weather. Luckily, I only got a few scratches. Would've been worse if I'd been driving faster.' She touched the scar again. 'My car was a write-off. But these are the only physical reminder of that day.'

Hunter breathed in and out, taking time to remind his tongue how to roll words off it. His mind scrambled to come up with something to steady him. To remind him this wasn't five years ago.

She's all right. You didn't even know her then. Everything's fine.

'Are you OK?' She gently touched his elbow, deliberately this time.

He rolled his shoulders, walking to the first stall. 'Yes, sorry. I'm glad you weren't badly hurt.'

'Me too,' she said quietly, her pensive expression smoothing her features.

A bay horse stuck its head over the stall's gate, nuzzling Hunter's open palm. 'This is Ringo Thunder. An ex-barrel gelding. He's twenty-two years old.' Hunter stroked Ringo Thunder's mane with his other hand.

'He's beautiful.' Caroline made a move like she was going to touch the horse but withdrew her hand. 'How long has he been here?'

'We got him in three months ago.'

Her eyes widened. 'He raced for that long?'

'There's not really a set age for horses to retire. Some go out younger due to soundness, injuries or illness. But some can race well into their twenties, if they're taken proper care of.'

Ringo Thunder snorted.

Caroline took a step back.

'Don't be scared. He's a gentle soul.' Hunter looked at her. 'Do you want to touch him?'

She didn't move a muscle. 'I haven't been around horses for over ten years.'

Hunter reached out a hand to her. 'I promise he won't hurt you.' Their eyes locked and Hunter's fingers tingled in anticipation. 'I thought you came here to get back in the saddle.'

'That was Anna's idea.'

He flexed his fingers, extending his hand a bit further. 'Don't you miss it?'

Even though he didn't elaborate, he could tell she knew exactly what he meant. It was as if a serene memory washed over her. Her green eyes glimmered in the patchy sunlight fighting to get inside the barn through the small windows near the roof. The dust motes danced between them, reflecting the browns and reds in her dark blonde hair.

If he could, he would take a mental picture to keep the image of this moment in the library of his memories so he could pull it out when he needed a reminder of something good.

Her fingers were cool as they touched his. A single lightning bolt shot right into his chest as she squeezed his hand.

'OK. But if that horse eats my fingers, it's on you. I haven't quite ruled out surgery as a potential speciality so kind of need my hands.'

'I hope you can think of more uses for your hands than medical ones,' Hunter said.

Caroline glared at him.

He chuckled. 'Fine, apparently not the right thing to say.' Without letting go of her hand, he tugged her closer. 'Just relax. He'll sense it if you're scared.'

'I am relaxed,' she bit out.

He raised both of their hands up, placing hers by Ringo Thunder's head. 'He likes being rubbed behind his ears.'

Caroline watched the horse warily. 'You're sure?'

Hunter moved to stand behind her. 'I'm sure.' He lowered his head over her shoulder. His chest was level with her back. He could feel every breath she took.

She cleared her throat, her curiously steady hand making a contact with the horse. Ringo Thunder let out a short snort, moving his head towards Caroline. He nuzzled her palm, just like he did to Hunter before.

Caroline beamed at the horse. 'He seems to like me.'

'He isn't the only one,' Hunter whispered into her hair.

CHAPTER FOURTEEN

Caroline

Caroline stiffened. The press of Hunter's chest against her back plucked the concerns from her mind one by one.

Being wary of the horse? Gone.

Wondering if any of this was a good idea? Forgotten.

Back-and-forth worrying about Finn? Erased.

She swallowed against a tightness in her throat. 'Hunter.'

'Caroline.' He trailed his fingers up her left clavicle without lifting his nose from her hair. 'Just say a word and I'll stop.'

She closed her eyes, taking a large gulp of air. 'I don't want you to stop.'

She wasn't sure if she had said it out loud. Maybe she wouldn't be sure of anything else ever again. Right now, right here, it felt like it was a real possibility.

Trying, and failing, to control her pounding heart, she whirled out of his embrace and looked into his eyes. Her cheeks burned.

She barely knew him. Why did he affect her this much? Sure, he was handsome. Very handsome. His looks, the way he dressed . . . The only thing missing from his wardrobe so far had been a leather jacket – that'd be the cherry on the cake to turn her into a molten puddle. He probably would wear one when the temperature dropped. He looked like a leather jacket kind of guy.

Adding to that his deep voice and accent . . . And the bloody perfect forearms.

There was no denying he was incredibly sexy.

It all added up to a physical attraction. But being able to objectively say that someone was good looking and not being able to keep your thoughts straight in their company were two completely different things.

At least, they used to be for Caroline.

Truth be told, she had never felt this way before. Not even with Finn. And it was unnerving.

She caught herself looking at his lips. The memory of how they felt against hers pushed to the front of her mind, making her want to taste them again.

Fuck, what am I doing? This is madness.

She took a step back. 'Look, Hunter. You seem like a great guy. And I'm flattered you asked me out, truly. But I'm not who you're looking for.'

His eyebrows shot up, his expression somewhere in between confusion and amusement. 'Oh? And who do you think I'm looking for?' He took a step towards her.

She closed her eyes, trying not to think about his broad, muscular chest. Feeling it pressed against her just moments earlier made it almost impossible. She was trying to ignore the earthy smell of his skin.

Her throat worked but no words came out.

He smirked, clearly satisfied with her reaction. 'I just want to get to know you better. That's all.'

'Why? I told you I'm going back to Scotland in less than a year.'

He laughed, raising his arms in the air. 'Honestly, I don't know why.'

He was close enough for her to practically feel the heat coming off his body. A mix of the unforgiving temperature outside and whatever this thing was between them.

Caroline tilted her head and looked into his eyes. 'You're not the problem. I am,' she whispered. 'I don't trust myself when I'm around you.'

He gazed at her. 'Caroline . . .' His hand closed over hers. He took a deep breath. 'Damn, I really want you. You have no idea—' He didn't manage to finish the sentence.

Caroline crushed her lips to his, pushing herself up on her tiptoes to reach him, her hands behind his neck, pulling his head down to her level.

Hunter wrapped his arms tightly around her waist. He kissed her back like an astronaut drifting into space, her body the only gravity worth holding on to.

They pressed against each other, so close she felt his heart beating against her chest.

Her mind went blank.

All she could think about were his hands travelling up her body, his tongue crushing against hers, the feel of his lips on hers. The way he kissed her was like she was the only air he needed to breathe.

She was floating in the ocean, and he was the only supply of fresh water. She wanted to drink him in until she was fully satiated, until she couldn't manage another drop of the delicious nectar of desire.

His teeth grazed her bottom lip, and her senses exploded. She moaned into his mouth.

He responded with a low rumble that vibrated through her, curling her toes.

Each kiss knocked the previous one off the top of the urgency chart. Soaked in honeyed need, Caroline's insides were on fire. If she was a believer, she would imagine her soul was about to rid itself of her body and ascend somewhere greater.

His hands slid under her top, his fingers caressing the smooth skin on her abdomen. He stopped just as he reached the level of her waist.

Caroline gasped to draw air, her lips zapping with electric protest to the loss of contact with his. 'Why did you stop?'

'I wanted to check you were good with this.' His hand slowly inched up over the base of her ribs.

She drew a shaky breath. 'Don't stop.'

His lips curled in a smirk. 'So, I take that as a yes?'

She groaned, grabbing the front of his shirt and finding the buttons. She unbuttoned the second one, pausing every other heartbeat for a breath.

Hunter's lips were on hers again and, somewhere halfway through, she lost count of the buttons, the heartbeats, and the breaths. It was a sweet oblivion, and gods, she was willing to burn in its bliss.

He pushed her against the wall of an empty stall opposite Ringo Thunder's, pinning her hands above her head. He kissed every inch of her bare skin – the top of her cleavage, her neck, behind her ear, her cheeks . . . He dropped a much gentler kiss over her eyes, and she was senseless.

If he wasn't holding her up, she was certain she'd sink to the floor, unwilling and unable to stand up.

'Boss, are you in here?'

They froze as the heavy footsteps entered the barn. Pulling apart from Hunter, Caroline's eyes widened in horror as the realisation of what she had done hit her.

She had never, *ever*, done anything like it in her life. Her hand flew to her mouth, still throbbing from the kisses and the biting, and everything else they did, and even more from the things she was certain they were about to do if they hadn't been interrupted.

One kiss in the bar when she thought she would never see him again was one thing.

This . . . whatever this was, was quite another.

She wanted to speak but no words came. Instead, her eyes welled with tears.

Hunter hastily buttoned his shirt back up. 'I'll come outside in a moment. Wait there!' he shouted to whoever was looking for him. Then, he looked at her, eyes full of concern, and tried to put his hands on her shoulders. 'Caroline, what's wrong?' he whispered.

She stepped out of his reach and backed towards the barn door.

'I'm so sorry. I shouldn't have done that. I'm sorry.' Her voice croaked.

'It's fine,' he tried, but she shook her head violently.

'No, it isn't! You don't understand. I'm . . . I'm married. I can't. Oh, God. I'm so sorry.'

She turned on her heel and ran all the way to Anna's car.

CHAPTER FIFTEEN

Hunter

Hunter was unable to move. His legs felt as if they were made of lead. He lifted his trembling hand, slowly touching his lower lip.

He'd kissed so many women in the past. Most of the time, kissing was just a prelude to what came next. It rarely meant anything. Hell, if he was being honest with himself, there were only two women in the past who had made him feel the way he felt right now. Weak in his knees, slightly intoxicated. Like he was drinking a dram of very fine whisky.

The first, Chloe Turner, was his first kiss. They had briefly dated one summer when they were teenagers. Understandably, one never forgot their firsts. And the next one was meant to be his last.

The kisses that came after her were all different. None of them particularly bad, but Hunter wouldn't call them memorable. Women he used to meet, usually at rodeos, were all the same type: attractive and eager. Wanting to have some fun just as much as he did. After a while, they all started blending into one. He wasn't proud of it, but he also didn't see any real harm in holding this view. They never asked him for anything, which was perfect, because he had nothing to give them beyond a good time.

He closed his eyes and dropped his hand.

Now, there was Caroline. And he felt like the ground moved beneath him when she kissed him. That one kiss made him feel more alive than he had in a very, very long time. It'd almost be poetic if only she hadn't run away.

His heart beat faster at the memory of how her bare skin felt under his fingertips, how he grazed the edge of her lacy bra . . .

I'm such an asshole, he cursed in his mind. Only then, when the initial shock and dizziness subsided, he remembered her words.

Married.

He wasn't judgemental and knew that everyone had a story. But he hadn't expected this. He tried to cast his mind back to their meeting at the bar. She wasn't wearing a wedding ring. He'd have noticed. When you start sleeping with women you meet at rodeos, you learn to look for the ring. Hunter once had a guy who looked like a bodybuilder run after him after he had started kissing, with full consent, a woman who'd hit on him in Austin. After that, he'd always made sure to look.

Maybe he was a spineless arsehole, but he didn't care if she was married.

That startled him, because he should care. It couldn't have been a great marriage, given she was in Oklahoma all alone and hadn't mentioned her husband before now. All the flirting, the kissing . . . Not that Hunter knew that many married women or was an expert in this area, but he didn't think that was the way they behaved.

There must be more to this. There must be a reason, something she isn't telling you.

Yes, that must have been it. He was certain there was an explanation.

Satisfied with straightening his tangled thoughts, he squared his shoulders and found that he was finally able to lift his feet and started walking.

When Hunter entered his parents' house, his mother was crouching over the kitchen counter, kneading dough for bread. It was her Saturday tradition, so that they had fresh bread for Sunday breakfast.

'Did Dr Kennedy leave? I haven't seen a car outside.'

She looked up as Hunter walked in and gave him a tight smile. 'Who? Oh. Yes, darling, she's gone. Apparently her niece wasn't feeling well. I packed them some carrot cake to take home. I know her wife is a great baker, but I'd say my baking isn't too shabby . . .' Mary's voice trailed off. She took her hands out of the dough. Her expression was unreadable and her gaze glassy, as if her mind was very far away.

Hunter's eyebrows knitted with worry. 'Mom, did Dr Kennedy tell you and Dad anything new?' he asked, focusing very hard on not letting his voice quiver.

Mary inhaled and exhaled, like she was struggling to breathe. She straightened her arms and stood taller, as if she hoped it would give her extra strength. 'His latest results came back. She said she shouldn't really tell us outside the office but . . . Well, your daddy asked, and she didn't want to evade the question.'

'What did she say?'

Mary turned away from him and faced the window. She clutched her hands on the edge of the stainless-steel sink.

'Mo—'

'They were bad, Hunter. He isn't improving. He isn't improving and they hoped he would. And, oh, God. There isn't much else they can do.' She closed her eyes. 'They're going to wait until the next round of tests and see. But if there is no improvement, she said she'd like to discuss palliative options with us.'

Numbness crept all over his body for the second time today. Although this time it was a completely different feeling compared to merely half an hour ago. *That* numbness was akin to butterflies in his stomach. Full of electric hope and desire. Now, he felt like he had been thrown into the depths of a black hole.

'When will they run the next set of tests?' he asked, her words still ringing in his ears.

'Early November.'

He nodded, although his neck was so tense that the gesture was barely noticeable. Wordlessly, he walked up to his mother and engulfed her in a hug. The moment her head touched his chest, she broke down in tears. He held her tighter, feeling her whole body shake.

'I'll show you something but keep it to yourself, OK? Under no circumstance can you tell Eve.'

'OK,' Hunter said slowly, eyeing Mitch suspiciously.

They were sitting in the small living room of Hunter's rented two-bedroom house in Purcell. They were set to watch the game, which was starting in less than an hour. Mitch had invited himself. Hunter suspected that he felt bad they hadn't spent more time together lately and wanted to be there for him. And after what happened earlier at the ranch he could use some distraction.

'Promise you won't tell Eve.'

'Fuck, Mitch. Why would I tell Eve?'

Mitch didn't respond. He reached for his denim jacket and looked at Hunter, grinning, as he pulled out a small blue box.

'I wanted to share this with someone and you're the only one I trust,' he said as he opened it.

Hunter's eyes widened at the sight of the shiny ring. 'It's an engagement ring,' he said slowly.

'I know we've only lived together for a few months, but I just know she's the one.' Mitch looked at the ring with a dreamlike expression, smiling softly. 'I was walking past the jewellery store the other day and noticed it in the window.' He looked at Hunter, his smile faltering. 'Do you think Eve's going to like it?'

'She'll love it.' Hunter's voice was thick. He looked away from the ring and felt like something was stuck in his throat. *Don't go there. Nothing good ever comes out of it*, an insistent whisper hissed inside his head.

Mitch closed the box and started turning it in his fingers. 'I'm sorry. I didn't think—'

'It's fine, don't worry about it.' Hunter cleared his throat and met Mitch's eyes. 'I'm really happy for you, man.'

'Thanks. I don't know when I'm going to do it. Can I leave it at your place, until I figure it out? Don't want Eve to accidentally see it.'

'No problem. I'll keep it safe for you.' Hunter opened his hand.

Mitch nodded and carefully put the box in Hunter's palm.

Hunter stood, walked across the room to a console table in the corner, and put the box inside the drawer.

'So, how are things with you?' Mitch asked, leaning back on the couch.

'I don't think my dad's going to make it.' It wasn't the first time Hunter had said those words out loud, but it was the first time that he'd believed them.

Mitch looked up at him, startled. 'What happened?'

'His oncologist came to the ranch earlier today and spoke to my parents. It seems that he isn't improving. He isn't getting any worse, not really, but the results aren't what they'd be hoping to see right now.'

'But didn't you say he's in a clinical trial? They can't really know what the results should be in that case, can they?'

Hunter shrugged. Mitch was probably right, but once he let his mind wander into dark places, it was hard to pull it out of them. Logic was the last thing that spoke to him in that moment.

'Hold on, his oncologist drove all the way from Oklahoma City to the ranch just to give him his results? Isn't that what the appointments are for? Also, isn't it, like, I don't know, a bit unprofessional?'

'She was there for something else. He asked her about them, and she didn't want to brush him off. Dad's been her patient for a long time now. He trusts her. I know it sounds a bit unconventional, but I really don't think I'd have done differently if I were her.' Hunter shrugged again.

'Why did she come then?'

Shit. He hadn't mentioned Caroline to Mitch.

'She wanted to take her niece out riding. Apparently, she rode when she was younger.' Hunter had to stop himself from pulling a face.

'Is that the reason you look like someone whacked your head with something heavy? The niece's hot?'

Hunter bristled. 'What? Why would you say that?'

Mitch grinned. 'Oh, come on. We've been friends for what, six years now? Give me some credit.'

Hunter rubbed his eyes, considering how much he should tell Mitch. 'Today wasn't the first day I met her niece. Remember when I asked you to go to The Rouge Scot with me?'

Mitch nodded once.

'Well, she was the reason I wanted to go there. We met there just over two weeks ago, shared some drinks, chatted, then we kissed. I met her at the Rouken Cancer Center, too. She works there as a research assistant.' He sighed. 'We were meant to go to Robbers Cave tomorrow, but I don't think that's going to happen now.'

Mitch's eyes grew wide with surprise, and he looked like he might burst into laughter. 'Wait, go back. You kissed?'

Hunter groaned. 'Is this the only thing you picked up on?'

'No! But you've got to admit that's the most important one.'

'Well, we did more than kissing earlier at the ranch . . .'

'*Excuse me?*'

Hunter groaned, thinking for a second this was a terrible idea. But even if he didn't share more details now, Mitch would still know something was afoot. So, he told him the bare bones: about the bar, the run in at the Centre, and then their meeting at the ranch today.

When he finished, Mitch laughed out loud. He fell back on the couch, clutching his stomach. 'Dude. You're just unbelievable.' His laughter abruptly stopped, and he sat up straight, suddenly looking very serious. 'How was it?'

'How was what? The kissing?'

'No, learning to tap dance!'

Hunter laughed. He knew what Mitch meant, but he had such a short fuse and irritating him was one of Hunter's favourite parts of their friendship. Most men didn't talk about their feelings. Or that's what society liked to believe. However, it was always different between Hunter and Mitch.

Mitch had been there for him five years ago when his world crumbled down, then again, when his father got sick. He knew him. And Hunter trusted him.

Hunter took a deep breath, trying to think of a way to put his thoughts into as few words as possible to describe the way kissing Caroline made him feel. 'Like it brought me back to life.'

He didn't look at Mitch when he said it, and now that he did, he reached over and lifted a glass of whisky from the coffee table. He took a long sip and shivered.

Mitch gulped and downed his whisky too. 'Wow. Man, that's . . . huge,' he finally choked out.

Hunter nodded once.

'What happened after?'

'She pulled away, said she couldn't do it, apologised, and ran away.'

Mitch let out a loud whistle, but he didn't laugh. 'That's it? Maybe it wasn't so great for her.'

Hunter opened his mouth, wanting to say that it probably had nothing to do with him and everything to do with the fact that Caroline said she was married. But looking at his friend, he remembered how happy he had been a few moments ago when he'd proudly showed him the engagement ring for Eve. It didn't feel right to tell him. No matter how much he trusted him. Plus, Hunter still felt a bit tainted when he remembered Caroline's horrified expression when they pulled apart. Not enough to compete with his desire to see her again, but enough to feel too ashamed to tell Mitch about it.

'Maybe you're right,' Hunter said, trying to seem nonplussed. He bent over and poured more whisky into both glasses. 'Although I'm starting to suspect that Caroline was never meant to be just a random woman I met at the bar—'

'Hunter Jackson, turning over a new leaf and a believer in fate, after all?'

'Oh, shut up, Mitch. I still don't believe in fate.'

'No? And under what category would you put what you've just said?'

He ignored Mitch's comment. 'I think I'm going to text her and see if we can still meet tomorrow.'

He hoped she would at least talk to him. Even if she didn't want to go to Robbers Cave or anywhere else, maybe they could go over things in messages.

'If she doesn't want to meet, you know you can always stop by my place, and we can go drown our sorrows. Or just talk.'

'Thanks.'

They were quiet for a moment, both staring at the muted TV screen. The game was going to kick off in a few minutes.

Mitch put his glass back on the coaster and cleared his throat. 'Do you want to talk about your dad?'

Hunter shook his head. He was still processing this piece of news and wasn't ready to discuss it.

'OK. I'm here if you want to, though.'

'Thank you.'

'Any time. Let's watch the game then, huh?'

CHAPTER SIXTEEN

Caroline

On the way back from the ranch, Caroline felt like someone had stuck tons of Lego pieces underneath her. She shuffled in her seat, pretending to look out of the window but not registering any landmarks. The sudden headache she had claimed to have come down with wasn't even an exaggeration – she felt nauseous and dizzy when she remembered what had happened in The Retirement Yeehaw.

When they passed the sign welcoming them back to the city, Anna cleared her throat. 'Are you OK?'

'Why wouldn't I be?'

Anna didn't answer straight away, and when she did, she sounded like she was weighing her words carefully. 'I feel like we haven't really had a chance to speak properly since you got here. I know we're both busy, and you got thrown into the deep end at work. But I still feel like there's something you're not telling me.'

Caroline pursed her lips tightly.

'I don't want to pry, please don't take it that way. I guess I'm just worried. You never mention Finn. I don't think I have even heard you speak to him on the phone.'

Caroline blinked, not turning her head to look at Anna. 'We're getting a divorce.' Her chest squeezed. 'Haven't signed the papers yet, but we will as soon as I get back.'

Anna was quiet.

'It's a good thing, really. The last four years, well, our entire marriage, has been . . . tough.' Caroline exhaled. 'It wasn't what I imagined.'

'Did he cheat on you?' Anna asked sharply.

'What?' Caroline's head snapped up. 'No! You know Finn. He would never do that.'

'What happened then?' Anna's voice softened. 'I mean . . . If you want to tell me.'

They stopped at the back of what appeared to be a long traffic jam.

Anna's grip tightened around the steering wheel. 'I hate driving in the city. All these roadworks . . . Whenever they finish something, they dig up somewhere else.'

Caroline snorted. 'It's the same in Glasgow. There are just more potholes, and they never seem to actually fix anything.'

Anna hummed in acknowledgement.

Caroline considered what she should tell her. They were close, always had been. Anna had been her shoulder to cry on when Ronan fell into depression after her mother died. She had taken a year out of her own career, moved to Aberdeen and helped them put back the pieces of their shattered hearts together. Or at least she had tried her best. It wasn't her fault that she couldn't bring Siobhan back. But she was still her aunt. Neither of Caroline's sisters knew about what happened with Finn. Erin was the only one to whom she had ever told the whole truth. She wasn't ready to reopen the wound that swallowed all the smaller scratches and bumps over the years like a vicious black hole, trumping them all.

Half a truth was better than a lie.

'Finn wants to have children. I don't.' She wrung her hands in her lap. 'I know this is something we should've discussed before getting married. But I didn't know I didn't want to be a mother then.'

'People told you you'd change your mind whenever you said you might not want to.'

'How did you know?'

Anna shrugged, turning on the right indicator. 'I overheard Finn's mother at your wedding. What's her name?'

'Orlaith.' Caroline winced. She despised the woman. 'That doesn't surprise me.'

'I'm sorry things worked out that way. But you're parting on friendly terms?'

Caroline thought back to her conversation with Finn. Her heart ached, wondering how he was doing. It was Saturday, so he might've gone out with his best friend, Robb. They normally either hit one of Glasgow's golf courses or the driving range. She imagined him on their three-seater sofa in the living room of their four-bedroom flat in the West End, flicking through TV series and films, choosing what he wanted to watch.

'You could say that,' she said in a low voice. 'It's been a mutual decision.'

'Good. That's good.'

Caroline swallowed a thick lump of regret. She remembered how she wasn't thinking about any of this just an hour ago. Wrapped in Hunter's arms, with his mouth on her skin . . .

She shook the memory off. He must think she was an awful person, after what she had said. If nothing else, she owed him an explanation. He needed to know she wasn't cheating, despite what her conscience tried to drum into her. Somehow, his opinion was important to her. She didn't want to leave what they'd shared tainted.

Out of habit, she touched her left ring finger. She rubbed the spot where her engagement ring's diamond used to rest.

They pulled into Anna and Gian's street and Anna took the turn to the underground car park.

Caroline took her phone out of her pocket. She unlocked it, ignoring the guilt telling her it was better to leave it alone.

> CAROLINE: *I'm sorry for running off like that. I'd like a chance to explain, if you still want to meet tomorrow?*

She put the phone screen down on her thigh.

Just as Anna pulled into her parking spot, the phone vibrated.

> HUNTER: *Looking forward to it. See you there.*

Anna put the car into park and unbuckled her seatbelt. 'You're coming?'

Caroline smiled to the screen, indiscernible excitement, relief and fear churning inside her. She got out of the car, practically running to the elevator.

People had warned her about the distances in the US. The other day, Gian announced she was popping out to see her parents but would be back in the evening.

She had driven to Dallas and back. Within a day.

Six hours in a car, if the roads were good.

Caroline was a good driver, but anything over forty miles was not a 'quick' trip in her book. When she had announced to Anna and Gian what were her Sunday plans, they blinked at her. *You might want to check how long it's going to take you to get there. It's . . . a bit of a drive*, Anna said.

It was a good job she did, because as it turned out, it was one hundred and fifty-eight miles. One way. Only about fifty miles less than the distance between Glasgow and Manchester, where Erin lived. Caroline had never driven there and back within the same day.

She probably should've checked the maps before she had suggested meeting Hunter at Robbers Cave State Park. But it was too late for that now. After running off like he'd burned her yesterday, she didn't want to cancel on him last minute.

She was also too proud to simply tell him she hadn't realised how far it was.

So, here she was at 5.30 on a Sunday morning, shooting incredulous looks at any driver coming from the opposite direction as she clutched the steering wheel of Anna's car. She turned up the volume on the radio, wanting to wake herself up with both the music and the black coffee she had poured into a travel mug on her way out.

'The views had better be worth it,' she muttered to herself as the joined the highway, following the route to the pinned location Hunter had shared with her last night.

He was already waiting for her when she pulled into the parking lot. 'Morning.' He flashed her a smile, touching the side of an orange-and-white trucker cap.

Caroline let out an exasperated breath as she jumped out

of Anna's car. She had got lost three times on her way. Tardiness flustered her, especially when it was of her own making.

'Sorry I'm late.'

'It's fine. I've got something for you.' He held out a brand-new copy of *A Lady's Guide to Scandal*. 'I felt bad yours got ruined.'

Caroline opened her mouth, then closed it. She tried again. 'You didn't have to.' A smile lifted her lips as her finger smoothed over the front cover. 'Thank you.'

'Least I could do. Hope you enjoy reading it.'

She looked into his eyes, shielded from the early morning sun by the cap.

Why are you so nice to me? I told you I'm married. You shouldn't be this nice, not after all the shameless flirting and kissing before I dropped that bomb on you.

A warm breeze rustled the air, weaving through Caroline's hair. She pushed a strand off her forehead and turned to open the passenger door to Anna's car, where her purple backpack sat. Unzipping a side pocket, she pulled out a satin scrunchie and pulled her hair into a ponytail.

She put her backpack on, adjusting the straps. 'Shall we? You promised me a walk.'

Hunter gave her a crooked smile. 'Let's go.'

CHAPTER SEVENTEEN

Hunter

Hunter bobbed his head towards a large map with a red marked-up path. 'Do you just want to follow the nature trail?'

Caroline considered the map. 'It says it takes about an hour. So, even if we stop on the way, we'll be back before the temperature goes up.' Her forehead creased. 'Hopefully there won't be many people this early on a Sunday,' she added, like it was the most important consideration.

Hunter's lips split in a smile. 'Is that a yes, we'll follow the trail?'

With a sigh, she cocked her head to one side. Her finger traced the path on the map, following it all the way to the Robbers Cave.

'You said you've been here before?' she asked.

'I used to come here with my grandad. Then with my dad,

after Grandad passed.' He glanced at the map. 'I can probably lead you to the cave with my eyes closed.'

Caroline let out a half-snort, half-laugh. 'Please don't. I didn't pack a first aid kit. And it probably takes a while to get any rescue up here.'

'You just assume that I'd hurt myself?'

'I like to be prepared for the worst scenario,' she murmured.

'Fine. I'll lead you up there with my eyes wide open.' He glanced, catching the end of her eyeroll. 'Left or right?'

She checked the map again. 'Let's go right. We'll see the cave on the way back.'

They set off on the main path. The rocky terrain could be intimidating for some people, despite the steps chiselled into the rock. But Caroline's back was straight, her shoulders squared, her face lacking any sign of worry. She looked like she not only knew what she was doing, but like she was in her element.

'You hike a lot,' he noted after they walked in silence for a bit, with only the shuffling sound of their walking boots against the path disturbing the serene morning.

'I used to. Growing up, we always had at least two dogs at home. We'd spend Sundays going on long walks with them. *Adventures* as my dad used to call them.' She smiled. 'I wish I could live somewhere where there were more opportunities for nature walks on my doorstep. I miss it.'

'I thought Scotland had plenty of green open spaces.'

She turned to him, not slowing her pace. 'Of course. There are country parks just outside Glasgow. We also have a gorgeous national park about forty minutes' drive away. It's just difficult to make the time.'

'With your work, you mean?' he asked.

She nodded, stopping at the foot of the slab steps, craning her neck. 'So many hiding spots around here.'

Hunter followed her gaze to the steep Sans Bois Mountains. 'Yeah, there are many legends about these caves, full of hidden treasure and outlaws.'

Caroline's face lit up. 'Treasure?'

He chuckled, placing his foot on the first step. 'Apparently, in the late 1950s, park employees found something like close to three hundred gold wedding bands. The theory was that they were left behind by a stagecoach robber, because they were near an old stagecoach line.'

A shadow crossed her face, twisting her lips in a grimace he hadn't seen before. 'All those wedding bands were stolen?'

'I guess so. It's just one of the tales.' He shrugged.

She remained quiet as they climbed up the steps.

Hunter wondered if the odd change in her demeanour was due to the mention of the wedding bands. Her left hand was the first thing his gaze had flickered to when she'd got out of the car earlier. And then, his eyes had found it again as they were walking. Twice. His memory hadn't deceived him – there was no ring on her finger.

He didn't ask her about it, waiting for her to start the conversation. She'd said she was going to explain. Maybe she was working up to it. Or maybe she had decided she didn't owe him an explanation.

He truly hoped it was the former.

'Who were the outlaws? The ones from the legends?' she asked, sidestepping to avoid a gaping hole in the ground.

Hunter cocked his brow. 'You like dangerous men, then?'

'Who said anything about men?' She winked at him.

He bit the inside of his cheek, forcing his eyes back on the path in front of him. He would be perfectly fine if he didn't look too closely at her face. Her lips were a clear danger zone, but it seemed that so was her nose, her chin, her eyes, her forehead . . . Her entire face, really.

'Confederate and Union army deserters, mostly. They used Robbers Cave, the one where we're heading, as a hideout spot. After the Civil War, the gangs allegedly used it too. See how steep the mountains are?' He gestured to them. 'They formed a perfect corral for horses. There are equestrian trails through the forests nowadays, too.'

'Have you ever ridden here?'

He didn't realise she'd got closer to him as the path narrowed. Her wrist brushed his, accidentally, he was sure. But his breath still shook as he tried to remember her question.

The horses. She's asked about the horses.

He cleared his throat. 'I have, though not in a long time. There's an equestrian campground. We used to make a weekend out of it.'

This bit of the trail was particularly tricky, with uneven, slippery stones. Hunter had seen people trip on here before. His arms were ready to catch her if the same thing happened now, but Caroline walked through the path without even a wobble.

'We?'

'Me and my older brother, Buck.' He scrunched his nose, browsing through his memories for the one of the last time he had been here. 'His stag was here. I was so thrilled my parents, and Buck, let me go.'

She shot him a sceptical look. 'How old were you?'

'Thirteen.' He laughed at the horror written in her face. 'Don't worry, I was only allowed to ride with the party during the day. When they were drinking and whatnot later, I was tucked in bed in the camp, reading.'

'I'd have pictured you as a teenager who would try to sneak into the party.'

Hunter mocked an aghast expression, taking a step back and pushing his hand to his heart. 'Me? Never.'

Caroline laughed, bowing her head to avoid crashing into a pine branch. 'Not sure I'm buying it.'

'Well, there was this one time I hid in Buck's car when I was seven. He was going to a party, and I buried myself under a pile of blankets on the back seats.'

She laughed, again, and her laughter put a smile on his face.

He didn't know many things about her. But he knew he could make her laugh. And just now, when there was no other soul in sight among the unfathomable vastness of rocks and greenery, this was a vital piece of information. Like a golden nugget hidden by the outlaws in the cave, Hunter tucked the sound of her laugh into the pocket of invisible treasures.

'Did he find you?' she asked.

He shook his head. 'No. I got out at the party. I was out there for maybe half an hour. Forty minutes? It was carnage. I walked in on a couple having sex in a closet, thought the girl was getting murdered, and screamed my head off. They were like *"Who is this kid? What's he doing here?"*'

'What did you do?'

'Ran, of course. I hid back in Buck's car. I don't think he ever found out it was me. If he did, he never said.'

Caroline stared at him. 'Unbelievable. Now I feel like my childhood was so boring in comparison.'

Then the smile slipped off her lips as she stopped abruptly, noticing the view.

The treetops looked like a carpet of the greenest grass from where they stood. The sun peeked over wispy white clouds, showering the landscape with bright summer glow. Birds chirped from all around, like they had plugged into the highest quality surround system.

'It's stunning,' she whispered into the windless air.

Hunter briefly followed her gaze, but when he realised nothing had changed since the last time he was here, his eyes bored into her profile. Her green eyes were like two large emeralds. The natural surroundings seemed to bring out their colour even more. He thought he had seen green eyes before, and he had, of course. But not like that. Not like hers.

'It really is,' he said, not taking his eyes off her.

Caroline walked up to the edge and looked down. Seemingly satisfied, she took two steps back and turned to Hunter. 'I think we should let it all go.'

He blinked, confused. 'Let what go?'

'All the bottled-up emotions. Come on, I can tell you have plenty of them. Even though you put on a good front.'

'Sure. Who doesn't? But I have no idea what you want me to do about them.'

She grinned, raising both of her arms in the air. 'Isn't it obvious? Release them into the air, let them crash over the edge. Sort of like a mental cleanse, metaphorically speaking.'

He reached her side, gazing at the horizon. 'I wouldn't have picked you for someone who believed in that kind of thing.'

'It's something my friend Erin taught me.' Her eyes darkened. 'Sometimes I struggle with expressing my feelings. I worry too much and don't talk about it. Then, suddenly, it's this monster of emotions and everything I wanted to avoid.'

'And how do you deal with them?'

Still grinning, she faced the untamed forest and rugged mountains and let out a long scream.

Hunter jumped back, startled. Somehow, he hadn't expected that.

The sound carried in the air, dissipating into the wilderness. Caroline screamed again, letting the sound mix with laughter.

She turned to him, hands on her hips. 'Your turn.'

'What is the—'

'Just yell. Scream your heart out. Trust me.'

He shot her an unsure glare. Then, he did just that. Opening his arms as if to throw out all the heartache into the outside world, he screamed.

For the unfairness of his father's cancer. For the concern for what was going to happen to his family when Alan was gone. For his own heart, crushed five years ago and never fully recovered. For his broken dreams and plans put aside, never to be picked up again. The wind mixed with the noise he made, but Hunter just kept going. Only once his throat had dried up did he fall silent, practically panting from the effort.

Caroline clapped slowly. 'Woah, that's what I'm talking about! How are you feeling?'

'Free,' he whispered, as that was all he could manage.

They looked at each other, an understanding and something deeper passing between them.

The knowledge that whatever flicker of attraction brought the first spark, if they weren't careful, they were going to go up in flames.

CHAPTER EIGHTEEN

Caroline

Caroline looked away first. Screaming at the top of her lungs into the crowns of the trees hadn't wiped out some things completely.

The guilt, from how far she'd let things get yesterday.

The shame, because she wanted more.

And so many more indistinguishable swatches of emotion swirling around in the pit of her stomach.

'We should get going if we want to be back in the A/C before it gets sweltering,' she said.

Hunter nodded, wordlessly rejoining the trail.

She followed him, dozens of thoughts fighting for space at the forefront of her mind. When he'd brought up the stolen wedding bands stashed away in caves, her heart momentarily froze. It only took a second. An internal gasp, followed by reminding herself things between her and Finn were done. That they were both going to be fine, although separate.

But it had reminded her about the explanation she owed Hunter. Despite her best efforts, she hadn't forgotten it. She had tried to push it off, told herself she would wait for the right moment. Then she realised that such a moment didn't exist.

She needed to tell him before they got back into their respective cars and set on the road, blasting the A/C and radios.

'Here we are. The Robbers Cave,' he announced.

Caroline halted. She wasn't really looking where she was going and almost walked into his back. 'Can we go inside?' she asked, collecting herself.

'Sure, if you're brave enough.'

'What's that supposed to mean?'

Hunter's eyes crinkled. 'Some people say that the ghosts of the robber from 1870, Lanky George, haunts the cave. He likes to search for jewellery and steal it, ripping necklaces and earrings off people's necks. A couple of years ago, a woman from Arkansas claimed she had lost a chunk of her earlobe.'

Caroline snorted. 'Lanky George, really?'

Hunter shrugged in mock helplessness. 'I didn't come up with the name.'

'I'm going in. You can stay outside, if you're scared.'

She walked around a thick tree trunk, marching up to the cave's entrance. Inside, she blinked, letting her eyes adjust to the sudden loss of sunlight.

Goosebumps erupted all over her bare arms. She hugged them to her chest, guarding off an unexpected shiver. She walked a bit further, then rested her back against the cool surface of the rock.

'I didn't think you'd actually be scared, it was a joke,' she called out, a smile playing on her lips.

'I'm not scared of Lanky George.' A twig snapped under

a heavy boot and Hunter cautiously stepped inside the cave. 'But what's that, is your left earring missing?'

Caroline's hand flew up. She touched her pearl stud, which was, of course, still there.

Hunter laughed. 'Got you.' He crossed his arms as he leaned over the rock next to her.

Caroline's consciousness prickled with the awareness of his body. It was so strange. Surely if this is how her body reacted to another person, it would've happened before, right?

You were in love with Finn since you were fifteen. You noticed other men but didn't really see them. Until now.

She grimaced, inhaling sharply. Now was just as good a time as any to tell Hunter the truth – or at least, part of it.

'So, about yesterday . . .' She paused, chewing on her bottom lip. 'When I told you I'm married and then ran off.' *Like the coward that I am*, she added in her head.

'You don't have to tell me anything you don't want to,' Hunter said softly.

Caroline crossed her legs at the ankles and shook her head. 'I want to tell you. It's just . . . difficult because I don't really talk about it.'

She swallowed, twisting her fingers in her lap. 'Four years ago, I married my first and only boyfriend. We met in primary school. We were friends for a long time before we became more. Anyway, we got married, and I really believed it was going to be my happily ever after. But things between us started going downhill.'

He mulled over her words with a thoughtful expression. 'Are you still with him?'

'No. Long story short, we're getting a divorce. We've been through marriage counselling, we argued until there was no more puff left in either of us. So, it's over.' She scratched her forehead, leaving a red mark. 'It's complicated. I love him, but I'm not *in* love with him anymore.'

As soon as she said it, her throat tightened, and her heart ached. Despite thinking about it many times, this was the first time she had found a way to put her feelings into words. It terrified her. Not only because it was the truth, but because she found it so easy to confide in Hunter. He was practically a stranger, for Christ's sake. *A stranger you kissed like a horny teenager lusting after him for days before that.*

'You aren't in love with him?' Hunter repeated, like this was the main takeaway he'd got from her monologue.

She shook her head, a sad smile tugging the corners of her lips. 'No. To be honest, I think I haven't been for a while.'

Caroline watched him with a mix of nervousness and anticipation, not sure what she was expecting or hoping for. She knew he made her feel hot and bothered. He was gorgeous, he was a great kisser, and based on the limited information she had about him, he was a kind, good-hearted guy.

Maybe this was all that she needed to know just now.

She shivered with surprise when he slid his hand into hers and gave it a firm squeeze.

'Is there anything else you want me to know? About your marriage?' he asked.

She shook her head slowly. 'No. But you see now why that kiss was impulsive and—'

He squeezed her hand again and it made her feel warm all the way down to her toes.

'And why there are tons of reasons why we shouldn't see each other again,' she finished clumsily. 'Like the fact that I'm only here for a few months.'

'Because you don't trust yourself around me?' He smirked, looking very pleased with himself.

She swallowed hard. 'Precisely.'

Hunter hummed under his breath, staring at the wall of the cave opposite them.

'If you tell me that this . . . this thing—' he gestured between them '—is completely one-sided and I've got it all wrong, then I'll walk away right now. But if you feel the same pull to me as I do to you, however stupid and incomprehensible it seems—'

She put a finger to his lips, and he stopped mid-sentence. 'I think you already know that I do. I kissed you, after all. It's hard to make my attraction any more obvious,' she smiled shyly.

Then, she pulled her finger away.

This was crazy. She must've gone completely crazy. How else could she explain throwing all her caution and moral backbone to the wind? This wasn't her. She was responsible, level-headed, and always putting others before herself. She was a people pleaser. And she had never, ever, done anything so out of character.

'Well, Dr Caroline . . . Damn, I just realised I don't know your last name.'

'O'Kelly. Caroline O'Kelly.'

'Dr Caroline O'Kelly, I think you're a woman worth dismissing the reason and logic for.'

They locked eyes with each other, still holding hands.

Her throat went dry and when she spoke, it sounded like a low whisper. 'The feeling's mutual, Mr Hunter Jackson.'

She squeezed his hand back.

Their names echoed in the hauntingly eerie Robbers Cave. If Lanky George heard them, he didn't make a move to disturb the clumsy attempt at whatever this was – a flirtation, of sorts, one with an expiration date and truckload of emotional baggage.

CHAPTER NINETEEN

Hunter

'I have to say, when you asked if I wanted to go to dinner, I didn't expect this.'

Hunter laughed, watching Caroline's eyes fill with curiosity as she took in the interior. He had asked her out in a vague text, only saying he knew just the right place for dinner and asking if she had any food allergies. She replied that she never says no to food, isn't allergic to anything, and that as long as it's good, she has no preferences.

They were sitting on wooden bar stools in a cramped pizzeria. There were only six to eight chairs stacked around the counter running alongside two short walls. The charcoal menu had six different types of pizza written down in white chalk, with prices noted next to it. These changed daily, depending on the availability of fresh ingredients that were in season. The only constant was a plain margherita, forever denoted with number one.

The wood-burning stove crackled with an inviting fire, and the smell coming out of it was as close to food ecstasy as one could get.

Hunter flashed her a brilliant smile, watching her take a big bite from a large triangle.

'I like to be unpredictable. We can go to a fancy restaurant next time, if you want, but I wanted to take you for the best pizza in the whole of Oklahoma. It's my go-to.'

She chewed slowly, nodding to herself. He noticed the moment her eyes lit up and she moaned with satisfaction. 'This is delicious!' she exclaimed with her mouth full.

He let out a half-suppressed laugh, trying not to make her feel uncomfortable.

She finished chewing and added, 'It's perfect, really. I will take good, authentic food over fancy any time.'

'You're trying to tell me you don't enjoy higher-end cuisine? Damn, there goes my plan to take you to the Michelin-star French restaurant next. Their snails are out of this world.'

She shoved his side playfully, and he took the opportunity to put an arm lazily around her waist.

Their eyes met for a split-second, and Hunter felt like his heart skipped a beat.

It was Thursday night, the first time they had met since the trip to Robbers Cave. Caroline had been busy at work; he had been busy at the ranch – tonight was the first time he had managed to get away earlier. His knuckles ached from all the late-night texting, though.

He still wouldn't call whatever it was proper dating. Even though a small voice in his head nagged him that it very much was precisely that. Dating as a verb felt like a big thing. A step Hunter wasn't sure he was ready for. Besides, even if he was, it would make no difference. She would still be leaving.

As much as he wanted to forget about it, the lack of any future for them was impossible to ignore. But it didn't stop his mind from trying.

'I like any good food. Though maybe not the snails.' Her body moved in a gentle, involuntary spasm as if the mere thought made her uncomfortable. 'All I meant was that so many people choose expensive over quality. Sure, they often go hand in hand. But I've been to so many places that had the trendiest décor and the highest prices, and yet the actual food failed to impress.'

She stopped, finishing the half-eaten piece. After taking a sip of lemonade, she continued. 'I just don't believe in paying a premium for the sake of paying more, if you can get the same or better for a lower cost.'

'What do you think are some of the things that are worth paying more for?' He bit into his pizza, his eyes not leaving her face.

Caroline shrugged, looking ahead. The pizzeria was on a busy street in Bricktown. Although it was a weeknight, the foot traffic was still heavy. People were walking past in pairs, groups or on their own. Laughter and conversation mixed with the sound of passing cars.

'Meat is probably one of the things. And seafood. Any fresh food ingredients, really. I'm not a big believer in the whole organic movement, but you can taste a difference in quality fruits and vegetables.'

He nodded in agreement. 'Absolutely. For me it's also pasta. Though nothing beats it fresh.'

Seeing him shrug, nonplussed, she laughed and put her hand on his thigh. They were already very close, their knees touching, but this extra contact with her body made him jolt inside.

He swallowed hard. 'But . . .'

'Rice doesn't make much difference,' she finished his sentence.

'Exactly. I think we'd both agree that good whisky is worth its price.'

'Of course it is. I'm also a big advocate for sustainable fashion and creating timeless, capsule-wardrobe looks. I think my favourite winter wool coat is six years old.'

'You'd look great in a garbage bag,' Hunter said before he could stop himself.

Her cheeks reddened and she gave him a small smile. 'One thing that I'm hopeless for is luxury make-up. I don't know, it's just my little indulgence. I always only have one of everything on the go, except lipsticks and eyeshadows, but it brings me joy. That and perfumes. Those are two things that I wouldn't be interested in trying to find cheaper alternatives for.'

He instinctively examined her face, which looked flawless. But to him, she never looked anything else, whether she had full, light or no make-up on, like when they had met at Robbers Cave. Biting his tongue not to say something soppy, he reached out for another piece of pizza.

The little bell above the door rang with increased frequency as the minutes passed, letting in a constant stream of loyal customers, most of whom walked away with steaming cardboard boxes. Apart from them, there were only two other people sitting inside. An older man and a girl who looked about ten.

Caroline finished eating and watched the duo, her forehead creasing with a deep frown.

'I miss my niece,' she finally said, her voice tinged with sadness.

'What's her name?'

'Victoria. But she's getting a sibling soon. My older sister, Clara, is pregnant.'

'Congratulations. That's awesome.'

She beamed at him. 'It is. She and her husband are very happy.'

'Do you see them often?' He noticed that her face fell a little at the question. She looked at the bushy-haired girl again.

'Not as often as I'd like. They live in Dublin. Though it's only a short flight away, it's hard to find time to visit. I sometimes wish they all still lived in Aberdeen but that's over three hours' drive, and I guess it really wouldn't make any difference. I still wouldn't be able to get up to see them more often than I do now.' She blinked and took a deep breath. 'Missing my family is probably the hardest thing about living in another country. At least there are video calls. They're not the same, but better than nothing.'

'It sounds hard.'

Caroline nodded. 'I read once that living away from home always holds a chunk of your heart hostage. You can never feel truly whole, no matter how happy you are, because there's always a piece missing.'

Hunter gave her a sad smile. 'That's beautiful and depressing at the same time.'

She laughed, sadness dispersing from her face. 'You're right. You have a niece as well, don't you?'

'I have one, and one nephew. Morgan and Cody.' He smiled affectionately. 'They're coming around for dinner on Sunday at the ranch. I'd invite you, but not sure it'd be the best idea. I wouldn't want to give my family the wrong impression about us, and they'd read too much into it.'

She didn't look at him, still looking ahead.

He noticed the sadness overtaking the green of her eyes. 'Unless you'd like to come?'

'No, I think you're right.' A strained smile split her lips but she blinked like she was trying to mask it. 'And is it just you and Buck?'

'I have a younger sister, Megan. She's a freshman at the University of Oklahoma, taking mostly pre-med classes. She said you led one of her biology labs on Monday?'

She furrowed her brow. 'I did, but there were too many students to pay attention to anyone. But how . . . Did you tell her about me?'

'No. Apparently Mom told her you and your aunt came over on Saturday. When she came back on Monday, she was all excited about that lab and you.'

'I see.'

'She also asked me if I was seeing anyone.'

Caroline quirked her brow. 'Oh?'

He shrugged. 'Apparently, I seem chipper.'

She snorted. 'Chipper?'

'That's what Meg said. My attempt at being mysterious and sneaky clearly was not as subtle as I thought,' he admitted.

She shook her head, amused. Leaning back, she rested her head on his chest, and he steadied her with both of his arms.

He could feel his heartbeat against her back.

'You're many things, Hunter, but you're not mysterious or sneaky. In fact, you're probably the most honest and no-nonsense person I've ever met.'

'I feel like there's a compliment somewhere in there . . . Never mind, I'll just take it as one.'

'You should.' She put her hand on his forearm. 'But why was she excited? It wasn't a particularly interesting lab. In fact, if I'd had to do four years of college the way you do it here, I'm not sure I'd have had enough motivation to carry on with medical school afterwards.'

'Oh, Meg's a massive science geek. I think she's thinking of medical school now, but she also wanted to be a forensic scientist, an anthropologist, a biochemist. You can see the breadth of things that'd interest her. But no, it wasn't the lab that caused the excitement. It was you.'

She pushed away from him, sitting up in shock. 'Me? But I didn't do anything exciting.'

'I think it was more just because you're you.'

She raised her eyebrows dubiously.

'No, honestly. I don't think you know how amazing you are,' he added.

She scoffed dismissively, shaking her head.

Before she had a chance to cut in and start denying it, he said, 'You are, Caroline. You said I'm the most honest person you've met. Well, you're authentic, passionate, and intelligent. I know it sounds cliché. But it's true.' He smiled at her earnestly.

'What did they put in this pizza? You're talking nonsense.'

He laughed. 'I hope there comes a day when you can see how wonderful you are. Don't respond, just file it in your mind for later,' he added quickly, seeing that she was opening her mouth to argue.

She closed it and continued wordlessly looking at him.

'Anyway, Meg wants to meet you. I know we talked about not meeting the entire family, but Meg's Meg. We've always been very close, and I feel like spending time with people who seem to inspire her would do her good, especially now . . .'

He could feel the unspoken words *'that our dad is probably dying'* hang between them. The truth was that one night when they were texting, Hunter had floated the idea of her staying over for dinner at the ranch. She'd said she wanted to come back and get into a saddle, and he was trying to be nice. Caroline had said she appreciated the thought, but it was probably better if they stuck to horse riding when they were at the ranch. On one hand, he was pleased – his mother would not stop nagging him if he brought Caroline for dinner. But, somehow, he was also a little bit disappointed. Even though he kept telling himself they weren't really dating.

'OK. When do you want me to meet her?'

'I don't know. No rush, just a thought for another day.'

Caroline nodded, finishing her lemonade and kissing him softly on the cheek. The simplicity and intimacy of this gesture surprised him, but he tried not to let it show on his face.

She jumped off the stool and threw the strap of her mustard yellow handbag over her shoulder. 'Sounds good.'

And with that, he followed suit.

They exited the pizzeria, arm in arm, into the cloudy end-of-August night.

CHAPTER TWENTY

Caroline

The corners of Caroline's mouth twitched as she forced a smile to see off another potential study participant.

'And that's us all done. Thank you very much for your time, Mrs Cortez. We'll be in touch after analysing the results.'

She put her forehead against the door after closing it behind Mrs Cortez. Even though it was just Tuesday afternoon, it already felt like she'd been here all week. She had spent the day interviewing new candidates for the Phase III clinical study they were hoping to kick off soon. Phase III trials were the last hurdle new treatments had to overcome before they got regulatory approval to be used on patients. This one was sponsored by one of the big pharmaceutical companies and involved using an oncolytic virus in the treatment of advanced bladder cancer. This new agent was causing waves of excitement in the oncology environment among both scientists and doctors. So far, the results looked very promising, and if they could achieve what they hoped for in Phase III . . . Even though Caroline was worn out by the extra work involved in starting a new trial, she was cautiously optimistic that it meant good news for hundreds of patients.

Her enthusiasm didn't take away from the difficulty of speaking with fifteen people who had exhausted all available lines of treatment. Caroline knew she should be used to these conversations by now, but it turned out they didn't seem to get any easier as time went on. Of course, she wasn't the person making the ultimate decision on whether someone made a good candidate or not. The type of patient who could be included in the study was very strict. You were either a match, or you weren't.

She took a heavy breath and sat back at her desk, trying to steady her racing thoughts. They were still very much filled by last night's text messages with Hunter. It was the second week of September. Since their trip to Robbers Cave, they had seen each other only three more times, including twice at the ranch, when Caroline had finally bit the bullet and decided to get up on the horse. Before that, Hunter had come to the city, and they'd had one of the best pizzas in Caroline's life so far. It didn't beat the pizza by the slice from the hole-in-the-wall pizzeria in Bologna she had tried during her solo weekend trip two years ago, but it came a close second.

Her lips were just starting to remember the way that Hunter's lips felt against hers when he'd kissed her goodnight before they'd exited the barn last night, after making sure no one else was around, when someone knocked on the door.

'Caroline, are you there?' Amira Singh poked her head round the door. 'I wanted to ask you about the upcoming congresses.'

'Yes, come in!' Caroline quickly pretended to busy herself with the printed-out forms scattered around the desk.

Amira came in, smiling sympathetically. She was wearing a burnt-orange hijab and dark red lipstick today. Over the last month, Caroline thought she must've seen her dressed in an iteration of every colour of the rainbow. The bright clothes made her look younger than she was. The other day, they were talking, and Amira had told her she was thirty-three years old. When Caroline just blinked at her, unable to hide surprise from her face – she had been convinced Amira was in her early to mid-twenties – Amira had just laughed and said, *'The importance of using a sunscreen!'*

'How's your day going so far?' Amira asked, settling herself on a leather chair opposite Caroline.

'Fine, yeah. I've screened—' Caroline consulted the computer screen '—fifteen potential participants so far.'

'Fifteen? Wow. You must be ready to call it a day.'

Caroline let out a short, bitter laugh. 'Oh, I really am. But that's not important. You said you wanted to speak about the upcoming congresses?' She decided that as much as she enjoyed Amira's company, what she wanted even more than a friendly chat today was clocking out on time, going home and preferably relaxing in a long bubble bath. As much as her mind had enjoyed riding again, her body was less pleased. The ache in her thighs was a painful reminder of how out of practice she was.

Amira gave a short nod and pulled out a sheet of paper from a manila envelope. 'There's ESMO, of course, at the end of October and that's in Madrid this year. We usually send at least two people from the centre to that. Jake was hoping to go, and Dr Russell, but if you were interested, I'm sure we could figure something out?'

Caroline scrunched her nose, digging in her memory for the acronym. 'ESMO is the European Society for Medical Oncology, right?'

'Correct. The most important oncology congress in Europe, and one of the most prestigious ones in the world.'

Caroline considered that for a moment but then shook her head decisively. 'Thanks, Amira, but I think I'll pass. I came all this way here and I'm not staying in the US for too long. I can go to ESMO next year when I'm back in the UK, if I decide to pursue oncology in the end.'

'Fair enough! If you don't want to go, I might see if I can swing it. It'd be nice to spend some time with Jake—' Amira suddenly blushed furiously and quickly averted her eyes to stare at her red Converse.

'Oh.' Realisation dawned on Caroline, and she grinned. Jake was their coworker – sweet and kind of gangly, always ready with a joke and, she suddenly thought, always with a cup of coffee and an extra snack for Amira. 'So, you and Jake?'

'No!' Amira almost leaped out of her seat. 'I mean . . .' She lowered herself against the cushion, growing even more red. 'I like him, and I think he's great, but he probably doesn't feel the same way.'

'You never know. I say go for it.'

Amira nodded nervously, looking like she was very eager to change the topic.

'Thanks, I guess . . . Anyway! Congresses. There's also APHA in November and that's in Atlanta.'

'APHA? I'm sorry, I don't think I'm familiar with this one.'

'American Public Health Association. It isn't strictly an oncology-focused congress like, for example, ESMO or ASCO, but it's interesting and we got funding to send someone over this year. Dr Kennedy thought it might be of interest to you, given your background.'

'And the fact that I can't seem to decide what I want to do with my life?' Caroline asked half-heartedly.

Amira chose to ignore her and cleared her throat uncomfortably.

So, she's still bitter I got the job, Caroline thought.

'Moving on, there's also ASH in the second week of December, it's in San Diego this year. Then I don't think there's much more on the calendar until ASCO next year.'

Caroline pondered that for a moment. ASH, American Society of Hematology, wasn't an oncology congress. She'd overheard that name in the cafeteria last week, where a group of doctors were discussing the paper one of them was due to present. She wasn't eavesdropping but the sound carried when it was busy. There were never enough tables in that place either, it seemed. She could count the number of times she had managed to sit by herself on the fingers of one hand.

She bit back a smile, remembering her shock when she'd found out oncologists didn't treat blood cancers; it was the forte of haematologists.

ASCO was the biggest oncology congress. It was organised by the American Society of Clinical Oncology, but she had heard about it even at medical school.

Her lungs squeezed with indecision. If only she knew what she wanted to do speciality-wise, the choice would be simpler. But she was already getting a good exposure to oncology here at the centre. Maybe this was another opportunity to explore what else was out there. Especially as haematology was one of her favourite blocks back in medical school.

Her mind made up, she looked to Amira. 'OK. If possible, I'd like to go to ASH. Not too keen on California's climate, but I've always been interested in haematological cancers. Think I'm going to skip APHA. I'd love to go to ASCO, should I still be here when it happens – but we can talk about that closer to the time, right?'

Amira nodded and signed Caroline's name under ASH's heading. 'Yep. Great, I'll pass it on to our coordinator and he'll be in touch to schedule your travel and make all the other arrangements.' She stood up, stifling a yawn with her left hand. 'Thanks for this, and, Caroline . . . please don't tell Jake what I said.'

'I'd never do that! It's up to you to tell him if you ever want to. But for what it's worth, I say go for it.'

Amira gave her a small smile as they said their goodbyes.

After her conversation with Amira, she saw another five potential participants for the oncolytic virus trial. She locked the door to her office as soon as the clock struck 5.30 p.m., which was the time she was supposed to finish every day. However, that was rarely the case. There were always more cases to review, more data to collate, more clinical study reports to read and more abstracts to draft.

Caroline got out of the elevator on the ground floor, ready to head out to the exit, when she heard a low sob. Frowning, she looked around.

This side of the building didn't see much footfall from patients and the public. The hospital part of the centre had a separate entrance. People dressed in white coats, scrubs, or smart attire walked up and down the corridor, their badges affixed to the lapels of their jackets or their waistbands. Their steps click-clacked on the tiled floor, carried with the hum of conversation. Every now and then, the elevator pinged.

Another sniff, louder this time, reached Caroline's ears. Her eyes zeroed in on the back of a grey couch stashed in the corner of the lobby.

Cautiously, not wanting to spook whoever was sitting there, she approached.

A pair of red-rimmed eyes, streaked with tears, goggled at

her. The girl, who looked to be in her mid-teens, sniffled again. She wiped her face with the back of her light blue hoodie, disturbing her straight black fringe in the process.

'Are you all right?' Caroline asked softly.

The girl nodded, even though she looked anything but that. 'Yes. I'm sorry I was loud.'

Caroline's chest squeezed. If sadness and heartbreak could have a face, it'd be this one. 'Nothing to apologise for. Can I sit?'

The girl blinked. 'I guess so.' She shuffled to the end of the couch. Her hands were pressed firmly into her knees, her back was straight, and her eyes flared with anxiety.

'What's your name?' Caroline asked.

'Yolanda.'

'That's a pretty name.'

Yolanda choked on a half-snort, half-laugh. 'It was my grandmother's. I'm not a fan but got used to it. My mom likes it.'

'I'm Caroline.' Her eyes scanned the lobby. 'Is your mum here?'

Yolanda nodded stiffly. 'She's a patient. I . . . I had enough of the hospital building. Needed a change in scenery. But this place looks the same.' She glanced at the large Ficus by the floor-to-ceiling window. 'Though the hospital lobby doesn't have plants.'

'Is your mum the reason you were crying?'

'That obvious, eh?'

Caroline gave her a sympathetic smile but remained quiet.

Yolanda slumped against the back of the sofa. 'She has liver cancer. I've been coming with her to all the appointments I could, after school and during vacations.' She swallowed. 'I thought that if I learned every medical word, knew all the jargon, read up as much as I could about her cancer and treatment options, that it'd somehow, I don't know, make a difference?'

'How long has she been sick?'

Yolanda's eyes filled with tears again. 'Three years. She got unwell just after I turned fourteen.'

Caroline took in a deep breath. She flexed her fingers, pushing away her own feelings and emotions; it wasn't about her. It was about offering whatever little kindness she could to a girl who shouldn't have been through this. She knew that Yolanda probably held her breath every time they waited for new scans or results. Hoping for remission, hoping for a miracle. Or even the little respite that months when the cancer hadn't progressed could bring.

'Who are you staying with when your mum's in the hospital?'

Yolanda shrugged, pointedly avoiding Caroline's eyes. 'No one. It's just the two of us.'

Caroline probably shouldn't interfere, but she couldn't help herself. She opened her mouth to ask more, but Yolanda beat her to it.

'Don't worry, my mom isn't staying in hospital. She comes in to the day unit for chemotherapy. That's why I'm waiting, I'll be taking her home once she's finished.' She checked her phone. 'In about an hour or so.'

'I'm sorry. It must be hard for you.'

In medical school, she was taught to always say things like that to people if they shared some bad news, like their parents or spouse passing away. *Oh, I'm so sorry to hear that,* or, *My condolences.* Because she said it so often, it became second nature. Not that she didn't feel empathy for her patients and their families. She did. It'd be hard to work as a doctor if she didn't. But in this moment, she really meant it. Somehow, she felt a depth of feeling for this young girl, one that she hadn't felt in a while.

A true agony of the loss likely to come. By gods, she hoped she was wrong.

Yolanda sighed. 'It's fine when she's home. Sometimes I do stay alone, when she needs to be admitted. My uncle lives at the other side of the city, I can pop into his place if I want to, but I like being home.'

Caroline nodded sympathetically because she understood. She had been the same at her age.

'You work here, right?' Yolanda asked.

Caroline nodded.

Yolanda glanced at her. 'Aren't you heading out? You must've finished for the day.'

Caroline had forgotten all about her tiredness and her wish for a hot bath. The time had just run away from her. It happened all the time at hospital; the workday just flew past. Working in research involved a lot more clock watching.

'I can stay until your mum is ready to go home. If you want me to.'

She caught Yolanda's smile. It was barely there, but it reached her eyes and transformed her face considerably. 'Thank you. I'd like that.'

Caroline put her bag next to her and settled more comfortably on the couch. 'What would you like to talk about?'

CHAPTER TWENTY-ONE

Hunter

Meg knocked once on his office door and walked in without waiting for an invitation. 'Hey, Hunt, can you give me a lift to the city? I need to get to Maya's birthday party, but I don't want to take the car.'

Hunter raised his eyes from the laptop screen. She was dressed in a pair of tight jeans and a silver sequin top. 'No problem. When do you want to leave?'

'Uh, like now?' She pointed at her outfit with a flourish and grinned widely. 'It's already six.'

He frowned and glanced at the dusty grandfather clock in the corner. A wave of tiredness suddenly overtook him as he realised he had been working on the ranch's accounts for the past four hours straight. Stretching his arms above his head, he let out a loud yawn.

Meg chuckled. 'You're still OK to drive? Looks like you could use some coffee. Or a nap.'

But he was already on his feet, keys to his truck in hand, and walking past her through the door.

'Or not.' She shrugged as she spun round to follow him.

They had just got onto the highway. Hunter was quiet, gripping the wheel with far more concentration than was necessary.

Meg turned a bit in the passenger seat and looked at him expectantly. She was probably the most observant member of their family. She had eyes and ears, and Hunter was certain that she had picked up on certain changes in his behaviour. Like the fact that he was smiling more. Or the fact that he stayed over for dinner more often, which made their mother very happy.

'What?' he finally asked, his knuckles blanching on the wheel as he tried to contain a smirk from spreading all over his face.

'Oh, come on. You really won't tell me?'

'Tell you what?'

'*Who is she?*' Meg practically shouted, jumping up in her seat, seemingly unable to rein in her excitement. 'It's a woman, isn't it? Mama says it's got to be a woman for you to be so . . . perky,' she finished.

Hunter laughed out loud. It was such a genial, light peal of laughter that it sounded almost foreign to him.

'"Perky", seriously Meg? First "chipper" now "perky"?'

She waved her hand impatiently. 'Whatever. You know this isn't the point. The point is, who is *she*?'

He just laughed again and shook his head. As much as he loved Meg, he wasn't going to tell her about Caroline. Mainly because there really wasn't much to say. At least, not yet.

They agreed to have fun. No expectations, no pressure, and most of all, no strings. They would simply enjoy each other's company.

And they decisively were not saying they were dating. It wasn't a relationship. Logically, he knew all that.

This would be much easier to deal with if only he didn't feel this magnetic pull to her. Whenever they were together, he felt a strange urge to touch her waist, to caress her cheek, to slide his finger across her neck. It was distracting, really. No one had ever made him feel this way.

Why did it have to be her? Why couldn't it be some nice girl who was fully single, uncomplicated, and easy to read? Of course, Caroline didn't even fall under the 'girl' category, either. She was a woman, in every sense of the word. It wasn't just her looks. It was everything about her.

He liked hearing her opinions on movies and books. It turned out neither of them could resist a good historical fiction.

He liked the way her whole face lit up whenever she spoke about medicine and science.

He just liked her, period.

'Earth to Hunter. We need to get off at the next exit unless you want to go all the way to Tulsa.' Meg's voice snapped him out of the trance.

He hit the indicator and turned to join the busier traffic heading into the city. Pulling the car in front of an apartment building, Hunter turned the engine off. 'What time do you want me to pick you up?'

'Why?' Meg looked at him suspiciously as she unbuckled her seatbelt.

'How else are you going to get home?' Hunter shrugged as if it was obvious.

Confusion flooded her face as she responded, rummaging through her handbag. 'Surely you won't be driving around for hours to kill time?'

'There are other ways to do that.' He smirked as her face lit up in a shocked but happy smile.

'Oh, you're going to see *her*? Tell me who she is!'

'Meg. Go have fun. I'll be around, OK? Just text me when you want to go back.'

She nodded happily and hurriedly got out of the car. As she was closing the door, he shouted after her, 'Two at the latest!'

She just waved, not turning back to look at him.

Hunter watched her press a buzzer and go inside the building. He shook his head but smiled to himself. When they were told about his father's cancer coming back, he was worried it'd weigh so heavy on Meg that she'd miss out on enjoying the college experience. He knew she was upset – hell, they all were. But he was glad she was able to still do typical freshman things.

He sat in silence for a moment, musing over his father's condition and what now seemed inevitable. Finally, he sighed and unlocked his phone. There was an unread message from Caroline in their conversation.

> CAROLINE: *What are you doing tonight? I know it's kind of late to ask but if you didn't have any plans, maybe we could meet later? I can borrow Anna's car and come to you.*

> HUNTER: *Well, what do you know? I'm in the city and would love to see you. Are you doing anything right now?*

She replied almost immediately, which brought a smile to his face.

> CAROLINE: *I've just finished helping Gian bake a*

trial pumpkin pie before rolling it in the bakery. OK, I mostly helped by tasting it. I was planning to finish reading a book, maybe catch up with my sister if she was available. That's about the extent of my plans. If you can top it with something more interesting, I'm all ears.

HUNTER: *No offence to your book and sister but I'm confident I can top it, even just with my company. Pick you up in 15?*

CAROLINE: *Feeling confident. See you then, cowboy ;)*

The bell chimed as Hunter pushed a creaky pink door, holding it open for Caroline. She brushed past him, casually skimming the side of his shirt. A simple gesture that got his throat bobbing with a hard swallow.

'A diner?' Caroline looked at him, amused, as they sat down opposite each other in one of the booths. She touched the worn-out pink leather seat and looked around with wonder. 'What happened to the promise of snails?'

He laughed. 'That can still be arranged, don't worry.'

'I always worry.' It sounded like a light-hearted joke, but he saw the truth to it in her eyes.

'Well, when it comes to me taking you out for food, don't. I know good spots.'

'I'm starting to see that.'

'Have you been to a proper diner before?'

She shook her head. 'No, never. Although I've seen many of these in movies and TV shows growing up. Do you know if they make those huge milkshakes here?'

'I don't know about what you'd class as huge, but they

have milkshakes. The food's good, just thought you might be hungry for something other than pumpkin pie.' He grinned at her. She playfully kicked his shin under the table. 'Ouch!'

'You wouldn't mock the pie if you tried it. Gian's baked goods are heavenly.'

'I'm not mocking the pie, I'm just not a fan of pumpkin.'

She frowned. 'In a pie?'

'In anything, really. Muffins, coffee, candles . . . You name it. If it has any pumpkin in it, I probably won't like it.'

Her frown deepened.

'I know what you're going to say – it's the most American fall thing, how can I not like it?'

'Well, no. I hate matcha and most people seem to love it, so I get it. It's just, you know, you seem like a guy who'd like pumpkin spice. You have this warm, autumnal aura.' She blushed and started examining her fingers with an alarming interest.

He opened his mouth to respond but was interrupted by a waiter who had come to take their order. Hunter ordered a double cheeseburger with fries and, to Caroline's visible delight, a chocolate milkshake. She gave the same food order but asked for a strawberry milkshake instead.

'You're not getting a beer?' she asked.

'Not in a diner. Anyway, I'm driving, so it's just soft drinks for me tonight,' he answered.

Someone put the jukebox on. A classic eighties tune filled the room, and he started humming along to it unconsciously.

She leaned back in her seat and watched him with a small smile.

His eyes met hers and he felt heat rising inside his chest. He stopped humming, barely able to hear the words of the song.

He didn't know why, but there were moments that just looking at her took his breath away. She was beautiful, but it wasn't just her looks that he found mesmerising. It was the way she held herself, the way the light played across her face and lit her green eyes. It was the way she smiled and the sound of her voice. Hunter could tell himself many lies, but he couldn't lie to himself about this. He was attracted to her in a way that lovestruck teenagers wrote poems about before they found out that what they felt was desire, not love. And that as much as they could eventually go hand in hand, it was usually the former playing tricks on their minds.

Caroline tugged a stray lock of her fair hair behind her ear and coughed, breaking the charged silence. 'So you don't like pumpkin spice. Anything else you dislike as much?'

Hunter pondered this for a moment. There weren't that many things he disliked. Sure, he had his preferences, but nothing felt particularly important to mention. 'I don't like when people try to please others at the expense of their own happiness.'

She let out a low whistle, leaning forwards on her elbows that rested on the table. 'Wow, diving straight into the deep end. I was expecting you to start the debate on chocolate versus strawberry ice cream.'

'Why should I bother, everyone knows there's only one correct answer to that.'

'Strawberry!' Caroline said quickly, raising her voice.

'Chocolate!' Hunter breathed out, practically at the same time. They looked at each other and laughed.

She pretended to put on a sad expression and said, 'No, this is just wrong. Now we won't be able to share dessert.'

'Maybe I'll bring you over to the dark side.'

'Aha, so you admit that liking chocolate is the dark side!'

She laughed again, and he shook his head in disbelief.

Their food arrived shortly after. Without waiting for him, Caroline eagerly bit into her burger. 'This is delicious. Have you been here before?'

'I come here with my dad sometimes after, you know . . . his appointments,' he finished clumsily, pretending to focus on his burger. He felt her worried eyes on him as he ate, her own burger back on the plate.

'It must be hard for you and your family.'

He nodded, focusing on his food.

'Do you want to talk about it?' she asked gently.

Hunter chewed slowly, considering this. Only now had it occurred to him that he had never actually told her about his father's diagnosis. He had assumed her aunt would've told her, but he remembered that she probably wouldn't have done due to doctor–patient confidentiality. And he didn't think Caroline would've asked her, for the same reason. *She must've put two and two together*, he thought. After they met at the cancer centre and later when she heard he took over the ranch after his father got sick.

He took a long sip of his milkshake and started the story. 'I went to college in Texas, studied biomedical sciences. I planned to apply to vet school afterwards. Always dreamed of becoming a vet. Shortly before my graduation, my mom called me. I remember like it was yesterday . . .' His eyes glazed over as he closed them. 'She told me Dad had fallen off a horse. Nothing major, she assured me. Just some broken ribs and a slight concussion. But the doctors were concerned with some abnormal blood results.' He paused, glancing at Caroline.

'It felt like weeks waiting for the results – it could only have been a few days – but when they came in, they asked my mom to come in to be with Dad when he heard the news. She's terrified of doctors, so she asked me to go too.'

It wasn't something he talked about often. With every word, the pain edged deeper inside his heart.

'Stage IV melanoma. The most severe stage with the worst outcomes, which I'm sure you know. When they found it, it had already spread to his lymph nodes. Then it started. Surgeries, scans, blood tests, oncology appointments, targeted combination therapy . . . everything that could get rid of the disease. And it did. He went into remission two years ago.' He took another shaky breath and went silent.

It took him a moment to notice that Caroline had placed her hands on top of the table. Before Hunter realised what happened, she took his hands in hers.

He breathed out, pausing for a second to soak in the warmth and kindness the wordless gesture offered. It anchored him, let him know she was listening. That he wasn't alone.

'Not long ago, we found out that the cancer was back. Only this time more aggressive. The clinical trial he's in right now, at the centre, is his last chance.'

'I'm so sorry,' she said, squeezing his fingers.

He tipped his head forward, his mouth forming a sad smile. 'Thank you. It is what it is but . . .'

'It's hard,' she finished in a whisper.

Hunter nodded. 'Yes.'

Caroline let go of his hands and bit her bottom lip. 'Did I tell you that my mother passed away when I was nineteen?'

He looked up. 'You told me she passed but didn't elaborate.'

'She had lung cancer. Even though she had never smoked a cigarette in her life. How ironic is that?' Caroline laughed but the tone sounded off. Like she couldn't convince even herself there was anything remotely funny about it.

'They only found it when it spread to her brain, and she started having seizures. By then, it was too late to do anything other than keep her comfortable and try to hold the pain at bay.' She shivered as if she suddenly went cold.

'I'm so sorry. You must miss her,' he said gently.

She nodded, continuing with a pensive gaze somewhere above his shoulder. 'Every day. Everyone tells you that it gets easier, that time heals the wounds. They're right, in a way. But you're never going to stop missing them. Losing a parent is inevitable, yet it doesn't make it hurt any less. I've always loved my dad, but now I try to appreciate every moment with him even more as I know how much it's going to hurt when he's no longer here.'

Taking a deep breath, she closed her eyes for a moment, and when she opened them, she returned to her half-eaten burger.

'Tell me about her.'

'My mother?'

Hunter nodded, popping another fry into his mouth.

Caroline lowered her hands and blinked, looking far away into her memories. He felt a warm pull inside when he noticed the exact moment the crease between her brows smoothed and she smiled.

'She loved the opera. I remember when she took my older sister, Clara, for the first time. I was so jealous and couldn't wait to go myself. When Clara came back, she had this air of mystery around her as if she'd become wiser over the course of one evening. She told me I'd understand when it was my turn.' She paused, taking a sip of her milkshake. 'When the time came, I was ecstatic. I put on my best dress and my mum did my hair with her curling iron. I thought I looked like a princess.'

Her smile widened and Hunter found himself smiling too. 'Anyway, even before the first act finished, I knew it wasn't something I enjoyed. I could barely make out what anyone was singing and found the whole thing rather boring.'

'I've never seen the opera.'

'No? It's good to experience it, at least once. Who knows, you might enjoy it.' Her smile faltered and she looked down at her hands. 'I wish I liked it more. After that one time, I never went back. Even though Mum asked me several times. I didn't even go with her when she got sick – it was always Clara or Caitlin, my younger sister, who accompanied her.' Her eyes became misty.

She continued in a broken voice. 'I . . . I wish I had more memories of seeing how alive she came when she sat there in the seat, completely engrossed in the performance. It made her radiant.' She finished, tugging at her sleeve.

Hunter took her hand in his again. He felt her shudder when their skin made contact.

'I'm sure she wouldn't have wanted you to pretend on her account.'

She looked at him, her eyes filled with unspoken gratitude.

'And I'm sure she knew how much you loved her. Opera or no opera. I think that being able to be honest with the people we love is the biggest gift we can give them.'

Neither of them said anything else for a while. They just focused on their food and milkshakes in companionable silence, like the connection weaving between them didn't need any words to add more fibres to its threads.

Hunter glanced at the clock on the wall behind the bar. It was 11 p.m. and Meg hadn't messaged him yet, so he had offered to get a round of coffees. After finishing at the diner, they'd driven to one of his favourite bars, which, as expected on a Friday night, was packed. The décor was a bit shabby, but the staff were friendly, and the atmosphere was always great.

Caroline thanked him as he handed her another glass of red wine and sat back down, sipping his Pepsi. 'You really weren't joking about drinking only soft drinks tonight,' she noted loudly, trying to speak over the noise of the conversations all around them and the upbeat country song playing in the background.

'I don't drink and drive, and I'll need to head back home when Meg's ready to go,' he replied.

She studied his face with curiosity as she took a gulp of wine.

'That's refreshing to hear. You know, we have a zero-alcohol policy when it comes to driving in Scotland. So, it isn't surprising exactly, but at the same time, it is a bit. Seems like most people around here don't care about having a drink or two and getting behind the wheel.'

He felt like all the blood drained from his face. Hoping she didn't notice, he hopped off the stool and extended his other hand to her. 'Dance with me, Caroline.'

'But . . . Nobody's dancing.'

As if on cue, three other couples moved to the small, wooden dance floor area and started swinging together to the country music booming from the speakers.

Hunter smirked, taking both of her hands in his and gently urging her forward. She looked like she was thinking about it, but finally nodded firmly and followed him. Just then, the song changed to a slow ballad. He put his hands on her waist, pulling her closer to his chest.

She smiled and placed her hands on his shoulders. 'This

seems like a good moment to tell you that I love dancing, but I'm not great at it.' She stood on her tiptoes, trying to speak near his ear.

He hugged her in response, bowing his head to her level. 'You said the same about conversing with strangers. And you did a great job then.'

'Oh, that was so embarrassing.' She shook her head, her cheeks going a bit pink. 'I couldn't believe I said it and felt like an idiot later.'

'If it makes you feel any better, I always dance like no one else is watching. Sometimes it gets embarrassing, but if you asked, I'd even do the macarena.'

They both laughed, still moving together to the music. It didn't take them long to find a comfortable rhythm.

In this moment, Hunter felt the closest resemblance to content that he had in a very long time. He wasn't thinking about his father or the ranch, he wasn't worrying about Meg or anything else. If he could have stopped time right then, he would. Just to prolong that weightless feeling for a while longer.

His fingers went up and down Caroline's arm, and he bit back a smirk as he felt goosebumps raise on her skin. He inhaled the scent of her perfume. He couldn't quite put his finger on the notes, but he knew one thing: it was a lot more woody than floral. Sensual. Somehow, he knew that smell would linger in his memory long after they untangled and left the dance floor.

The song finished but neither of them moved. They stayed, dancing to half a dozen songs after. Some of them slow, some upbeat. When a very lively one came on and everyone started doing the two-step, Caroline stepped away. Her cheeks were flushed, and her eyes glowed with raw happiness.

'I think I've had enough of dancing for tonight!' she choked out. 'Plus, I don't know how to do this . . . this thing.' She gestured towards the dance floor, where the dance party continued merrily.

'Two-step? I can teach you,' he offered, checking his phone. Meg had messaged him fifteen minutes ago asking if he could pick her up in an hour. He looked at his watch and then at Caroline. 'But maybe not today. Looks like Meg will be ready to go home soon. Sorry.'

She waved her hand, dismissing his apology. 'Oh, don't be! This has been so much fun.' She was resting her back against the panelled wall, looking as happy as she sounded.

He stepped closer, lifting her chin up with his fingers. The buzz of excitement from the dancing, the music and the closeness of her body were still filling his head as his gaze dropped from her eyes down to her lips.

Caroline slowly reached to the nape of his neck.

'I had a great time too,' he managed to say in a low, husky voice. His whole body ached to touch hers. Being this close to her and not kissing, not touching her, felt like torture.

But then their lips crushed together in a heated, passionate kiss. He wasn't sure who kissed who first.

She didn't pull away, and he sensed that she'd permitted herself to enjoy this moment. This kiss lacked the guilt, the shame . . .

It wasn't a spark. It wasn't even a sparkler. It was a whole damn firework display.

Hunter pushed her against the wall. His hands slid under her ass, lifting her up. Her legs wrapped around him, heels of her boots pressing into the muscles at the back of his thighs. Her calf cut into his waist, and he wanted all the weight of her against him.

Caroline let out a sound somewhere between a moan and a gasp as he bit the soft skin at the base of her neck. Her fingers sunk into his hair, pulling at the roots, hard.

He kissed her again, their tongues battling against each other, like they wouldn't survive if the contact was severed.

It was like they both had forgotten themselves and where they were.

Finally, they broke apart and Caroline wobbled as he lowered her to the ground. She pressed her forehead against his and drew a shaky breath, fingers of one hand curled in his belt loops.

'To be continued another time?' She bit her lip, locking eyes with him.

Hunter kissed her again, slowly this time, feeling her smile on his mouth. 'I'll be counting down the minutes.'

CHAPTER TWENTY-TWO

Caroline

'Next up is Deacon Clade, champion from Wyoming! Let's see how he fares against Thor's Hammer. Come on!'

Caroline held her breath and pushed her fingernails into her palms, watching the enormous brown bull practically fly out of its chute with its rider grasping the flat rope that was looped tight around the animal's chest. His other hand stayed above his helmet-clad head.

'And he's down early! 4.13 seconds.'

She watched the rider go down, diving face-first into the sand. The metal cage of his helmet cushioned the fall, and he rolled sideways to avoid the thunder. With quick instinct, he shot up and scrambled away from the bucking bull. A trio of bullfighters stepped closer, distracting the animal and ushering it back to the chute with the help of pickup men.

Caroline craned her neck to look up at a big digital

board where the scores were displayed. Deacon Clade got no score.

'What do you think?' Hunter leaned in, raising his voice so she could hear him over the chatter in the stalls.

She slowly turned to him, wide-eyed. 'Are you serious? This is nuts!'

He chuckled in response.

'I mean it. Why would anyone ever willingly do something so dangerous?'

When Hunter had asked if Caroline was free on Saturday, going to a rodeo was the last thing she'd expected. Yet here she was, trying to blend in with her brown leather cowboy boots and a new hat she'd bought for the occasion.

She peered down at the arena, where Ted Toad from South Carolina was just announced next in line. He held on better than Deacon Clade, though she thought his bull wasn't bucking as wildly as the last one. Eight seconds were up before she could blink, and Ted jumped down, landing on his feet and pelting away while the bullfighters lured the furious bull towards the chute.

'Because it's fun?' Hunter shrugged, handing her a half-full plastic cup. 'The physicality, the excitement. It's unpredictable – the ultimate adrenaline rush. Plus, you listen to this crowd, they love it. It's easy to feed off that.'

Ted got a score of forty-seven.

She wordlessly took the cup and took a long sip of soda. 'I think it's reckless.'

'Well, yes. I won't argue with you there.' Hunter smirked, taking the cup and chugging back the rest of the liquid.

'Did you ever do it? Ride bulls?' she asked cautiously, looking at him.

His eyes met hers and he flashed her a wide, confident

smile. 'Not bulls. But I did quite a bit of bareback bronc riding, only stopped a couple of years ago.'

'What's that?' Caroline asked, not able to resist watching the next rider up in the arena from the corner of her eye.

'Another type of what's called rough stock events. Bareback bronc riding is the oldest rodeo sport. It's similar to bull riding but you're riding a bucking bronc not a bull. Bronc is the term for an untamed horse that habitually bucks. You need a free hand too, and another hand goes on a riggin', which is customised to the rider's grip and gets attached to a piece of leather; all that is wrapped around the bronc's girth.'

'So, a bit more than just a rope,' she said, motioning towards the arena.

'Yeah, people describe it as a suitcase-style handhold.'

Caroline shook her head, feeling a small smile tug on her lips. *Suitcase-style, honestly.*

The last of the bull riders didn't last eight seconds, and a break was announced before the next event – barrel riding.

'Come on. Let's get another drink.' He took her hand in his, helping her up.

As they slowly weaved through the crowd, she felt a bit self-conscious with her clearly not local accent and no knowledge about where they were going or what was going on.

Hunter, contrary to her, looked like rodeos were something he did all the time. His crisp, navy shirt was tucked into his dark, faded Wranglers with a buckled black belt. His black leather jacket made him look effortlessly sexy. She couldn't help it – she'd always had a thing for guys in leather jackets. Matching black cowboy boots and an elegant Stetson completed the picture. She knew that this was just the way he dressed. But she also noticed the number of women who smiled at him, batting their eyelashes. He nodded several times to acknowledge them. She couldn't work out whether he knew them or was just trying to be polite.

It's none of your business. You'll be gone soon. This is just casual . . . Well, whatever it is.

'Did you ever get injured when you did the bronc riding?' she asked, trying to push the jealous thoughts away.

'Sure.' He shrugged, slinging his arm around her shoulder as they passed a group of giggling teenage girls, men putting bets on the team roping event, and four middle-aged women gathered at a tall round bar table.

'Don't know anyone who hasn't. But it was never anything serious,' he added quickly, seeing concern creep up on her face. 'Some bruises, mostly. I broke my wrist once,' he said, lifting his left hand. 'But that's it.'

'Good.' She instinctively put her hand on his wrist and gently tugged it down. Her palm slipped into his, fingers intertwining. 'I'm glad you don't do it anymore.'

'Why? Would you be worried for me?' he asked in a teasing voice.

She stopped, not letting go of his hand. 'Do I even need to answer that?'

'No, but can you blame me for wanting to hear it?'

She rolled her eyes and shook her head. 'I think I'd find it hard to feel sorry for you if you got hurt doing something like that. An accident? Sure. But this? This is just silly.'

'Oh, come on, I'm sure you wouldn't tell me I deserved it if I really got hurt.' He briefly untangled his arm from hers to let a large group of people pass. When he reached for her hand again, Caroline felt a jolt of electricity shot through her, from the tips of her fingers all the way up her arm.

'I'm glad we don't have to find out,' she said, feeling her cheeks go warm.

Hunter just laughed in response.

'Mr Jackson! What a small world, we were just talking about you.'

They both stopped when they heard a male voice behind them. Hunter slowly turned round, and Caroline couldn't help but notice how his smile faltered fast when he faced three middle-aged men.

'Mr Tealey.' Hunter tipped his hat in greeting, but his expression remained cloudy. He looked to the other two men.

'Oh, of course, you haven't met. These are my colleagues, Mr Fox—' Mr Tealey nodded towards a taller, bald one '—and Mr Yates.' The shorter, rounder man with wispy, blonde hair also gave a curt nod. He looked at Hunter but he didn't say anything.

'Well, I hope you enjoy the rodeo,' Hunter said.

Caroline could swear he was about to turn back and walk off, when Mr Tealey said, 'Did you receive the letter we sent two weeks ago?'

'You mean, did my father, who's the owner of the ranch, receive it?' Hunter asked with a stormy expression. 'He did. I think it ended up in the trash.'

The corner of Mr Tealey's mouth twitched. 'Mr Jackson, you must see that in the current climate, selling up is a great solution for many family ranches. We're happy to discuss our offer further, perhaps we could—'

'No, we couldn't. My father already told you where you could put that offer,' Hunter said in a stern voice, squeezing Caroline's hand harder and pulling her away from the men. 'Have a good day.'

'Are you OK?' she asked when they were standing in a long line to the bar.

Hunter took a deep breath, looking into the distance. When

he let it out, she thought he looked a bit deflated, more tired. He wasn't holding her hand anymore.

'Those bastards have no conscience. They know my dad isn't well, yet they keep pestering him.' He rubbed his hand on his temple. 'They want to buy our land and plant alfalfa there. Two other ranches in the area went down last year. Now they want to expand here and ours is the biggest target.' He shook his head. 'They came to the ranch last year, after they bought Williamson's ranch.'

'I take it that didn't go well?'

'Dad ran them off the ranch with a gun.'

Caroline looked at him, horrified, but when she saw his amused expression she laughed. *Americans.*

'We thought that was the end of it. Seems that they're more stubborn than we gave them credit for,' Hunter said.

'Would you sell it, if it was up to you?'

He pursed his lips. 'It isn't up to me.'

Caroline knew that she shouldn't push the conversation. She noticed how, when he spoke about the ranch, it was in a way that he felt the duty to his family and people working there. It sounded like he accepted that responsibility without dwelling on whether it was what he wanted to do. She hoped he'd figure it out, whatever it meant to him. But knowing that his father didn't have long left . . . It probably wasn't the right time to think about it now.

'Look. A photo booth.' Hunter pointed towards a square red box not far from the bar. 'Should we do it?'

Caroline looked ahead. The queue wasn't moving very far, and she wasn't that thirsty. Besides, they didn't have any photos together. It wasn't the first thing on her mind, and it wasn't like they were a couple. Or something. But she always found photo booths to have this nostalgic feel about them.

Like something that could help freeze a precious moment in time.

'Let's go.'

This time it was her turn to tug on his hand.

The inside of the photo booth was tight. It also smelled vaguely of beer and fried onion, not the most pleasant combination.

Hunter reached into his pocket, taking out some coins. He pushed them into the marked hole and the light above their heads came on.

'It's definitely cosy,' he said, squeezing in next to her. 'I think you might need to—'

'I can move this way if—'

'Ouch, that's my rib.'

'Sorry! I didn't mean to,' she said quickly, reaching for his chest. She put her right hand flat against the left side of his ribcage, feeling how his chest rose and fell when he breathed.

Hunter shuffled closer to her. 'You know, it might be best if you sit on my lap. Just saying, no one will get injured then!' He tried to lift his hands up in defence but there wasn't much room to extend them.

Caroline cleared her throat, a wave of heat throbbing in the bottom of her belly. Without saying anything, she tried to carefully lower herself on his lap but he grabbed her waist with both hands and helped her with the movement.

He grinned widely. 'That's better, no?'

'That depends.'

'On what?'

'On whether you'll continue grinning like an idiot to yourself or kiss me already.'

His lips touched hers, his arms wrapping tighter around her waist. She opened her mouth, welcoming his tongue into a languid dance.

She could tell the flash went off once, twice, three times . . . But she didn't look. She had just a vague awareness of her surroundings, because her head was spinning. Beer and onions forgotten.

'Is that what you wanted?'

'Well . . . This is more like what I had in mind,' she whispered, grazing his bottom lip with her teeth.

He moaned against her mouth, grabbing a handful of her hair. When he kissed her neck, she felt like she was struck by lightning. Any kind of neck action from Hunter had the power to arouse her, fast. He just seemed to know exactly the right spot to awaken her senses.

They jumped apart when a loud beep signalled photos being printed and vended outside. Caroline's eyes sparkled as she picked up the strip. Her breath froze mid-exhale as she stared at the people in the photos. Laughing, smiling. Carefree. They looked like they were a couple of teenagers in love.

She swallowed the bunch of butterflies swatting their wings inside her throat.

Not dating. Not a couple. There's a ticking clock on this thing, a voice in her head nagged and her heart skipped a beat.

Whatever happened from now on, she would hold on to this photo strip. Not because she loved him – that would be preposterous. It was a reminder that there was joy in her. Whenever she would inevitably forget it, she could pull up these photos and remember herself in this moment. The freedom of being who she never got a chance to be after her mother got sick. She had missed the fun part of her late teens and her early twenties; afterwards, things had only got more serious.

These photos, these memories, were priceless because they proved to her that whatever part of her soul had been broken before was starting to heal.

CHAPTER TWENTY-THREE

Hunter

Warm late September wind coloured Caroline's cheeks as she closed her eyes, sticking her face to the sun setting behind the treeline.

'You're a natural,' Hunter said.

'Flattery won't get you far, Mr Jackson,' she said, gently giving the reins a pull. Star, the beautiful palomino mare she was riding, came to a stop. Caroline looked to her left and grinned. 'Although it does seem like she's taken a shine to me.'

He chuckled, pulling Dallas to a stop as well. 'She's not the only one.' Her blush widened his smile. 'But I mean it, you're a great rider. It's hard to believe you haven't been on a horse in years.'

'Well, this is like the third time. Don't forget that I almost fell off the first time you brought me here.'

He waved his hand as if it was a minor detail. 'That was

my fault; I chose the wrong horse for you. Should've known better. Pringle isn't fond of strangers. I'm just glad it didn't deter you from trying again.'

'It'd take a lot more than that to deter me. I told you; I do love horses.' She leaned forward and brushed her hand through Star's thick white mane. 'Plus, you caught me, so technically I didn't fall.'

'I'll always catch you if I can.'

Their eyes met and the air grew thick. Hunter cursed in his mind. What was going on with him? He wasn't one to throw clichés around. It just seemed that with Caroline, he often spoke before thinking. Fortunately, she just smiled and didn't seem to mind. He coughed, trying to compose himself. 'But I don't think you'll need assistance anytime soon. You seem to grow more comfortable on her every time we go riding.'

'Well, practice makes perfect, right?' she said, now patting Star's golden neck.

The wind picked up in intensity and he instinctively reached up to hold his hat in place. He turned Dallas round, facing the sand path they had come by earlier. 'Looks like the weather's turning. We should get back.'

Caroline shrugged, but soon Star was facing the same direction. She straightened herself in the saddle, pushing her hair away from her face with her left hand, the right one still holding the reins.

She grinned. 'It's a shame you're refusing to race me.'

'I don't want you to get hurt. Although you're doing well, I think it's way too soon for galloping, never mind racing. Plus, do you really think you'd ever beat me?' He laughed confidently, setting Dallas off at a walk.

Caroline followed, keeping behind on the narrow bit of

the path. After they reached a wider stretch, she caught up with him and raised an eyebrow.

'I might. Or you might be inclined to let me win.'

'Why would I ever want to do that?'

She looked at him and her whole face lit up in a genuine smile that reached her green eyes. Despite the grey weather surrounding them, they shone. 'Because if I'm in a good mood, I might feel like celebrating. That's usually better with someone to share the moment.'

As soon as she said it, she leaned forward, raising herself slightly from the saddle. Before Hunter could say anything, she was off, her laugh ringing through the air. She didn't look scared, and Star seemed to move in perfect harmony with her.

He shook his head and, despite his better judgement, felt a wave of warmth spread in his chest.

Without wasting time, he urged Dallas into a gallop to catch up.

'Well? I told you I would win!' she announced triumphantly as she got off Star's back.

Hunter jumped off Dallas. He didn't want to tell her that he deliberately didn't even try to go as fast as he could, because he didn't want to encourage her.

When he caught up with her, Star was going at a nice, steady pace. It was a fast canter but remained sensible, not quite reaching a gallop. He probably should've told her that she was being irresponsible and could've been thrown off the horse. That he had seen more experienced riders than her hurt in a reckless attempt to gallop before they were ready for it. But as soon as he looked at her face, all he saw was pure joy. And a good dose of pride. Her cheeks were flushed from the cold and the wind. Her hair was tangled. Her boots and pants were specked with mud.

She looked like the most beautiful thing he'd ever laid eyes on.

'I think you're just annoyed I managed to ride so well,' she added teasingly, starting to lead Star towards the western barn.

'You did ride well. I think you must have a good teacher.'

'Or maybe I'm just a natural, as you said earlier.'

'Can't it be a combination of both?'

'I suppose it can.' She took the saddle off Star, and he did the same with Dallas.

As soon as they reached their respective stalls, which were conveniently next to each other, she took the bridle off and picked up a brush from the shelf.

Hunter closed his hand over her wrist. He leaned over her shoulder and said in a low voice, 'Leave it. Janice will brush them later. She told me off the other day for always doing it myself. Apparently, I don't have monopoly on these two.'

He felt her body shiver. Caroline put her hand into his and turned round, facing him.

They were mere inches away from each other.

'And what will we do with all that extra time?' She ran a finger down from his cheek to his waist.

His whole body tensed at this small yet maddening gesture. 'I can think of a couple things.'

She smirked, lacing her finger through one of the front belt loops of his jeans. She leaned in, pressing her body against his. 'Only a couple? That's disappointing.'

He let out a growl, capturing her lips in a searing kiss. She responded with eagerness that matched his. He was kissing her with all the built-up tension and desire, like he had never kissed her before. His mind went blank to everything, and it only focused on the feel of her tongue and her lips on his. When they finally pulled apart, they were both breathless.

'I hope you added many more *things* to your list now.'

In response, he kissed her again. He wanted to do so much more, but this wasn't the place to do it. He wasn't one of those guys who thought the first time with someone new should be perfect, because there was no such thing as perfection when it came to sex. But a dirty barn where anyone could walk in on them, including his parents or sister, was definitely very low on the list, even by his standards.

Putting both hands on her waist, he looked her and said, 'What do you say we get out of here?'

CHAPTER TWENTY-FOUR

Caroline

Hunter turned the key in his front door with nerves bundled up in a furry ball in his gut. 'Here we are. It's not much, but it's home; at least for now.'

As he closed the door behind them with a slam, Caroline turned her head and tried to take in the surroundings.

He watched her eagle-eyed, looking for any shadow of disappointment or disapproval. 'I could live at the ranch. It probably would be more practical, and then I also wouldn't have to pay the rent. But I really wanted to have a place where I could close the door on all the outside noise and breathe freely.'

She smiled. 'I like it.'

'There isn't anything interesting to see. Here is the kitchen.' He gestured to the left where the small but functional area with slate-grey units was separated from the living room by a breakfast bar. 'Here is the living room.' Another uninterested gesture towards the area with a tired-looking leather sofa, an armchair and a TV. 'There's the bathroom, a cupboard, the office and the bedroom.' He finally pointed to the white door on the right.

'I guess we'll be heading there?'

'Caroline.' He looked into her eyes, his expression suddenly serious. 'Just because we came here doesn't mean we have to do anything you don't want to or are not ready to do. I don't want you to feel in any way pressured.'

She stood on her tiptoes and kissed him in response. 'I know. But I want to.' She kissed him again. This time it wasn't a quick peck. It was all the longing, all the imagination and all the hopes she had. And then they weren't just kissing.

It was all teeth, and tongues, and moans, and groans.

Molten lava filling in the space in her lower abdomen.

His hands slipped underneath her shirt.

She lifted her arms; he pulled the material up, taking it off. A shiver consumed her body as she swallowed, suddenly feeling fully naked.

Hunter's fingers moved from her back to her chest. He trailed one of them all the way down from her neck to her belly button. He leaned in, kissing the base of her throat. 'You're so gorgeous,' he muttered against her skin, and her eyes fluttered shut.

It felt amazing, until he was slowly pulling down the strap of her bra, his breath warm against her neck, and she froze.

A memory pushed underneath her eyelids. One she would do everything to forget.

'Are you all right?' Hunter's voice sounded far away even though she was still right here, in his arms. He wasn't kissing her anymore, but his hands were still on her waist.

Her knees shook, her legs almost buckled underneath her.

She breathed out, trying to focus on Hunter's voice. His face was blurry, and it seemed like the walls behind him were closing in on her. Taking in a deep breath, she closed her eyes. *One . . . Two . . . Three . . .*

Exhale. Inhale. Repeat.

You're fine. It's nothing, just a memory.

'I'm sorry, I just remembered I told Amira I'd dog-sit for her tonight. Totally slipped my mind.' She put on the most convincing smile she could muster and looked at him. 'Rain check? Sorry.'

She bit her lip, cursing how weak this excuse sounded. Dog-sit? She wasn't even sure if Amira had a dog. But Hunter wouldn't know any different.

'No need to apologise.' He took a step back. 'Caroline, if you aren't ready—'

'It's not that.' Her voice sounded sure even though she wasn't. 'I'll text you later, OK?' She planted a quick kiss on his cheek.

Hands shaking, she bent down and picked up her shirt. She put it back on, her back to Hunter. She didn't think she could look at him just now.

Without a backward glance, she rushed out of the apartment. They drove here in two cars, so it would be easier for her to get back to the city. She fumbled in her bag searching for the car keys.

'Caroline!'

Her hand stopped between her wallet and a leather-bound calendar, keys clutched in her fingers.

Hunter ran up to her, out of breath and wide eyed. His expression screamed, *I don't understand.*

Neither did she. Not really.

'What just happened?' he asked.

Her eyes bore into her cowboy boots. Pink roses were embroidered in caramel leather, with other patterns rising up to her calves. She inhaled sharply, trying to count the number of roses on each shoe.

Counting helped her whenever she had a panic attack.

'Hey.' He reached for her hand, gently taking it into his. 'Talk to me. What's the matter?'

Tell him. He won't judge you. If you don't tell him he'll think he's done something wrong. And it's not his fault.

Caroline raised her head, looking right into his eyes. 'Can we go inside?' She hugged her arms to her chest, looking around like she expected to find someone listening. 'It's not the parking-lot kind of conversation.'

'Of course. Whatever you need.'

He led her back inside his house, glancing concerned looks in her direction every now and then. She felt every single one of them. They were like butter knives warmed in a bowl of hot water before they sliced right through her soul.

Hunter sat in the large leather armchair, leaving the entire sofa for her. A pang of warmth shot through her heart when she realised he was giving her as much space as she needed.

The couch sunk underneath her as Caroline settled at its very end. She laced her fingers together, looking at the floor. It was too difficult to look at Hunter.

'I grew up Catholic. So did Finn. Some Irish Catholic families are . . .' She paused, looking for a word. 'Pretty hardcore. Not mine, but Finn's family are very much in that category.'

Her cheeks burned and she felt ridiculous as the next part of the story rolled over her tongue. 'He wanted to wait until we got married. With sex, I mean. I didn't, on the contrary. But I was so in love with him that I probably would've agreed to anything back then.

'Besides, even though I stopped going to church myself after my mother died, it was hard to set aside everything I was taught my whole life. That sleeping with someone outside the marital bed was a sin.'

Her eyes flicked up to check Hunter's reaction, but he was sitting in the same position he had been in before. It didn't seem like he had moved a single muscle. His expression was attentive, and she knew he was taking in every word.

Caroline blinked, taking in her bottom lip between her teeth. 'Anyway, we waited. All the way until our wedding night. I was so excited, so bloody eager.' She let out a short, bitter laugh and shook her head. 'So stupid. Bought a special bridal set of lingerie, ordered room service to our suite and a bottle of his favourite champagne. I thought it was going to be the best night of my life.'

She took a brief pause, letting the memory in. If she could, she would go back in time and tell her younger self it wasn't her fault. In that moment, it didn't feel like it. Her fingers brushed her cheeks, wanting to wipe away tears reminiscent of those she had silent sobbed into the satin pillowcase while Finn peacefully snored next to her.

'Did he hurt you?' Hunter's voice pulled her back to the present.

She startled, only now meeting his gaze. 'What? No. It wasn't like that.'

His eyes softened but he didn't say anything.

Caroline exhaled. 'It just didn't happen. At all. He said he was tired. I thought he was just saying it because I was tired too. I went to the bathroom to change, and when I got back, he was already asleep.'

She bit back a laugh. When it happened, she didn't feel particularly amused. But now it was funny. Just a little bit.

'It was a very strange start to a marriage. We talked about it – well, I tried at least. He made it sound like it was my fault. Said not many people even have sex on their wedding night.' She shrugged. 'Either way, it happened on the third night of our honeymoon in Santorini.'

She looked to Hunter. 'I don't have to keep going if this is making you uncomfortable. It isn't like . . . I don't know. Not a normal topic to talk with another guy about sex with your ex-husband.'

Wordlessly, he shook his head.

She continued. 'It was sloppy, rushed, and painful. He behaved like he wasn't himself.'

Caroline's mind wandered back to that night. She remembered how Finn had pulled the straps of her dress off her shoulders and pushed her down on the bed. How hurriedly he'd undone his belt and shorts' zipper, throwing both on the floor. How he'd hoisted himself over her, propping himself up on his elbows. How, without even looking at her, he'd positioned himself at the opening to her vagina and thrust hard inside.

How she had clasped her hand over her mouth, trying to stop herself from letting out a howl of pain. For a second, she had thought she might cry. But she didn't. Instead, she bit her lower lip and drew blood.

How Finn had seen neither her pain nor discomfort.

Because his face was buried in the pillows the entire time.

'It was over in a blink of an eye. I . . . I didn't think it was going to be like that.'

As she finished her story, she let out a shuddering breath. Erin was the only person she had ever told this to. The wild beat of her heart against her ribs reminded her she was alive. Saying it out loud didn't open a black hole in the ground that would swallow her whole.

Hunter's hands were balled into tight fists. 'Bastard,' Hunter uttered, his voice nothing but an angry growl.

'It's fine. I mean, we talked about it over the years. He didn't mean to hurt me.'

'But he did.'

When they later talked about it, Finn was horrified to hear how she had felt that night. Another one on the list of things that shouldn't have happened between them, but it did.

'I'm not angry at him,' she stopped, unsure if she should say more. But then she decided she should. Not for Finn's sake, but for her own. 'He isn't into it. Sex, I mean.'

Hunter just stared at her like she had just told him the aliens were real and they were about to invade the Arctic to set up a colony of tomato growers.

'We both tried more times after the honeymoon. It just wasn't good. At all. Eventually, we stopped trying.' She shrugged, like it was the most natural thing to say. 'We had an honest conversation, and it turned out trying made both of us miserable. Just for different reasons.'

'Is that the reason you're getting a divorce?'

'Partly.'

When he just blinked at her, she added: 'It's also because he wants kids. I don't.' She glanced at her bare ring finger. 'I tried to make myself fit into the space I thought I should be able to occupy. First, holding off sex until the wedding night. Then, telling myself that I didn't need sex because everything else was great – I'd married my best friend. We loved each other. But I just . . . I don't know.

'A time came that I just couldn't give away pieces of myself. When I turned thirty last year, I had an epiphany. I realised I had too much life ahead of me to throw it away on compromising my own happiness. Finn felt the same way, both about me and about his own life. We came to a decision that we just didn't work. That the best thing we could do for each other was to let go.'

Silence enveloped the room in a hug. The words hung in the air, dissipating against the backdrop of a healing heartache.

Caroline felt lighter. Whatever Hunter thought about her, about her situation, she had unburdened herself from something she had been holding on to for years now. Every night she had sat on the bathroom floor, every night she had sneaked out of bed and wrapped herself in a blanket on the sofa, wondering what she had done wrong, what was wrong with her for Finn not to be interested in her the way she wanted him to be . . .

Deep down, she knew it had nothing to do with her. Months of marriage counselling and inching farther and farther away in their king-size bed had told her that much. It was just one of those things. Yet it was still hard to completely forget.

'And you haven't been with anyone else?' Hunter asked.

Her cheeks heated. 'No. Never.'

He scratched his chin, like he was processing it. 'If I'd known—'

'Don't. Really. Why would you have? I'm a thirty-one-year-old soon-to-be divorcee. How could you know.'

'Still. Thank you for telling me.'

'I didn't want you to think that I panicked because of you. It's just . . . when you pulled down the strap of my bra, it suddenly became real. And it scared me. Not that you scare me, quite the opposite. But I just . . .' She drew in a shaky breath. 'I wanted to. Everything we've done, I really enjoyed it.'

'We don't have to do anything you don't want to do,' he said, and she remembered his words from just before things took off.

It felt like hours ago. Like they had crossed another dimension since then. Or leaped off a cliff. Either analogy seemed appropriate.

'That's the thing though. I want to.' Her cheeks burned, and she could only imagine the violent pink covering them. 'I think I just need time.'

'We can go as fast or as slow as you want. You're in total control, OK? If you ever feel uncomfortable, you can just tell me. Doesn't matter how far in we are,' Hunter said with an earnestness that brought tears to her eyes.

She looked into his eyes and saw that he meant it. 'OK.'

Her heart shed the heavy armour of embarrassed worry, and soared into the uncharted territory of something akin to hopeful excitement.

CHAPTER TWENTY-FIVE

Hunter

Hunter sleepily walked into the kitchen, pouring himself another cup of black coffee. He hadn't slept well, thinking about his father, the ranch and Caroline.

His hands curled into fists when he remembered her haunted eyes and the ice in her voice as she confided in him. If he could, he would get on a plane to Glasgow, find her soon-to-be ex-husband, and have words with him. Although that was a very polite way of putting it.

He wanted her like he hadn't wanted any other woman before. Mitch, who had no idea that she was still married, laughed that it was the chase. The thrill of it, sleeping with her being the prize. It should feel that way. It was disturbing how far from the truth all that was.

Her admission she didn't want to have children sped up his pulse. It hadn't felt like the appropriate time to go into further details, or say he felt the same, but she had answered a question that had been on his mind. One he had been too afraid to ask. After all, they kept telling themselves they weren't dating. They weren't together.

But aren't we?

Taking a large sip of coffee, he closed his eyes and massaged his left temple. He looked at his phone: 6.38 a.m. This was about an hour later than he would normally be up and out of the door but, lately, he had been trying to take his father's advice and delegate more. *'Trust your people, Hunter. They're the ones doing the work. You need to give them enough freedom to take initiative. They won't work well if they feel like you're breathing down their necks.'*

He took a deep breath and put the empty cup in the sink with a thump.

Words of wisdom aside, he didn't know what to do with himself inside his place. Being idle led to overthinking and that was dangerous territory, particularly with the date for his father's medical tests coming up. He didn't want to keep track, but he couldn't help himself. It was like a heavy anchor that he couldn't shake off, no matter how much he tried.

He checked his phone again. No new messages. Glancing around at the empty, tidy living room and kitchen, he decided there was no point in delaying his departure. He put on a mahogany leather jacket and a baseball hat, grabbed his keys and walked out, closing the door on the emptiness inside.

'Guess who I saw again today.'

Hunter heard Meg's cheerful voice as she walked into the office, but he didn't look up from the laptop screen.

She stood next to him. 'Don't you want to know?' She sounded annoyed at being ignored.

'Meg, I'm busy. I'm trying to buy this bull. We could really reinvigorate . . .' He stopped as she rolled her eyes. Still keeping one eye on the screen so he wouldn't miss the bids coming in, he tried to feign appropriate interest. 'Fine, I'll bite. Who did you see today?'

'Dr Caroline O'Kelly. She led my bio 101 lab today, again.'
He turned round, startled.

'Ha! I knew that'd get your attention,' Meg exclaimed.
'Why would that get my attention?'

'Mama also told me you've been riding with her several times now. I put two and two together, plus your totally goofy expression just now. She's the woman you've been seeing, isn't she?'

'I guess you could say that.' He sighed, defeated. He forgot about the auction for a moment and swore in his head when he noticed that it had finished and he'd got outbid. Annoyed, he slapped the laptop closed.

Meg shot him a watery smile. 'I'm sorry, didn't mean to distract you from work.'

'Don't worry, there are other bulls out there.' He pulled out a stool from under the desk and patted it, inviting her to sit down.

She dropped the pretence of being apologetic and eagerly pulled it up. Resting her elbows on her knees, she grinned at him. 'So, when are you going to introduce me?'

'What? Introduce you to who, Caroline?'
'Yes, Caroline! Who else?'
'I thought you said you'd met her?'

She waved her hand impatiently. 'Being in two labs led by her doesn't count. Did she tell you she does some teaching and laboratory work at the university? Anyway, it was very cool. She's so beautiful and, like, I don't know . . . I want to say elegant, but that makes it sound like I'm talking about some snobby sixty-year-old lady. But you know what I mean. And she's *so* smart. Like, goals. I want to be her when I grow up.' She kept talking excitedly, and Hunter found himself smiling because Caroline was all those things and more. 'So, when can I properly meet her? I didn't introduce myself or anything, that'd have been creepy.'

'Meg, I can't just let you tag along on our date—'

'So, you *are* dating?' She leaned forwards, almost knocking the half-full glass of water off the desk.

He considered her for a moment and shot her an exasperated look. 'For our meeting. Rendezvous. Whatever you want to call it. Doesn't matter as you aren't going anyway.'

His rule of not calling it dating or a relationship due to possible lack of any future for them was in a very grey area. Besides, he refused to think about her going back to Scotland. Maybe if he didn't think about it, it wouldn't happen. Or he was just becoming more naive.

'We could go somewhere together, the three of us. Or you could ask Mitch to come as well.' Her eyes sparkled mischievously.

Give me strength, Hunter thought as he looked at the ceiling.

Meg seemed to harbour some teenage infatuation with Mitch, who was way too old for her and treated her like he should – his best friend's little sister. That didn't deter her; she never missed an opportunity to bat her eyelashes at him. He was glad that Mitch saw it as more humorous than anything else and didn't mind too much. She'd met Eve, too. That also didn't deter her. Hunter was just about to say they should also invite her but then remembered Mitch told him she was away in Nashville, dealing with some publicity drama involving Lionel Webster. Again.

Hunter had listened to some of his music, and the guy had talent, but sounded like trouble.

He remembered that Caroline had already agreed to meet Meg at some point when he had asked her about it at their pizza date. She did say she'd be fine with it.

Feeling a bit more relaxed about the idea, he sighed. 'Fine, whatever. We can go somewhere. Me, you, Mitch, and Caroline. If they both agree. Now, will you please stop bugging me and let me get on with some work?'

'Can we go to Friday night karaoke in The Crocked Boot? It's cancelled this week but back on next. I love it there,' she asked hopefully, pulling the oldest trick in the book: the puppy eyes.

'Sure, whatever. Now, will you please go?'

She jumped up and briskly walked out. He could swear she was humming to herself.

'Only if Mitch and Caroline are up for it!'

But she continued walking, pretending she didn't hear him.

CHAPTER TWENTY-SIX

Caroline

Despite the weather turning colder and windier as September gave way to October, Caroline felt a comforting warmth inside that radiated all over. Because she was still so used to shift work, she didn't exactly dislike Sundays per se. But this felt just like perfect Sundays looked in her imagination. She turned on her side and was just about to close her eyes and reminisce about yesterday and the long, lazy make-out session on Hunter's sofa after they had been out riding again, when there was a knock on the door.

She sighed and sat up. 'Come in!'

Gian pushed the door open, trying to balance the contents of a laden breakfast tray. She was fully dressed in a pair of smart navy trousers and a grey cashmere jumper.

Caroline jumped out of bed and rushed to help her. 'I'll get it.' She took the tray from Gian, who smiled at her gratefully.

'Thank you,' Gian said, massaging her right wrist.

Caroline noticed it looked quite swollen and red. 'Gian, you shouldn't be bringing me breakfast. Looks like you're having a flare up?' Caroline put the tray carefully on her bed.

Gian followed her and sat on top of the crumpled duvet. 'May I?' Caroline asked.

'Sure.' Gian extended her hand, letting Caroline examine both of her hands. As she moved her fingers from joint to joint, Gian grimaced in pain.

'I'm sorry.'

'It's fine. I took the meds, hopefully it'll be better in a bit once they kick in.'

Gian looked deep in her own thoughts for a moment, and then she grinned, breaking up a piece of toast from the other plate. 'No point in worrying. Where were you last night? You got back quite late.'

'Eleven p.m. isn't that late.' She sipped her juice and tried not to look at Gian.

The wide grin and suggestive wink could only mean one thing. Feeling her cheeks go hot, she tried to put on an indifferent tone. 'I went riding at Jackson's Ranch. Then, I met up with a friend.'

'Was it the horses or a certain cowboy that kept you so occupied?'

'I mean . . .' Caroline finished her juice and took another bite of food. She realised that, despite thinking it was wrong on the surface and feeling like she had to make up excuses, deep down she didn't feel even a shadow of embarrassment. She smiled brilliantly at Gian. 'I guess you could say it was both.'

'Oh, I bet it was. *Hey!*' Gian laughed as Caroline swiftly

put the tray on the floor out of the way and hit her with a pillow. 'No need to get so defensive. I get it. I mean, I've never actually seen him, but from what Anna said, he's good looking. As far as my opinion on men goes.' She shrugged.

'Yeah . . .' Caroline sat with her thoughts for a moment. 'Can you please not say anything to Anna? I'll talk to her myself, if there's anything to tell. It isn't really anything serious, just a bit of fun.'

Gian shot her an affronted look. 'Of course. I won't tell her if you don't want me to.' She smiled. 'And has it been fun so far?'

'It really has,' Caroline said earnestly, biting back a grin. Over the past few weeks, she had grown a lot more comfortable around Gian. Between her clinical role and working on the trials, Anna spent a lot of time at the hospital, which often left Caroline and Gian to their own devices. They both seemed to have fallen into an easy camaraderie.

Gian chuckled and shook her head. 'That's good then. Anyway. Do you have any plans for today?'

'No, no plans. I want to call my dad and Nora later, but I told them it'd be around three p.m. our time, so I'm free until then. What did you have in mind?'

'I thought that if you're so interested in cowboys now, we could visit the National Cowboy and Western Heritage Museum.'

Caroline rolled her eyes but didn't lose her smile. Gian said it in a light-hearted, joking way but she jumped out of bed and decided it sounded like a good idea.

'Why not? I do want to see some local sights, after all. Let's go play tourists. Well, you'll play, I don't need to.'

'Wait. You're telling me you've been here three months now and you haven't been to that museum?'

Caroline shrugged. 'I'm not big on museums. But if you want to go, I'll make an exception.' She winked at Gian.

Caroline waved goodbye, smiling with fondness at the camera. 'Love you, Dad. Speak soon.'

Her father smiled back and a moment later the call ended.

She closed her laptop and reached for her phone. She hadn't had a chance to speak with Erin since yesterday, when she got back from Hunter's flat and noticed she was showing as online. She turned up the volume on the Bluetooth speaker, which was playing 'Tennessee Whiskey' from her playlist and started typing.

CAROLINE: *I really want to sleep with Hunter.*

ERIN: *Well, good evening to you too. I could act surprised but we both know I'm not a good actress. What's stopping you then? Seems like he's even more keen than you are, from what you said.*

She hesitated, typing a couple of letters and then pausing.

ERIN: *Caroline. I can see you're typing. Spill.*

CAROLINE: *We almost did it the other day.*

ERIN: *!!!!!!!!*

CAROLINE: *Hold your horses, nothing happened. Well, nothing beyond what we've done before.*

ERIN: *I don't understand. Why?*

CAROLINE: *I sort of had a panic attack? What do you know, it killed the mood.*

ERIN: *Oh, Car. I'm sorry. I should've thought it might be difficult after what happened between you and Finn. I didn't think.*

CAROLINE: *It's fine. Don't worry. Anyway, I did tell him about it.*

ERIN: *Woah. Like . . . Everything?*

CAROLINE: *Everything.*

ERIN: *You must really like him. And trust him.*

CAROLINE: *I do.*

ERIN: *What did he say?*

CAROLINE: *That we can take it as fast or slow as I want. And we don't have to do anything I don't want to.*

ERIN: **swoons**

CAROLINE: *OK, stop! Haha. But yes. It was what I needed to hear.*

ERIN: *And now you want to sleep with him.*

CAROLINE: *My body has wanted to for a while now. It's my mind that's the problem.*

ERIN: *Just see how things progress. If it's meant to happen, it will. Don't put pressure on yourself. You've sounded like the old you. Before the marriage and everything. I've missed that Caroline.*

CAROLINE: *Yeah, I've missed her too.*

CHAPTER TWENTY-SEVEN

Caroline

Caroline typed in the password on her work laptop and opened the email app. There were two new messages from the medical communications agency she had been working with: one about scheduling an author kick-off for the new manuscript on the multiple myeloma trial, and the second asking her to confirm travel details for the upcoming congress.

After she signed up to attend ASH, Caroline had approached one of the haematology attendings, Dr Matthias, and asked if she could tag on to a multiple myeloma trial he was overseeing. Dr Matthias was delighted by her enthusiasm, and, after clearing it with Anna, Caroline was now dividing her time between the oncology and haematology teams.

The medical communications agency was hired by OnyxRex, the pharmaceutical company behind the new multiple myeloma treatment she had been working on. Before she had started working as a research assistant, she didn't know much about the medical communications industry. She vaguely remembered that someone she went to medical school with posted on their social media that they had transitioned from clinical work to medical writing.

Maybe if she didn't go back into a clinical role once she got back to Scotland, she would look into that career option.

She pulled up her calendar and responded to the first email with her availability for a call. Then she clicked through to December and studied the listed time for departures and arrivals to San Diego.

'You're looking at flights for ASH?' Amira walked up to her desk, focused on rubbing the front of her shirt with a damp cloth. She noticed Caroline looking. 'I'm a clumsy idiot. Spilled an orange juice on this.' She patted the material with the cloth aggressively. When there was a big wet patch, she threw the cloth onto her desk by the window.

'Yes, not sure if it's better to fly there the morning before or the afternoon. The morning flight option is quite brutal.' Caroline winced, checking the time again. 'Yeah, not a fan of seven a.m.'

Amira snorted, leaning against Caroline's desk. 'I think I'm going to go with the one at 2.15. Still early enough to rest up, enjoy the evening and get a good night's sleep before the first day.' She crossed her arms over her chest and looked at Caroline. 'If you want, we could travel together. I usually go on my own, so it would be nice to have someone to talk to for a change.'

Caroline smiled at her. 'That sounds good. Which return should we go with?'

Amira took a pair of glasses from the breast pocket of her bubblegum-pink shift dress and put them on. She moved closer to the screen. 'Hm . . . Let's go with the one just after eight p.m. on the last day of ASH. It's always tiring travelling on the same day, and it ends up being an awfully long day. But at least you get to start your day back home the next morning.'

Caroline nodded in agreement and responded to the email with their chosen times. She hit 'send'. 'Done. Thanks, Amira.'

Her phone vibrated, and she glanced at it, unable to bite back a smile.

HUNTER: *Us, out of town for an overnight stay. You're in?*

CAROLINE: *Thought you'd never ask x*

Caroline stroked her hand gently up and down Star's soft neck. 'Atta girl.'

They had just got back from their first solo trail ride. Caroline was surprised at how fast she had fallen back into a familiar riding routine. After a few weeks, she had understood Star's body language, temperament, and personality much better. She could now notice subtle things, and marvel at the ordinary, like the movement of Star's ears bobbing slowly in front of her and stretching back and forth when she approached. Star loved jam sandwiches and had an inexplicable hatred towards cattle trailers. Whenever they passed one, even in the distance, if she heard its noise, she'd try to buck Caroline up.

I'll miss you when I go, gorgeous, she thought, looking at the mare.

Sitting in the saddle gave her a slightly different perspective on the world. Yes, it was only a few metres off the ground.

But she could still spot things she normally wouldn't. Every ride brought a new adventure, a sense of peace and a feeling of freedom.

Hunter told her that when he was riding, he couldn't help but live in the moment. Being one with the horse and nature, because there were no other distractions.

'I think it's unfair how much she likes you; she's supposed to be my horse.'

Caroline didn't have to turn around for her mouth to shape into a warm smile.

'I'm sorry I couldn't join you.'

'Don't worry, we had an amazing time, right, girl?' Star neighed as Caroline faced Hunter. 'Did you manage to find the runaway heifer?'

'The runaway heifer?' He laughed heartily. 'That sounds like a comedy title. But yes, we found her just over our western boundary, on Leacher's pasture.' He stroked Star's mane. 'Luke roped her, and we loaded her onto the truck. She must've got spooked by something; she was still scared when we found her. But she's back with the rest of the herd now.'

'Good.' She pulled him closer by the collar of his shirt and looked into his eyes.

He grinned widely, planting a single soft kiss on her lips. 'Let's get out of here before my mom sees you.'

Caroline let him take her hand and lead her to his truck, parked outside the back of the barn. She tried not to let a hint of sadness show in her expression. It was her idea not to get too attached. It was her idea that whatever they had should be purely casual. But trying to avoid running into his family, and even not meeting them, was starting to weigh down on her.

And she couldn't understand why. After all, she was the

one who kept saying to herself – and him – that this was purely casual.

Is it though?

'Where are we going?' she asked, her voice filled with tempered excitement. She wasn't a fan of surprises, but when Hunter said he had one for her and that it'd be an overnight one, she was curious. She noticed a sign for Chickasha, and they joined Route 44, heading south.

'You'll see, we're almost there. How was your work today?'

'Good.' She turned from the window and looked at him. 'Booked the flights to San Diego for ASH, that congress I told you about. Amira and I are going to go together, which will be nice. Did I tell you I got asked to speak at the panel discussion?'

He shook his head, eyes not leaving the road.

'It's on haematologic emergencies and their acute management. I met someone from OnyxRex, the company behind the multiple myeloma trial I'm working on, last week. She was thoroughly impressed with my background and work at the centre. One thing led to another, and she brought my name forward as an "up-and-comer" who would be well-suited to take a seat on the panel. I said yes today.'

'Caroline, that's wonderful.' For a split-second, he turned his head and beamed at her. 'It sounds like an amazing opportunity.'

She smiled back at him. 'Yes, but it's also terrifying.'

'Why?'

'Well—' She paused, realising she hadn't told Hunter about her anxiety. Being a private person, she rarely shared it with people. Sometimes, it was easy to forget about it. She didn't take any medication at present, and it had been a while since she had been to a therapy session. Most days, she just got on with her life. It felt easier that way. 'I struggle with public speaking. It makes me very nervous.'

Hunter didn't say anything, but she could tell he was listening, giving her space to say more if she wanted. Somehow, he always knew when she needed it.

She cast her mind back to the day she'd heard that one sentence that showered her with unexplainable relief: *You have generalised anxiety disorder.* It suddenly all made sense. Her higher-than-normal stress levels over things that most people didn't understand. The sense of impending dread, fixating on knowing that something bad was surely going to happen. Panicking when someone she cared about wouldn't respond to her texts for hours, to the point where she wasn't able to focus on anything else until her phone pinged with a response.

People liked to judge or misunderstand. Caroline couldn't count the number of times she had tried to say she struggled with anxiety, and people had told her to *'just relax'* or *'don't worry so much'*. Anxiety didn't work that way. She couldn't just flip the switch and 'not worry'.

But Hunter wasn't like that. Sometimes, she tried to remind herself that she hadn't known him long. The voice of reason told her she didn't really know him at all. Another voice, which was getting louder, insisted that it wasn't the length of time that shaped connections. What mattered more was their depth.

She stole another glance at his profile. Then, she took a deep breath and shared more than she'd shared with anyone, except her therapist. And Finn.

'It isn't just a bit of nerves, it's overwhelming. I've always had this . . . this overconsuming worry in my chest. For a very long time, I thought this was just normal for everyone. I didn't know anything else.' Her lip trembled. 'When my mum died, I couldn't cope with the anxiety and how it made me feel. That was the push I needed to seek help.'

She paused again, sensing Hunter hanging on her words. 'My first counselling session felt like a eureka moment. I left it feeling like I could finally draw a normal breath. I went to therapy, was on medication for a while . . . unpacked a lot of emotional baggage and just learned to acutely cope with the symptoms.'

'How are you doing with it now?' His voice was kind, but she noticed his eyes grew distant, filling up with sadness.

'Mostly fine. There are days or things that make it worse. Like public speaking.' She tried to smile but only managed to move her lips in a weird twitch. 'Normally, it's low-grade and often feels like one constant that I can always count on. It might sound odd, but it often reminds me I'm alive when I need grounding.'

'Sometimes the pain reminds us we aren't dead yet,' Hunter said in a low, broken whisper.

She didn't know if he had said it to her or to himself.

There was a fleeting sadness to his features. Caroline realised he must've thought about his father. Without thinking, she reached out and put a hand over his on the gear stick.

He attempted a smile, but it didn't quite reach his eyes. 'I'm sorry, you shared something important with me; it's not the time or place for my fortune-cookie wisdom.' His hand moved back onto the wheel. 'How do you manage, with public speaking? I know you enjoy teaching – in a way that's also public speaking, isn't it?'

'Yes, but it's different.' She fiddled with her ring finger, feeling an urge to twist her rings around – but of course, they weren't there. She felt around the finger, touching the smooth, worn skin surface where they used to sit. Trying not to dwell on it, she continued. 'Students are usually eager to learn, at least some of them. It's different when I'm speaking in front of colleagues, most of whom, if not all, are my superiors. I'm afraid of stumbling on my words or saying something stupid.'

'Does it get any easier, the more you do it?' he asked, hitting the left indicator and turning off the main road.

'Sometimes it does.' She looked out the window. 'Where are we going?'

'You'll see.'

She sighed, folding her arms across her chest. She knew when the cause was lost. He wouldn't tell her anything until they reached their destination.

CHAPTER TWENTY-EIGHT

Hunter

Hunter switched off the engine and the doors popped unlocked. 'We're here,' he announced, a wide grin across his face.

Caroline turned to him, her eyebrows raised. 'And here is . . . ?'

'Lake Lawtonka, Comanche County.' He pointed towards the modest log cabin at the top of the gravel driveway. 'This is where we're staying.'

She chewed on her lower lip, but he could see a shadow of a smile. Encouraged, he jumped out of the car and strode to the passenger side. He pulled her door open and reached out a hand to her.

She chuckled, shaking her head in disbelief. 'A gentleman, indeed. I should've had more faith when you told me that.'

'A woman like you should be treated like a lady.' He said it before he thought it through. As soon as he did, he started berating himself in his head for how cliché it sounded; she didn't seem to mind.

Smiling, cheeks flushed a bit, she let him take her hand and they stepped onto the driveway. 'Wow.'

His eyes didn't leave her face as she took in the surroundings, spinning slowly in a full circle. Her eyes paused over the top of the treeline, right in front of Mount Scott, its smooth outline striking against the orange hues of the setting sun.

'It's beautiful.'

'I thought you might like it.' He had hoped she would but wasn't sure. She'd told him she didn't like surprises; he loved them. 'It's a family cabin. My father bought it as a gift for my mother for their tenth wedding anniversary.'

'How romantic.'

'We used to come here often when I was growing up.' He fished a set of keys from his pocket. 'I don't think I've been here for maybe three years or so. Buck comes here whenever he can. Either for a little getaway with his wife after dropping the kids off at the ranch, or with Cody. They go fishing together.' His voice trailed off and he realised he was feeling a bit nervous.

The mere thought of the last time he had been here brought tears to his eyes. Five years ago, celebrating what was meant to be the start of his happy-ever-after.

'Are you OK?' Caroline asked cautiously.

He looked up, meeting her concerned glance. 'I'm great.' He blinked rapidly, trying to will the tears away. 'Just a lot of memories. Shall we go in?'

Before she answered, he retrieved a cooler bag and another big green duffel bag from the trunk. He also took Caroline's travel bag and started walking up the narrow driveway.

* * *

'I haven't seen these many stars since I went to Skye,' Caroline said in wonder, wrapping the blanket she'd found on the sofa tighter around her arms.

Hunter didn't respond; he was just observing her from the other side of the open fire they'd started outside. He watched how her face lit up as her eyes travelled through the vastness of the dark, starry sky. He noticed how she brushed away the stray lock of her light hair that fell over her left eye. All he could see in her just now was joy. It was the kind of joy that was contagious – he couldn't help but feel the warmth reflecting in his own face.

'The view's definitely stunning,' he said without looking away.

She must've felt his eyes on her as she looked back at him with a blush.

Silence filled the night air, its stillness interrupted only by the insistent cicadas and wood crackling in the fire pit.

Hunter stoked the fire with a long, carved stick. 'I think I promised you dessert, right?'

'I hope you brought marshmallows. That's the best you can do over an open fire.'

'We're going to do better than that, we'll have s'mores.' He reached into the material tote bag behind him and took out a packet of big white marshmallows. Tearing it open, he said, 'Have you tried s'mores before?'

'No, but I've heard about them. It's like a cracker sandwich with chocolate, right? And marshmallows.'

Hunter smiled at her, popping two plump marshmallows on the stick. Carefully, he balanced it so that it stayed over the fire propped up by stones. 'Yeah, but if you haven't tried it, you don't really know what it is.' He took one graham cracker and broke it in half. 'It's my favourite thing on Earth as far as food goes. Perfect comfort snack.'

He covered one half of the cracker with Hershey's chocolate pieces. 'Also, it's the first thing I learned to make when I was a kid. In this very same fire pit.' He checked the marshmallows. Both were roasted, with a slight golden tinge on their edges. Holding the stick, he laid the marshmallows on the chocolatey graham cracker half. Lifting the other half of the cracker, he covered the toasted marshmallows and pressed down firmly, removing the stick with his other hand. 'Here you go. Try it, it'll change your life.' He grinned, handing the squashed sweet sandwich to Caroline.

She laughed as she grabbed it, taking a bite. Her eyes closed and she chewed each bite slowly, deliberately.

He watched her, not making a sound. Finally, she swallowed the last piece and gave him a smile so bright it lit up the night. 'You're right. It's delicious. Let's make some more.'

A little while later, when they ran out of marshmallows, they decided to open a bottle of bourbon. The fire was still going strong, helped by his vigilance and a steady supply of firewood.

'Thank you for bringing me here. It's been a great night,' Caroline said, pouring herself another glass of amber liquid. 'I think it might've been just what I needed.'

She passed him the bottle, and he held it for a moment. 'The night isn't over yet.'

'Oh? And where do you see this night going?' Her eyes sparkled over the rim of the heavy crystal glass.

He licked his lip, eyes not leaving hers. 'Wherever we want it to go.' He put the bottle on the grass. 'I, for one, think that making out by the open fire is underrated.'

'Never tried it.'

'No? As I said, it's not quite as popular as it should be.' He put his hand on her knee and shuffled a little bit closer. She had come over to sit on his blanket when they were making s'mores and was now just inches away. He could almost feel the heat radiating from her, mixed with heady smell of the burning fire.

'I think I can see the appeal,' she murmured, putting her hand on his chest. Without another word, he leaned in, gently tasting her lips.

The gooey s'mores and warming bourbon.

Caroline kissed him back, lacing her fingers at the back of his neck. Pulling her legs over his lap, his hands moved to her waist. Without breaking their kiss, he rolled a strand of her hair over his finger and brought it to his face. Their lips parted and they both took deep breaths.

Hunter closed his eyes, burying his face in her hair. 'Your hair smells so good, like mango and some other tropical fruit . . . pineapple?' As soon as he said it, he felt her whole body stiffen in his embrace.

She held her breath and didn't even flinch.

He pulled back. 'Caroline? Are you all right? Did I say something wrong?'

'N-No,' she stammered.

Her hands were shaking. Alarmed, his first instinct was to put his arm round her and draw her close. But he stopped himself, unsure whether it would make matters worse.

'What is it?' he asked gently.

She shook her head, letting out a low laugh. When she spoke again, her voice dripped with bitterness. 'Finn used to comment on my hair the same way. It's a shampoo I use, or rather, used in the past. I haven't washed my hair with it for almost three years. But then, what do you know, Gian bought the exact same shampoo, and I forgot.' She laughed again, sounding even more grim. 'I didn't realise until you said what you did.'

'I didn't know. I'm sorry.'

The anger, which had been bubbling away on a steady heat in the pit of his stomach since the night she had told him about Finn, flared. She had deserved so much better.

Hunter vowed he would show her how good sex could be. How it should feel. He'd worship her body, so she'd see stars rivalling the ones adorning the sky above them. If she wanted that, of course. He really meant it when he told her they'd go only at the speed she was comfortable with.

'Don't be sorry. It's not your fault.' The tone of her voice changed slightly. 'It's just . . . I feel like I'm trying to run away from my real life when I'm with you. And it feels great. But it doesn't change the reality. Legally, I'm still married.' She took a deep breath. 'If I believed in God, I'd think Hell was waiting for me.'

'If they put the souls of people like you in Hell, they'd have run out of space back in BC times.'

That made her laugh. 'You think I'm a good person. I'm really not.'

'I think good and bad are such relative, narrow-minded terms that it's hard to really pin either to a living and breathing human.' The gap between his brows narrowed.

She sighed and stretched her legs in front of her.

He didn't probe her further, thinking that she needed space to make sense of her thoughts. Instead, he added more wood to the fire and poured himself another glass of bourbon. He stole a glance at her profile; she looked so serious.

'Do you want to tell me about him?'

'You want me to tell *you* about Finn?' Her question came in a high-pitched squeak, which sounded nothing like her.

He swore in his mind, already regretting those words. But there was no going back now. 'How did you meet? I know you said you were children. How old were you?' He was ashamed that there was some audible jealousy in his question. He knew he had no right to it. It made no sense. But he couldn't help it.

'We—' She closed her eyes as she took in several deep breaths. When her ragged breathing slowed down, she looked at the lazily roaring fire. 'We were eight. He was a new kid who transferred to my primary school. The teacher made him introduce himself. I remember he said he liked dragons and pirates.' She smiled wistfully, eyes still on the dancing flames. 'I came up to him after the class ended, saying I liked dragons and pirates too. And that we could play together sometime.'

She paused as if checking whether he wanted to say anything. But he didn't interrupt her, so she continued. 'We became fast friends. *Best friends*. When we were fifteen, I realised I liked him more. I found myself thinking about kissing him . . . It became like an obsession.' She chuckled to herself, drawing her knees up to her chest. She hugged them, closely wrapping the blanket further round herself.

'And I did kiss him, one night after he walked me home from the cinema. He didn't say anything. I felt like an idiot. I think I stayed up all night, tossing and turning, thinking I'd ruined everything. The next day, he found me after History and gave me a shy peck on the lips. Then he said, "*I like you that way, too*", She pulled up the blanket even tighter round her neck. 'That's it, really. We were the "golden couple" at school. Everyone thought we'd be the ones who made it forever.'

'You never had another boyfriend?'

'No, never. Finn was my one and only. He's supposed to be my one true love, my soulmate.' She gritted her teeth, tears welling up in her eyes.

Hunter felt an urge to touch her, to comfort her somehow – but he knew that wasn't a good idea. It sounded like she needed to say all this. He knew far too well how therapeutic speaking out loud about one's feelings was.

'He planned a surprise trip to Slovenia after my med school graduation and proposed when we were there.' She rubbed her temples. 'We got married. And you know what happened after that.'

She poured herself more bourbon and downed the glass in one gulp.

He watched her cautiously, afraid to say or do something wrong. Then, he relaxed a bit as he saw a small smile on her lips again.

'How about you? Any serious relationships?' she asked, slowly lowering herself on the blanket. She lay down, staring at the stars.

Hunter followed suit. They were so close their arms were touching.

'No, only fleeting romances.' He grinned. 'I don't like the idea of settling down or being tied up. I like to spend time having fun.'

'Then our arrangement seems to be right up your street.'

'Indeed. I'm only hoping you're having as much fun as I am.' He turned his head and saw her smile. Something tugged at his insides.

'I certainly am.'

Then she kissed him, and he momentarily forgot that he felt like a complete idiot.

CHAPTER TWENTY-NINE

Caroline

Hunter kissed her back, and that kiss was everything a kiss should be. His hands were on her waist, her hands were on his neck . . .

Her body tingled. Her core heated.

This was what she wanted to focus on.

They stumbled into the cabin, breaking apart only to take in more air.

She took off his cowboy hat and threw it on the old armchair covered with a patchwork throw. She sunk her fingers into his soft, dark hair.

He pushed her against the wood-panelled wall, hands travelling up her stomach to her chest. When he hooked one finger over the V of her shirt, he looked at her, wordlessly asking for permission.

She nodded, her own hands untucking his shirt from his dark jeans. Very slowly, he started unbuttoning it. She shivered as his hands touched her now bare skin. She wanted more and she wanted it faster. Fuelled by a rush of impatience, she pulled off her shirt and threw it carelessly on the floor.

Hunter smiled widely as he drunk in her topless form.

The intensity of desire in his grey eyes caused her stomach to flip a bit.

'Gosh, you're perfect,' he said in a low voice.

She blushed. What was she going to say to that? Thank him? She didn't want to make it so obvious that this felt so different from anything she had ever experienced. This felt so good, and they hadn't even done much yet.

Truthfully, she was a bit nervous. Although they had never discussed Hunter's romantic past, she was sure he was more experienced than her. And he had kind of admitted as much by the fire. It wasn't just because he was handsome. There was a certain way he carried himself, the confidence he radiated. She couldn't be the only one that noticed it. But for her, the strong attraction she felt towards him wasn't confined to his tall, muscular body or his devastatingly deep eyes. His sense of humour, his intelligence, his devotion to his family, his absolutely-no-bullshit approach to life and his kindness were all equally important.

Caroline stopped herself from thinking any further as she realised this was veering into dangerous territory.

She pulled his hips towards her and slid the shirt off his arm.

Joining his lips with hers, Hunter freed his other arm from the sleeve. His shirt fell onto the floor, next to Caroline's. Pressing her back to the wall, he left a trail of fiery kisses all the way down from her neck to her belly button. When his hands squeezed her ass, she moaned, cupping his face and kissing him urgently.

She lifted her leg, trying to pull his body as close to hers as she could. She wanted to rip the remaining clothes, to free them both and fully feel his body next to her. It wasn't even a want at this point; it felt like the most urgent need. The kind that would bring down a plague of locusts upon them if it went unfulfilled.

Breathlessly, she whispered in his ear, 'Can we go to the bedroom?'

Before she realised what was happening, Hunter lifted her off the floor.

Her breath caught; her heart stopped.

Despite her relative inexperience in real life, her imagination was vivid. Fed by scenes of passion on and off the page, she had often imagined herself as the heroine moving the handsome male lead to unholy, torturous acts that would bring her to the most delicious orgasm.

Regaining her composure, Caroline wrapped her legs around his waist as he effortlessly carried her to the bedroom. Or at least she assumed that's where they were heading. Unless it was to look into his eyes, she had no interest in opening her own.

It felt like a continuation of their make-out on the periphery of the dance floor. The memory of the ache as the heat pooled between her legs, when her mind had screamed at her it was not nearly enough. Sometimes, she wondered if there was such a thing as enough.

Maybe it was her ravenous sexual hunger which had never been satiated before. She had of course masturbated and used various toys, but somehow it didn't feel the same. The pleasure was short-lived, always missing something. Like an almost-finished jigsaw with a piece or two that fell under the table, never to be seen again.

Her body sweltered under the imprints of his fingers tattooed on her skin. It was like falling into a fever dream.

Hunter kicked the door open. Gently, he lowered her onto the bed, and she pulled him down, not pausing the all-consuming dance of their tongues.

Her hands blindly found the front of his jeans. Fingers trembling with excited anticipation, she undid the belt buckle, the button and pulled the zipper down.

'I think we're both still overdressed,' she teased, her right hand reaching below the waistband of his underwear.

Hunter grinned, standing up. He took his jeans and socks off, staying in just a pair of black boxer shorts.

'Better?'

Caroline's eyes caressed every inch of his spectacular chest and legs. 'Well, no – you still aren't naked.'

'I think we should first rid you of your jeans, don't you think?' He smirked, kneeling on the bed beside her.

She shook her head in mock annoyance and started wiggling her bottom and thighs to take them off. 'You could help me, it's not as easy as it looks when you're lying down.'

He chuckled but grabbed the fabric and rolled it down. He pulled her socks off and sat down next to her.

Covering her hand with his, he took in her body. She smiled without a hint of embarrassment this time. She was wearing one of her favourite sets of lingerie: emerald with gold lace, which she had bought not only because it was her favourite colour, but because the shop assistant had commented on how good it would look with her colouring.

Hunter clearly shared this sentiment as he coaxed her up to a sitting position as well and grazed his finger over her nipple through the fabric.

'As much as I think this looks great on you,' he said, now

lifting his left hand up as well, 'I think you're going to look even better without it.'

Eyes not leaving hers, he unhooked the bra at the back. All it took was one swish hand movement. No fumbling, no awkwardness, no needing to do it herself.

Caroline pulled away. Wordlessly, she pushed the right bra strap down her arm, inch by inch, her eyes burning into Hunter's. She didn't know what had got into her, but she took her time, every movement the slowest motion. Seeing the tantalising undoing etch deeper and deeper into his features every time her fingers grazed her own skin, her confidence surged.

'You're killing me here,' he groaned.

'Patience is a virtue.'

His eyes darkened. 'I've never been a virtuous man. Or a patient one.'

She shook her head, biting back a smile. 'So, you prefer this off?' Her fingers tugged on the left strap, the only thing keeping the bra still on.

Hunter pushed himself up on the bed in between her open knees. 'Off,' he growled.

'Are you sure though?' she taunted. 'I quite like it on.'

He stared at her with an intensity that stoked blazing fire at the end of her every nerve.

She swallowed, dragging the strap down in one swish motion. She barely had time to throw it elsewhere on the bed before Hunter was in front of her, so close she thought that their bodies might become one from the maddening nearness alone.

Hunter let out another growl, this one almost primal. Roughly, he cupped her breasts, drawing slow circles over her areolas. He bent his head, and she shivered as his tongue touched the same path his fingers had been tracking.

He worshipped them the way no one ever had – licking, sucking, massaging. With every shot of building orgasm, Caroline's mind lost some sharpness. She knew some people were able to experience nipple orgasm; never did she think she could be one of them. It was uncharted pleasure territory, one she ached to explore further.

She drew in a sharp inhale. Her nipples stiffened as arousal pooled in her lower abdomen. 'That feels so good,' she murmured, not intending to say it out loud.

Hunter chuckled. 'Darling, this is just the beginning. I plan to make you scream over and over again, until you lose your voice.'

Caroline moaned in the acknowledgement of his promise. Closing her eyes, she lolled her head backwards to give him better access to her neck, which his mouth moved onto.

His penis pressed hard against her belly. She was growing more and more relaxed, wetness between her legs clear evidence of her desire. Without wanting to wait any longer, she tugged at his boxers and pulled them down. Then, she slid her underwear off.

He stood up, heaving deep breaths. 'Are you sure you want to do this?'

'Yes,' she said, rolling her eyes as she brushed hair off her forehead.

He nodded.

She noticed he was trying hard to mask how happy her '*yes*' had made him.

'Before we do, though, tell me what you want.'

She blinked. 'What do you mean?'

'I want you to come for me before we climax together.'

Caroline's lips formed into a soundless 'O'. Finn had always said foreplay was overrated. They had never . . . This was . . .

She kicked the memories and thoughts square in the chest, sending them into the abyss of insignificance. She was getting what she had craved for years: a memorable journey in sexual exploration. Her closely guarded fantasies opened in her mind like a catalogue ready to be browsed.

'I want you to go down on me,' she said, surprising herself with how easy it was to voice.

Hunter's lips split in a devilish grin. 'Good choice. Lie back.'

She did, letting him pull her legs close to the edge of the bed.

He kneeled on the floor, opening her legs. His hands burned into the inside of her thighs. 'How do you want it, Caroline? Slow or fast?'

She gulped. She had no idea what she liked, but she didn't want to say that. Thinking back to different sensations she experienced, what felt good, she pulled a pillow under her head. 'Start slow and then go fast.'

She didn't know if he nodded or smiled; the next thing she knew, his fingers grazed her labia majora. 'Damn, you're already so wet for me.'

Caroline was just about to reply to that, when her words were swallowed by an involuntary groan escaping from deep down her throat.

His fingers splayed out on her outer thighs. He got his tongue to work, starting slowly, as she asked. He dragged in agonisingly languid circles over her clitoral hood.

She grabbed the metal headboard with her left hand, needing something to hold on to. Her right hand sunk into his sweat-licked hair. Her feet dug into his shoulder blades.

His tongue picked up the pace as he moved on to her clitoris, drawing gasps and shivers from the very bases of her lungs; sounds she had only ever heard in the movies. She was no longer able to tell which part of her vulva he was pleasuring because it all blended into one breathless build-up to the best orgasm in her life.

Her hips bucked in tandem with the pressure building from the inside. Her moans grew louder, and she was saying things without recognising the words; she could've been begging, or laughing, or swearing – she had no idea, and it didn't matter.

All that mattered was the earth-shattering sensation that washed over her, from the top of her head to the ends of her toes.

Just when she thought she couldn't take another second of it, that it was in fact too much, that she would combust on the spot and reduce to ashes, Hunter didn't let go. His tongue was moving fast, his fingers joining in at her vaginal opening to draw out every last whimper, every last moan.

Her back arched.

And then she screamed like she was a woman possessed. She wriggled, twisting the sheets in her fists, waiting for the bones to regrow in her body. Until the ecstasy raised, leaving her behind. She didn't know how long it took.

When she finally regained some semblance of senses, she propped herself up on her elbows and looked down.

Hunter didn't get up from the floor. He watched her with an indescribable glimmer in his grey eyes. He waited until her whole body stopped shaking, kissed her inner thigh and smirked.

'I told you I'd make you scream.'

She laughed, collapsing against the pillow. 'You did.'

'You're ready for round two?'

Her eyes flared in alarm. 'What?'

'Another orgasm,' he said, like it was obvious. 'I personally think two orgasms before the grand finale is a good number.'

Caroline stared at him. *It'd be less strange if he suddenly sprouted another head*, she thought. 'What about you though?'

'Oh, don't worry about me. Number three is the finale, remember?' He winked.

'But it's not fair. You should enjoy it, too.'

He trailed his fingers up her thighs, all the way to the base of her breasts. Squeezing them in both hands, he flashed her a smile as she swallowed the sensation.

'Trust me. I'm enjoying it immensely.'

And she had no more objections or anything else to say. This time, she thought she knew what to expect, but every time his tongue touched her, she exploded from the inside a little bit more. When she recognised another orgasm building up, she reached down to find Hunter's hand. Weaving her fingers with his between her breasts, she clutched it like it was the only thing keeping her from falling.

Then, with another scream, she fell over the edge of another cliff of ecstasy.

She might've temporarily zoned out afterwards; she wasn't sure. When she recovered, she looked at Hunter. She wanted to say something, but words failed her. To thank him didn't seem suitable, yet it was the first thing that her brain came up with. He had taken her into a world she had only been told about before.

You can thank him in other ways, her mind supplied.

'Come here,' she said. 'Finale time.'

'Your wish is my command.'

Hunter bent down, reaching into his jeans pocket and took out a colourful, square foil package.

Caroline bit her lower lip. Her skin was in almost physical pain when he wasn't next to her. She leaned back on her feet and raised her hands to her own breasts, her eyes never leaving his face. They were swollen to her touch, the nipples tender from where he had drawn them into his mouth.

She moaned at the memory prickling her skin. Then, she shuddered as she remembered the sensation he had awakened when his face was buried between her legs.

He unrolled the condom over his shaft, then captured her lips in a long kiss, his hand in the middle of her back until he had lowered her down onto the bed. She spread her legs wide, bursting with need, and pressed her hips up to meet him.

When he entered her, a gasp escaped her lips. They lay there for a moment, mouths searching each other, savouring the heat of each other's body. She shuddered as he pulled slowly back, then sank deeper insider her caressing her with each thrust.

At first, Caroline felt like she didn't know what she was doing. But any worries she had disappeared as quickly as they entered her mind. They danced in a rhythm as old as time.

It all was too much; she didn't know anymore which feeling to concentrate on. Ecstasy started building in her from the very core of her being. She groaned in pleasure, barely conscious of making any sound at all. Her throat became hoarse, her chest heavy with a tightness she didn't recognise.

All she wanted to do, in this moment, was fade into Hunter. Into his heart, into his head, into his bed. Their bodies felt like they melted together, there was no trace any longer that one was once two. She felt like she would break out of her skin, the feeling of passion driving her to new heights.

They rode it together until finally the dam broke and she climaxed, for the third and most intense time that night.

CHAPTER THIRTY

Hunter

The morning sun cut through the drawn curtains. Birds chirped outside, and there was a distinct soft October chill in the air. The serene silence of blissful seclusion of the cabin gave a delusional impression that time had stopped. That, beyond the wooden walls, the rest of the world didn't matter.

Hunter looked down at Caroline's face, pensively running his fingers through her hair. She was lying sideways with her head resting on his abdomen. They had been awake for a while, both too tired to get out of bed. Neither of them got much sleep last night. He gulped at the flashback of the mind-blowing sex. Mere reminiscing about it was getting him hard. But what pleased him the most was that she had a great experience. One she should've had the first time and every time since then. The sheen of satisfaction in her eyes was possibly the most arousing thing he had seen.

If he could stop time, even for a little while, he would press 'pause' right now.

'You never told me what's your favourite whisky,' Caroline said, her fingers drawing lazy circles across his chest.

He barked a surprised laugh. 'Really? That's what you want to talk about?'

'Yes.' She lifted her head, propped herself on her elbow and flashed him a brilliant smile. 'Go on, spill. Unless you're embarrassed.'

'What?' He shook his head. 'Of course I'm not. It's an easy question. Royal Lochnagar.'

She looked at him enquiringly.

Hunter bit his lip and said, 'It's from a small distillery up in Aberdeenshire, near Balmoral Castle.'

'Oh, I know it. I'm from around there. Just surprised you do.'

He pushed himself up against the headboard to get more comfortable and opened his arm, making a space for Caroline, which she pressed herself into, sliding her arm over his chest.

Her hand rested above his heart and he thought she could probably feel its erratic beat.

'Of course you'd know it, I'm sorry. It didn't click.'

'It's a good whisky. And the Royal Deeside is gorgeous.' She sighed. 'I miss it very much.'

'Why won't you move back up there?' Hunter asked.

'I'd love to, eventually. It sounds a lot easier than it is for doctors in the UK to move around. We have very little power over where the centralised system allocates us. Well, you can apply wherever you want to, but it isn't given you're going to get the job you want.'

'Did you apply to Aberdeen at all?'

Caroline winced. 'Not as a doctor, no. I got into medical school there but . . .' She pressed her hands to her eyes, rubbing them like she wanted to disperse some uninvited sadness pushing to fill the corners of her mind. 'I couldn't stay there. Not after my mother died. It was just too much. Everything was too raw. If I'd stayed, I'd have walked the corridors of the very hospital in which I lived the worst days of my life during my clinical placements. Even just the thought of that was haunting.'

Hunter felt her tense. He hugged her tighter to his side. 'I can only imagine how hard that would've been.'

She let out a shuddering breath against his skin. 'That's why I didn't even think twice when I also got into Edinburgh. It was far enough to squeeze the memories out of my consciousness.'

'And then you got a job in Glasgow?'

'Yes. Finn got a job there, too. So, it made sense. But now, with everything that's happened, I think I'd like to try to get back to Aberdeenshire.'

'You miss it, then?'

Caroline dropped her hand from his chest, untangled her legs from his and sat up. Pulling up the cover almost up to her chin, she smiled. 'It's home. Even though my entire family has moved on, I feel a peace there that I haven't felt elsewhere. I'd love to move back, if I can.'

Hunter nodded, more to himself than to her. 'It is a beautiful part of the world.'

She furrowed her brow. 'When did you go there?'

'My grandmother was born in Scotland, not far from Balmoral, actually. Three years ago, when her health was declining, she wanted to visit her homeland one last time. As my dad was already unwell, I volunteered to go with her. I couldn't miss a chance to check out some distilleries when there and that's how I discovered Royal Lochnagar.'

Caroline looked as if she was deep in her own thoughts. She rested her head on his arm but didn't interrupt the silence between them for a long while. When she finally spoke, it was in a barely audible whisper directed towards his neck. 'Did you like it?'

'It was beautiful. And so peaceful.' He smiled, pulling her in closer. 'It was the first time I contemplated living somewhere other than Oklahoma. Imagine that.' He chuckled, shaking his head.

The notion of moving to the north of Scotland should be utterly absurd, but Hunter found himself thinking back to that trip. To the misty hills, the clear rivers, the dense forests, the charming villages and the fields.

Maybe you'd enjoy it. Maybe a change would do you good.

For a quick, fanciful spark of a moment he imagined himself on a hike up one of the snowy hilltops, Caroline walking by his side with her cheeks flushed from the cold, her eyes bright in the fresh air.

You have responsibilities here. The ranch needs you. Your family needs you. You can't just take off and move to Scotland.

Caroline put a hand on his bare chest again and leaned in, her mouth just inches from his, bringing him back to the present. 'You have good legs to wear a kilt.'

She tried to kiss him, but he moved to the left, and she missed his mouth.

'Are you mocking me?'

'I wouldn't dare.'

He kissed her, and something roared inside him when she responded, eagerly kissing him back. And then, their bodies joined in a passionate dance again. Her fingernails were gently scratching his back up and down. His hands were moving all over her body.

It was fire on fire.

Afterwards, she covered her breasts with the duvet. 'Should we get up and make some breakfast? I'm quite hungry now.'

Hunter laughed and got out of bed, pulling the duvet with him.

'Hey! That was mine!'

'Technically, it's mine. Let's move this party to the kitchen.' He watched her pull on her pants and a shirt, leaving her bra on the floor.

She pushed her fingers through her tangled hair. 'What?' she asked when she caught him staring at her.

'Nothing. Last one in the kitchen washes up.'

He knew that, logically, this was going to end in nothing but heartache when the time came for her to go back to Scotland. But he couldn't help himself.

He was falling in love with her.

CHAPTER THIRTY-ONE

Caroline

CAROLINE: *I slept with Hunter.*

ERIN: *I knew it! How was it?*

CAROLINE: *Fantastic.*

ERIN: *Oh, come on! That's all I get?! I need details! I still don't even know what he looks like. You could really send a friend a photo or two . . .*

CAROLINE: *He doesn't have social media. What am I supposed to do, snap a photo of him and say, 'Oh, my friend is nosey'?*

She wouldn't mention the photo strip from the rodeo. They'd ended up getting two – she had one, and Hunter had kept the other. Just the thought made her cheeks burn. Those felt private. A keepsake she wanted to hide just for herself.

ERIN: *This is exactly what you should do. I'm sure he'd be flattered. But you're avoiding the question. How was it, really? I know you haven't been with anyone other than Finn.*

CAROLINE: *I don't really know how to describe it. You know the feeling that everything just seems right, when you aren't thinking about anything else, the whole world and the worries and silly things fade away, and you just focus on the moment you're in?*

ERIN: *I guess?*

CAROLINE: *Well, it felt like that. I mean, physically it felt bloody wonderful. I didn't think there were different types of orgasms, but no vibrator has ever felt like that. And it was great the first time, and the second . . . I don't know. I feel like I've been missing out before.*

ERIN: *You clearly had shitty vibrators (just kidding). The second, hm?*

CAROLINE: *Don't judge! The oral sex was great, too . . .*

ERIN: *Oh, trust me, I don't. I'm just happy for you for feeling happy. You deserve to feel all these awesome things. And yay for some tongue action! That's one thing they haven't invented yet – my theory is that men know once we get toys like that, we won't need them.*

CAROLINE: *Erin!*

ERIN: *What? It's true!*

CAROLINE: *I just hope that it wasn't a mistake.*

ERIN: *Things that feel this good never are. My grandma told me once to never regret anything that made you smile. Because it couldn't possibly be wrong.*

CAROLINE: *That's a bit of a stretch, don't you think? But anyway . . . I appreciate it. I just don't want him to get too attached.*

ERIN: *He's a guy. Why would he? It's like a perfect scenario. He has all the perks of spending time with you on all levels without the fear of any commitment. He knows you'll be leaving, right?*

CAROLINE: *Of course he does.*

ERIN: *Then it's all good. I'm more worried about you.*

CAROLINE: *Me?! Why?*

ERIN: *Because I know you. I know that even though you tell yourself that this is just a bit of fun, you aren't the kind of person who can keep her feelings in check. You don't compartmentalise, Car.*

CAROLINE: *I'll be fine.*

ERIN: *If you say so.*

The following week passed in a blur. Jake was off sick, so Caroline and Amira tried to help with his work on top of their own. It was a lot of long days and late nights. When Friday finally came, Caroline couldn't look at Excel spreadsheets and study protocols anymore.

She hadn't seen Hunter since they'd got back from Lake Lawtonka on Sunday morning. Maybe it was better that way. Whatever casual label they stuck on their relationship, deep down Caroline feared her hands were slipping off it. She needed to readjust her grip on reality, reminding herself that it was just a bit of fun for them both. She was going back to Scotland. And now that she had decided she really wanted to go back to Aberdeenshire, there was nothing that could persuade her otherwise. Especially not if it involved staying in the States.

No, it was better all round if she kept any theoretical feelings from blossoming.

They texted throughout the week, but it was very sporadic; it seemed that there was a lot going on for him just now too. He'd called her yesterday to check that she was still up for going to karaoke with him, Meg, and Mitch.

'Of course. I'm looking forward to it', she'd replied.

The audible happiness in his voice stirred something in her. He apologised for not being able to pick her up, but he had a riding lesson scheduled just before and wouldn't be able to make it. Then, he told her the name of the bar in Purcell where they'd meet.

'See you there', was all she'd said as she hung up.

The Crocked Boot was unlike any bar Caroline had been to in Oklahoma City.

She walked in through the wooden saloon-style door that could have used a fresh lick of paint. Immediately, she was hit by the warmth and sound of loud chatter over the country music playing in the background. There were so many people inside that she instinctively took a step back, worried she'd get squashed against somebody. The tables were stashed closely together and were all occupied. Everyone seemed to know one another, with people walking from the bar with drinks in hands stopping on their way back to their parties, exchanging smiles and greetings with other patrons. At the back of the room there was a small stage, with a TV screen mounted on the wall directly opposite it. There were no instruments in the vicinity, but there were a few big speakers and a couple of microphones on stands. Caroline assumed this was where the karaoke would start shortly.

'Hi. Glad you found the place OK.'

Her head snapped to the right and an instant smile spread across her lips when she saw Hunter.

'It isn't exactly Oklahoma City,' she replied.

He grinned with slight disbelief.

'Fine, I did use Google Maps and had to do a little circle round to find a parking space.'

That made him laugh. 'I thought I remembered you saying you were terrible with directions. Anyway, I'm glad you're here now. Come meet Mitch and Meg.'

His fingers found and intertwined with hers, as if it was the most natural gesture.

She didn't pull her hand away. All her earlier reservations and reminders it was just casual took a backseat.

Hunter led her slowly through the cramped area, smiling and nodding at some people shouting their hellos. When they reached the corner table, both people sitting at it stopped their conversation mid-sentence and looked at them.

He let go of her hand, pulled up a chair for her and slid

onto the one next to a shorter man with ruffled blonde hair, who looked maybe a couple of years older than him. 'This is my younger sister, Megan.' He nodded towards a teenage girl in a rust-coloured jumpsuit and a long ponytail. 'And this is Mitch, my best friend.' Another nod towards the man sat on his left. 'Meg, Mitch, this is Caroline.'

She was relieved that he didn't include any definitions of who she was in his introduction.

Putting on the friendliest smile, she extended her hand first to Megan, who shook it eagerly, excitement dancing in her eyes. 'Hi, so nice to meet you! Officially, I mean.'

'Likewise. Hunter told me you were in one of my biology labs. I'm sorry I don't remember you from there, so many students. And teaching is still quite new to me, so I get rather nervous.'

Megan waved her apology off and stared at her in disbelief. 'Really? You didn't come across as nervous! Most of my classmates really enjoyed both labs. I hope you'll be taking on some more this semester?'

Caroline gave her a grateful smile. 'That's so nice of you to say, thank you. It's only two more just now, I'm afraid. My work at the centre is ramping up with the clinical trials, and I'm also going away for a congress in December.'

'What clinical trials are you working on? And what congress?' Megan leaned over the table with such enthusiasm that she almost knocked Mitch's beer over.

Caroline chuckled, but Hunter shook his head. 'Meg, enough. You don't need to interrogate Caroline. It's meant to be a nice, relaxing evening for all of us.' He looked at his sister in mock annoyance.

The siblings started quickly talking between themselves, momentarily forgetting about Caroline and Mitch.

Taking this as his cue, Mitch turned to Caroline. 'These two are always at it. I guess that's how sibling dynamics work,' he finally said, breaking the gaze and taking a long sip from his pint glass.

'I guess it is. I have two sisters myself, and no matter how old we get, bickering always seems to be our default mode,' Caroline replied.

'I'm the only child, so I don't have any experience myself, but I always find it amusing to watch.' Mitch shrugged. 'Are you hungry? There's an excellent taco truck outside through the beer garden. We'd be back before the start of karaoke.'

She raised her eyebrow in suspicion at the sudden change of topic.

Mitch picked up on it and let out a laughter that sounded genuine. 'Don't worry, I won't kidnap and kill you. I just thought we could chat. And I'm starving.'

Caroline locked eyes with Hunter, who seemed to catch the end of it with one ear.

'The tacos are good. Would you bring us some too? Don't want to leave the table as it seems we won't get seats when we get back.'

'Oh, yes, please!' Megan cut in. 'Plain chicken ones for me.'

'Sure thing.' Mitch got up and waited for Caroline to follow him. 'We'll be back soon.'

The fresh air was just what Caroline needed. It wasn't that much quieter outside as there were several groups of smokers chatting, but the music was barely audible, and the sound carried differently.

She could feel Mitch's eyes boring into her again. Pushing her hands into her dress pockets, she moved in the direction of a lime-coloured truck, which gave off a delicious smell that spread across the beer garden.

As soon as they joined the queue, Mitch cleared his throat. 'He's a good man, you know,' he said. 'He doesn't deserve to have his heart broken again.'

Caroline bristled. 'I know he is. And who said I'm going to break his heart?'

'Well, it's a given, isn't it? You're going back to the UK in what, July, is it? It might just be a fun fling for you with a hot cowboy, but I know Hunter. Trust me, this is anything but casual for him.'

She looked up. The queue moved but she didn't flinch to move with it. Instead, she walked off towards a swing bench under the string of fairy lights.

Mitch followed her without a word and leaned on the wooden pole, crossing his arms over his chest.

She bit her lip, trying to think of the most coherent way to convey her thoughts.

Mitch, however, didn't seem to feel very comfortable in the hanging silence. He took a deep breath and continued, 'Look, you seem nice enough. Hell, you must be more than nice if he likes you this much. You're clearly beautiful and accomplished. I don't have anything against you as a person. But he's my best friend and life's already been too hard on him.'

Hunter had told her that he hadn't told anyone she was still legally married. She wasn't sure if it was for his benefit or hers, but it probably wasn't the proudest moment to announce to your family and friends that you were seeing a married woman. Technically divorced, but not really. The unsigned divorce papers felt like a mark against her, even if it was only visible to her.

'He's an adult. And I've never lied to him or made him any promises,' she said.

'I know you haven't. That's not the point. It's one thing if you both want to lie to yourselves. Maybe it's true for you, I don't know. He sure says that it's all casual and just good fun. As I said, I know him. The way he looks at you . . . I just want you to know because he won't tell you this. But he cares a hell of a lot.'

'He strikes me as a heartbreaker type who doesn't get too attached. I'm sure in a year, he won't even remember me.'

As soon as the words left her mouth, Caroline knew she didn't believe them one bit. True, this was the initial impression she'd got when they first met. But now? Now she knew there was so much more to Hunter.

Mitch smirked and shook his head, running a hand through his hair. He sat down on the opposite end of the swing and looked wistfully in the distance. 'He didn't tell you that he was engaged, did he?'

She looked at him blankly and he nodded, as if this is what he'd expected. 'I thought not. But . . . Although no. Not my place to tell.' Mitch shut his mouth, pushing his hands deeper in his pockets.

Her head was spinning. A wave of nausea washed over her. She had asked him about his romantic past, last weekend by the fire. Before the night that had turned her world upside down.

No, only fleeting romances.

Why did he lie to her?

She looked at Mitch with a new appreciation. He was just trying to be a good friend and look out for Hunter. She'd do the same for Erin in a heartbeat. Especially given the situation.

She wiped her eyes with the back of her hand, pushing

away the tears that threatened to spill over. 'Thank you for telling me all this, Mitch.'

'I'm not sure I should've, but here we are. Make of it what you want.' He shrugged and they joined the queue for the food truck.

'Finally! I was starting to think you drove all the way to the city for these.' Megan grabbed the small tray with three tacos from Mitch's hands and took a large bite.

Hunter raised his eyebrow at his sister. 'Hungry?'

'Well, they've been gone for ages.' She ate her first taco in three chews and had started on the second one before Caroline and Mitch had a chance to properly sit back down.

Caroline passed Hunter a tray with mixed tacos and set another one in front of herself.

He searched her face for a second as if trying to see any imprint of her and Mitch's conversation. 'You have been gone for a while. Was the queue that long?'

'Oh, come on, Hunt. The queue was a bit long, but we also just chatted for a while. Getting to know each other and that. This was the whole point of tonight, right?' Mitch said in a cheerful tone that Caroline hadn't heard before. He looked a lot more relaxed now, his initial icy demeanour gone.

Before Hunter could respond, a redhead middle-aged woman walked up to the stage and announced through the microphone, 'Howdy Purcell! Hope you're having a good time this Friday night?'

A few murmurs of agreement and some whistling followed.

She beamed and continued, 'Good, the night's just starting! We're officially opening our karaoke – who is brave enough to go first?'

More whistling and laughter, and a confident hand shot up in the air from a guy sitting at the bar. 'Awesome, let's give a round of applause to Trent Gorey!'

Caroline leaned over to speak into Hunter's ear over the noise of the commotion that accompanied Trent's walk to the stage. 'How does she know his name?'

Hunter wiped his mouth with a napkin, swallowing the last of his food. 'Everyone knows everyone around here. Trent went to school with my brother, Buck. He often volunteers to go first at karaoke nights.' He looked at Trent, who chose a song that was met with a loud round of applause from the crowd. 'Sadly, he doesn't have the greatest voice, but you can't fault his enthusiasm.'

He was right, too. Trent was singing one of the classics – 'Austin' – which was the song that had introduced Caroline to the world of country music.

She winced when he missed note after note in the chorus.

After Trent, there were two women who looked to be in their late thirties. They sang a duet and received a warm round of applause, which was a step up from the polite response to Trent's performance.

Starting to enjoy the music and cold beer, Caroline felt the tension leaving her body. She still didn't understand why Hunter had lied to her. She knew she couldn't be upset, not really, but it was hard to rein in her feelings. Whatever they were, tonight wasn't the time to get into this with him.

She swapped seats with Hunter so she could speak with Megan, who seemed like she wanted to absorb everything Caroline had to say like a sponge. They mostly talked about medicine and Caroline's job.

About five more karaoke performances later, the emcee made another announcement. 'I can see that our karaoke favourite is here tonight. Hunter Jackson, would you come up and sing something for us?' Her eyes and those of a dozen others among the audience landed on Hunter, who blushed under the brim of his hat.

He shook his head. Mitch elbowed him in the ribs and said something that Caroline couldn't hear. He shook his head again.

'Come on, Hunter. One song?' Mitch teased.

It didn't take long for the whole bar to start chanting '*One song!*' and clapping their hands.

Finally, Hunter raised his hand in capitulation and downed his lemonade.

Caroline raised her eyebrow, amused. She moved her chair closer to him. 'I didn't know you could sing.'

He just blushed a deeper shade of pink.

'No? He's actually quite good,' Megan said with a hint of pride. 'We used to come here every Friday before I started college and, well, the regulars got used to hearing a song or two from him.'

'Don't exaggerate, Meg.' Hunter stood up and sighed. 'Guess I don't have much choice.'

His walk to the stage was accompanied by loud applause.

He pulled up the microphone stand to match his height and looked across the room. 'You got your wish, here I am. Any song requests?'

'"Head Over Boots"! Jon Pardi!' A muffled shout from the bar area was met with approving nods and several people repeating the title.

Hunter nodded once, and the woman clicked some buttons on the console. The lyrics came up on the screen, with music playing from the speakers. He started singing in a low, smooth, and confident tone.

Caroline straightened in her chair, entranced. She had never heard this song, but it seemed that most people knew it well, as they soon started tapping and even singing along.

Megan was happily bobbing her head to the music.

Mitch was snickering to himself, arms crossed across his chest.

'What's so funny?' Caroline asked him.

'Making fun of him after this never gets old. He plays a guitar too, if you didn't know. But I do like the song.'

'He is good though,' she responded, turning back to look at Hunter. When the chorus came again, their eyes met.

The words kept flowing from his mouth, his earnest grey eyes not leaving hers. He didn't even glance at the lyrics on the screen.

Something heavy flipped in the pit of her stomach. Suddenly, she felt too hot. Her cheeks burned from the inside, but she couldn't look away.

Hunter was looking at her like she was the only person in the crowded bar.

Her eyes glistened with something uncomfortably unfamiliar.

A few people at the front of the stage turned round to see what had Hunter so captivated. One woman in a navy denim dress turned to her friend and whispered something in her ear. Both smiled and looked at Caroline with interest.

She didn't pay them any attention. It didn't matter.

His voice filled her ears and set her whole body on fire. She achingly recalled the taste of his lips on hers, the feel of his hands on her body and the moments just after, when she felt only happiness. The ecstasy and everything else bundled up in an iridescent glow.

Hunter's darkened gaze stripped every layer off her. No one had ever looked at her like that. It was hard to explain but she thought the way she looked at him was somehow new as well.

It felt different.

Her body just seemed to respond to him in a manner she didn't fully understand. Like it had a power to bring her the greatest happiness and the biggest heartbreak, all in one.

The song finished to a round of rapturous applause.

Megan jumped off her seat and joined in.

Mitch, smirk still plastered to his face, did too.

But Caroline was glued to her chair and couldn't move.

Mitch was right. This wasn't casual for Hunter. And to her greater dismay, it was getting impossible to pretend she had no feelings for him.

Which made the lie he'd told her burn even more. Why did he do it? This question had been playing on her mind since Mitch had told her Hunter had a fiancée. Not just a girlfriend, not a long-term partner. *A fiancée*.

Of course, she wasn't going to get hung up on that. She was the last person who could. But she'd been honest with him, well, pretty much from the start. He could've told her.

He didn't have to, she knew that.

Yet, the fact that he hadn't still hurt.

CHAPTER THIRTY-TWO

Hunter

Hunter wrapped his arm round Caroline's waist, pulling her sideways to him. He could feel her body stiffen as soon as he touched her. Puzzled, he stopped and put a hand on her shoulder. 'What's wrong?'

'Nothing's wrong.'

'Caroline . . . I might not have known you long, but I think I know you quite well by now. I can see something's wrong.'

She huffed, taking a step back. 'I wish I could say the same about knowing you.'

His hand slowly dropped. 'What is that supposed to mean?'

'You lied to me.' Her tone was now a bitter whisper.

He looked at her, perplexed. 'I have no idea what you're talking about.'

The Crocked Boot's saloon door swung towards them as a group of four locals exited the bar, waving and tipping their hats to Hunter in a goodnight greeting. He nodded to each, not certain who they were. As soon as they stumbled far enough not to overhear their conversation, he looked at Caroline.

She shook her head. 'Let's not talk about this here,' she said, as more people went past, accompanied by jolly laughter.

He stepped towards her and touched her elbow. 'We can go to my place. I don't think you should drive back tonight anyway.' She opened her mouth but before she could protest, he hastily added, 'We can leave your car here overnight; Zac won't mind.'

She gave him a curt nod, turned on her heel and started walking briskly towards his house.

He followed her, trying to rack his brain and come up with an explanation as to what happened. When did he lie to her? He had no idea. Maybe Mitch or Meg had said something to her, and she'd misunderstood . . . Yes, that was probably it.

Feeling a bit calmer, he sped up and caught up with her outside the front door. 'Do you want anything to drink?' he asked, as they stepped inside.

Caroline shook her head fervently.

Hunter dropped his keys into a bowl by the door and flicked the light switch. He pursed his lips and reached inside the fridge door, taking a bottle of beer for himself. He popped it open and took a long swig.

She wasn't even looking at him.

Cautiously, he left the kitchen and sat on the leather armchair in the corner. 'Caroline. Talk to me. When did I lie to you?'

'At the cabin. When I asked about your serious relationships. Not that I'm such an expert but I'd say that having been engaged is pretty serious.'

He felt like someone had kicked him in the abdomen,

knocking all the air from his lungs. He took a deep breath, clutching the beer bottle harder in his right hand. 'Who told you?'

'Mitch.'

'He had no right—'

'He was worried about you. He thought—' She broke off, and he looked at her, unsure which emotion he could see playing across her face. She shook her head. 'He thought that you were falling for me, and he didn't want to see your heart broken. *Again*.' She put an emphasis on the last word.

Hunter swallowed hard, fighting the things he wanted to say. He was furious with Mitch. *Why the hell would he tell her?! And why would he make it sound like he was developing feelings for her?*

Because you are, dumbass.

He wanted to growl in annoyance. She couldn't know how he felt. And because of that, he couldn't tell her the real reason why he hadn't said anything. This wasn't what they'd agreed to.

'Mitch is delusional,' he rasped, taking a gulp of cold liquid.

Caroline raised an eyebrow at him, sitting down on the sofa with her arms crossed. 'First, he's your best friend, now he's delusional?'

'Being my best friend doesn't stop him from being delusional. He sees things that aren't real. And—' He considered it for a moment. 'He shouldn't have told you. It isn't his story to tell,' he hissed.

Heavy breaths and pounding of his heart mixed, pulsating loudly in his ears. Feelings of annoyance and anger were fighting for the top spot in his mind. And then he was also trying to control his stomach as nausea threatened to overtake him.

'Well, if you *didn't lie* to me then I wouldn't have had to hear about it from Mitch!' she snapped loudly, jumping to her feet.

Hunter winced. This was the first time he'd heard her raise her voice.

'I'm sorry.' Their eyes met, and he looked at her imploringly. 'You're right. I should've told you.' He sighed and buried his face in his hands. *It shouldn't be this hard.*

Caroline sat down on the carpet, crossing her legs. She pried his fingers away from his eyes, squeezing them gently. 'Why didn't you?' Her tone went back to normal, anger seemingly set aside.

'I don't know,' he answered, hoping she wouldn't pick up on the hint of hesitancy in his voice. 'We shook hands on sex and fun, not heavy conversations and sad stories.'

'It's a bit late for that, don't you think?'

Hunter nodded. He knew she was right. They had become so much closer than just two people having a good time. He still couldn't tell her how he felt about her. Not the whole truth. He could tell her more though, explain further . . .

Maybe she'd understand him better.

'Probably.' He let out a low laugh, burying his face in his hands again.

Damn you, Mitch.

'You told me you only had fleeting romances. Is this all I am to you? A mindless fuck?' She tried to hide the hurt in her eyes, but he noticed how crestfallen she looked.

'No!' he cried out, knocking the empty beer bottle over as he stood up. 'It's not like that with you,' he blurted, not sure what to say next or how to phrase the explanation without revealing what he wanted to stomp over and keep hidden.

'What is it like then?'

'I . . . We . . .' He bit his tongue, stumbling over his words. He strode to the window and looked into the stormy sky. Heavy rain had started pouring after they'd got inside.

He pushed his hands into his pockets, turning to her after he composed himself.

'I'm in awe of you, Caroline. You're probably the most interesting person I've ever met. I like spending time with you, I adore our conversations. And I enjoy our physical connection.' He exhaled sharply.

If he could pat himself on the back for avoiding saying '*love*', he would.

'But if you're asking me to put a label on what we have, I can't.' He couldn't read the expression on her face.

She looked so stoic.

'Can you?' He tried to keep any hint of hope, any hint of longing from his tone.

He wanted to close the distance between them and tell her the truth: he hadn't told her because he'd have to explain how much he felt for *her*. He'd have to deal with all the guilt, and he wasn't ready for it. And he was worried she'd then run for the hills because falling for her wasn't what he was meant to do.

He wanted to tilt her chin up, kiss her and tell her how much she really meant to him. But that'd be a mistake. He didn't deserve her. He certainly didn't want her to fall in love with him. Not that he thought she would, but just in case . . . It couldn't happen.

Caroline looked like her mind was elsewhere. When she spoke, her voice was calm. She even attempted a small smile. 'No, I can't.'

He felt his nerves relax a bit.

'Regardless, you lied to me.'

'I didn't lie.'

That seemed to have drilled something in her as her smile faltered. Hunter realised he shouldn't have said it then and tried to reach for her, but she stepped away.

'Lying by omission is still lying,' she said quietly. 'I enjoy your company too. And I don't want to lose what we have.' She looked into his eyes, and he held his breath. 'But you can't lie to me again. Lying is one thing that I can't get past.' Her bottom lip quivered, and without thinking, he lifted his finger and put it to her lips.

'I'm sorry.'

A roar of thunder rumbled through the air, fat raindrops slamming against the windows.

Caroline's mouth was open, just a little bit.

Hunter found himself unable to resist its invitation. He leaned down, brushing his own lips softly against hers.

She kissed him back.

He couldn't help but think that something had changed between them tonight. Something vital.

Then her lips were on his, her hands touching his chest, pulling his T-shirt over his head. And he stopped thinking at all.

'Take off your clothes and lie on the floor,' Caroline demanded, unbuckling his belt. 'No three rounds tonight – just one. And I want to be in control. If you agree.'

Hunter's eyes darkened as a shiver ran down his spine at the sound of her confident voice. 'Your wish is my command.'

He rid himself of his clothes like they were on fire. Lying on the scratchy carpet, he looked to Caroline.

She smirked, peeling off her own clothes.

He didn't think he blinked even once as the material slid down her skin; first the strap of her dress, then her bra, her underwear . . . He held his breath as she stood naked over him. He was already so damn hard, but the view from below her was like an extra metal ring wrapping around the shaft of his penis.

She straddled his hips, her face all mischief.

It suits her, Hunter thought. He promised himself he was going to make sure she wore that expression more often.

'What now?' he rasped.

Her hands reached out to his and guided them above his head. She held them there. 'Now I'm going to ride you, of course.'

Her breasts pressed to his chest, hard nipples squashing against his muscles.

Hunter's hips bucked involuntarily underneath her, aroused just from that simple sentence.

'Woah, easy, cowboy. We haven't even started yet. At this rate, you'll come way before me.' Her mouth hovered near his ear, and her teeth nipped his earlobe.

'I think you talking this way might be my new favourite thing.'

Caroline let go of his hands, pushing herself up to a seating position. She pressed her palms against her thighs, studying his face. 'I've never done this but always wanted to.'

'Darling, you can do whatever you want to me. I'm at your mercy.'

She dragged her teeth across her bottom lip and tilted her head. 'Anything?'

'Anything.'

Her fingers wrapped around the head of his penis. 'Good. I haven't decided how merciful I'm going to be.'

Hunter slammed his eyes shut as her hand went up and down, a low groan escaping his throat whenever she moved over his glans. He reached his hand to cup her right breast, but she pushed it away.

'Did I say you could touch me?' she asked in a teasing tone.

'No.'

'Then, hands off.' She chuckled and looked round. 'Where are your condoms?'

Hunter turned his head to where his jeans lay in a heap. 'Back left pocket.'

Caroline stared at him with amusement. 'You carry condoms in your pocket?'

He looked into her eyes. 'It's a new thing. I've met this gorgeous doctor recently and she always turns me on.'

'Always, huh?' She grabbed his jeans, pulling out the foil wrapper. Tearing the top off, she wet her lips with her tongue, and Hunter bit back a moan just from the sight itself.

She rolled the condom over his penis, and pushed herself up, her thighs pressing his hard. 'Do you want to touch me?'

'God, yes.'

'Don't bring God into it. But maybe I'll allow it.' She raised her brow. 'One hand only.'

Hunter didn't have to be told twice; he squeezed her right breast, his breathing growing more laboured as it elicited a delicious moan from her.

Slowly, she lowered herself onto his penis, and his breath caught.

'Two hands, please.'

She chuckled, her fingernails pressing the sides of his ribs. 'Hm. I don't know.' She moved in an agonisingly slow circle. 'You think I'd like it better?'

'Yes,' Hunter growled, his voice becoming raspier with every motion of her hips. He held her left buttock with his other hand, digging his fingers into it hard. 'I think you'd like it.'

She moaned, her eyes closed, her head threw back with her hair spilling over her bare shoulders. 'Hunter.'

It was just his name, but he took it as not only permission but a sign. He moved his hand away from her ass and onto her breast.

As their joined bodies moved in rhythm, going from slow to soon more frantic, Hunter's mind went completely blank. It was all the feel of her around him, the walls of her vagina, her thighs, her fingers on his chest . . . His hands on her breasts, her ass . . .

Hot and sweaty mess.

Hunter wasn't sure if there was lightning flashes outside, but he was sure struck by one when Caroline came.

Her scream liquified his insides and pushed him over the edge.

CHAPTER THIRTY-THREE

Caroline

Caroline tried to convince herself there was nothing to tell and that there wasn't any need to bring Hunter up at work. Well, if she was honest with herself, maybe she didn't want to bring him up at all. Despite what she had told Gian, she hadn't found a way to start the topic up with Anna yet.

She didn't think she and Hunter were crossing any ethical lines. But sex had changed things. It somehow always did, either not having it or having it.

Most importantly for her, having it was the first time that she'd allowed herself to get lost in the moment. To enjoy the undeniable, electric connection that was developing between them and kept on pulling her in. She knew that she wouldn't be able to stay away. She didn't want to either.

Maybe she should feel guilty. Despite their mutual decision to split up, legally Finn was still her husband. And she *did* love him. But not like that. He had never made her feel the way Hunter did.

Her body felt hot every time she thought about their limbs tangled up in a passion she hadn't known was even possible.

Right now, Erin was the only one who knew the whole truth, but not for long. Caroline knew she had to speak with Anna to see if she should step away from the melanoma trial. It didn't feel right to keep working on it while doing whatever it was she was doing with Hunter. Of course, it wasn't him who was enrolled on the trial, it was his father. And she wasn't Alan's doctor, just someone who collected and analysed the data. The trial was an open label, which meant that all the participants received the active treatment. There was no risk of putting herself in a situation where she would have to choose between the trial's integrity and Hunter's father's health. However, it still didn't feel right.

What if Hunter asked her about the results? Or any other confidential information to which she had access, like the protocol or interim data? She'd never been in such a situation. They covered different situational judgement scenarios at medical school and beyond. *What should you do if a patient asks you out on a date? What should you do if the patient asks you for your social media profile? Why is it inappropriate to discuss medical care if you meet the patient in a supermarket?* But these were all based in the clinical setting.

Here, she felt a bit in the grey, and she didn't like it. She was still a doctor, although she wasn't currently practising. More to the point, she had a very strong sense of right and wrong. She didn't want to go any further in her personal life until she sorted this out.

At exactly 10.45 a.m., she finished adding in comments to a draft manuscript with recent data read-out from the multiple myeloma clinical trial and circulated it to the remaining authors. She checked Anna's Outlook calendar and felt a mix of relief and nervous anticipation when she saw an hour-long opening until lunchtime.

Now's as good a time as ever, she thought resolutely.

'Come in!' Anna's voice called through her office door as soon as Caroline knocked.

She took a deep breath and stepped inside.

It was a spacious, sunny room filled with modern, sharply designed furniture. Everything, from the big windows to the minimalistic bookshelves covering the entire wall to the neatly organised desk, was very different from the maximalist, moody décor in Anna and Gian's apartment.

The only personal touch seemed to be the photographs. There was one of Gian, proudly taking up space on the desk. Then there was one of a much younger Caroline, Clara and Caitlin; it must've been taken the last time Anna visited Aberdeen. The final photograph she recognised was of a younger Anna with a light-haired, radiant woman wearing red lipstick. *Siobhan.*

Caroline looked sadly into her mother's unmoving eyes but turned her head away before she got sucked into melancholy.

Anna looked up from her computer and gave Caroline a tired smile. 'Is everything OK?'

Caroline settled into the chair on the other side of Anna's desk, pushing herself tightly into the back of it. She folded her hands together on her lap and bit her lower lip. This felt a lot more embarrassing than she'd expected. She wasn't just talking to her aunt. She was about to have this conversation with *her boss*.

'I wanted to ask if I should step away from the melanoma

trial. Either Amira or Jake could step in and take over for me.'

Anna furrowed her brow and studied Caroline's face for a long moment.

'Why?' Anna's voice echoed with suspicion. 'When you got here, I asked if you wanted to work on this study. You said yourself that it was probably the most impactful one out of all the ones we're currently working on. Besides, neither Amira nor Jake are particularly interested in this area. Why would they want to take over on it?'

'Because it'd give them broader experience? Plus, it's a Phase III trial. We're already working on an important manuscript, which the company is hoping to publish in *New England Journal of Medicine*. It'd be a great opportunity for their résumés.'

'What about *your* résumé?'

'I'd still be working on other trials.'

Anna took a deep breath and looked at Caroline the way her mother had used to when she was worried about her. 'You didn't answer my initial question. Why do you want to step away from this trial?'

She slowly raised her head and looked straight into Anna's eyes. Without blinking, she said, 'I don't really want to step away from it. But I probably couldn't continue working on it if I was sort of involved with someone's family member, could I?'

If Anna was shocked, she didn't let it show. 'Whose family member?' she asked in the calmest voice.

'Alan Jackson's son.'

'Hunter?'

Caroline nodded, and that seemed to put an end to Anna's stoic composure. She stood and started pacing between her desk and the window, lacing her hands behind her neck. 'What do you mean by "*sort of involved*"?'

'It's a bit of a crazy story. You won't believe it.'

Anna stopped and gave her a stern look that said, '*Try me.*'

Caroline took a breath and started her tale.

When she finished, Anna asked slowly, 'The *friend* who you keep going out with? It's been Hunter the whole time?'

Caroline nodded, crossing her legs at her ankles.

Anna stopped pacing and sat back in her leather chair. 'But this has been going on for weeks. Months, even. Why are you only asking about stepping away from the trial now?'

'Because I like him a lot, Anna. It didn't feel right to keep going in deeper until I stepped away from the trial.'

'He isn't in the trial. And you're neither his nor his father's doctor,' Anna reminded her.

'I know,' Caroline said quietly, staring at the wall above Anna's shoulder. 'But it just doesn't feel right.'

'Well, I'm the principal investigator of this trial and I don't think there's any objection for you to continue working on it. You've done a lot of great work to date, especially on data analysis and writing up the draft manuscript. I don't even think you've met Alan in the centre, have you?'

Caroline shook her head. 'No, I haven't. Neither in the centre nor outside it. But what if Hunter asks me to discuss the study?'

'I don't know him well, but he doesn't strike me as the kind of person who would. Plus, if he does, you can just tell him that it's confidential and you can't talk about it. He'll understand. Besides . . .' Anna paused, chewing her bottom lip. She looked unsure of what she was about to say next. 'Look, I know you have access to all data, but this isn't something that is necessarily written down anywhere. What I tell you now is just between you and me. Promise me you won't tell Hunter, or anyone else about it.'

'Of course, I won't tell anyone,' Caroline replied, sitting up a bit straighter.

'I really shouldn't be telling you this,' Anna said, pushing her hair behind her ears and taking a deep breath. She looked at Caroline, conflict clearly written on her face. 'But . . . Damn. I told myself I'd never break patient confidentiality.'

'Then don't tell me,' Caroline said quickly, realising what this was about. 'You don't have to.'

'But I do.' Anna bit her lip and hesitated for another moment. 'I don't think Alan has much time left. His results aren't improving, and we're out of options. I'm afraid it's likely he's going to decline rapidly soon, and there won't be much anyone can do to help other than ensuring he's as comfortable as possible.'

Caroline felt her chest constrict as if something heavy was pushing against it. 'Do they know?' she asked quietly.

Anna gave a curt nod. She sighed and leaned back in her chair. 'Alan's been my patient for quite a while now, even before he joined the trial. I really hoped that we'd beat the odds for him, but it seems that cancer's winning once again.' She looked tired and somehow defeated.

'Have you discussed withdrawing from the trial? If he really doesn't have much time left, switching fully to palliative care might be a kinder option.'

'I told him as much. Well, I tried to. He's a very stubborn man. He's adamant that if he must go, he wants to do some good while he's still here. He truly believes that him staying in the trial might help the study and, ultimately, help another person in the future.'

'He isn't wrong,' Caroline said, mostly to herself.

This attitude wasn't unusual among terminally ill patients. She remembered her mother's resolve to do something '*good*' once she realised she wouldn't get better. She raised money for charity, wrote articles and even gave a radio interview to raise awareness of lung cancer in non-smokers. She was very passionate about telling others about her experience, hoping that it would ultimately lead to reducing the delay in diagnosis and improving the outcomes.

As if she could read her mind, Anna reached across the desk and took her hands in hers. 'What I'm trying to say is that Alan's most likely going to die, and soon. We're going to run another battery of comprehensive tests next week, but I can't say I'm optimistic. Hunter's very close with him. He's been accompanying him to every appointment, every surgery, scan – you name it. Even when you think you're prepared for it, you really aren't. He's likely going to need a lot of emotional support in the coming months. And you're only here for what, another seven or eight months . . . I just don't want you to get hurt, that's all.' Anna's voice trailed off as she finished clumsily.

Caroline pulled her hands away from her aunt and looked at her with a mild disbelief. 'So, you aren't bothered by the fact I'm working on this trial and seeing him privately, but you're worried that I'll, what, care too much?'

'It's not that! I just know that things between you and Finn are complicated and that you're in a vulnerable spot. Not just when it comes to Finn but with your career. You wanted to focus on what comes next for you – isn't that why you came here?'

'This is separate. And please don't bring Finn into this. I told you we're getting a divorce, there's no coming back from that.' Caroline swallowed. 'Hunter is like a breath of fresh air. I just feel happy when I'm with him. That's all. I know nothing will ever come of it, but if two adults want to enjoy each other's company, surely it isn't wrong?'

She felt her cheeks grow warmer.

Anna pinched the bridge of her nose and pushed the loose strands of her chestnut hair behind her ears. She closed her eyes, took a deep breath and when she spoke again, she looked and sounded very serious. 'You really do like him, don't you?'

'I do.'

'I can tell. I think you might find yourself more drawn in than you're thinking now.'

'It's . . . not like that. He's five years younger than me. He runs a family ranch in Oklahoma. Even though I'm not sure what I want to do, the past months of working here made me realise I don't want to give up practising medicine. I just need to figure out what exactly that looks like for me. But I can't stay here, I want to go back to Scotland.'

'We often make decisions we didn't think possible when it's about love.'

Now it was Caroline's turn to laugh. 'Love?' She shook her head. 'He's handsome, funny, and so easy to talk to. Maybe if I was someone else, I could let myself think it could lead to more than it ever will. But given that I'm me and the circumstances are what they are, this will never be more than a bit of short-term fun. We'll end up going our separate ways and keep hold of some fond memories, that's all.'

Anna grinned, shaking her head. 'Oh, honey, this is how all the greatest love stories start.'

Caroline opened her mouth but then closed it again. She couldn't think of a suitable retort to this. Instead, she got up, brushed the invisible dust off her trousers and coughed. She suddenly remembered the real reason why she was in Anna's office.

'So, you're OK with me staying on the melanoma trial?'

Anna stood as well. 'I am. But only if you are.'

Caroline nodded, feeling like a weight had been taken off her shoulders. Without thinking, she walked to the other side of Anna's desk and gave her a tight hug.

Anna hugged her back, kissing the top of her head. She then leaned down and whispered in Caroline's ear, 'Things will work out just fine, you'll see.'

CHAPTER THIRTY-FOUR

Caroline

Next morning, Caroline realised her headache from last night was mostly gone. The inside of the apartment was quiet. Anna and Gian had gone to Gian's cousin's engagement party last night and stayed over.

She pulled her navy woollen cardigan tighter around her chest as she walked into the kitchen.

Anna and Gian were great hosts. She had got used to living with them, the sound of their voices and laughter. Often, they'd also have the radio playing in the background. Happiness seemed to bounce off the walls.

The suffocating silence this morning reminded Caroline of her and Finn's place. It hadn't always been that way, but for the past four years it had grown progressively quieter. Like the flat itself became oversaturated with resentment and hurt. It was a vicious circle of her trying to get closer and Finn pushing her away. Repeatedly, until it all bubbled over, and they agreed divorce was the only option left.

Without realising what she was doing, Caroline practically jogged to the breakfast bar where a cream-coloured radio stood, and eagerly pressed the 'on' button. Turning up the volume on one of the country music stations, she closed her eyes.

Last year, she couldn't even bring herself to imagine a situation in which she'd even consider going out with anyone else but Finn. And yet here she was.

There were no words in her repertoire to truly describe what she felt for Hunter. His probing question from the night after the karaoke last Friday nagged her mercilessly.

But if you're asking me to put a label on what we have, I can't. Can you?

Always a high academic achiever, she used to be the one with an answer to every question. If she didn't know something, she would go off to the library or track down a teacher or an older student who was able to tell her the answer. She'd search the internet, not leaving any stone unturned.

Yet, she had no answer to the question about her feelings for Hunter. Worse, there was not a search engine she could ask.

Trying to steady her shaking hand, she reached into the fridge and took out a half-empty carton of juice. She poured herself a glass, but then left it sitting on the counter. Her breathing came in ragged spasms, and she was trying to hold on to the present moment. A single tear rolled down her cheek. She ignored it, standing motionless.

It scared her how much Hunter not feeling like he could tell her about what happened to his fiancée bothered her. It shouldn't have; they weren't together. It had nothing to do with her.

And that's why it petrified her. Somewhere between spending time with him and getting to know him, she had started caring.

Even admitting that much made her wince.

It's because of the physical bond. It's because it's new, and exciting.

But if it was just about the physical bond, why had she been dreading seeing him again after what Anna had told her yesterday about Alan's prognosis? She knew she'd struggle keeping her emotions from her face. Finn had told her in the past she'd make a lousy poker player, and she had to agree. Her face was an open book.

How was she meant to look Hunter in the eye, pick up where they left off, and not tell him the one thing that would shatter him?

Deep down, she knew the answer to that question. Any extra day, hour or minute of hope was worth its weight in gold. It never felt like it in the moment, but once the hammer of despair came crushing down, the knowledge it had been delayed as much as possible could sometimes be soothing. Not immediately – later, often much later.

She dried her eyes and reached for the glass.

For her, that realisation had only come in the final year of medical school. Seven years after her mother passed away. And even now, it didn't make losing her any easier.

HUNTER: *I'll swing by the centre this afternoon. My dad left his glasses behind when Buck took him for scans yesterday. Any chance I could see you?*

Caroline stared at the unanswered message on her screen for what felt like the tenth time that morning.

'You know, phones usually don't bite when you pick them up,' Amira teased from her desk.

'I know they don't,' Caroline replied. *Though this one might*, a voice whispered in her ear.

It should've been an easy answer. She hadn't seen him for a few days and wasn't meant to until Saturday. Another three days. She wanted to see him. But at the same time, she didn't.

If Alan had his scans done yesterday, they were preparing for the multidisciplinary team meeting to discuss his case next week. The meeting Anna had told her about. One that likely was not going to go well.

'Are you all right? You seem to be somewhere far away,' Amira said again, a dose of concern injected in her question.

Caroline swivelled away from her computer screen to face her. She really appreciated the friendly work relationship that they had managed to build, despite the shaky start when Amira hadn't even tried to hide her distrust and suspicion. There was often an unspoken animosity between bench scientists and medics, an easy trap to fall into between ambitious perfectionists. Caroline had briefly experienced it during medical school, but thought it was more about competitive streak between different degrees at the University of Edinburgh, rather than the medical field itself.

Chatting to Amira made her workdays go faster.

'I'm fine. Thanks for asking,' Caroline gave her a grateful smile. 'How are things with Jake?'

Amira paled, her spine straightening like someone had replaced it with a metal rod. 'Why? Did he say anything to you?'

Caroline raised her brow. 'I haven't spoken with him since before he went on leave the other week.'

Amira slumped into her chair with relief. 'He's moving his gran into a care home in Florida. He'll be back next week. We've been . . . texting.'

'Texting?'

Amira bit her bottom lip, grinning from ear to ear. 'Texting. Nothing serious.'

'I'm happy to hear. He's a good guy.'

Amira blinked. 'Nothing to hear because nothing's going on.'

Caroline chuckled as she turned back to her desk. 'If you say so.'

She stared at Hunter's message again. With a heavy sigh, she picked up her phone and typed: *Depends what time you get here? I can get away at 5 but not before. And I have plans for lunch.*

He replied almost instantly. Seeing his name pop up on her screen twisted a knife in her gut. Normally, he didn't have time to text during the day. It was too busy at the ranch. If he was able to message her right away, it meant he was either taking his time or stressing over Alan's results.

> HUNTER: *I'll come round just after 4 and meet you in the centre's lobby? P.S. Lunch plans, huh? Should I be jealous?*

> CAROLINE: *Sounds good, see you then x Hope you find your dad's glasses! P.S. Yes, jealous of a seventeen-year-old girl – I told you about Yolanda, right? It's Wednesday – her mum's having chemo and we're having lunch together.*

She put her phone into a desk drawer so it wouldn't distract her again and opened another Excel spreadsheet with interim results from the bladder cancer trial.

Yolanda wasn't at the usual table in the hospital cafeteria.

Caroline sat on the uncomfortable plastic chair, watching the faces of the people milling in and out, searching for the characteristic black fringe.

Twenty minutes had passed and there was no sign of her.

She didn't have her phone number, and even if she did, what would she say? They weren't friends or colleagues; they weren't family. Yet somehow, over the past few weeks, they had fallen into a routine of chatting over lunch.

As a doctor, this kind of arrangement would be inappropriate when it came to a family member of a patient. But Caroline wasn't a practising doctor just now, and Yolanda's mother wasn't her patient. A half-hour chat over lunch was completely different from what she and Hunter were doing, but the principle was similar.

Don't get attached. Don't get involved.

It seemed that she had been failing in more than one instance.

'Is this chair taken?'

She looked up at a man in teal nursing scrubs who stood by the table.

Caroline shook her head, rising. 'I was just leaving.'

Checking her watch, she decided she would check the centre's lobby, where she and Yolanda first met. Maybe she'd sought refuge there today.

And if she's not there, you're just going to get back to work and not dwell on it.

Yolanda was awkwardly perched on the black sofa, just as

she had suspected. As soon as Caroline stepped into the lobby, she knew.

Yolanda didn't even look her way. She didn't say anything. But Caroline knew. It was like a thick blanket of unmistakable grief had wrapped around the girl. Which could only mean one thing: her mother had died.

Caroline sat on the sofa, right next to her. She didn't say anything, just sat there. Hoping that her presence could bring her even a small semblance of comfort.

'My mom's gone,' Yolanda croaked, her voice broken and throaty, like she had been crying for hours on end.

'I'm so, so sorry.'

Yolanda just nodded. She kept nodding, slowly rocking back and forth, her eyes glazed and distant.

'Do you want to talk about it?' Caroline asked softly.

Yolanda shook her head.

'OK. I'll just sit here for a while, and if you change your mind . . . Well, I'll sit here.'

She heard Yolanda swallow hard, her breathing laboured. 'I'm just so relieved that she isn't suffering anymore. I really am. But . . . I just don't know who I am in the world without her.'

In that moment, it took Caroline every ounce of strength she had not to tear up. It would be unprofessional, and it wouldn't help Yolanda.

She balled her hands into fists and took a steadying breath, before speaking. 'It'll be like this for a while. Nothing will make much sense and you're going to miss your mum every day. At first, it'll be a constant ache in the pit of your stomach. The kind of pain that will make you think you're going to fall apart.' She reached for the girl's hand. 'But you won't because you're strong. Your mother loved you very much. Don't ever forget that.'

'I know she did,' Yolanda whispered, fresh tears slowly rolling down. 'I loved her too. I'll never stop loving her.'

A small piece broke off Caroline's heart, the pain visceral.

'It just feels like I'll never laugh again. Like there'll be no more joy.' Yolanda sniffed. 'It sounds stupid, but it feels that way.'

'Eventually, you'll start enjoying life again. Little things at first, like the taste of food or smiling during a funny moment in a movie. Then, the guilt will come. You'll feel bad for laughing and living while your mother isn't there to share these moments. In the end though, the pain will ease up and you'll be able to breathe again. However, it'll never fully disappear.'

Yolanda looked at her as if seeing her for the first time. 'How old were you when your mother died?'

Caroline blinked and when she opened her eyes, she felt like she was nineteen again, clutching her mother's limp hand, her father's arms dragging her from the side of the hospice bed, repeating in a voice so raw and unlike anything she had ever heard: *'She's gone, honey. She's at peace now.'*

Her bottom lip quivered. 'Nineteen. I was your age when she got diagnosed.'

Yolanda sniffed again.

'I'm sorry you had to join that awful club of motherless women,' Caroline said.

'Me too.' Yolanda reached for Caroline's hand. 'Thank you. For talking to me. Not just today, but over the last few weeks. It . . . helped.'

Caroline squeezed her hand warmly. 'Is your dad coming?'

Yolanda had told her before her parents were divorced. Her father lived in Las Vegas with his second wife.

'He is. He said he's going to stay here with me until the end of the academic year, so I can finish high school.'

'That's nice of him.'

Yolanda let out a half-laugh, half-snort, all puffy eyes and unspeakable heartache. 'Yeah. It was a surprisingly decent offer.' She wiped her eyes. 'I guess he isn't the worst, after all.'

Just as she said it, her phone vibrated in her pocket. She took it out, glancing at the screen. 'That's him. I probably should take this.'

They stood and Caroline gave Yolanda a sad smile. 'Again, I'm so sorry. Take care, OK?'

The girl nodded. 'I will. Who knows, maybe I'll even become a doctor. And save someone's life, like my mom's.'

Caroline's chest squeezed tightly. This was the reason she had applied to medical school. She wanted to help people. She wanted to keep up to date with all the latest research, see the day when a patient who would've died fifty years earlier not only lived, but thrived. She wanted to do her best for patients – the ones she could help, and the ones who she couldn't.

It was a naive notion of a young girl.

And it was breathtakingly beautiful in its purity.

Tears clouded her vision, and she was glad that Yolanda had already walked outside.

I can't give this up. I don't want to throw it away.

She swallowed a silent sob.

The sharp clutches of reheated grief let go of her throat when she spotted Hunter.

He stopped right in front of her, his smile warm, and her freeze-dried heart thawed.

'Hi,' he said.

Caroline threw her arms around his waist, pulling him in for a hug. 'Hi,' she whispered into his leather jacket.

She breathed in his familiar scent, and her heart rate normalised.

His hand rested at the back of her head. 'Did something happen?'

She let go, taking a wobbly step back. 'Just a long day. It's good to see you.'

'The feeling's mutual.' He lifted a glasses case in the air. 'Got Dad's glasses. The nurses had found them in the changing room.'

Caroline laughed. 'He seems to forget his glasses a lot.'

'You have no idea; it's a whole thing.'

She looked into his eyes. The guilt from carrying with her the knowledge capable of destroying his world right here, right now, weighed heavy on her shoulders.

Would it have helped Yolanda? Or me? Knowing, when there's nothing that can be done? And the results might be better than Anna thinks; maybe all isn't lost. Maybe Alan beats the odds.

'I was thinking of going for a walk by the river. Want to come?' Hunter asked.

Caroline nodded. 'Sure. Let's go.'

She took his outstretched hand, simultaneously trying to channel her strength into his heart, and take some of his warmth to keep hers from breaking; for Yolanda, for herself, for him.

CHAPTER THIRTY-FIVE

Hunter

Hunter had always thought the passing of time a strange concept. There were days that dragged mercilessly, usually when he was waiting for something good to happen. Then there was time that almost equated to a heartbeat. In principle, he knew time was measured and went by the same way. An hour was always an hour, however you looked at it. Yet, the weeks they had waited for the next set of tests for his father had brought on a low-grade, underlying but ever-present heaviness in the pit of his stomach. And they'd gone by before he knew it.

Today was the day they were going to find out what the results meant after the battery of tests and scans last week.

Hunter got out of his truck, zipped up his jacket and looked at the imposing building of Rouken Cancer Center. Trying not to let his mind race, he took a deep breath and walked round to open the passenger door.

'Here, Dad.' He helped Alan step down onto the pavement.

Alan coughed and shook his hand off, taking his best black Stetson off and checking it out. He made sure the shape was correct and put it back on.

'Is Buck coming?' Alan asked, pushing his glasses up his nose. He tried to sound carefree and conversational, but Hunter detected hesitation.

Hunter nodded. 'He called me this morning when he was setting off. Said he'll meet us there.'

Alan opened his mouth but then closed it. He looked like he'd aged another couple of years in the past few weeks. His arms trembled, but he shook the feeling off and started walking with purpose towards the entrance.

Hunter followed him.

Buck walked into the conference room on the fourth floor, letting the door slam behind him. 'Dad.' He enveloped Alan in a big hug and didn't let him go for a long moment.

When they separated, Alan sat back down and crossed his arms over his chest.

Buck settled on the uncomfortable chair next to him and nodded to Hunter in acknowledgement. Words weren't necessary. They both wanted to be here for their father. But the love they had for him, and for each other, didn't help with making the day feel any less unbearable.

None of the Jackson men spoke while the clock ticked away the minutes to 1 p.m. Half an hour felt like half a day . . . Finally, the door opened again. Dr Anna Kennedy walked in first, putting on a warm smile.

'Good afternoon, Alan. Hunter.' She nodded the greeting to him. 'And Buck, nice to see you again.'

Two men and a tall woman walked in all wearing lanyards

with the centre's staff ID cards. They followed Dr Kennedy's lead and sat at the top of the table.

Dr Kennedy looked to Alan. 'Are we waiting for anyone else?'

'Not from our side, Doc.'

'Mary isn't here?' she asked, her voice a bit quieter.

Alan chuckled good-naturedly. 'You know, she was beating herself up for days. Changing her mind all the time. First, she wanted to come. Then she didn't. I figured she felt she needed to, for me. But I didn't want to make it harder on her.' Alan met Dr Kennedy's eyes and held her gaze.

'Not after what happened last time. She still has nightmares after I died and came back to life after that surgery. It's going to be hard on her anyway, won't it? I can tell by how solemn you all look. Hope you don't play poker as that ain't a good face for it. Just get straight to it, Doc.' Alan slumped in his chair.

Hunter had never seen his father look more equally defeated and at peace. He seemed to have already decided what the results meant before they'd even heard them.

Dr Kennedy leaned against the top of the table and laced her fingers together. 'Alan, we have your test results. I invited some of my colleagues from our multidisciplinary team to help me walk you all through them. Dr Travis Rourke is a neurosurgeon, Dr Susan Ceehil is our palliative medicine lead, and Mr Alex Kim is one of our community nurse practitioners. I'll ask them to step in to help me explain the results as we go.'

She pressed a button on the remote and stood. The big TV screen mounted on the wall flickered to life and the first scan showed up. 'The symptoms that you've recently been experiencing, including the headaches, some balance issues, and weakness in your arms and legs are all likely connected to the new metastases in your brain.' She zoomed in on the scan and outlined the white blobs with a laser pointer.

Hunter held his breath and thought he'd never let it out again. There were seven blobs, big enough for him to see from the other end of the table. He instinctively looked at his father, who just nodded slowly.

Alan looked more resigned than surprised. 'And these brain things . . . Can we treat them? Like we did with the earlier ones?'

Dr Kennedy looked to her right side and gave a small nod to Dr Rourke, who cleared his throat. 'Unfortunately, these are very different from the metastases you had removed before your cancer returned. To start with, five out of seven of them are in your frontal lobes. It's this region here.'

Dr Kennedy used the pointer again, drawing a rough circle as Dr Rourke continued speaking.

'This part of your brain is essentially responsible for making you who you are. They have an important function in voluntary movement, language skills, behaviour, and emotions. If we were to attempt surgical removal of these lesions, due to their size, it'd come with damage to this area. This could lead to a variety of symptoms, from paralysis to loss of speech. You could also experience mood fluctuations, changes to your personality or behaviour . . . That's if the surgery was even a success.'

Dr Rourke paused and consulted a sheet of paper on the table. Hunter could see his eyes move as he read. Then, he looked up, meeting Alan's eyes. 'I must say, after reviewing all your history and current results, I'd strongly advise against the surgery. We can of course investigate it, if this is something you want to explore, but that would be my professional recommendation.'

'I see.' Alan nodded slowly. He furrowed his brows, staring at the image of his brain. He bit his lip and, looking directly at Dr Kennedy, said, 'If we don't do anything, these are going to kill me, right?'

'Yes. Not on their own, but as you know this isn't the only place your cancer has spread to. And sadly, it isn't responding to treatment.'

The atmosphere grew heavy with the effort Alan was putting into avoiding eye contact with his sons. Keeping his focus on Dr Kennedy, he asked, 'How long?'

'It's always hard to estimate and put an exact number, but it's likely weeks, not months. I'm so sorry, Alan. There isn't much else we can do. We're at the end of the road we discussed before.'

Hunter closed his eyes. There was a difference between thinking you're prepared to face something and experiencing it. His mouth went dry, but he felt like he was drowning from the inside.

Buck sneered and kicked the table leg in frustration. 'Aren't surgeons meant to want to cut people open? What's the point of saying you don't recommend it? Isn't it worth the risk if it can save his life?'

Dr Rourke looked to Buck with a mix of sadness and empathy. 'As Dr Kennedy said, there's unfortunately not much we can do. We could try to remove the lesions, but given your father's overall health and prognosis, it most likely wouldn't save his life in a way that we all would like it to. In the best-case scenario, it could add a few months. The lesions would most likely grow back within a year . . . And he could experience all the symptoms I outlined. That is, if he survived the surgery.'

'But there's a chance! You said it yourself. Maybe you're

wrong and they wouldn't grow back. You keep saying "*most likely*", "*could*" . . . Not much certainty, is there? I say we should try.'

'No!'

They all jumped in their seats as Alan's voice boomed through the room.

He pressed his lips tight. 'I don't want to try. I put all the fight I had in me to try to beat this thing. Looks like it won, after all . . . I want to spend my last days in peace. Not being prodded and cut open. I want to be myself when I meet my maker.'

His expression softened as he looked at Buck. 'I'm ready, son. Let's not fight over this. I want to eat my favourite food, maybe re-read my favourite book. I want to go on one last ride. I want to hold your mother in my arms and cherish all the memories we've made over the years together. I want to fall asleep and wake up in my own bed. For as long as I can. And when I go, I want to go quietly. Pain free.' He looked to Dr Ceehil and Mr Kim. 'That's why you're both here, right?'

They started discussing the options for managing his symptoms and maintaining his quality of life. Hunter knew he should be listening, participating, and taking note of all they said. But he couldn't. Everything that followed his father's speech felt like an out of body experience. One that would recur often in weeks to come.

The sun had set over an hour ago. Hunter had watched it travel south and disappear behind the horizon while he rigidly sat in the armchair. An untouched glass of whisky sat on the coffee table, next to his phone. The eerie silence in the small, rented house normally made him uneasy. He usually put on some music in the background or the TV, just to draw a thin blanket of noise over the loneliness. Right now, though, he was glad for the stillness.

It felt appropriate.

After the meeting at the centre, Buck had insisted on driving their father back home. Alan didn't mind whether he got into a Ford or a Chevy, so there wasn't much argument on his side. When he'd closed the door behind him and fiddled with fastening the seatbelt, Hunter and Buck had faced each other on the outside. With awkwardness and unfamiliarity, they had both made a move as if they wanted to embrace each other in a comforting hug but thought better of it.

Hunter had followed them to the ranch, and all three of them had walked into the house together. Mary had been sitting at the kitchen table, messing around with some crocheting pattern. She'd leaped to her feet when she heard the creak of the opening door.

Her hopeful smile had faded into despair as soon as her eyes met Alan's. Hunter and Buck had given their parents some privacy and sat quietly on the veranda.

They could still hear their mother's cry and their father's broken voice as he was trying to comfort her.

Snapping out of the earlier memory from the day, Hunter picked up the whisky glass. He rocked it gently from side to side, intently gazing at how the amber liquid swirled against the sides. He raised it to his mouth, but instead of taking a sip, he sniffed it.

The aroma woke a memory of drinking the very same whisky with his father on his twenty-first birthday. Alan thought this was the first time his son had ever tasted alcohol. It wasn't, of course. But Hunter had never told him. He'd faked an eager anticipation as his father slowly poured a modest single measure into two glasses on the veranda. They'd sat in comfortable chairs; the sun was just setting. It was the middle of the summer. Hunter had come back home from college and was helping at the ranch, while training for some rodeos. Alan had explained how good whisky should be appreciated, and how you should always smell it first. *'You don't drink good whisky to get drunk on it. You drink it because you enjoy the taste. You appreciate its history, its flavour and the process that went into producing the bottle in front of you. You can get drunk on cheap beer or vodka. But never whisky.'*

Back in the present, Hunter tipped the glass and felt the warmth spreading from his tongue all the way to his gut. His breath caught and he continued drinking, downing the rest. As he was getting ready to pour another measure, he heard a timid knock on the door. His brows furrowed. He got up, walked to the door and stepped back in surprise.

Before he could say anything, Caroline threw her arms around his neck and hugged him tightly.

His body was rigid at first, but the warmth of her touch chased some of the tension away. Only then did he realise that this simple gesture was something he had been needing all day.

Sighing, he hugged her back, burying his nose in the crook of her neck. They stood like this for a moment, just frozen in an embrace more powerful than any words. When she let him go, she took a step back and gave him a small, sad smile.

'After you called, I just thought you needed a hug. I borrowed Anna's car and drove here. I can leave if you prefer to be alone.'

'You drove almost forty miles just to give me a hug?'

'Like I said, I just thought you needed one.' She took a deep breath.

He looked at her with wonder. He'd called her after he left the ranch because he didn't know who else he could talk to. Or, if he was more honest with himself, he didn't want to talk to anyone else.

And she came.

His chest heaved, filled with unbearable emotions he had been holding at bay all day. He hadn't shed a tear, trying to be strong. Trying to be the shoulder to cry on for his mother and Meg. Now, it felt like the floodgates of sadness opened.

'Thank you. It means more than I can say,' he finally managed, his voice broken.

'I'm so sorry you're going through it, Hunter. I wish there was something I could do to help . . . But no matter what I or anyone else says or does, it won't change anything.' She looked at him. 'If you want me to go, I'll go. If you want me to stay, I'll stay. But if you need it, I can be someone to lean on through these coming weeks. Just let me know what I can do to help.'

Caroline took his hand in hers and the moment their skin touched, something cut through the last thread of his restraint.

Violent sobs rocked his entire body. He collapsed onto his knees, letting out everything he felt but couldn't say. Tears were rolling down his cheeks, and he cried for his father. He cried for how unfair the world was.

And he cried for himself, since he couldn't picture a world in which his father no longer existed.

Caroline kneeled beside him, tentatively touching his elbow.

He looked at her through tears, wordlessly asking her to stay.

She enveloped him in a surprisingly strong embrace, rocking

back and forth on her feet. Her presence felt like the anchor amid the storm. Right now, this was all he needed and wanted to focus on.

Trying to stay whole.

CHAPTER THIRTY-SIX

Caroline

As November drew to an end, the rich autumn foliage was replaced by darker brown and black rotting leaves. Everywhere Caroline went, she could swear there was a lingering smell of pumpkin spice and cinnamon. The last Monday of the month came round fast, starting the final countdown to Thanksgiving. Initially, Anna and Gian had wanted to throw a small party for some close friends. However, the list had quickly grown from five to twenty-five.

Caroline had spent most of the weekend helping Gian with shopping and putting decorations together. Their big dining table was now fully extended with extra chairs assembled around it. Anna had ordered food from the local restaurant that offered catering, but Gian had insisted on making all the desserts herself. Anna didn't put up much of a fight against that idea, which was probably wise. No one was able to match Gian's brilliance in this department.

Although Caroline couldn't wait for the day and the food itself, she was also longing for some time off work, even if it was just two extra days added onto the weekend. Lately, her days had been full to the brim. In the run up to the ASH congress, it seemed like her work never finished. In addition to the clinical trials and teaching at the university, she'd got involved in writing up a qualitative study run by the centre on quality-of-life outcomes reported by patients with bladder cancer.

As the time passed, her conviction that she wanted to apply to oncology training once she got back grew stronger. The only reason why she hadn't considered it before was simple: her own wounds were still too raw. She'd thought emergency medicine would shield her from forming emotional attachment. It was meant to protect her. You only got to briefly see patients coming through the door, without any risk of building a longer rapport. Working on clinical trials and meeting patients with cancer had rekindled her passion. She hadn't been ready for it during medical school or after she finished her foundation training. But she believed she was ready now. Meeting Yolanda, their last conversation, had played a significant role in that.

Oncology wasn't going to be an easy speciality, she knew that. There would be high highs and very low lows. Yet if the good outweighed the bad, if she could make even a small difference in one patient's life, she hoped it'd be worth it.

She'd kept the word she gave Hunter, too, on being a shoulder to lean on whenever he needed it. Following the karaoke night, her first instinct was to distance herself from him. After all, there couldn't be any way forward for them. It didn't matter that they couldn't define what they had. She couldn't quite put a single word or emotion on these feelings, but he wasn't just a handsome guy she enjoyed sleeping with. Although their sex was *so great*.

Caroline had had this vague idea that sex should be pleasurable when she was younger. At first, it didn't bother her when all her friends started having it and exchanging tales of their first times. She'd listened and nodded, asking some questions to show interest. However, as she'd got older, she'd felt a physical void every time Finn pulled away from her when they were making out.

She wanted and needed more.

Caroline bit her lip, thinking how naive she was. But she hadn't known any better. Hunter had showed her pleasure, in its fullest meaning. When they were together, she felt drunk on the ecstasy. There was nothing that could compare to that moment, right before she came. When it felt like every single nerve cell in her body was on fire.

Sometimes, she wondered whether meeting Hunter was the biggest blessing or the most horrible curse. He had showed her exactly what she'd been missing. Before, she'd had no idea. But knowing it now, could she see herself giving it up?

Caroline was sitting in her bedroom, looking over the ASH agenda and highlighting which sessions she wanted to attend, when the doorbell rang. She didn't get up as she knew Anna was in the living room. But then it rang again.

'Caroline! Can you get it? I'm busy with something just now.' Anna yelled over the high-pitched sound.

Caroline pushed herself away from the desk and strode through the hallway to open the front door. As soon as she did, her jaw dropped in a mix of shock and delight.

'See, I told you Anna and Gian kept the secret! Car, you look like you've seen a ghost!'

The taller, older woman chuckled as the younger one, who looked so like her, elbowed her, clearly amused.

Caroline realised her mouth was still open, so she closed it, still gaping at her sisters.

'Oh, come on, I know we don't look the best after travelling all the way from Dublin, but I thought you'd be happy to see us.' Caitlin shook her head with mock disapproval and pulled her into an enthusiastic hug.

Once she let go of her, Caroline looked at Clara. 'Of course I'm happy to see you but . . . What are you doing here? Who's staying with Vic?'

'She has a father, doesn't she?' Clara shrugged, wide grin moving across her lips. 'It's great to see you, Car. We've missed you.'

'I've missed you too.' Caroline observed Caitlin moving their suitcases into the hallway. 'But I don't understand, why are you here?'

'Well, they wanted to spend Thanksgiving with us.' Anna walked out of the bathroom, beaming at the sight of all three of her nieces. She hugged both Caitlin and Clara in greeting. 'I can't believe how grown up you are, Cait!' she exclaimed. 'Remind me, how old are you now? I swear you were like ten when I saw you last.'

'I'm twenty-six, and you saw me at Caroline's wedding. It wasn't that long ago.' She rolled her eyes, but Caroline noticed a barely noticeable smile tugging at her lips.

'Four years,' Caroline whispered, more to herself than to anyone else.

They all looked at her.

Clara was the first one who broke the charged silence. 'Anyway! We're here now, and that's all that matters. We're staying for a week, and hope to stay up late, see the sights and hear all about your adventures.'

Anna shot her a meaningful look.

'And your work, of course,' Clara added.

Caroline walked up to her and threw an arm round her shoulders. 'This is the best surprise ever.' Then she looked down at Clara's baby bump. 'And you're pregnant!'

Clara laughed, putting her palm on her belly. 'I am! Twenty-two weeks yesterday.' Her eyes glowed with happiness.

Caroline beamed at her. 'You look so great.'

'She won't shup up about the miraculous anti-sickness pills she's been taking this time round,' Caitlin supplied. 'Honestly, I've lost count of how many times I've heard about it.'

'Well, they literally kept me sane in the first trimester.' Clara shrugged.

With that, Anna took them to another guest bedroom, which she'd managed to get ready for their arrival without Caroline noticing.

Caroline's cheeks hurt from smiling and laughing. She couldn't remember the last time they had spent so much time together, just the three of them. It must've been before Clara's wedding. Caitlin was still too young to drink. They'd gone to Croatia, passing the days with sightseeing and trying local cuisine, and the nights dancing under the stars.

The memory of that week made her pensive. So much had changed since then, but when she looked at Clara and Caitlin, she realised that all these changes made them who they were today. The best sisters a woman could ask for.

'Why are you so quiet, Car? Hope you aren't secretly plotting how to ditch us.' Caitlin popped another black olive in her mouth and turned round, trying to locate a waiter to order more wine.

They'd come to a family-owned Italian restaurant in the neighbourhood. Their chicken parmigiana had quickly become Caroline's favourite dish since her arrival. They'd invited Anna and Gian to join them, but they had refused, saying they needed to finish preparations for the party. Caroline suspected that they were trying to give the sisters time to enjoy one another's company.

'What? Of course I'm not!' Caroline jabbed the last olive from the starter sharing dish with a wooden stick and looked at it for a moment before eating it. 'I was just thinking about the last time we spent real quality time together.'

'Croatia.' Clara nodded, corners of her mouth raising in a content smile.

'Ah, that was the holiday . . . Though I'm still not over the fact you were so strict with my drinking,' Caitlin cut in, having ordered another glass of merlot.

Clara stared at her. 'You were way too young. Plus, it seems like you're making up for lost time.'

Caroline snorted as she saw Caitlin go wide-eyed at Clara.

'I knew I should've never told you I was planning to come. Could've had a lovely Thanksgiving without you.'

'Really? You had no idea how to book the flights. And who paid for them? Who's going to pay for your meals and drinks out? Either me or Caroline, because we're the ones with real jobs. We've grown up, which you don't seem to know how to do,' Clara uttered.

Caitlin's face went red and she dropped her eyes onto the white cotton table runner.

Caroline took a deep breath and put a hand on Clara's wrist. She leaned over to her and said in a low voice, 'can you give her a break, please? I'm grateful you're both here, but don't fight. You can do it on the way back. Or whenever. You see each other often enough. I don't get to see either of you nearly as much as I'd like. Let's just have great, sisterly bonding time this week.'

Clara licked her bottom lip and sighed. She turned to Caitlin. 'I'm sorry, Caitlin. That was mean.'

'It was. But apology accepted,' Caitlin responded, tension draining from her face.

Their main courses arrived, and Caroline felt instant relief. Not only because the food smelled amazing, but also because the timing was just right to naturally bring in a change of topic.

They spoke about Victoria, and their father and Nora. Then they discussed Thanksgiving and made some plans for the coming days. The atmosphere almost got back to what it felt like when they'd entered the restaurant. Almost.

As Caroline chewed her chicken, she had a feeling that this week was going to be a long one.

HUNTER: *Do you want to come over later tonight? I know you have this big party, but after everyone's gone. We could have our own Thanksgiving, with less food and more things to be thankful for . . .*

CAROLINE: *I'd love to, but I can't. My sisters are here. They've come for a week as a surprise, to spend Thanksgiving with me, Anna and Gian.*

HUNTER: *That's great! I know how much you've missed them. Sounds like you're going to have amazing time together. I won't bother you then while they're here.*

CAROLINE: *You aren't bothering me. But I also thought it might be better. I wouldn't want to distract you from the holidays with your family.*

HUNTER: *You're right. After all, it's my Dad's last one.*

CAROLINE: *That's not why I said it.*

HUNTER: *I know. But the realization just hit me.*

Caroline continued looking at her phone, but no further message arrived.

It was Thanksgiving morning, and she was still in bed. Hearing the faint sound of chatter from the kitchen, she swung her legs over the edge of the bed and put her slippers on. She pulled on her dressing gown and brushed her hair, pulling it into a messy ponytail. There'd be time to properly get ready later. The guests wouldn't arrive until 4 p.m. Her reflection smiled at her widely from the square mirror.

Just as she was about to leave her room, her phone buzzed with an incoming message. She unlocked it and felt an ache in the middle of her chest.

HUNTER: *Buck, Lorna and the kids are coming over so it's going to be a good one, too. We're going to make memories to fill us with joy for the time when he's gone. It's weird, thinking about it like that . . . But I guess, in a way, it's a bit poetic, isn't it? Anyway. Have a wonderful day. Enjoy your first Thanksgiving! Hope it's as grand as you imagined.*

CAROLINE: *You too, Hunter. Make those memories.*

The party was a roaring success.

Caroline felt like a character in one of the special holiday episodes of an American TV series. She knew this was going to be the best turkey she had ever had, and it was outstanding. It wasn't just the way it tasted, but the whole ritual of watching Anna, already tipsy on some cocktail concoction courtesy of Clara, carve it at the head of the table. And listening to all the guests gush over Gian's desserts, then seeing her blushed but proud face. Caitlin sampling pumpkin pie for the first time and trying to hide that she hated it. Caroline had to stop herself from laughing out loud when she ran into the kitchen and, after checking no one had followed her, spat it into a napkin and quickly dumped it in the bin.

'You don't fancy the pie?' Caroline mocked, taking out another bottle of Riesling from the wine cooler.

Caitlin didn't answer, reaching across for her sister's glass instead and downing the half that was left in it.

'Hey! That was mine.'

'Sorry, Car.' She wiped her mouth with a grey cardigan sleeve. 'Had to get rid of this taste. It's official, I hate pumpkin. Why do they ruin perfectly good pies with it?'

Caroline shrugged and recalled her conversation with Hunter on the very same topic. She smiled in a way that people with sweet secrets did.

Caitlin narrowed her eyes and walked up to the counter. They stood there for a moment in companionable silence until Caitlin blurted out in one breath, 'What's going on with you and Finn? I messaged him several times when I was thinking of coming here to surprise you. Asked if he wanted to tag along. He hasn't responded. It's so unlike him.'

Caroline bit her lip. She turned round, took the corkscrew, opened the Riesling, and poured herself a generous volume.

'Well . . .' She poured another glass and handed it to Caitlin. Then, she told her sisters everything.

* * *

'I can't believe you didn't come to me with this. It's been going on for years. You were so miserable, and you didn't say a word!' Clara's voice was filled with hurt.

The party had finished over an hour ago. The three O'Kelly sisters were sitting on the couch, the air in the living room filled with the weight of Caroline's tale. Anna and Gian had gone out for some after-party drinks with their friends, leaving them alone.

Caroline's eyes were tired, and her calves ached from wearing high heels all day. She was mentally exhausted. The only thing she longed for was sleep. But here they were, dissecting her life into gross anatomical pieces. Caroline and Caitlin had swapped wine for herbal tea, but that didn't make her feel any better. Clara had been sipping non-alcoholic apple cider all night but even she looked ready for her head to hit the pillow.

'I should've told you both before. But I was ashamed. I blamed myself for a long time,' Caroline said.

'It wasn't your fault,' Clara replied with surprising softness.

Caitlin wordlessly nodded.

'I know that now. You know how people always say that if they could turn back time . . . Well, I'd go back to being newlyweds and tell *that* Caroline that it's got nothing to do with her.' She wrapped her arms around her knees and pulled them up to her chest. She put her head on her knees and stared at the fluffy carpet. 'I just wish he'd told me the truth before it all got so messed up.'

'What would you have done if he did?' Caitlin asked.

Caroline let out a short, sarcastic laugh. 'Honestly? I've asked myself that question dozens of times. And every time my answer's different.' She paused. 'But I think I'd still have married him. I'd want to work things out. Who knows, maybe I'd be happy now.'

'I don't think you'd be happy, Car.' Clara handed her another steaming cup and sat cross-legged on the carpet next to her. 'Not if you always thought that piece of intimacy is missing. Besides, children on their own are the deal breaker. No one should ever compromise when it comes to that.'

'True.' Caroline sighed. 'And it's not all intimacy. It's just sex. Kissing, holding hands, hugging . . . We had all that. Well, until things went so south, we lost that too. And besides. I didn't actually know what I was missing.'

Clara pensively stared into her mug. 'I get it. I mean, not how you're feeling but we sort of have the reverse situation with Sean. He enjoys sex but, if I'm honest, I could go without it. And I wouldn't miss it,' Clara said.

Caroline sat up in surprise. 'What? You never told me.'

'What is there to tell? We talked about it and learned to compromise. I don't really care for that side of marriage.' Clara shrugged, taking another sip of her cider. 'There's so much more to marriage than love or sex. But you shouldn't feel bad for wanting something, like sex. No one should willingly compromise trying to get what matters to them.'

'Ditto.' Caitlin raised her mug.

Clara looked at her, confused.

'What? I agree with you. I know I'm not married, nor have I ever really been in any kind of long-term relationship, but even I know that love itself is just a concept that society feeds us. There are so many kinds of love. Yet, love never seems to be enough. With or without sex. Although—' she smirked '—I'd never give up sex. But it would be nice to fall in love, too. I seem to be getting all the sex but never anything besides it.'

Clara suddenly coughed as if attempting to mask an outburst of laughter.

Caroline watched her, eyebrows raised, waiting for another fight.

When she recovered, Clara said, 'You will, Cait. When you meet the right someone.'

Caitlin looked at her suspiciously, as if she was waiting for a double-edged sword to land, but Clara didn't say anything else.

'How do you know if you've met that someone? How do you know when that love is enough?' Caroline asked, and they both looked at her with a new interest.

'I guess you just know. I knew with Sean, and I don't think I made a mistake,' Clara answered.

'So, you're just meant to cross your fingers and wish for the best? That you won't get hurt?'

'Oh, Car.' Clara scooted over to where she was sitting and put her palms on Caroline's knees. She looked into her eyes and said slowly, 'No one can guarantee you the best or that it won't hurt. What you can gain though . . . Totally worth it.'

'I'm not sure that's the truth.' Caroline sighed and rubbed her eyes.

Looking at both of her sisters, she felt a wave of gratitude. They didn't always get along, but they had one another's backs. However mad they got, they'd always make up. She knew she could tell them anything, which she'd forgotten for a while. But tonight reminded her how good it felt to share her worries with them.

She hesitated, before letting the words tumble out. 'I've met someone since I got here. But it'd never make sense to fool myself that anything can come out of this.'

'Why not?' Caitlin asked.

Caroline raised her head and looked at her sisters, brow furrowed. 'For starters, he's five years younger.'

Clara snorted and covered her mouth with her hand. 'Sorry. But that's irrelevant.'

'OK . . . The fact that he runs a ranch in Oklahoma is. And he was engaged, no idea what happened there. He just won't open up about it. I won't even start on the fact he didn't tell me about it himself; I found out from *his friend*. That suggests he isn't over it yet. Now his father's dying . . . I think it's going to take years for him to get over all of this.'

'How is that a problem?' Clara raised an eyebrow, any shadow of amusement gone from her expression. 'We still miss Mum and it's been years. He's always going to carry that with him.'

Caroline raised her hands, exasperated. 'Did you hear what I said? He's a *cowboy*. Like, an actual cowboy – running a ranch, herding cattle, going to rodeos . . .' She closed her eyes, trying to calm the wave of anxiety lurking in the background. 'Besides—' she pursed her lips in a tight line '—he'll probably want children. Maybe not now, maybe not in two or three years. But eventually. I couldn't cope with another split like that, not after Finn.'

She drew in a loud inhale. 'Plus, what if Finn was my one true love? My soulmate? And now that it's over, I'm destined to be alone forever?'

Caitlin scooted over closer to her now; she had one sister on her right, the other on her left. They took her hands and Caroline felt the heavy feeling building up in her chest start dissolving, slowly.

'You know that the myth about there ever only being one person out there for us is just that – a myth, right? It'd be a very sad life if we could only get one chance at being happy.' Caitlin squeezed her hand and put her head on Caroline's shoulder.

'Cait's right. It'd be depressing if there was a limit on the love we get.' Clara's mouth twitched a little in a half-smile.

'Or maybe I should think less about Finn and Hunter and focus on what I came here for: figuring out what to do with my career.'

'Well, yeah that'd be helpful,' Caitlin said. 'The career bit, no judgement otherwise.' She let out a heavy sigh and slowly lowered herself on the floor, lying on her back. 'I think I had too much wine,' she moaned, closing her eyes.

Clara snorted into her cider. 'You both did.'

As if on cue, they all burst into laughter.

CHAPTER THIRTY-SEVEN

Hunter

Thanksgiving, for the first time in Hunter's life, was just a family affair. In the past, his parents would dress up one of the barns and invite what always seemed like the entirety of Purcell. Food, music and happiness shared among friends and acquaintances. However, this year, it was just them.

There was no party, no music. Even the food tasted like it was missing something, some of the usual joy. His mother tried her best to put on a smile and make the memories they all needed. But even she looked like she couldn't shake off the veil of gut-wrenching sorrow.

Hunter's heart ached every time he looked at her when she thought no one was there.

At the same time, no one wanted to speak about what was to come. The Jacksons thought that if they didn't say the words 'terminal' or 'cancer' out loud, then maybe somehow

Alan could cheat death a little while longer. Maybe it wouldn't be their last Thanksgiving together. Maybe the doctors were wrong, maybe a miracle would happen.

All the *maybes* made Hunter dizzy.

So, they all prayed among the congregation. Hunter noticed that his mother was never without a rosary tucked away in her pocket. She'd take it out several times a day, close her eyes and mutter prayers while her unsteady fingers moved from bead to bead. Hunter had stopped going to church shortly after turning twenty-one. He hadn't been back, not even now. No one commented on it. They were all coping the best they could. For his family, it was church and prayer. For him, long, lonely rides on Dallas. Even the worsening weather didn't bother him.

When he was home, he felt helpless. All the ranch employees had banded together and were really doing a fantastic job navigating the day-to-day tasks without his input. He had finally officially promoted Luke, one of the guys employed by Alan years ago, to foreman. Unofficially, Luke had been doing the job for a good few months now.

Hunter trusted Luke and he was well liked among the rest of the crew. He only deferred matters he couldn't handle himself, like accounts or phone calls with suppliers or businesses, to Hunter. And because Alan's condition was widely known, people tried not to bother the Jacksons if it wasn't necessary.

He should be grateful for having time to focus on his father and his family. Instead, he felt lost and useless. He had all this time to reminisce about his childhood, how much his father had shaped him into the man he was today.

And to imagine the days in which he wouldn't be with them.

'You look like you could use one.'

Hunter opened his eyes. His lips crooked in a small smile, and he wordlessly showed Buck an empty chair on the veranda.

Buck popped open a beer bottle and passed it to him. Then he sat down and lifted his own to his lips. Taking a big gulp, he looked at Hunter. 'How are you holding up, Hunt?'

'Probably as well as you are, Buck.'

His brother chuckled and shook his head in mock disapproval. 'Eh, you're right, stupid question. How are things with the mysterious woman Meg told me about – Caroline is it?'

In other circumstances, Hunter would be annoyed at their sister's love of gossip. But right now, all he could muster in response was a sigh. He swung the green glass bottle and drank a bit. Bitter, cold liquid went down his throat and he looked directly into Buck's eyes.

'Caroline's fine. Things with Caroline are fine.'

'You're very chatty today.'

'What do you want me to say?'

'Oh, I don't know. Maybe why, after the chat we had at the café about you being ready to meet someone, you didn't tell me about her?'

'There's nothing to tell though. We aren't together in that way,' Hunter said evenly. He took another sip of his beer.

They agreed on keeping things casual. He didn't need to 'make things official' in a social media post or something – not that he was on any – but they both said they wanted just a bit of fun.

Buck glanced at him with a furrowed brow. 'Aren't you though? From what I heard from Meg and Mom, and even Luke, you've been fooling around with her—'

'I'm not fooling around with her,' he interrupted, anger rising.

'No? You said you're not together. You're not fooling around. What are you doing then?' Buck paused, waiting for an answer.

If only he knew . . . Time had passed, feelings that he didn't want to allow into his headspace and heart had developed . . . She wasn't staying. She'd be gone, and soon. The invisible clock ticked away hours to certain heartbreak.

You don't deserve happiness anyway, not after what happened with Tamara.

Hunter swallowed over a hard lump of complicated, self-inflicted guilt. Logically, he knew he wasn't the one to blame. Sadly, love and logic didn't go hand in hand.

Buck leaned forward and looked at him earnestly. 'Hunt, come on. Talk to me.'

'What is there to talk about?'

'Well . . . Do you like her?'

Hunter rolled his eyes, reaching for another beer. 'No, Buck, I willingly spend time with someone I dislike.'

'Don't get smart with me. What I meant is do you *like* her, you know . . . that way?'

'I like her just fine. Now, can we stop with the interrogation?'

'Whatever. Forget I even asked.' Buck bit off, finally tearing his eyes away from his brother's face.

They sat in silence for a long while, staring at the darkening sky and listening to the sounds coming from the nearest cattle barn. Hunter knew Buck was hoping that time would loosen his tongue – but it couldn't.

He was afraid that if he talked about it, then he'd let himself think about it. And that couldn't happen. What was he going to tell Buck? That he was sleeping with a woman who was technically divorced but not legally, who had a clock on her stay in Oklahoma? That he thought about her a lot more than he should? That it wasn't just about sex?

No, he couldn't say any of that. Saying nothing was easier.

Besides, he should be focusing on his family, not on whatever this unlabelled thing with Caroline was.

Hunter quietly opened the door to the guest bedroom at the end of the corridor on the ground floor. It had been transformed into Alan's bedroom the day after the meeting in the hospital. A single, adjustable bed stood in the centre, with an IV drip stand next to it and morphine syringe driver. A soft melody of classical music came from a small CD player on the windowsill.

He swallowed uncomfortably, trying to coax himself to look as unfazed as he could. Every day he thought he'd get used to seeing his father as he was now; yet every day it hit him anew. Alan, who'd already lost a considerable amount of weight in the past year, seemed to get thinner and thinner every day. His pale, paper-like skin was stretched over his bones, which were becoming more pronounced.

One unchanged thing in his appearance were his kind, blue eyes. They came alive with warmth when they landed on Hunter.

'Come in, son.' Alan's voice was quiet but firm.

Hunter nodded and slowly approached the bed.

'Here, take a seat.' Alan took off his glasses and set them on his lap.

Hunter sat on the old, worn-out armchair which he and Buck had dragged down from the attic. Neither they nor Meg minded sitting on a stool, or even standing by the bed, but Mary usually sat by her husband's side into the small hours. When Buck walked in on her, all unnaturally twisted on a hard, wooden chair at five in the morning, he'd asked Hunter to help him move the big armchair downstairs. They knew they couldn't persuade their mother to sleep in her own bed, but they could at least make sure she was a bit more comfortable.

'How are you feeling, Dad?' Hunter asked, anxiously studying his father's face for any sign of pain. All of Alan's medications had been withdrawn, apart from high doses of opioids, anti-sickness medications and a handful of other medications from the palliative team. At first, Alan had refused even them, as he said they made him groggy, and he wanted to enjoy the remainder of his time with the family. He managed to get through Thanksgiving while still mobile, but two days later his condition deteriorated rapidly. Unwillingly, he'd accepted the offer of intravenous pain relief and now spent most of his time in bed. He had started having seizures, each one lasting longer than the previous one. He was too weak to walk on his own, and some days he wouldn't get out of bed at all.

Last time Hunter saw him up in the chair was yesterday morning.

'I'm feeling the same as I did six hours ago when you asked. Which is not bad at all, not bad . . . These meds—' he gestured towards the syringe driver. '—are good. I'm not in any pain. Just feeling more and more sleepy as the days go by. But we know that's how things go.'

Hunter swallowed and focused on keeping his expression unchanged.

His father didn't need to worry about him or try to spare his feelings. It wasn't about him, and Hunter knew that he was the only one Alan was honest with. He didn't want that to change, not now, when his father needed him the most.

'That's good,' Hunter said in an even voice.

Alan nodded. 'It is. But this isn't the reason why I asked

you here.' He paused, his eyes meeting Hunter's. He held his gaze. 'I wanted to talk about my will. As you know, I made sure all my affairs were in order last year. Dick Rothley has all the paperwork. I named you as the executor. It just seemed natural, considering you've been running the ranch and helping me through treatment . . .

'Buck, Meg and your mother are all included in it as well. But I want you to be the one making sure everything goes like I envisioned.' He paused again, like he expected Hunter to say something. Maybe in protest or in confusion.

But Hunter remained silent, his eyes not leaving Alan's face.

Alan cleared his throat and carried on. 'I won't go into detail as it's all there in black and white . . . You'll read it soon enough. I just want you to promise me you'll read it all and know that it's what I want.'

'Of course I will, Dad. I promise.'

Alan smiled softly and reached out, opening his right hand.

Hunter squeezed it tightly, as if holding on to his father's hand would anchor him in this life, protecting him from the inevitable.

'Thank you. You know I'm so proud of you, right? You grew up to be a kind, honest and considerate man. I always knew you were smart. To a parent, their children are all extraordinary. You, Buck, and Meg are all so different. Yet, you're also so alike. I hope you also feel that your mother and I raised you well.'

Hunter's eyes welled up with tears. Part of him wanted to tell his father to be quiet, that he didn't want to hear any of this. That it wasn't time yet. But he knew, deep down, that if Alan was saying it, it was bringing him peace. And who was he to deny his dying father peace?

'I love you, Dad. I promise you I'll take care of Mom and

Meg. I'll take care of the ranch and make sure it's passed on to the next generation.'

'This is what I wanted to tell you, Hunt. Remember those men from that big fancy company who came knocking on our doors? They wanted to buy the ranch and all the land to expand their agricultural business or something . . .'

'Of course I remember. You ran them off the ranch with a gun, and said that if they ever come back, you'd shoot them in the asses.'

Alan let out a raspy laugh that quickly turned into a cough.

Hunter instinctively helped him sit up and tipped a plastic cup to his mouth.

Alan took three small sips of water, leaned back against the pillows, and breathed in. 'Thank you.' Another deep breath. 'You saw the letter they sent recently, right? They renewed their offer. They must've got wind that I was on the way out and thought they might have a chance again.'

'I know. I also ran into them at Stillwater rodeo. Ignored them, no point dealing with bastards like them.'

Alan didn't rise to Hunter's outrage and continued calmly, 'The offer is even higher than what it was last year.'

'Well, we'll just tell them to go to hell. Again.' Hunter shrugged, anger still ringing in his voice.

Alan clasped his hand into both of Hunter's and looked at him with such pure fatherly affection that Hunter instantly felt ashamed of his outburst.

'I'm sorry. I'm just annoyed that these vultures won't leave us alone, even now,' he mumbled.

'I asked Dick to get in touch with them and say they'll have to speak with you after I . . . well, after I'm gone.' Alan swallowed and tried to mask the fear with a smile that didn't quite reach his eyes. 'I know that running a ranch was never your dream, Hunt. It's neither Buck's nor Meg's. They're both going their own way, doing what they want to do – and I'm happy for them. You already gave up your dreams to help us when I got sick, I don't want you to feel like you're tied down to this place. I want you to have options. To have dreams again. You can finally go to vet school.'

Hunter shook his head, trying to keep tears from spilling. 'I don't want to go to vet school anymore.'

'Still. You can dream a new dream. You're only twenty-six, you have a whole life ahead of you. If running this ranch is what you truly want to do, then I'm happy, and forget I said anything about the sale offer. But if you don't, if you want to do something – anything – else then I'm also happy.'

'The ranch has been in the family for decades. I can't just sell it.'

'I'm not telling you to sell it. I'm just telling you that I want you to be happy. I want you to carve your own path. My father was a rancher. I became a rancher because it was all I knew. I didn't have options back then. But you do. Just . . . promise me you'll think about it. Think about what you want. Speak with Dick. He knows all the details; he'll talk you through everything – in both instances, whether you decide to keep the ranch or sell it.' Alan paused, taking in more ragged breaths.

His chest was rising and falling in quicker succession, and Hunter could tell that this conversation had taken a lot of the little energy he had left. Fresh tears pricked the corners of his eyes with renewed urgency.

'And before you say anything, your mother would be taken ca— care of.' Alan's breathing became even shallower. 'She knows about the offer on the table, she's fully supportive of my decision to empower you to choose. If you . . . if you sold the land, the company stipulated they'd leave the house itself untouched and fence off a good-sized area around it, so that your mother can live the rest of her life here. Only afterwards the house would go to the company.'

Hunter blinked, no longer able to hold the tears at bay. His father was smiling at him through glassy, thoughtful eyes, trying to mask the enormous effort this conversation took.

'I . . . I—' Hunter coughed, taking the moment to compose himself. He wasn't often lost for words but right now he didn't know what to say. 'Thank you.'

Alan nodded, as if he understood. Exhaustion crept up on his face and he put his head against the pillow, closing his eyes.

Hunter took it as a cue to leave. He squeezed Alan's hand once more as he stood up. 'I love you, Dad.'

'I love you too, son.' Alan smiled weakly at Hunter. 'And there's one more . . . thing.' He breathed out, closing his eyes.

'You're tired. Whatever it is, it can wait.'

Alan shook his head with more vigour than he had showed since Hunter entered the room. 'I know you loved Tamara. But she's gone and you can't grieve forever. It ain't right. Give love another chance. I don't want to sound like your mother, but . . . but a dying man can be blunt.' He grinned weakly. 'Let someone in. Life's a long slog on your own. It's always easier when you have someone who you can lean on.'

Hunter swallowed. 'What if I do that but it doesn't work out?'

'Then that's just life. Things don't work out. Relationships fail. People change and grow apart. But . . . in all my years, I've heard fewer people regret taking the risk than those who missed their chance.' Alan took in a deep breath. 'Don't be the one with regrets, son.'

Hunter found his head bowing in a curt nod, which surprised him as genuine. Deep down, he must've known this for a while now. His father was right.

'Can you ask your mother to come in here?'

He nodded, kissed his father's forehead, and walked to the door. As he put his hand on the handle, the door creaked ajar and his mother squeezed into the room. He didn't know whether she had been standing by the door listening or how much she had heard, but she gave him the most encouraging, loving smile as she walked past, following Alan's voice calling her name.

Hunter remained standing by the door as she reached Alan's bed and sat in the armchair.

She picked up an old-looking book from the bedside cabinet and started reading out loud. Her soft, warm voice brought a glow to Alan's tired face. He looked peaceful; his eyes closed as his hand stroked Mary's fingers.

Hunter left the room, not wanting to disturb them.

CHAPTER THIRTY-EIGHT

Hunter

Alan Melvin Jackson died on December 11.

The printed obituary bore coffee stains.

The days after his father died all blended together for Hunter. He was numb from shaking hands and nodding his head respectfully while accepting countless condolences. He had listened to tales of his father's friendship and generosity, his heart heavier after each one.

Alan had made all the funeral arrangements ahead of time so there wasn't anything left for them to take care of. Hunter knew that his mother was grateful for that. She was trying to put on a brave face and surprised him with her emotional strength. She seemed to have adopted the approach of feeling grateful for the time she and Alan had spent together. For the love and the life they had built. Hunter knew she'd been through all stages of grief when Alan was still alive. Now, when he was gone, it wasn't necessarily easier, but she looked prepared for whatever might come next.

He admired her for that.

On the day of the funeral, Hunter woke up with a headache. He cursed under his breath. He didn't drink yesterday to precisely avoid this scenario. Annoyed, he dragged himself out of bed and trudged into the kitchen. He made himself a cup of strong, pressed black coffee and settled into the armchair.

The sun was barely above the horizon. Cold, December misty air enveloped Purcell. He swallowed two acetaminophen and washed them down with coffee. His phone vibrated with an incoming message.

>CAROLINE: *How are you holding up?*

>HUNTER: *Hanging in there. It feels like today's going to make it real. I know he's been dead for a week but watching the coffin with his body lowered into the ground and buried . . . That's final, isn't it.*

>CAROLINE: *I don't know what to say. I'm so sorry you're going through this. Are you sure you want me there today?*

>HUNTER: *I know you didn't know him, so please don't feel like you must come. But I want you to be there. I probably won't be able to spare a lot of time during the actual ceremony as Meg's a mess and Morgan still doesn't understand why she can't see Grandpa again. Knowing that you're close, being able to steal a glance at your face . . . It'll help.*

CAROLINE: *I'll be there. I won't get in the way but if you need anything, a chat, a hug, you'll be able to find me.*

HUNTER: *Thank you.*

There are these well-known phrases people say to describe a funeral. It was well attended. It was a lovely ceremony. The readings were emotional. The stories shared by the family made people laugh and cry at the same time.

Hunter had only been to two funerals prior to today. But even if he'd been to forty, it wouldn't have made today any less painful. Nothing could.

He fidgeted, trying to release his arm from Meg's hold. His tie was too tight.

She looked up at him with puffy, glassy eyes.

The pastor was in the middle of talking about Alan's contribution to Purcell's community. How well regarded and well liked he was.

Hunter grabbed the knot on his tie and loosened it, feeling like he couldn't breathe. His eyes searched the crowd with a mild panic. All these people, all dressed in black . . . He didn't stop until he found Caroline.

She was standing at the back, a bit out of the way next to Dr Kennedy. They both looked fully focused on the sermon.

Hunter's breathing and heart rate slowed down, his eyes remaining fixed on her. She must've sensed his gaze as she tilted her head. Their eyes met, an unspoken understanding passing between them.

Buck subtly elbowed him in the side. The pastor was finishing up, and it was Hunter's turn to say a few words. They'd had an argument about it the night before. Buck hated public speaking. He used to stutter at school and kids had bullied him for it. Hunter thought it wasn't fair he was the one who had to come up with some eloquent words in these circumstances. He'd even tried pulling the age card, which didn't go down well. In the end they settled it like men: rock, paper, scissors. Hunter lost.

'Now Hunter, Alan's younger son, is going to say a few words.' The pastor stepped to the side, letting Hunter past to stand next to the microphone.

He took a deep breath, looking at his family. 'Thank you, Pastor. I thought about what I could say here today and drew blank for hours. After all, how could I possibly condense my father's life into a few sentences?' He flexed his trembling fingers. 'But . . . then I remembered what he always taught me: speak from the heart. That's why I didn't write anything. So please bear with me, I might ramble a bit.'

Mary gave him an encouraging smile, tears glistening on her cheeks.

'My father was the greatest man I've ever met. I know this is a cliché, but he was my hero. He taught me so much, yet at times it feels like it wasn't enough. He didn't teach me how to live after he's gone. I know that he wouldn't want us to be sad – well, at least not for very long. He loved his life, and he loved his family. He was grateful for what he had, and he accepted the fate that he was dealt. He cared more about other people than himself.'

Hunter stopped, his eyes wet. 'He wanted everyone to be happy. He was there for me in the darkest time of my life. He showed me patience, and kindness, and told me that better days would come. Eventually.'

He bent down, reaching for a bottle of whisky. He poured it into two glasses, putting one on the grass. He raised the other one. 'Dad . . . A million words wouldn't bring you back. I know because I've tried. Neither would a million tears. I know because I've cried. We love you and we'll see you again.' He downed the shot of whisky and heard Buck's disapproving laugh.

'Now, this is just the perfect example of the weird sense of humour my Dad had: he specifically requested Alan Jackson's "Remember When" at this point. He said to tell you all that although it was by the lesser Jackson, the lyrics are what he'd want to say to our mother, Mary. And that if love was enough, he'd still be here with us.' He looked at his mother with aching affection.

She shook her head, overwhelmed, as the music started playing from the speakers. Lorna touched her arm and enveloped her in a big hug.

Buck had his arm round Meg. He caught Hunter's eye and gave him an understanding nod.

Hunter picked up the full glass of eighteen-year-old Bowmore from the ground. He peered into the hole, looking at the chestnut wooden coffin on top of which rested Alan's favourite black Stetson.

A big stone lodged in his throat when he realised someone had put Alan's glasses on the coffin, too – the ones he always misplaced.

He stood there for a moment, looking down.

Goodbye, Dad.

Hunter poured the whisky onto the coffin.

He felt her presence before he saw her.

'It only now clicked for me that your father's name was the same as *the* Alan Jackson.'

He chuckled, although the sound was foreign, like it

belonged to somebody else. 'You couldn't make it up if you wanted to . . . He always said that at least he was talented, and he didn't share a name with some godawful DJ or something.'

'That would've been tragic.' Caroline touched his elbow, but he flinched involuntarily.

He took a step to the side, trying to put some distance between them. If she noticed it, she didn't comment on it, raising her head high.

'How are you feeling?'

'How do you think I'm feeling?' he bit off. He didn't mean to sound so spiteful, but he couldn't help it. He didn't feel like himself. What was worse, right now he didn't think he'd ever feel like himself again.

'I can't even begin to imagine,' she whispered, dropping her gaze to the grass. 'I'm so sorry for your loss.'

He knew she was only here because he'd told her he wanted her here. And now he was behaving like an asshole. He wanted to respond, but no words came to him. Instead, he gave her a stiff nod.

'If there's anything I can do to help—'

'You can't bring him back. And that's the only thing that would help.' He swallowed hard, feeling hot, angry tears pooling under his eyelids. 'Although there is one thing you can do to help,' he added quietly, turning to her. He put his hands on her waist and pulled her to his chest, lifting her chin and capturing her mouth with his.

Rough, hungry. Full of grief and anger.

'Hunter, stop.' She pushed him away, her voice trembling. 'That isn't what I meant.'

'You said you wanted to help,' he murmured, feeling his heart beat fast. He could almost hear his blood pumping through his veins. Reminding him that he was alive. His father wasn't. He was alive in a world without his father.

'I do, I really do.' She tried reaching for his hand, but he shoved it in his jacket pocket. 'But not like this. If you want to talk—'

'And what good will talking do?!' He let out a strange, distorted laugh. 'I don't want to talk. I don't *need* to talk.'

'You're grieving,' she said, nodding. Her face was almost white. 'This isn't you.'

Their eyes met and the shock and hurt he saw in hers made him feel so ashamed.

It hadn't hit him that his father was truly gone until he'd seen the casket lowered to the ground.

He couldn't see past the pain, not now. Maybe not ever.

Looking at Caroline, all he could see was that she'd soon be gone. Not tomorrow, not even next week, but soon. She'd go back to Scotland. He'd lose her too.

He was so sick and tired of losing people he cared about.

'I'll let you go be with your family,' she said in a small voice.

He had so much to say, but he had no words, so he just watched her walk away. He wanted to call after her but when he opened his mouth, no sound came.

CHAPTER THIRTY-NINE

Caroline

Caroline had been staring at the ceiling in the darkness for what felt like hours. Every now and then, she heard a sound outside the window. A passing ambulance. A car with a modified exhaust. They interrupted the uneasy silence of the strange time between night and day, when it wasn't really morning yet, but it wasn't quite the middle of the night. Annoyed at not managing to keep her eyes closed, she reached for her phone and checked the time.

4.17 a.m.

It had been a week since Alan's funeral.

Later that night, Hunter had sent her a text she had since re-read more than she wanted to admit.

> HUNTER: *There are not enough words to apologise for my behaviour earlier. I'm so sorry, Caroline. I didn't*

mean to say what I did, it just . . . Came out. I feel broken, numb, dissociated from the reality. Like someone froze my body into an ice sculpture and smashed me with a sledgehammer into millions of tiny pieces. I'm not whole and I fear I might never be whole again.

She accepted his apology. Told him not to worry about her or her feelings. To focus on himself and his family. They could talk later.

Because she knew how he felt. There were no words for that scathing emptiness.

Pulling the duvet over her head, she opened her mouth and let out a soundless scream.

Just before she'd learned about Hunter's father's death, everything had started to fall into place. ASH turned out to be one of the most intellectually stimulating events in Caroline's life. The panel discussion went so well that she was still feeling the adrenaline rush when she got back to Oklahoma City. She had presented the thirty-six-month data and didn't stumble even once. She shook hands, introduced herself, discussed ground-breaking studies and met people who had a common goal with her: improve the lives of their patients.

She'd felt as if she was a medical student again. Wide-eyed, fascinated and feeling like she wanted to be part of the exciting future of medicine. Right there, standing in the medical booth of another pharmaceutical company doing research into non-Hodgkin lymphoma in the enormous exhibition centre, Caroline had decided.

Haematology wasn't for her. But oncology was.

She had already started looking into what she needed to apply for oncology speciality training for next year's intake.

Thinking about something other than Hunter helped her fall asleep. *This* was something she felt like she could handle.

Hunter picked her up from the centre on Thursday, the last day of work for her before the New Year.

He put both of his hands on the steering wheel and looked at her. 'I'm sorry.'

She felt a pang of sorrow in her chest as she took in his dishevelled appearance. 'You've apologised already. You're grieving, you don't have to make sense.'

'Still. I was a dick.'

'Just a little bit.'

'I can live with being a little bit of a dick,' he said, a small grimace resembling a smile tugging at the corners of his lips. 'What do you want to do? Are you up for a drive?'

'Why not? I'm officially on leave through Christmas and the New Year now.'

She didn't ask him how he was feeling. She didn't ask where they were going. It didn't really matter. Because as much as she wanted to fight it, she wanted to be near him. She didn't think past *right now*.

Hunter nodded and turned the engine on.

They ended up having sex in the bed of his F-150, somewhere off the beaten track on the Jacksons' ranch land. She made a joke once about doing it, told him that it was something a she wanted to try.

'You know, I wasn't serious when I suggested it,' she said, pressing her head closer to his chest. It was a chilly and quite breezy night, but there was no sign of snow anywhere.

'I know.' Hunter pulled one of the thick blankets higher to cover her up to her neck. 'And doing it in December probably wasn't the best idea. Might've been better in the summer.'

'Very likely,' she said, shivering a bit. He wrapped his arm tighter around her. 'But I didn't feel the cold during.' She raised her head and looked into his eyes. 'I hope you don't normally drive round with a duvet, pillows and three thick blankets in your truck.'

He laughed. It was a short, not very cheerful sound. But it was the first one she had heard from him since his father died. 'Of course not.'

'Good. I wouldn't lie on them if you did, they'd be mouldy.'

He didn't respond and she couldn't think of anything else to say. She pushed away from his chest and lay on her back, head on the pillow. The night sky looked like one stolen from a photograph. Velvet black, adorned with so many stars.

Caroline smiled. 'It reminds me of when we went to Lake Lawtonka.'

Hunter turned to his side, propping himself on his elbow. 'Yeah?'

They got fully dressed after they finished, and her eyes landed on the buttons of his jacket. She reached to the top one, running her fingers through its smooth surface. 'Yeah.'

'We did have the fire to keep us warm then.'

Her smile widened. 'True, but body heat is better.'

Hunter reached to her face and pushed a strand of hair from her forehead. 'No arguments from me.'

She knew they should've talked more, but it didn't seem like a good time. She had tried, gently, asking how he felt on the way here.

He had shrugged it off. It was plain he didn't want to talk about his father, and she understood.

Everyone grieved differently.

Some people turned into walking and talking memorials, reminiscing about their loved ones, spending their days recalling memories of their lives. Others reached for a bottle or other substances. Some people, like her, turned to therapy. Or decided to make something of themselves, like when she went to medical school.

And some, it seemed, turned to sex. Numbing the pain with physical intimacy, reminding themselves they were alive.

She didn't judge him for the way he decided to handle his grief.

Maybe this was the way she could help him, through sex and just being there.

Maybe it was as simple as that.

CHAPTER FORTY

Caroline

ERIN: *This is just sad, Car. You really weren't invited anywhere?*

CAROLINE: *I told you. I don't really have friends here. Amira and Jake finally took the plunge and went out on a few dates. They're away to Amira's parents' lake cabin in Michigan. They have it all to themselves as her parents went to Hawaii.*

ERIN: *Couldn't you tag along with Anna and Gian? They're going to a charity masquerade ball, right?*

CAROLINE: *Ha, ha. Because I love to third wheel so much.*

ERIN: *They're your aunts.*

CAROLINE: *Doesn't make it any less third wheeling.*

ERIN: *True. What about Hunter?*

CAROLINE: *What about Hunter?*

ERIN: *Didn't he want to spend NYE with you? I find it odd.*

CAROLINE: *Erin, his father just died. Besides, I'm perfectly capable of spending a night on my own. His grief's still fresh. I'm trying to keep my distance a little bit.*

ERIN: *Riiiight . . . Trying *rolling eyes*. It doesn't sound like either of you is putting much effort into doing that. I must just assume it's a very difficult, tactical mission.*

CAROLINE: *You're the worst.*

ERIN: *You know you love me. Anyway, I'm away. I sneaked out of the party to chat to you, but Rithvik is texting me asking if I'm trying to dodge the midnight kiss.*

CAROLINE: *Have fun! And Happy New Year to you both.*

ERIN: *I have a feeling it's going to be a year to remember.*

Caroline closed the app and put her phone on the coffee table. She was perfectly content spending the night on Anna and Gian's sofa, armed with a bowl of popcorn, a bottle of champagne and a remote.

How to Lose a Guy in 10 Days was the first movie up in her queue. There was something oddly comforting in rewatching the same romcoms. A little after 10 p.m., she was trying to decide between *The Proposal* and *27 Dresses* while waiting for a new batch of popcorn to finish popping in the microwave, when she heard a loud knock on the front door. She jumped, startled. Trying to remember where Gian said they kept the baseball bat, she slowly approached the door.

'Who is it?'

'It's me.'

It only took her a split-second to recognise the voice. She opened the door, puzzled expression written all over her face. 'What are you doing here? I thought you were in Tulsa.'

Hunter squeezed through the door, closing it firmly. Water was dripping from his dark hair onto his flushed face. His jacket was soaked through.

Caroline put her hands on his shoulders and looked him up and down.

He pushed the hair away from his eyes, reaching into the inside of his jacket. 'I was in Tulsa. I was sitting in Buck and Lorna's living room, and there were some of our cousins there, and Mom and Meg . . . Everyone was chatting and starting to have a good time. They wanted to reminisce about Dad and it was nice, at first. But—' he cupped her cheek '—then I looked around and realised that there wasn't a single person there who I wanted to welcome the New Year with more than you.'

Caroline raised an eyebrow, which made Hunter let out a

short laugh. 'So, I said my goodbyes and wished everyone a good night. Then I drove here. Bearing gifts.'

He held out a bottle of Taittinger, her favourite champagne.

She took it carefully, a shiver running through her body as she touched the cool glass surface. 'You drove just over a hundred miles on New Year's Eve to kiss me at midnight?'

'The roads were quiet. It didn't take that long.'

'It's still over one hundred miles.'

He shrugged, a small smile playing on his lips. 'What is one hundred miles? Nothing, really. Besides, I still remember you drove to Purcell to give me a hug when I needed one. And you came all the way to Robbers Cave to go on a date with me.' He grinned.

'That was my idea.'

'But you still came.' He shrugged. 'I didn't want you to see New Year on your own.' Their eyes met.

Hunter reached out and stroked her other cheek with his thumb. 'And it wasn't a totally selfless act, you know. I missed you.'

'Well, when you put it that way . . .' She threw her arms round his neck, pulling him into a kiss.

His hands splayed across her back, pulling her closer.

Caroline could taste all the longing and a desperate need for closeness. She parted her lips further, letting his tongue meet hers in a frantic collision.

That was how it had been lately between them. All the sex, very little talking.

She wished she could make him feel a bit better, even if it was just for a fleeting moment. She tried not to expect anything, always tried to let his mood guide whether they met and what they did. She had tried talking, but he seemed bent on trying to numb the pain, in the most literal meaning. So, they were having a lot of sex, which was amazing. Mind-blowing, even.

That's what she wanted from their arrangement from the start. Wasn't it?

Hunter groaned, releasing her from his tight embrace. 'Damn it, Caroline. We won't last to midnight at this rate.'

'Who said we have to wait until midnight? I was thinking we could finish the year with a bang.'

He chuckled softly in response. The sincere sound of it made her heart leap. She hadn't heard it in a long time.

She lifted her hand, brushing a strand of hair from his forehead. 'We can do whatever we want.'

'In that case . . .' He stepped away from her, slid off his wet jacket and hurriedly put it on the coat hanger. Wordlessly, he took the champagne from the round console table she'd put it on and pulled off the wrapping from the cork. 'I say we pop this bottle and see where the night takes us.'

She leaned her back on the hallway wall, observing him twisting the metal cap and uncorking the bottle. There was a loud *pop* and he looked up to her, grinning.

'I'll get some glass—'

Before she could finish, he laughed and took a long swig from the bottle.

Caroline looked at him aghast. 'Hunter!'

'What?' He passed her the bottle.

She furrowed her eyebrows, looking at it suspiciously.

'Don't you want some? We can get glasses if you want, I'm sorry if I offended you or—'

She let out a small noise – half-laugh, half-sigh, and shook her head. 'No need.'

She squeezed his fingers back and took the bottle from him. Taking a slow sip from it, she observed Hunter.

His face was pale, creased with worry lines that visibly aged him.

If she didn't know better, she wouldn't know he was five whole years younger than her. His grey eyes, although focused on her with warmth, hid bottomless grief. The kind that wasn't even buried deep. It was just there, a constant reminder of what struggles his life held. Somehow, that realisation made her insides ache.

'Here, let me have some too,' he said, taking the bottle from her. He lifted it to his lips, not moving his eyes from her face.

She blushed under his unblinking attention – his eyes might as well have been undressing her right there.

'On second thought,' he murmured in a low voice, setting the bottle back on the console table. 'I'd prefer a taste of you.'

He closed the distance between them before she could open her mouth and slid his hands under her T-shirt.

'Do you make a wish for when the clock strikes midnight?'

'No, do you?' Hunter propped himself on the pillow, checking the time. 'we have six minutes.'

'I used to.' *When I still believed in love and happily ever after*, she added in her head. Visibly, she just shrugged, pulling the duvet further up to her chin.

He shook his head, amused. 'You know I've seen you naked, like . . . I don't even know how many times. You don't have to hide from me.' He touched her wrist and something heavy lodged in her throat.

'It's different.'

'Is it?'

'Yes. When we're busy kissing and—'

'Getting hot and sweaty?' he offered, with a wide smile.

Caroline grabbed the pillow from under his elbow and smacked his head with it.

'Hey!' He laughed, trying to shield his head with his arms. 'I surrender!'

'Good.' She put the pillow down, avoiding his eyes. 'And I know all that. But after feels a lot more *intimate*,' she finally said, turning her head away. She felt like an idiot. She was thirty-one years old. Yet with how everything had turned out in her adult life, she still felt inadequate and very young when it came to certain aspects of relationships.

'Hey.' He lifted her chin and forced her to look at him. 'It's just us.'

And somehow, that simple sentence was enough.

She nodded, pressing her forehead against his.

'You're right . . . On that note, you know you can talk to me, right? About your dad, about how you feel . . .'

Hunter dropped his hand so quickly she opened her mouth in a silent '*oh*'. He sat up against the metal frame of the bed, eyes darkened with an unreadable expression.

'I—I don't know how to. Talk about it,' he choked out, his voice strained.

She reached for his hand. He didn't look at her.

'You don't have to know. No one knows; that kind of sorrow is unspeakable.' She felt his fingers twitch in her grasp. 'And I'm not pushing you. Just . . . if you want to talk, know that I'll listen.'

'I know.' He pulled her towards him and tangled his legs through hers under the duvet. 'And I really appreciate it. Even after how I behaved after the funeral,' he said, placing a hand that felt way too heavy on her waist.

'I told you it's forgiven.'

'I still shouldn't have said what I said.'

'You've apologised more than enough times. It was an impossible day.'

'It was. But you being here for me made everything a bit better. I know I haven't talked about how I feel. I can't. It makes all the difference though, knowing I could if I wanted to.' He swallowed. 'You have no idea how grateful I am that you're here right now, Caroline.'

Their eyes met and for a moment, time froze.

She knew that the longer they carried on, the more it was going to hurt when she left. But with Hunter, she knew they didn't have to fix each other. They didn't have to stay forever; they just had to be right there. Together in a blissful undefined construct of their messed-up feelings.

Of course, she'd never admit any of this to anyone. Not even to him.

'It's 11:59!' she shrieked, looking at her phone. 'Quick, get the champagne!'

He did, bending down to reach for two flutes – they had both agreed a midnight toast did call for flutes. He handed her one, raising his. 'Make a wish.'

'You make one, too.'

'Mine would never come true,' he whispered.

Neither would mine. The bitter thought flooded her mind. She'd never admit any items from her wish list out loud, but they were etched deep in her soul. Getting onto oncology training programme in Aberdeenshire was number one. Befriending someone with a cute dog she could borrow for hikes on her days off was on the list too, as she knew the amount of time she'd be spending in the hospital wouldn't be fair on a pet and so couldn't have her own. Smaller items – travel bucket list and such followed, but there was one thing she was too scared to wish for. An impossible unicorn of a dream she hadn't even known was in there.

She wanted Hunter. Not just until July – she wanted him throughout the next autumn, and winter, and likely all the other seasons to come.

That was never going to happen. He wouldn't leave his family. Especially not now. She understood it, of course. Her heart's desire was just pathetically tragic in its out-of-reach simplicity.

She took a deep breath, looking at the seconds ticking away on her smartwatch.

'Five . . . Four . . . Three . . . Two . . .'

Before she could finish the countdown, he leaned towards her, his mouth so close to hers she could taste it, and murmured, '*One*. Happy New Year, Caroline.'

And then he kissed her, taking her breath away.

CHAPTER FORTY-ONE

Hunter

Hunter woke up early when it was still dark outside. Groggily, he reached towards the nightstand and grabbed his phone. Only 5.03 a.m. He yawned, throwing himself back against the pillows. It was a Sunday, early February. A slow day at the ranch. Going back to sleep would be the logical thing to do.

Trying to keep his eyes shut, he turned to his left side and pulled the pillow to his face. It smelled like her. The mix of the coconut leave-in conditioner and lavender pillow mist.

He knew this realisation shouldn't have surprised him. Over the past month, she had spent a lot of time right here, in his bed. He didn't have to dream to still see her green eyes, her lips wide open and the blush on her cheeks. He didn't have to fall asleep to hear the sounds she made, and he didn't have to imagine how it made him feel. His imagination never measured up to the real thing anyway.

And the real thing was epic.

Every. Single. Time.

Since New Year's Eve, Hunter had existed in a suspended state of grief mixed with denial. His days were filled with his family, trying like hell not to fall apart whenever he thought about his father, and keeping up pretences of normality with the ranch hands and Mitch. The world kept turning, even though his father was no longer there. So, every morning he got up. Went to work on the ranch. Rode horses. He had even restarted riding lessons for new sign-ups, and had found that he actually enjoyed it more than he remembered. He made a point of staying over for dinner almost every night, so that his mother felt a bit less alone. It was hard to tell whether it was helping. But he still did it.

And then there was Caroline. Even just the thought of trying to figure out his feelings for her was too much.

Resigned that he wouldn't be able to fall back to sleep, Hunter got out of bed. He put on a fresh pair of socks, pulled up his old, dark Levis and paused. Feeling an inexplicable pull towards the wooden nightstand, he sat back on the bed and slowly opened its single drawer. After hesitating for a couple of minutes, he gently lifted an ornate rectangular box and let his fingers clasp over its lid.

It was finally time to say a proper goodbye to Tamara.

The paint on the iron gate was mostly peeled off. Hunter tried to remember if it looked like this before.

It was eerily quiet. His black truck was the only car in the parking lot. He switched the engine off and pulled the key out from the ignition. Feeling a bit queasy, he realised he was gripping the steering wheel like it was a lifeline.

The sun was starting to travel up, lazily peeking over the

eastern horizon. Even though it was rather chilly, his black leather jacket suddenly felt too heavy. He tried to take a deep breath, but his throat was too dry. Coughing, he realised his heart was pounding.

Another twenty minutes or so passed. He didn't put the radio on. He didn't take his phone from his pocket. He didn't loosen his chalk-white knuckles' grip on the steering wheel.

It's OK. You're OK. You can do this. But you don't have to. It's up to you, Hunter.

A small, soft voice he heard inside his head wasn't his. His heart ached, but its rhythm slowed down a bit.

Lub-dub. Lub-dub.

He closed his eyes and put his right hand on his chest, pressing to the left, over his heart. Focusing on breathing in and out, he tried not to think. There would be time for that later. For now, he just needed to get out of the car. He needed to close the door and walk. Which he did, clutching the ornate box close like it was his most precious possession.

Even though he had been here only once before, he knew where he was going.

Neatly cut grass shimmered in the faint morning light. It felt soft beneath his heavy boots. The rows of marble and stone headstones looked as if they were aligned perfectly. Etched on their surfaces the letters composing names and dates followed him as he passed. Some were new. Some were old. Some had flowers next to them.

Hunter noticed one brown teddy bear, dressed as a pirate, leaning against a small cross at the end of the row.

Tightening his grip on the box, he continued. Four long steps forward, two steps across . . .

And then he stopped.

The sight of the white marble headstone crushed him anew. He fell to his knees, dew soaking through his denims.

Of course there was a grave. It had been five years. Hal and Pauline Clark wouldn't have let their only daughter be buried under anything less than the best they could afford.

Yet, seeing it for the first time made him feel ashamed.

He hadn't come here after the funeral. He couldn't bring himself to even drive past the cemetery for months.

It felt easier to try to patch up the open wound without being reminded about the finality of it. It didn't matter that it felt like trying to put a tiny Band-Aid on a deep penetrative cut to his very core. Maybe if he put enough Band-Aids over it, it'd finally stop haemorrhaging. A temporary fix. A short respite. A chance to forget . . .

Although he could never do that.

He didn't even come here after his father's funeral. It was on the opposite side of the cemetery. He'd thought about it but decided he couldn't.

'Hi, Tammy. It's me. I know I didn't come here. I'm sorry.' He paused, shifting his weight to settle more comfortably on the ground. 'I can't believe it's been five years. Some days it doesn't feel like long enough. But most days, it feels even longer—' His voice hitched. 'I . . . I can't remember the sound of your laugh anymore. I tried to the other day, and I realised I couldn't.'

Another deep breath. He looked away from the surface of the headstone. 'Damn, I miss you so much. You might meet my dad there now, wherever you are. He always liked you.'

He didn't care that he must've looked like an idiot talking to himself. It felt good to put his thoughts and feelings into words and say them aloud.

'Even though I can't remember your laugh, I'll never forget

your smile. It could warm up the worst cold.' He felt a genuine, shy smile in the corners of his mouth.

With a metallic click, his fingers twisted the lock on the box he'd brought.

They'd met in high school. It was one of these teenage love stories people wrote love songs about. They'd stayed together when they went off to college, Hunter to Texas A&M University, Tamara to Tulsa. They did long distance and saw each other as often as they could, driving back and forth. Before they headed off for their senior year, Hunter had proposed, and Tamara said yes.

He lifted the lid, revealing a stack of photos in polaroid style. The one on the top had a bent corner and looked like it had got crumpled sometime in the past.

Hunter smoothed it with his hand and took it out.

He remembered how they'd taken it within an hour of getting engaged. She had wanted to have a keepsake that'd remind her of the immeasurable joy. Her black, curly hair filled up most of the photo. Her face was turned away from the camera. She was resting her chin on Hunter's shoulder and her nose was pressed against his neck. Her left hand, lifted in the front, showed off a thin gold band with a perfectly red ruby. Her cheeks were flushed.

Hunter looked at the photo closer, even though he could draw it from memory. Only a third of his face was visible, but he knew how happy he was in that exact moment.

'We were meant to be forever. I'm so, so sorry. It was all my fault.'

There was water on his cheek. He moved his fingers up to brush it off and felt more tears slowly streaming down. His hand dropped, letting them flow.

He remembered the evening when Tamara's father had

called him and told him that Tamara was taken. Hunter didn't understand – had someone kidnapped her? Was she hurt? What did Hal mean by *taken*? So, Hal told him.

How a drunk truck driver had swerved into the incoming traffic lane. He had fallen asleep behind the wheel. Head-on collision. Tamara had died at the scene.

But why was she on Route 45 to begin with? Hunter didn't understand.

She was driving down to surprise you, Hal replied.

A seven-hour drive. Over four hundred miles. All because he had cancelled his visit to Tulsa the weekend before.

She told us she missed you so much and she thought she'd go for the weekend. She was meant to text us when she got there.

It happened just outside Centerville. She had almost made it to College Station.

Almost.

The guilt had hit him with a crashing force as soon as Hal hung up. He wasn't driving that truck, but he was the reason she was in that car on that route on that day. He hated himself for it. How could he ever deserve happiness again after this?

Five years was a long time and, logically, Hunter knew it wasn't his fault. But deep down, the guilt was still there. Lurking in the shadows of the darkest parts of his mind. The only reason he hadn't seen her the previous weekend was because he was too hungover from a fraternity party the night before. Which was no excuse at all.

He sighed. Slowly, he leaned forward and put the photo next to the headstone. There was a small heart formed from seashells and stones at its base. *Probably something Tamara's young cousins did*, he thought. Instinctively, he lifted the biggest seashell and put it over the photo, anchoring it in place.

'I . . . I met someone. And although it probably won't work out, for the first time since you . . . since you—' His voice broke again, and he impatiently wiped his eyes with his jacket sleeve.

He couldn't finish that thought.

He inhaled deeply and moved on. 'I care about her. It scares the hell out of me because I only ever cared about you and . . . Well, it's just . . . complicated. And I know I'm a fool and if you saw me now, I'm sure you'd get a right kick out of it. But you're the one who told me I was a hopeless romantic. Maybe I hid this part of myself for too long, and now it's like the floodgates of idiocy have opened. Who knows.'

Hunter stopped, realising he had said all he wanted to say. He started looking over the remaining photos from the box.

So many memories.

So many life-changing events.

So many firsts.

So many smiles.

One immense loss.

When Hunter finally got up, the winter sun was already up in its daytime position. He looked up at it and nodded, like greeting an old friend. Or saying goodbye to one.

He looked back at the headstone. There were no more tears left in him.

Walking back to his truck with the box in his hand one photo lighter, he felt different. More resigned than peaceful, but at the same time he knew he had to let himself keep on living.

If just over four months was all the time he had left with Caroline, he didn't want to waste it. His heart was already stuffed with suffocating regret. He had promised his father he'd try opening himself up again. Even if it meant getting hurt.

Maybe the cosmic forces would align and somehow it could work out. Maybe he could move to Scotland, at some point – he had liked it there a lot. Maybe the universe would decide he had suffered enough and had some goodness coming his way.

Or maybe he was just a hopeful fool. Either way, he was done denying how he felt. If he stripped all the confusion and confounding factors away, layer by layer, all it really boiled down to were three words.

He loved her.

And he was going to tell her, when the time was right.

CHAPTER FORTY-TWO

Caroline

'Do you want to do anything on Friday?' Hunter asked, walking back into his bedroom in nothing but a pair of boxers.

'Why?' Caroline flipped to the next page of the book. It was one of those reads she had thought of not finishing but decided to push through; two chapters later it got so good she didn't want to put it down. Even though it was 7 a.m. on a Monday morning and she had to get up for work.

A wet towel landed at the foot of the bed, and she felt the mattress go down a bit as Hunter got back in.

'No reason.' He pushed himself up, peeking over her shoulder. 'Any good?'

'You know it's good,' she responded, feeling a warm smile on her lips. 'You read it first.'

'Ah.' He pushed the cover down, letting his hand rest on her left thigh. 'But our tastes sometimes differ.'

She held her breath, desire rising within her as his fingers lazily drew circles on her skin.

'Don't you agree?' His hand slowly climbed up, reaching the fabric of her underwear. He paused there and looked at her, eyes filled with lust.

She bit her bottom lip, as his hand sneaked up half an inch further. 'I think you know my taste better than anyone.' Without looking, she closed her book and threw it on the floor. Her hands reached for Hunter's head, sinking her fingers into his dark hair, still damp from the shower.

'I agree,' he said in a raspy voice. Without a warning, he pushed past the material and stroked her.

Caroline took a deep breath and closed her eyes.

'Right now, I think we both want me to go down on you. I know how much you like that.' His playful, unarticulated question hung in the air.

Her cheeks were already hot, her heart rate already up . . . She opened her eyes, just a little bit. When they gazed into his sparkling grey ones, she let out a loud sigh which resembled a moan.

'Hunter . . .'

'I'll take that as a yes.' He didn't waste time on any further foreplay, hungrily pushing her down on the bed. Untying her pyjama top, her mouth found his and their lips commenced a delicious dance of quick, uncontrolled passion.

Before she knew it, he had pulled her underwear off.

She opened her legs, and he got up to kneel on the floor. She shuffled her bottom further down the mattress, stopping only when his hands steadied her sides. He looked up and their eyes met again. A shiver ran down her spine. Legs wrapped round his back, one hand in his hair . . .

When his tongue touched her, it was like a lightning stroke

to her insides. Before she knew it, she couldn't think. All she was able to do was focus on the building pleasure – then, to cry out in a release so powerful it felt like the earth shattered beneath her. She wished she could stay lying here. She wished she could bottle up that relaxed feeling after.

It never lasted long enough.

'I'd better go, otherwise I'm going to hit the rush hour traffic.' She bent down and placed a quick, soft kiss on Hunter's lips.

As she turned on her heel, he caught her wrist and tugged on it.

'Hunter.' She tried to put on a stern expression but couldn't stop her mouth from curling up.

He smiled and kissed her again, ardently. When they separated, she felt a little bit dizzy. He smirked, satisfied. 'I'll see you on Wednesday.'

'Are you sure you can last that long?' She shot him an exasperated look on the way to the bathroom.

Half an hour later, Caroline was stuck in roadworks just outside the city centre. The digital clock on the dashboard stated she still had twenty-five minutes. Agitated, she turned up the radio and started drumming her fingers on the wheel to the music. A wave of warmth washed over her as the next song came on. Her fingers went still, and her mind flicked back to New Year's Eve.

'That was a song from this week's spotlight artist. Very romantic, don't you think? Just the right tune to put you in that mood for Valentine's Day on Friday. What are you up to that evening? Text—'

Caroline froze, switching off from the rest of the radio presenter's talk. *Valentine's Day*. That's why Hunter had asked her if she wanted to do anything on Friday. He was so casual, so *him* that she didn't even think about it. Until now.

How could she not have realised? An instant wave of anxiety rose in her chest, speeding up her heartbeat. They weren't close, in that way. Were they?

She swallowed hard, trying to analyse the past few months, particularly the past month. They had a good time together. They were there for each other. She enjoyed his company, and she knew he enjoyed hers. But that was surely it, wasn't it? Because the alternative was . . .

An angry honk from behind snapped her back to the present, a mere three seconds after the temporary traffic lights turned green.

The alternative was scary and completely unacceptable.

But you've been thinking about it. Wishing for it.

Maybe she was catastrophising. Maybe it really wasn't as complicated as she made it out to be. Maybe feelings were a good thing.

She lifted her hand in apology and drove through the single file stretch of road. Ten minutes later, she pulled in to the car park. Her cheeks were still a shade of pink when she walked into the building.

Since travelling to San Diego for ASH together, Amira had become even friendlier towards Caroline. It was nice to have someone like her at work; she was a great colleague, maybe even a friend.

'I met Jake's parents on Sunday. After only three months of dating! That's too soon, right?'

When Caroline didn't answer her, Amira let out a melodramatic sigh and put her hand over her forehead. 'I knew it was way too soon! What was he thinking?!'

'I'm sure he was just excited to introduce you to them. Didn't he say he had a crush on you since, like, day one?' Caroline said, closing the Excel spreadsheet on her computer. The Monday workday was finally over. 'How were they?' she asked, typing a quick email to a medical writer with whom she'd been working on a slide deck for an upcoming steering committee for OnyxRex.

'They're fine, I guess,' Amira huffed, turning round in her swivel chair. 'But he has three younger sisters – *three*! Do you know how long the dinner felt when they all ganged up on me? The CIA are probably less intense during their interrogations.'

'The CIA, huh?' Caroline asked, not taking her eyes off the computer screen. She clicked several times, exiting all open applications and shutting the system down. 'I'm sure they weren't that bad.'

'But they really were! Can you imagine that—'

Caroline stopped listening. Her eyes bore into the vibrating screen of her personal mobile phone.

Why would he be calling?

'I'm so sorry, Amira, but I have to take this.' She jumped up to her feet and almost jogged out of the office, phone in hand.

Once she was safely in the empty hall, she took a deep breath and pressed the green button. 'Hello, Robb. How are you?'

'Caroline. Hi.' There was some crackling at his side of the line. 'I'm fine, both me and Annie are. I'm sorry to call you over there—'

'Don't be silly,' she interrupted, trying to keep her voice steady. 'What's going on?'

'I . . . Well, damn it. I'd better get right to it.' More crackling in her speaker. 'I know that you and Finn have agreed on a divorce. I also know what happened between you.' He paused. Caroline didn't say anything. Robb took it as an invitation to continue. 'I never wanted to get in the middle of whatever it is that you guys are going through. But Annie's been bugging me about it for weeks and . . . Fuck, I'm worried about him too.'

'What are you talking about?' she choked, in a voice that didn't belong to her.

'Finn's had those headaches; they don't seem to go away with any meds. And he's lost the hearing in his left ear.'

Caroline flinched, feeling a sharp pain in her hands. She looked at her left hand and saw red marks where her fingernails dug in.

'Do you know if he's seen a doctor?'

'Well . . . that's the thing. He's been getting various tests and whatnot for weeks now. We were meant to meet up yesterday for a round of golf. But he didn't show.'

Her mouth felt dry.

'I went to check on him, still have the spare key, and found him unconscious on the floor. He's in hospital, but they're saying he has a mass in his brain.' Robb paused, tension mixed with worry palpable in the cross-Atlantic connection.

'I . . .' She was lost for words.

'I'm really worried about him, Car. I'd have never called you if I wasn't. But is there any way you could come back? I think he wants you here but is too proud to ask you himself.'

Silence.

Caroline didn't know what to say and clearly Robb expected her to say something. She clutched her mobile tightly, swallowing the bitter taste of guilty tears. 'I'll be in Glasgow on the earliest flight I can.'

She hung up, walked back into the office in a daze and mumbled something about needing to get back home to Amira. Before she had realised how she got there, she was back in Anna and Gian's apartment. Hands shaking, she bought the plane tickets and pulled out her suitcases from under the bed.

Somehow she managed to type out a hurried message to Hunter: *I need to go back to Glasgow immediately. Finn needs me. My flight's tomorrow. I won't be coming back. I'm so sorry.*

That was all she was able to say. Pressing the letters on her screen made everything real. If she told him more, if she explained why she had to go . . .

Don't think about it. Finn's going to be fine.

Caroline didn't know how long she had been aimlessly wandering around the room, dumping her belongings in unorganised chaos into the open suitcase. Hours might've passed.

She ignored her buzzing phone, walked to the wardrobe and pulled down another handful of hangers, then threw them over the large pile of clothes on her bed.

Another buzz.

Her hands paused over a half-folded black alpaca cardigan. No, she wouldn't look at the screen. She knew who it was. Childish as it seemed, she just couldn't speak to him right now. Steadying herself, she returned to packing.

'I don't think this is a good idea . . .' She heard Gian's voice from the kitchen as loud footsteps approached her room.

The door opened, bringing in a whiff of crisp February air.

'What the fuck, Caroline?! You won't answer my calls or texts now? Were you really going to disappear without even a goodbye?'

She closed her eyes, not turning to face him. 'I texted you.'

'To say you're flying back to Glasgow tomorrow and you won't be back?! Fuck this.'

Hunter started pacing across the small bedroom.

Her heart ached the moment he stepped into the room. She wanted to disappear into his arms. She wanted to be held by him, to be told it was going to be OK. That Finn would be all right. That they still had the months they'd thought they would have, that they'd ride together at sunset as the warmer weather rolled in . . . She wanted him to know how much strength it took to make this decision. The only right one in these circumstances.

But she couldn't show any of it. There was only one thing she could do.

She calmly put the folded pair of navy suit trousers into the suitcase. 'I *was* planning to say goodbye,' she said quietly. Slowly, she turned round and looked at him.

His eyes met hers. The despair and the longing written in them made her breathless.

She coughed, pulling on the mask of indifference even tighter. 'I just needed to finish packing first. My flight is tomorrow afternoon.'

'I don't understand why you're even going.'

'Because Finn needs me. You won't understand it.' She turned back to her suitcase and put another pair of trousers in.

'Then help me understand.' His voice trembled, some of the anger disappearing. 'Please,' he added, and she felt cold spread through her.

'You want to understand? Fine!' She threw her hands up in the air, starting to pace between the bed and the desk. 'I married my best friend. An amazing guy. But it wasn't the fairy tale I imagined, so I took off, fleeing to another country and leaving him in the name of what?!'

'Happiness?'

Irritation rose in her again. 'Happiness, really?' She let out an exasperated growl. 'You think I'm happy? Living in this fucked-up fantasy that has a time limit on it? Not even the best sex can make me forget that I don't deserve any happiness. I don't deserve anything good!'

Hunter grimaced. 'So, suddenly you remembered your husband. Wow.' His body shook slightly, and she saw his legs almost give way under him. He rested his back against the chest of drawers in the corner of the room. 'I don't even know what to say.'

'You don't have to say anything,' she muttered.

She didn't have the heart to tell him the reason. He was still reeling from his father's death; it would stir in too much for him. And talking about it . . . talking about it made her think about the worst-case scenario. That Finn was going to die.

She simply couldn't let herself imagine that.

Hunter laughed. It wasn't the usual bright, warm laugh. It didn't sound like anything she'd heard from him before. It sounded low and dark.

'And you think I'm going to believe that after everything, *everything* that's happened between us, you're really going to go back to him? Is a transatlantic flight all it takes to forget this?' He crossed the room in three long steps, pulling her in a rough kiss.

Despite herself, her body responded eagerly. A moan of pleasure escaped her mouth as Hunter deepened the kiss. Her mind went blank, and she didn't want to think. It took all her willpower to pull away from him.

Caroline crossed her arms over her chest, taking in a few steadying breaths. 'It's not about forgetting you. It's about remembering that as nice as it was while it lasted between us, we both knew it was just temporary. True, we thought there was more time. But maybe it's better this way.'

'Oh, it's certainly not better this way,' he bit off. He was so close she could feel his chest rising and falling as he breathed. 'And speak for yourself regarding temporary. I know that's what we said at the very beginning, but it went much further than that.'

'Did it?' she asked, the strain it took to keep her face impassive unbearable.

Hunter let out an impatient groan. He tugged at his hair, then his hands went down to his face and covered his eyes for a moment. When he pulled them away, he looked a bit taller. Like he wouldn't back away from whatever he decided.

'I wasn't going to say it now. I wanted to wait for the right moment. Hell, the fact that I will probably makes me the most selfish bastard in a twenty-block radius. If you're leaving anyway, I might as well say it now. It probably won't matter to you. It won't make you change your mind. But it'll give me peace. And I think I deserve at least that.' He took a deep breath. 'I love you, Caroline.'

Caroline froze. She felt like someone had stolen her voice. The room spun in front of her eyes. No, it wasn't spinning. *It's just your anxiety. The room's solid. You're solid. You're fine.*

This was unexpected and not at all how she'd planned. It took her a long moment to gather her thoughts. Then, she felt anger rise in her.

How could he? Whatever his feelings, now was really not the time for this. Plus, how could he *love* her, really?

'Why?'

Hunter blinked, staring at her in disbelief. When she didn't say anything, didn't even move a muscle, he said, 'Why? Because you drive me fucking crazy and yet I still want to spend every waking moment with you. *That's why.*' He took a step back, sadness extinguishing the last of the fury in his eyes. He watched her in anticipation, his eyes willing her to say something.

'Oh, this is just brilliant.' She laughed grimly, shaking her head in disbelief. 'You think that you can tell me that you love me and that'll, what, make me stay?'

'Why wouldn't it?' He took another step towards her and tried to take her hand, but she shook him off.

'Love isn't simple, and it isn't enough to make things work. And even if I played along with it, how do you exactly imagine us ever working out?' She crossed her arms tighter, daring him to say something that wouldn't just add fuel to her fire.

'You could move here. Doctors can work anywhere in the world, right? You like the area, Anna and Gian are here—'

Caroline scoffed, closing her eyes. 'Why am I not surprised that all of this hinges on me giving up my own life to fit around yours?'

'How can you say that after the past months?!' His voice was raised now as well, and he went back to nervous pacing. 'I told you that I love you and you're getting hung up on the details.'

'You think these are details? My career, my life? That's *just details*?!' She didn't mean to shout but maybe if she said it loudly enough, it'd ring truer. 'I can't move here and be a doctor, just like that. Even if I managed to, it'd certainly not be oncology. And that's what I want to do,' she said quietly. 'The confession might be huge for you. But it's just words to me.' She looked at him, her eyes full of resolve.

It was never meant to end like this but was there even a

way to make it hurt less? Looking into Hunter's grey eyes, she knew there wasn't. And it was all her fault.

There was only one thing she could do. She took a deep breath and forced herself not to look away.

'I should've known better. If I'd known you were going to end up falling in love with me, I never would have started it.'

CHAPTER FORTY-THREE

Hunter

Hunter slammed his front door with such force that he was surprised it didn't fall off the hinges. After he stormed out of Anna and Gian's apartment, he managed to calm himself a bit in his F-150 before he started driving. Now that he was home, he ripped off the mask of pretence.

He shuddered, an unbearable sensation of hot and cold overtaking him. He walked to the kitchen counter and felt a strong urge to swipe his hand through the surface, taking off everything in his way – from the utensils to the block of knives, coffee machine, kettle, stack of stoneware mugs . . .

Everyone I love leaves.

He flexed his fingers and looked down at his hands. They instantly stopped shaking. He inhaled again. Without switching the light on, he slumped into the armchair.

Why did he tell her that he loved her? How could he go from not being able to even think about what he felt to saying those three words, eight letters that he naively thought would make her stay?

She didn't even let him finish saying that if she didn't want to move here, he could maybe move to Scotland. That he'd already started thinking about it.

He didn't know how long he sat in the complete darkness. His mind raced, overwhelmed by an enormous strength of different feelings and emotions. He was furious. Angry. Hurt. Frightened. *Broken.* Terrified that he was never going to feel this way about anyone else.

If he could hate her, he could clutch on to that. If he could hate her, he could be happy that she was disappearing from his life. And it was just what she would do. There was no risk of bumping into her while shopping or awkwardly seeing her across the bar or restaurant. He wouldn't pass her in a workplace corridor or see her as he drove through the Oklahoma City streets. She'd be gone. In a different country, on another continent. An ocean and thousands of miles away.

He felt his heartbeat quicken as the realisation hit him.

He'd never see her again.

'You left so fast I forgot to give your keys back.'

He heard her open the door, but Caroline didn't switch the light on. Her voice was almost a whisper. Gone was the confident, high conviction from just a few hours ago.

He grunted in acknowledgement.

'I'll just leave them here.'

He heard the keys being placed in a glass bowl on the shoe cabinet by the door.

'Are you going to be OK?'

'Now you want me to believe that you care?'

'That isn't fair. You know I do.'

'Do I?' Hunter stood, feeling a bit wobbly. Like he had a

hangover even though he hadn't had a drink in two weeks. He reached over to the floor lamp next to the TV and switched it on. 'I thought I knew you well but, apparently, I was wrong. Never in a million years would I have thought you'd say you're going back to your husband.'

Caroline hesitated, but then she closed the front door behind her. The darkness swallowed her without the faint glow of the outside area lighting. She took an uncertain step towards him.

'I'm not going back to him.'

Hunter furrowed his brow as she took another step forward. 'Then why are you going? Please, Caroline, help me understand. Because it makes no sense.'

She was so close now that he could see her green eyes in the light from the lamp. They were glassy and full of sadness. 'Finn has a mass in his brain. His best friend called me today and asked me to come. I can't . . . I can't—' She burst into tears, choking on the words.

Wrapping his arms around her was like instinct. He pulled her to his chest, holding her tight as her tears soaked through his shirt. His senses froze when she'd said the two words that ripped the makeshift bandage over his barely beating heart: mass, brain. Images of his father's brain on the big screen in the conference room at the hospital flashed in front of his eyes.

'You need to be there for him,' he whispered into her hair. He wasn't sure he'd said it out loud but he felt her chin move against him as she nodded.

'I love him.'

Hunter's jaw tensed but there was not even a flicker of anger left in him. He knew what she meant. Finn was important to her. He would always be important to her, in a complicated and messy way. If it was Tamara, if there was anything he could've done . . . If he could've been there for her in the end . . .

He wouldn't have hesitated. He would've bargained with the very essence of who he was if that meant she lived.

'I know.' His own eyes pricked with tears.

She wriggled out of his arms and took a step back. Her face was red but her eyes appeared to have run out of tears. 'I don't want you to think that *we* didn't matter. Because it isn't true. I'm only sorry that it got this far.'

'I'm not sorry.' Her head snapped up at his thick voice. 'I could never be sorry that I got to know you.'

Caroline looked down at the floor. 'I never wanted to hurt you.'

Hunter took her hand into his. 'You asked why I haven't told you I was engaged before.' Her body stilled. 'Her name was Tamara. She was killed in a car accident not long after I proposed. It was five years ago, and between the heart-ripping grief of losing her and my father getting sick . . . I wasn't living. I was merely existing. Until I met you.'

He ran his thumb over her knuckles, struggling to breathe through his rumbling heart. 'You brought happiness back into my life. You showed me that I can be happy again. Don't ever be sorry for that.'

'I am though. I didn't want things to end this way.' She sniffed. 'Why didn't you tell me about her?'

'I didn't tell you the night of the karaoke because I was still making sense of my own feelings. She died on her way to see me. I felt responsible even though I wasn't the drunk truck driver who killed her.'

'It wasn't your fault.'

Hunter gave her a sad, barely there smile. 'I know that,

now. But it's only something I've come to terms with recently.' He swallowed hard. 'I understand why you need to go.'

'I wish I didn't need to. I wish we had more time.'

They looked at each other and Hunter felt a spark within his stomach. It spread across his chest, up to his throat. 'I don't know how to say goodbye to you,' he choked, avoiding her eyes.

Caroline cupped his cheek, wiping away a tear, which slowly created a wet streak. 'I don't know how to either.'

He looked at her and his breath hitched.

It defied all reason. Yet, he covered her hand with his and looked deep into her eyes. Their eye contact was more intimate than words could ever be.

She was motionless, holding her breath in anticipation.

'I suppose . . . if this is goodbye, we should leave with no regrets. No sadness.' He looked down to her mouth, which was open slightly. He leaned down, stopping mere inches from her lips. 'I want you to remember how it felt when we were together.'

She blinked.

Hunter wasn't sure who moved first – he thought it might've been her, but the distance between them closed as their lips crushed together.

They had had sex countless times. Each time, it was both familiar and new. Exciting. With every touch, he'd felt like he was peeling away new layers of her inhibitions and worries. He'd learned how to coax the most pleasure out of her. How to make her scream and want more. She'd done the same to him. They had become attentive to each other's needs, learning their deepest desires. Despite all that, right now, he was like a nerdy kid stumbling into the most exquisite library. He didn't know if it was the finality of it. This was the last time he was going to make love to her. And his body somehow knew that. The intensity, the desperation . . . Both made him feel like he was on fire.

He didn't think it was possible to feel this much desire.

In a frenzied dance of passion, they stumbled to the table.

Caroline cocked her head to the side, a curious expression on her face. 'You know, this is one surface we haven't done it on yet.'

'I think it's a perfect opportunity to remedy that.' He watched, mesmerised, as she took off her blue shirt dress; it pooled at her feet. Next, she pulled down her bra strap, exposing both of her breasts.

He peppered her bare clavicle and shoulder with fiery kisses.

She moaned, jumping on the table. 'Agreed.' She sank her fingers into his hair and tugged on it slightly.

He groaned, feeling a stab of pain. His teeth marked her arm. She lay down, back pressed against the table. Hunter positioned himself over her, finding her lips with more dizzying kisses. After she hooked her leg round his waist, after she took her bra off, after he clumsily rid himself of his shirt, the heady affection overtook him. He lost track of time. He felt like he was losing his mind. It was perfection. *She* was perfection.

'Caroline . . .' He looked at her as he climbed to the top of ecstasy. Her eyes were closed, mindless, all-consuming pleasure etched on her beautiful face. He kissed her, dragging his teeth over her bottom lip. She whimpered, green eyes flying open. This was all he needed to come.

'Hunter – I—'

They rode on the high of pleasure together, collapsing in each others arms as the trembling subsided.

'Can I stay? One last night?' she murmured into his neck.

And she did. Because he didn't want to refuse her. And, selfishly, he wanted to cherish being able to fall asleep while holding her in his arms. If this was the last time he could do it, he wanted to remember every detail. How she looked when she opened her eyes in the morning. The weird little noises she made as she was falling asleep. He knew he was thoroughly pathetic and that he should've told her to go.

But if being pathetic was what took for him to deal with losing her, then so be it.

In the morning, Hunter watched her get dressed. Caroline was jumpy, unfocused, and forgetful. She slid on her shoes, took her handbag, and looked round the room awkwardly.

'I...I—' Her voice broke a bit, but her eyes were clear. 'Goodbye, Hunter. I'll never forget you, that's for sure.'

'I'm not going to say goodbye to you. Because as idiotic as it might sound, I believe we might meet again. Someday. Somehow.' His voice croaked and he felt his chest tighten. This was ridiculous. How could this be happening?

'I hope you know how much you mean to me,' she said, not looking at him.

He jumped out of bed, not caring that he was completely naked.

She blushed as he stood in front of her. Wordlessly, he pulled her into a kiss like no other. It was the kiss into which he tried to put everything he didn't know how to say. He wanted her to know how *he* felt. Not like the ridiculous, childish outburst of yesterday's declaration; that was a moment of weakness. He was too scared to let her go.

'You mean everything to me.'

'Hunter—'

'Don't.' He shook his head, holding back tears. He knew

he wasn't meant to fall for her, that it was just a temporary – what did people call it nowadays, a situationship? He was certain Meg had mentioned that term to him recently. He leaned down again, stopping a mere inch from her lips.

She closed her mouth, pulling away from him.

Tears shone in the corners of her eyes.

'Goodbye, Hunter,' she whispered.

He reached for her hand, but she turned away from him and practically ran out the door. He kept on holding on.

It was never meant to end like this. Standing alone in the middle of his quiet house, Hunter felt like his heart, which had just started to heal after losing Tamara, broke anew.

The evening came and with it, Hunter found himself sitting at the bar. He was flicking a cardboard coaster in a shape of a beer bottle back and forth between his fingers. The memory of their first meeting barged into his mind, and he dropped the coaster like it burned. Feeling a deep resentment, he looked at the clock.

'Hunt. That's like the fiftieth time you've looked at that clock within the past hour.' Mitch shook his head.

'Her plane will be taking off . . . right about now.' Hunter leaned back, emptiness filling him to the brim. He lifted the whisky glass in front of him and took a long sip.

Mitch studied his profile carefully. 'I don't understand. Why did you let her go?'

'What was I supposed to do, Mitch? Tie her up? Steal her passport? She needed to go be with Finn. There's not more to it than that.'

'You could've gone after her. Chicks always fall for that in the movies.'

Hunter shot him a disbelieving look. *If only that would've changed anything.*

'What? They do. Everyone loves that shit. The guy runs through the airport, confesses his love and then they live happily ever after.'

'Remind me never to let you pick the movies.'

Mitch shrugged.

'You know what they say, Mitch. If you love someone, set them free.' Hunter downed the rest of his whisky. 'She's never been anything but free with me. I respect her, and myself, too much to go and do something like that. She knows how I feel.' He signalled the bartender to pour him another double of Redbreast.

Ironically, Scotch reminded him too much of her, so he'd ordered a twelve-year-old Redbreast. Then, he'd realised how twisted that was, considering she was Irish.

He chuckled to himself.

'And you didn't tell me she was still married.' Mitch's voice had an uncomfortable edge to it.

'I was going to tell you, at the beginning, but it was the night you asked me to keep Eve's engagement ring and decided against it. Honestly? I was ashamed.'

'I wouldn't have judged.'

'I know.' He gave Mitch a grateful grimace. 'But it wasn't my proudest moment.'

He didn't mention his fanciful musings about moving to Scotland. This wasn't the time for it. What if her husband didn't recover? What if he needed long-term care? What if he died? She needed space for whatever transpired once she got back.

He continued watching the clock tick away, knowing that with every minute, Caroline was moving further away from him, forever.

CHAPTER FORTY-FOUR

Caroline

Caroline had lost track of the number of times she'd questioned her decision to leave Oklahoma. It clung to her like an octopus as she walked through the airport, as she went through security, as she looked over the Atlantic through the small window, as she disembarked for her layover in Amsterdam, and as she took the taxi ride from Glasgow Airport to the hospital.

It still lingered, although in the background, as she briskly walked through the familiar entrance.

She had made her choice, and she knew she'd have to just live with it. At first, she told herself she had no choice. But that was bullshit. She'd read once that people always had a choice, even if that choice was limited.

Was there really any question she'd go? Of course there wasn't.

Finn had a mass on his brain. Very likely a brain tumour. Probably cancer.

There was no world in which she wouldn't have come. Whatever happened, he was Finn. She had loved him for more than half her life.

Caroline stopped before walking through the door to the neurology ward. It felt strange being back here. When she was in Oklahoma, time had passed differently. Some days, being a doctor was like a distant memory. Others, she'd missed it like it was the air she breathed.

It was always easy to forget about it all with Hunter.

The mere thought of him made her ache with regret.

Tears of sorrow streaked her cheeks, and she tried to stop the flow with her hand.

In an act of desperation, Caroline had asked if they could delete each other's numbers before she left. *I can't do it otherwise. I'm not strong enough*, she'd told him. Hunter hadn't seemed thrilled by this idea, but they did it. Together. That moment was, in a way, like *'The End'* to their story. Beautifully unfinished. Maybe this was all they were ever meant to be.

She wiped her tears with the sleeve of her blouse. She wasn't sure who they were for. Finn? Hunter? Probably a little bit for them both. Worried for Finn, regretful for Hunter.

Selfishly heartbroken for herself.

Then, she took in a deep breath and pressed the button to open the ward door.

One of the nurses led her to Finn's room. With every step closer, her heart thundered. There were too many possibilities of what she could expect. She knew too much. The curse of knowing the likely ending to a life story married to a diagnosis.

But even though she had all that knowledge, all those years of training, when she saw Finn lying in the hospital bed, her heart dropped to the floor.

He was awake, propped up in a half-seated position. His face was turned to the window.

She saw his reflection in it; he saw hers. Caroline noticed the exact moment his eyes flickered with shock.

'Hi,' she croaked, cautiously approaching the bed.

Finn was pale, and there were dark circles under his eyes. But aside from that, and the medical equipment surrounding him, he hadn't changed. He hadn't visibly lost weight, an observation that gave Caroline a tiny glimmer of hope that maybe it wasn't cancer.

'Car. What— How . . . I don't understand.'

She smiled through tears pricking at the corners of her eyes. 'Robb called me. Did you really think you could collapse and I wouldn't find out?'

'It's nothing. I'm fine.'

Caroline pulled up a chair. 'Finn. Why didn't you call me?'

He avoided her eyes, feigning interest in a cannula attached to the top of his hand. 'We're getting a divorce.'

'And you think that means I automatically stopped caring?' Her voice trembled. 'If it was me, would you have dropped everything and come?'

Finn looked up, meeting her glare. 'In a heartbeat.'

She let out a shuddering breath, reaching out for his hand. 'Our marriage is over. But you're still you and I'm still me. I love you.'

His lip quivered as he swallowed. 'I ruined your research exchange. You really didn't have to come. I'm sure it's going to be fine.' He squeezed her hands.

'Forget about it, it doesn't matter. All that matters is that you get better. What did the doctors say?'

Her throat constricted, she rolled her shoulders and cleared her throat. This she could do. Talk through possible diagnoses. Discuss the results. Research treatment options. Take him to the appointments. Help him at home. These were all tangible ways she could be useful.

'I had tons of tests before I passed out. They ruled out a bunch of stuff, but they think it's a tumour.'

Not a single muscle twitched in Caroline's face. Her mind raced, combing through different brain tumour types. But she didn't want to worry Finn, or herself.

'What time are they rounding?' she asked instead.

'Should be soon. Do you want to stay?' Finn gave her an unsure smile. 'You might understand what they say. My accounting degree is hopeless against medical jargon.'

She nodded. 'Of course.'

'Thank you. Now, tell me about Oklahoma,' Finn said, holding on to her hand.

Neither of them let go until the consultant neurologist came in with several residents and two medical students trotting behind him.

'Mr McCarthy, how are you feeling today?' the consultant asked from the foot of the bed, checking his chart.

'Same as I did yesterday. Eager to finally know what's wrong with me. Now that my wife's here, I might even understand what's going on.'

'Caroline O'Kelly. Long time, no see.' Short, square-jawed with a shaved head, the resident grinned at her. 'Last I saw you, we were both languishing in the Ayr's emergency department chasing away that bird . . . Was it a pigeon?'

Caroline snorted, standing to shake his hand. 'It was a crow. Hi, Justin.'

The consultant looked to her. 'You're a doctor?'

Caroline bit the inside of her cheek. She hated to be put

on the spot. 'Yes. Though I'm taking a year out from the training. Figuring out my speciality options.'

The consultant grunted. 'I'm Dr Henry Roering, consultant neurologist. I've been looking after your husband.' He looked to Finn. 'Are you happy for your wife to stay in the room, Mr McCarthy?'

Finn nodded.

Dr Roering asked one of the residents to present the case, asked if anyone had any questions. Caroline had a distinct feeling of déjà vu observing the set up.

It's going to be you again soon.

'So, Mr McCarthy. We finally have an answer to what's been going on with you. You have a clear cell meningioma in your left cerebellopontine angle.'

Caroline let out a semi-relieved breath. It wasn't good news by any means, but it wasn't the worst news.

Finn blinked. 'What's that?'

'Your brain and spinal cord are covered with different layers; they're called meninges. They are membranes that essentially act like protection barriers. Meningiomas are tumours originating in these layers, and they can start anywhere in your brain or spinal cord. They're actually very common – nearly one third of all brain tumours are meningiomas.'

'Is it cancer?' Finn asked.

'No. Most of these tumours are benign. There are three different grades we use to classify them and various subtypes. Some we can just watch and wait, and nothing needs to be done for them immediately. But, unfortunately, yours is grade two. It's a rare subtype which can grow fast and is what we call an aggressive tumour.'

'You're going to operate?' Caroline asked, barely feeling

her fingers as Finn crushed them in his hands harder with every sentence coming out of Dr Roering's mouth.

'Yes. I'll have a neurosurgeon specialising in them come and meet you either later today or tomorrow to discuss the surgery further.'

'Is that it? The surgery's going to cure it?' Finn asked.

'Unfortunately, these tumours have a high relapse rate. They can recur in more than two thirds of patients after the surgery. So, we're going to design a course of radiotherapy for after the surgery. That's going to reduce the relapse risk.'

'What if it still comes back, despite radiotherapy?'

'We'll monitor you closely and can take it from there. More radiotherapy or radiosurgery are all viable options. But our hope is, of course, that we're going to cut it out, do a course of radiotherapy, and it'll be gone.'

Dr Roering looked at both Finn and Caroline. 'Do you have any questions just now?'

Finn shook his head slowly. 'No . . . It's a lot to take in.'

'Understandably.' Dr Roering put his pen back in his shirt pocket. 'I'll let you digest it all, and talk. I'll come back in the afternoon, and we can talk some more.'

The medical entourage exited the room, leaving Caroline and Finn alone with the buzzing words filling the air.

'Not cancer,' Finn repeated, staring at the wall. 'That's good, right?'

'Yes.' Her voice was thick with emotion; there were so many things that could go wrong, the possible complications of the brain surgery alone being huge. But she didn't want to take away from the positive note.

'I'm sorry I called you my wife. I thought it'll be easier for medical appointments and all . . . You're still my next of kin. I thought it'd be too difficult to explain.'

'Of course.' Caroline squeezed his hand again, looking into his eyes. 'We're going to get you through this. You'll be fine.'

She wasn't sure who she was trying to reassure more – him or herself.

CHAPTER FORTY-FIVE

Hunter

Summer was Hunter's favourite season. Although it often got too hot and tornadoes were quite common, he still would happily extend summer to last longer. July was the warmest month. And this year, you could really feel it.

'Damn, I'm going to miss this place. I know the house is staying but it won't be the same,' Buck said with nostalgia, looking at Rory leading Pringle inside the barn. 'Did you tell the crew?'

Hunter nodded, taking a sip of his beer. 'Told them last week.'

They were sitting on the veranda, warmed by the evening air.

'We still have time until the end of September.'

'Are you having second thoughts?' Buck asked.

'Weirdly, no. You?'

'Once or twice.' Buck shrugged, emptying his bottle. 'But I never wanted to run the ranch anyway.'

'Neither did I, not really.' Hunter furrowed his brow. 'I always thought that I had to. Because you didn't want to, neither did Meg, and someone had to do it. I thought that's what Dad wanted.'

He found that speaking about his father didn't throw him off balance these days. He'd never forget him, but every day it hurt a bit less. The anger and injustice he'd felt after he died was slowly replaced by being grateful for the time they'd had together. It was a slow process, like taking out single squares from a Rubik's cube and replacing them with new, lighter ones. But it was still progress.

'Well, he surprised us all. He hated to be predictable.' Buck smirked, opening the portable cooler standing by his reclining chair. 'What are you going to do, after the ranch is gone?'

'I'm not sure.' The crease between Hunter's brows deepened. 'I know I want to work with horses – that's what I really enjoy. Maybe I'll buy a much smaller ranch exclusively for horses and run it myself.' He took the new bottle of beer Buck offered him and popped the top off it. 'Or maybe I'll take off and travel a bit. I feel like I haven't really been anywhere.'

'Do you have a place in mind where you want to buy the ranch?'

Hunter didn't answer straight away. The idea had taken seed in his mind a while ago, but he hadn't shared it with anyone yet. It was solely his; a happy thought he could escape to.

'I was thinking of Aberdeenshire.'

Buck choked on his beer. 'As in, Scotland?'

'Yeah. Where Gran was from.' Hunter bit back a smile. 'I loved it there when I took her. Just felt like a place I could rediscover myself in. There are too many memories here, of Tamara, of Dad . . . I just want to start afresh.'

It was also Caroline's place. Her home. As ridiculous as it would sound, there was a tiny glimmer of hope that maybe, just maybe, he would see her again. Although he didn't kid himself that it would be easy. If her husband was sick, if he died . . .

He pushed the thoughts away. He didn't know him, but he hoped he pulled through.

'Well, moving across the pond is pretty drastic.'

Hunter shrugged. 'It's just something I've been thinking about. Might not even happen. The visa process is a bit tedious, from what I've found out so far. But I think I'm going to give it a try.'

'So, you don't want to go back to school, become a vet?'

Hunter shook his head. 'No. I think I let that dream go a while ago. Now that I could do it, I've realised I no longer want to.'

'Fair enough.' Buck shrugged, looking at his brother with a small smile. 'It's a lot of money. Lorna couldn't believe when I told her how much it was.'

'Yeah. It is.' Hunter ran his fingers through his hair, pulling at a tight knot he felt. He winced as the hair came out. 'Meg is the happiest, I think. She was ecstatic when she announced she didn't have to worry about taking out loans or working during medical school.'

The money they'd got from the sale of the ranch was beyond what any of them had imagined. After ensuring there was a tidy sum left for their mother to keep her comfortable, they had divided the rest into three. Hunter was worried about the ranch hands losing their jobs at first, and that had been his biggest concern when they were discussing if they should sell. But that conversation went much better than he'd thought. Before he told them, he had spoken to some other ranchers in the area and managed to find jobs for some of them. He vowed to help others, too, if that's what they wanted.

'At least one of us ended up with the brains,' Buck said offhandedly.

Hunter chuckled at that. 'I think you meant it as an insult, but I agree with you. I'm glad Meg can just focus on her studies. And that Mom will be taken care of for the rest of her life. She'll never want for anything.' He nodded to Buck, who raised his bottle in wordless cheers. 'What are you and Lorna going to do with your part?'

'Buy a new house, then set some money aside for Morgan and Cody. Whether they go to college or not, it'll be there to give them a head start in life.' Buck sighed. 'Lorna told me that's what responsible parents do. I was all up for investing in a baseball team or something.'

Their eyes met and they both erupted into laughter.

Hunter wiped a tear from his eye, trying to calm himself down. 'A baseball team, honestly, Buck.'

'What? I could've got some shares in maybe lower league or something.' Buck shrugged. 'We're also taking the kids to Hawaii for Christmas.'

'That'll be nice. I'm sure you'll have a great time.'

'And how about you? Have you been having any good times lately?' Buck looked at Hunter, suggestively raising an eyebrow.

'What kind of question is that?' he asked, pursing his lips.

'Just trying to check on my little brother. Make sure you're doing all right.'

Hunter bit the right side of his lower lip, taking a deep breath.

Caroline was meant to go back home last week. They would've had five extra months together. There were times, especially in the middle of the night when he was lying alone in bed, when he had wild ideas of packing his bags and jumping on a plane to Glasgow. But when the morning came, it all looked different. More rational. He didn't even know her address. They had deleted each other's phone numbers. He didn't really have any means of contacting her.

Then, the desperate and stubborn part of his longing helpfully fed him the idea of overcoming every single obstacle with a single action. *You can go to Anna and Gian and ask them.*

But he couldn't, not understanding all too well why she'd had to go. Why she needed to be there for Finn.

'Of course I'm OK,' he said, taking a very long swig from the bottle.

CHAPTER FORTY-SIX

Caroline

Caroline was staring out of the large bay window in their first-floor Dowanhill flat. It was six months since she'd got back to Glasgow, and they had been the most gruelling time in her life. She hadn't got back to work, hadn't even started thinking about properly applying for higher speciality training.

Finn's health had been the only thing on her mind.

The surgery was successful in fully removing his meningioma, and he had just finished the last course of radiotherapy two weeks ago. He would be getting follow-up imaging regularly to check for potential recurrence, but the doctors were optimistic.

And so was he.

Caroline had been there for every appointment, every bad night he'd had, and every doubt-filled early morning, answering questions like *'What if this is it? What if this is not going to work?*' She'd bitten her tongue so often after Orlaith, Finn's mother, swooped in from Dublin and rented an Airbnb around the corner from them.

Even though she didn't let herself admit it out loud, she had been so scared he would die. Or experience the scary complications.

He was doing well and she felt like she was finally able to breathe again.

'Are you busy?' Finn walked into the living room, wearing a pair of tracksuit bottoms and a hoodie. He had shaved his head before the surgery and the hair was starting to slowly grow back.

'No.' She sat up, closing a book on her lap. 'What's up?'

He put a stack of documents on the coffee table.

Caroline raised her brow. She knew what it was. 'The divorce papers?'

Finn sat down opposite her in an armchair. He sighed. 'Yeah. I've already signed them.'

'I didn't know you wanted to get it done so fast.'

His brown eyes crinkled. 'I feel like it's been a formality. I can't thank you enough for coming back, the past few months . . . I don't even want to think about it. But you've been there for me when I needed you most. And I'll always be thankful for that. You have no idea how much it's meant to me.'

She nodded, swallowing a thick lump in her throat.

'But I'm doing better now and feel bad keeping you tethered to this place, to me. It isn't fair on you.'

'I'd have always come back. There was no question about it,' she said, and she truly meant it. 'You're a part of me, Finn. No matter what happened or happens, that will never change.'

He gave her a watery smile. 'Maybe we can be friends. I

know this is the worst line to say, but in our circumstances, I think it makes sense.'

She laughed. 'I thought we were already friends.'

'We are. That's why I know I need to set you free. Especially because I know you're in love with another man.'

Caroline's eyes widened. 'Wh—What?'

Finn sighed and reached into his shorts pocket, pulling out *that* photo strip. One she had been using as a bookmark for all these months. That single token, the only reminder that the memories she had were real. That it wasn't just a dream.

Finn handed it to her. 'That's the guy you went out with after you called me, right? The cowboy?' He pointed at the photos. 'I always thought those hats were so tacky. But, never mind.' He cleared his throat. When his eyes met hers again, there was no sign of anger. Just deep, profound sadness.

Like they both knew this was really the end.

'It wasn't just sex, was it? He means something to you,' Finn said.

She considered her words carefully before responding. 'He told me he loved me before I left.'

Finn let out a low whistle. 'Wow.' He glanced at her. 'Do you love him?'

The tightness squeezed in her chest again.

'You don't have to answer. It's written all over your face.'

'It doesn't matter. That's all in the past.' She put the bookmark on top of the book, not looking at it. 'Do you have a pen?'

Finn handed her an elegant, metal pen.

Caroline pulled up the top sheet from the coffee table, staring at her name and dotted line next to it. With a heavy breath, she signed it and pushed both the papers and the pen away. It might've felt a bit dramatic, but she'd had her own solicitor looking over the details beforehand; she knew this was coming. She just didn't expect to be signing it so soon.

'Thank you,' Finn said.

'For what?'

'I don't know. In general? This went much better than I had imagined.'

'I never understood how people who loved each other, even if it was all in the past, could be cruel to each other,' Caroline said.

'Maybe those people never actually loved each other.' He lifted his hand, brushing his fingers against her cheek. 'I know I messed up.'

'We both did,' she said. 'We loved each other. We hurt each other. We're not the only ones who didn't get the happily ever after.' She looked deep into his eyes, smiling through the tears welling in her eyes.

'For what it's worth, every word I said, every feeling I had . . . I'll always mean it.'

'Me too. Every word.'

Finn kissed her cheek. It was such a simple gesture, but it was wistful, carried so much sorrow and felt final.

It was the goodbye they both needed.

CHAPTER FORTY-SEVEN

One year later
Caroline

'Dougal, come back here!'

The black Scottish terrier stopped in the middle of the path, turning his head towards Caroline. He regarded her with disinterest, but reluctantly waited and let her clip his lead back on.

Caroline scratched the spot behind his right ear. 'I know you want to explore, buddy. But you can't just run off in the distance. What would your mum say?'

Dougal just panted in response.

She sighed. *Great. Now I'm trying to have conversations with a dog*, she thought as she set off again, Dougal happily trotting in front of her.

Twenty minutes later, they reached their destination. She hooked Dougal's lead round her wrist and reached for her phone. Clara had got into *Outlander* on her recommendation and now was just a little bit obsessed with anything remotely to do with the series. Clune Hill Stone Circle was no Craigh na Dun, but she'd still appreciate the thought. Smiling, Caroline took a photo of the view, slid the phone back into her hoodie pocket, and looked round.

It had been five months since she'd moved to Banchory, and she still couldn't believe it sometimes. The day she found out she'd got into North of Scotland Deanery for her medical oncology training was the first day since leaving Oklahoma that she felt truly happy.

Aberdeenshire was truly home.

She loved her job. It was tough, and there was a lot to learn, but she never doubted her decision to choose oncology. For now, she was enjoying the natural beauty of Royal Deeside. She had even found time for some hobbies, long walks and mountain biking included. Excluding these and work, she was busy figuring out who she was. Which, at thirty-three, probably sounded a bit strange. But this was the first time in her life that she had lived alone. She didn't have to please anyone but herself.

Caroline had even been on several dates since she'd moved here, another set of new experiences ranging from very good to disastrous. One time she went for dinner with a radiographer she had met at the hospital. He'd asked her out and, because she found him rather attractive and there were no immediate red flags in the few conversations they'd had, she had agreed. The evening went well at first, until he asked if he could paint her toenails red and take photos of them. She'd suddenly remembered something important she really had to do right at that second, and had been avoiding him at work ever since.

At least the stories kept Erin and her sisters entertained.

Not all of the dates went this far south from the start.

Some ended with great sex. And then they parted ways, amicably knowing they'd had a good time and that's all it was. Then there was this one divorced architect in his early forties who she'd seen for about three weeks. He was handsome, fun to be around, and they had a lot in common. However, after those weeks, he had realised he was still in love with his ex-wife and booty-called her when lying in bed with Caroline. *You can be out of here in ten, right?*

She still thought about Hunter from time to time. Then she'd scold herself for being an idiot. Surely he was happy with someone else by now. Maybe even engaged or married . . . Who knows? She certainly wouldn't.

'Thank you for looking after Dougal while Nana's been in hospital. With Sarah away and me trying to juggle work and visiting Nana, I'm sure he was more comfortable here.'

'No problem. He's the best company.' Caroline smiled at Dougal and handed his lead to Tom, her childhood friend and grandson of her elderly neighbour.

He looked at her gratefully. 'That's good to hear.' Tom took the lead in his right hand and pushed his left one inside his jacket pocket. He took his car keys out and nodded to Caroline. 'You should come to the Inn – drinks are on the house after your help.'

'I'll happily stop by but will pay for drinks.'

'Nonsense.' He waved his hand. 'I want to repay you for your kindness towards my Nana. She's always been fond of you.'

'I like her a lot too.' Caroline's smile widened. 'How is she feeling? I know she's coming home today.'

'Yeah, she's fine. Given, you know, everything.' Tom shrugged. 'How are you settling in? It must be different being here again after all the years in Edinburgh and Glasgow.' He leaned over the kitchen cupboard. Dougal sat down at his feet.

'It is, but in a good way.' Caroline walked to the kettle. 'Tea?'

'That'd be lovely, thanks,' Tom responded.

She nodded and clicked it on. She opened the grey kitchen cupboard, taking out two porcelain mugs and putting a teabag in each.

'I missed it here. It's funny, because years ago I would've grasped any chance to go away. But now this is home, you know,' Caroline mused. The kettle boiled and she poured water into the mugs. 'Sugar? Milk?'

'Two sugars and a small splash of milk.'

She laughed. 'You haven't changed the way you take your tea since high school.' She measured two flat spoons, added the milk, and handed Tom the cup.

'Cheers.' He blew on his tea.

Caroline added cold water to her mug filled with black tea. 'I'm glad I decided to live in Banchory and commute. Don't think living in Aberdeen would have the same appeal it had when I was young.' She took a sip. 'I love my work just now and I'm feeling really content otherwise. The only thing maybe missing from my life is a decent guy.' She laughed, shaking her head. 'Sorry, that must've sounded pathetic.'

'Not at all.' Tom looked at her warmly over the rim of his mug. 'No luck with the dating apps?'

'Not since you witnessed that disastrous scrolling session at the Inn a couple of weeks ago.' She sighed. 'But never mind.'

'I can maybe help with that,' Tom said, scratching his chin as if he was thinking. 'There's a guy who moved to the area not long ago. He looks to be a similar age to you. I don't know him that well, but Sarah deemed him to be "a real catch".' Tom raised his eyes to the ceiling as if embarrassed on his girlfriend's behalf. 'He comes to the Inn regularly for food, sometimes a drink, but always takes a taxi home afterwards. Doesn't seem like he enjoys cooking for himself.' He scratched his chin again. 'He bought that equestrian facility, just outside Aboyne? Think it's called Windswept Hooves.'

Caroline froze. The place where she had learned how to ride. The place her mother took her to, watching her over the fence and smiling, like seeing her middle daughter on top of a horse was the best view. 'I didn't know McCluskeys went out of business.'

'About three, four years ago now? They retired to Spain.'

'I'm glad someone bought the place.' She *had* planned on getting back in the saddle, eventually. Riding was another thing she missed when remembering her time in Oklahoma. But she hadn't found a good time to do it, at least not yet.

'Anyway, the guy seems to be, you know, normal. As in, not a psycho or something. I could set you up on a date if you wanted to?' Tom looked up at her, grinning. 'Like a blind date? That'd be so cool.'

'Well . . . OK, I guess,' she finally said, wincing. 'Guess I have nothing to lose.'

'Only your time.' He shrugged and they both laughed. 'Is that a yes then?'

'Sure. What's his name?'

'If I told you, it wouldn't be a blind date, would it?'

CHAPTER FORTY-EIGHT

Caroline

Caroline fumbled with her necklace, frowning at the cleavage of her dress. She had almost decided she wouldn't come. What was she thinking, agreeing to go on a blind date?

She snorted into her glass of red wine.

The whole situation was ridiculous. But she needed to get back out there. Hunter had shown her everything she had been missing in her life; she didn't want to fall off the saddle, now that she learned how to stay in it.

So, here she was, at Tom's pub in Aboyne. Dressed in one of her favourite purple dresses, waiting for the guy whose name she didn't know. It'd be thrilling if she didn't feel so stupid.

'Caroline?'

Caroline stiffened. She took a deep breath and closed her eyes, trying to calm her nerves. This wasn't possible, was it?

It could be a complete coincidence that the accent sounded so familiar.

Slowly, she turned towards the direction of the male voice. As soon as she did, she thought she was going to pass out. She blinked twice, not daring to believe her eyes.

A tall, muscular, dark-haired man in a checkered shirt tucked into a dark pair of jeans casually leaned over the bar counter next to her.

Time seemed to have slowed down. Their eyes met. Caroline felt like she was falling deep into sweet nothing. She hadn't realised she'd jumped down from the stool. She didn't remember her legs moving towards the man. Before she knew it, they were standing face to face.

'How . . . Are you real?' he whispered, surveying her with glassy eyes.

She bit her lip, forcing the tears not to fall. 'Hello, Hunter.'

Before she could say anything else, he took her face in his hands and kissed her, releasing butterflies that had been firmly locked away since she left Oklahoma.

EPILOGUE

Caroline had lived her entire life adamant that there was no such thing as fate. It was easier to believe that, given all the bad things happening in the world. The idea that all the heartache, all the tears and the trials she had experienced in her life could've had a purpose was awful. But maybe, just maybe, there was something to be said about things working out the way they were meant to.

It had been a year since she reunited with Hunter at Tom's bar. She still couldn't believe that Tom had plotted the whole thing with Anna.

Apparently, Hunter had run into Anna in the pizza place he had taken Caroline to. They'd chatted for a while, and he told her he was moving to Aberdeenshire and showed her the equestrian facility. Anna, not wanting him to move somewhere he didn't know a single soul, gave him Tom's number. She had known his entire family since he was a boy; conveniently, she omitted telling Hunter that Tom was Caroline's lifelong friend. She also hadn't told him Caroline had already got into the oncology training in Aberdeenshire and was living in Banchory. Anna and Tom got in touch and schemed to get

Caroline and Hunter back together. They had come clean only after she moved in with Hunter, which arguably didn't take long – only a month.

Initially, Caroline feared Hunter had only moved to Aberdeenshire for her. Knowing how close he was with his family gnawed at her every time he mentioned them; she knew all too well what it was to miss the people she loved. She thought he would regret it and leave; and she didn't think she could bear it.

But weeks passed, months. He threw himself head first into renovating the rundown Windswept Hooves equestrian facility, dreaming up big dreams of reopening a riding school alongside applying for a planning permission to add further stables for boarding. It was plain to anyone who looked his way that he was truly content.

She was so happy, so thankful, that he'd taken that leap. He was the right person who she met in the wrong place, at the wrong time. Now, her heart permanently soared in the air like a robust kite incapable of losing wind.

Aberdeen used to be her home. Hunter had taken over that special place in her heart. The fact they got to live where her soul belonged was the most delicious icing on the cake. For a time, Caroline had worried that Hunter would want children. They had talked about it so much, possibly more than any couple who had children. He had assured her he didn't; that it wasn't because of her, but that he enjoyed being a fun uncle.

Dallas and Star came to a stop on the path, bowing their heads to drink from the River Dee. Despite how much of a nightmare navigating horse export from the States was, Hunter had managed to bring them over. When Caroline came round to meet Star again, she had a distinct feeling the mare recognised her. They had spent hours trekking the area, alone and with Hunter and Dallas.

It was a Saturday morning. Summer was in full swing, putting to shame all the jokes people liked to make about how dreadful Scottish summers were. Caroline was off work for the entire weekend, having prepared for something special. One thing that could make her even happier than she already was.

She loosened her grip on the reins, fumbling with the saddle bag.

'What are you looking for?' Hunter asked, stroking Dallas behind his ears.

'Nothing,' she replied in a sweet voice. Pushing around the contents of the bag, she smiled when she found it.

'No, seriously, what are you up to?' he asked, approaching her from behind and sliding his arms around her waist. 'Is it something naughty?' he whispered into her ear.

Caroline shivered, swatting his arm away. 'Bedroom is the only naughty area.'

'Tell it to the living room carpet. We're lucky we don't have any neighbours close by. Given you're a screamer.' He winked.

'You're the cause of those screams.'

Hunter chuckled. 'I know. I'm a very skilled man.'

She swallowed, closing her hand around a pair of cool metal objects. 'Hunter. About your visa issues—'

'Don't worry about it. I'll get it sorted.'

'Yes, I know. But what if you didn't have to? What if there was an easier way?'

'What do you mean?'

Caroline grinned. 'Isn't it obvious? Marry me.'

He just stared at her. 'Darling, you don't mean that. I know you don't want to get married again. I get it. We don't have to.'

'I know we don't have to. But I want to.' She put her hand on his chest, right over his heart. 'I love you. I don't want a wedding, but I want marriage if it's with you.'

She opened her other palm, revealing a pair of gold-rimmed spurs. 'I didn't think a diamond ring was your style so I got you these.'

Hunter's eyes widened. 'These were my father's. How did you—'

'Your mum sent them over when I told her what I needed them for.' She smiled.

Gently, he lifted the spurs from her hand. His throat bobbed as his fingers moved over them. 'I don't know what to say.'

'Say yes. Marry me, Hunter Jackson.'

Their eyes met, and Caroline wasn't sure whose were filled with a thicker curtain of happy tears.

Hunter hugged the spurs to his chest and put his hands on her waist. 'Of course I'll marry you. I'd have asked if I knew you were open to the possibility.'

She rested her forehead against his. 'I know you would. But I wanted to do this.'

He tilted her chin up, pulling her in a kiss sealing the promise of the future they had both thought they wouldn't get.

She truly believed that their love was going to be enough.

ACKNOWLEDGEMENTS

I love reading acknowledgments and always go to them first. So, naturally, I must've rehearsed what I wanted to say here a hundred times or so. Even before I knew this book was going to get published. Even when I put it in the drawer. Even when the imposter syndrome kept telling me this was never going to happen. Yet here we are.

There are so many people who helped me get to this stage, not only when it comes to *Back in the Saddle*, but the beginning of my writing career overall. Here goes a list of 'thank yous', though some are hard to put in to words.

To Avon Books UK team, for picking up this manuscript from their open submissions pile. I've already moved on from it, when I got the first email asking if it was still available, and I couldn't believe it. Thank you for taking a chance on me.

A special thank you to my fantastic editor, Emma Grundy Haigh. This book felt like a story I was almost able to tell, but not quite; like it had legs but it didn't know how to run. Thank you for helping me fall back in love with Caroline and Hunter. Also, a big shout out to Maddie Wilson – I appreciate all your help, keen eye for detail and patience in responding to all my silly queries.

To my agent, Rachel McMillan, for believing that me and my writing were worth betting on.

Before *Back in the Saddle* became the book you're holding now, it was called *Love is Not Enough* and it won the first prize in I Am In Print Novel Award 2023. A big shout out to Elane and Sarah, for organising such amazing opportunities for budding writers. You're both awesome.

To Rebecca Ryan, who told me I write sex very well – I hope you still think so if you got through this version! Your sense of humour is fabulous. I admire you so much as an author and I'm very glad that we met. Thank you for your developmental edit of *Love is Not Enough*, which helped me get it in to the shape that not only won the award, but also got me my first book deal.

To Emma Steele – I don't even know where to begin with this one. You were the very first person who believed in this story, rooted for these characters and understood my vision. I'll always hear the phrase 'whip it in to shape' in your voice. Thank you for so many things but most of all, for your time, guidance and kind words when I wasn't very kind to myself.

To Melissa from Dark Grove Press, for working on editing the previous version on this book, helping me elevate my writing and for giving me encouragement when I needed it the most.

There are also some people who have helped me make my writing better overall, even though they haven't worked directly with me on this book. Anna Britton, thank you for the mentoring and developmental editing with my other contemporary romance; I really hope that one gets into readers' hands soon too. I've learned so much from you and will always think of you whenever I see cinnamon buns. Odie appearing in my stories always brightens up my day. Andie Smith, you've been an immense help with my other romance book. I love your keen eye for detail, your enthusiasm and for just being all around lovely. Rebecca Carter, you've helped me shape the book *Of My Heart* into something I'm proud of. I really hope that story sees the light of day soon. You're a rockstar.

As someone who hasn't been to the US (yet) – or knows much about horses – I wanted to thank my beta/authenticity readers, who were instrumental in piecing together the setting of this book. Holly Allan, Becca Innes and Emily Machin, thank you for your equestrian expertise. It's a bit trickier to list everyone who answered every single silly question I had about the US or Oklahoma in general, as it'd be a very long list, but special mentions to: Teal Brechtel, Elizabeth Draths, MaryJo Holden and Deidra Duncan.

And to MaryJo Holden, again, for telling me Liam was not a name for a cowboy, and giving me Hunter instead.

I often say that the best part of writing has been meeting other writers and it's true. I would've given up very early on if it wasn't for the love, encouragement and the space to vent and bounce ideas off. In no particular order, thank you to Lindsay Beck, Noreen Nanja, Deidra Duncan, Tara Sexton, Emily Krempholtz, Melissa O'Connor, Ally Zetterberg, Allissa Lewis, Felicity Beaumont, Esha Patel, Nyla Deen, Hannah Brohm, Isabelle Martinsen, Sasa Hawk, Megan Murphy, Briana J. Newstead, Chloe Ford, Lauren Okie, Nicola Knight, Linny Mack, Cara Collins, Ashley Detweiler, Natasha J. Hastings, Georgia Stone and many, many more people. I'm thankful for every conversation, every hearted snippet and every time when I felt heard. If I missed anyone off the list,

I apologise, but know that I appreciate every single person who I met on my writing path.

To Kelly Beck, for just 'getting it'. The good, the bad and the frustrating. You were the first person who read the new opening of this book, and your message made me teary. You're such a talented author and I can't wait to hold your book in my hands soon.

To Haley Phelan, for writing the most swoon-worthy books which I can't stop obsessing over. Your writing makes me want to be a better writer.

To Leona McKerna, for supporting me and my big dreams from the very start of my writing journey. You're the best, love you and I hope we get to meet in person one day. Now, go and write that cowboy romance, too!

To Lauren Ford, for the long-winded conversations about writing, books and life; photos of Busy; writing some of my favourite characters and just being wonderful. I know I can always tell you things and that means a great deal.

To Donna Marchetti, for making me laugh and grin like an idiot, both on the pages of your books and in our chats. Our back and forth laughing emojis after every message often make my day.

To Sophie Cass, just for everything. I don't even know what to say here but I hope you know how much I appreciate you. I love your words, passion, heart and tenacity. And for Rune. May you write many more love interests that I get obsessed with that hard.

It's also so important to have non-writer friends and I wanted to give a special shout out to three of mine.

Gaby, for being there for it all: the good, the bad, and the ugly. Career changes, degrees (so many degrees between us, ha), drama and joys. You're the person I'm comfortable being silent with and it's beautiful. P.S. Also, for telling me you were bored of the beginning of the very early draft of this book. You were right. It sucked.

Aga, for working on sharpening my sarcasm since high school. No distance or time passed can get in the way of how much love I have for you. Thank you, for entertaining my writing delulu, listening, reading and always being there for me.

Justyna, you're the best friend I have. Thank you for being the most amazing person. Erin is my love poem to you and our friendship, and I hope people loved her as much as I love you.

To my sister-in-law, Bobbie, for being my favourite bookish person. Thank you for always being there to get hyped about all the recent releases and Taylor Swift, of course.

To the best sister, Monika, even though you probably won't read it because it isn't a thriller or a horror. I'm so proud to see how you've grown and see the kind of woman and mother you became. You're amazing, today and always. Love you to the moon and back.

To my gorgeous nieces, I wish I could see you more often, but I'm trying. I'll try harder, I promise. Hopefully by the time you're old enough to read this book, I didn't just try, I managed.

To Fergus and Hamish, for forcing me to leave my laptop behind to go on walks that probably made sure this book even happened; for the hugs and just being the best dogs.

To Martyn, for everything. It's cliché but it's true. You're my best friend, my favourite person in the world and my love. There would be no romance books if I didn't have an example of the kind of love I want to portray. I love you.

AUTHOR'S NOTE

As a teenager, I thought country music was 'lame'. My friend made some headway in convincing me otherwise back in high school (thank you, Monika), but it wasn't until my then boyfriend, now husband, became obsessed with it that I completely flipped my view. My taste turned by 180 degrees. Today, I've been to more country music concerts than I can count, loved every minute of every single one of them, and I hope there are many more in my future. The idea for *Back in the Saddle* came to me when I was in the height of that country music era – the summer of 2022, just before I started medical school.

I think the best thing about country music is the range of emotions it can evoke in the listener – you can go from an upbeat to a ballad ripping your heart into shreds within seconds.